# The Legend of Lake Marilee

W. Kyle Hammersmith

PublishAmerica
Baltimore

First printing

At the specific preference of the author, PublishAmerica allowed this work to remain exactly as the author intended, verbatim, without editorial input.

ISBN: 1-4137-7788-0
PUBLISHED BY PUBLISHAMERICA, LLLP
www.publishamerica.com
Baltimore

Printed in the United States of America

*To Tammy, my love and my destiny, divinely placed on my path at the Brown Swan Club.*

# PROLOGUE

A pink bathing suit—a girl, stunning, perches cross-legged atop an elephant-sized rock. Balanced and gracefully propped with arched back, she waits and watches. Her chin is high; her jaws are clenched, eyes gazing skyward towards me.

Boulders blaze below her—smooth, massive, and menacing in the sunlight. Water glimmers like shattered glass. A pounding cataract shreds the surface into glittering fragments.

Step, step, step—leap! In midair my body hovers, floating—no, falling—falling, clawing at empty space. Wind blasts past my ears, deafening the din of crashing water. She screams—a piercing, horrific wail. I kick and flail and reach at nothing, falling, falling.

An egg-shaped boulder, white under the morning rays, its belly blackened by shadows, zooms closer. The end is here. God, are you there? The boulder is upon me now—no, I upon it, an unavoidable disaster. Can't stop it. Flash! —I clench my eyes and wait for the pain. It never strikes, but the boulder does, silently. Now, only darkness, black, and sudden, and final. The girl in the pink bathing suit—she stoops behind me now.

The stony surface is cool upon my cheek. She is sobbing, heavy, convulsive sobs; I can't breath. I am leaving. My mouth is clogged with something lukewarm and familiar—blood. A chill laps the calf of my dangling left leg—water. Warmth oozes out from under my chest, up my neck, and drips like a faucet from my chin.

No pain, only regret. I am so sorry.

A voice whispers, *Jimmy Grandstaff didn't fall from that cliff. It was cold-blooded murder. Evidence is at falls. Go find it. Yours truly, John Doe.*

Sensations fade in the morning light, linger briefly in the shower, and the phantasma is wholly forgotten before I dry off. It would all return in nine months.

# CHAPTER 1

## *The Ghost in the Mirror*

When I turned sixteen in the spring, I wanted my life clearly defined and my future firmly shaped. I needed a model, a prototype of a self-made man towards whom I could aspire. I wanted a hero.

So I determined on my birthday that of all the adults I had met in this world, the only one whom I truly respected was my history teacher Mr. Gray. I'd had him for the past two years: World History in ninth grade and Government and Economics in tenth. I was hoping to get him next year in American History, but he doesn't teach it. Mr. Gray said he didn't really like teaching about America anyway; we've gotten too rich and too powerful for our own good, he said.

His were honors classes, and, to be honest, I was in them because I'm a fairly smart kid—at least that's what the guidance counselors said last year. They enrolled me in honors everything: biology, English, algebra, and Spanish. I would've been in honors phys-ed, too, if they had one. I was athletic *and* smart. I batted third and played shortstop on the JV team, *and* I was in the National Honor Society. I don't like to brag, but that's the way it was for me. There was a group us bright kids with the same class schedule, so that we didn't have to waste our education away in a classroom full of schmucks.

It was fine being one of the smart kids, but sometimes I felt like I was the only cool guy in the group. The rest were mostly girls, some of them *were* kinda cute; the guys were nerds who didn't do or say anything except meet on Friday nights for LAN parties—some type of computer geek tournament.

I know it sounds like I'm stuck up or something, but by the time you're halfway through high school, you've got to know who you are. I was a fortunate one—getting good grades just came natural to me—I hardly had to try, not like Sally Peterson who studied her rear end off to keep her 4.0 GPA to be our class valedictorian. The funny thing about her was how hard she tried in Mr. Gray's Gov'n'econ class when she really didn't have to.

Honestly, there was nobody better than Mr. Gray. He didn't just teach you stuff—he forced you to think, and he made you develop your own opinions about things. None of those crappy worksheets and screwy writing assignments. His teaching style was deep and profound, kind of like being in college. He used to teach at a college in California, but now he was teaching us to "reach the unreached" he said. The importance of history, he told us as freshmen, isn't measured by what is written about the past, but its importance resides in how we see it. Deep stuff, Mr. Gray's class.

Some people, especially Sally Peterson, didn't like him because he was an outspoken atheist, but that never bothered me. In fact, that's what added to his authenticity as a free thinker, and it's what I found so appealing about him. He was his own man—his own source for truth. As for my own high school self, I didn't know for sure if God existed or not. I had some friends who were Christians and things, and Mr. Gray was right about them—they'd believe anything written in the Bible without question and then tell you *you* were wrong if you didn't believe it. Mr. Gray openly questioned the Bible; he questioned everything written, for that matter, even the history books from which he taught. I found him fascinating.

Early in the fall he said something in class that I wrote down in my notebook, word-for-word, to keep as a source of inspiration. He said, "Trust yourself—you're the only one you can count on with absolute certainty." I liked it; it was purposeful and empowering. I copied the quote on an index card and taped it to the mirror above my dresser. Ideas like that made me feel enlightened, as if I had reached a new intellectual plateau far and above the average person. I made the quote my maxim for my entire sophomore year.

"Trust yourself," I would say just before a test, an at-bat, or a hot date. "Just trust yourself—you're the only one you can count on with absolute certainty." I typed it into the screensaver on my laptop, and I saw my life becoming more defined. I was ready to tackle the universe.

Months later, on Tuesday morning, the ninth of June, I whispered the maxim again. I was in my Mustang ready to leave home for the first time.

It was the beginning of the most fascinating journey of my young life, one that would alter an identity I had so recently defined, forever changing the way I think and the person I hoped to become.

I'll never forget that morning. She had been crying; her forehead and cheeks were veiled with pink blotches. "Don't drive too fast; take your time and pull over if you get tired," my mother fussed, leaning through the driver's window.

She hugged and a kissed me and told me to call as soon as I got to Abbeyville. I could sense the tears in her voice; she was going to miss me terribly. Never mind that it was all on account of her that I was leaving in the first place, but there she was starting to blubber when I started the engine. Frailty, thy name is Madeline Barrett.

Piled on the passenger seat were a road map, my Hilfiger jacket, and a small lunch cooler holding two ham sandwiches, a bunch of green grapes, and a sixteen-ounce bottle of Mountain Dew. In the back seat were a paperback copy of *The Great Gatsby* and a hardback version of *The Last of the Mohicans* (my summer reading for 11th Grade Honors English). The novels rested on top of two enormous, bulging, red nylon gym bags that were stuffed with T-shirts, shorts, blue jeans, socks, and underwear, including six brand new pairs of Fruit of the Loom still in their packages. Mom insisted I'd need them when she bought them for me the night before.

I was anxious to pull out of the driveway, but Wesley, my stepfather, was still snoring in bed—no surprise—paying absolutely no attention the biggest day of my life. He could've stayed there until he died, for all I cared. We had been at each other like hornets for the past six months, almost as bad as he and Mom had been at it for the past year. Like I said, my teacher Mr. Gray was the only man I respected in this world, and my stepfather Wesley was his antithesis.

"I can't believe I won't see you until Labor Day," Mom fretted, her voice cracking again. She was too predictable to appreciate.

She hugged me one more time through the window and, at last, I released the brake, coasted slowly to the end of the driveway, beeped the horn for affection, and turned left out onto Blackstone Drive. In a matter of hours, six hundred miles would separate me from every person I had ever known in my entire life. "Trust yourself," I whispered, as I pressed the accelerator and abandoned my mother in her crying fit.

I didn't feel a scrap of fear or loneliness; I was actually relieved to be getting away. I considered this newly begun journey to be an adventure, or better yet—an exodus. Call it anything, as long as I was escaping Mom and Wesley and their crappy life.

My destination: Abbeyville, New York, a tiny summer resort town, two hundred miles north of New York City. My employer: The Brown Swan Club, "a ritzy getaway nestled along the shores of Lake Marilee in the heart of the Adirondack Mountains." That's how the glossy brochure described it. That and hundreds of stories my mother told me about her teenage days at the Brown Swan Club were all I knew about the place where I would be spending the next twelve weeks.

The drive was long but I savored every mile of it. Sixteen years old and on my own for the whole summer. Boy, I was rather proud of myself. The wind pounded through the open windows and music blared through the speakers, until radio reception was lost up in the mountains for the last hour of the trip. I never felt a tinge of homesickness—only absolute, pure freedom for the first time in my life.

Freedom. I wanted nothing more than a summer of freedom. To exchange the horrors of that house and the imminent divorce for twelve weeks of freedom was all I had thought about all spring. Wesley or Mom had never actually mentioned a divorce, but I was certain it would happen sooner or later. Nobody who fights like they did could possibly love each other. But who cared now? As far as I was concerned, I was finding my wings—escaping their insidious relationship—and sensations of independence and peace rushed through my mind like the wind through the open car windows.

As mile markers shrank rapidly away in my rearview mirror, I frequently looked at my road map and was impressed with how far away from home I was actually going. The town of Pokeville, N.Y. was just a small speck on the page, about one centimeter below a slightly larger dot representing Abbeyville. It was the closest exit before Abbeyville, and finally, after ten hours of driving on Interstates 71, 90, and 87, I followed Mom's directions and took the Pokeville exit.

It was at that moment when, for the first time, as I drifted off that wide-open interstate onto the narrow ramp, I began feeling unsettled and uncertain. This was foreign territory: all I had was me, the map, and mom's memories; everything else was unknown.

At the end of the exit ramp, I followed the less-traveled Route 7 into a tiny little town, and the scene hardly lived up to the charming impressions of Mom's summer stomping grounds she had painted for me. Instead of an enchanting little village full of her childhood tales, what I saw in Pokeville was nothing but sad and disappointing barrenness.

All the town offered was a tiny, white-painted church, sagging under the weight of an over-sized steeple, and a main street consisting of one city block's length of weathered, groaning buildings in which small businesses had withered away and died. It was a town of white, peeling paint, shards of dust-gray glass, and crumbling, ash-colored pavement. A single rust-on-white pick-up truck that was parked along the curb provided the slightest intimation that a human being might be somewhere inside a building, most likely in skeleton form. I didn't see a living thing anywhere. Not even bugs.

I needed gasoline. The light above the gas gauge had begun to fade on and off after I went through Albany well over an hour ago. Now it was glowing bright orange, and I also had to go to the bathroom. My bladder was as full as my gas tank was empty. A thirty-two ounce Mountain Dew from Burger King wobbled empty on the floor. Next to it was a sixteen-ounce plastic bottle of the same beverage, its contents having been consumed after my first gas stop near Buffalo five hours ago.

I crept to a stop sign at the town's only intersection. A white street sign with black letters was nailed to a telephone pole, indicating that a left turn would put me onto Dreary Creek Drive. It was the whole town that was dreary, if you ask me. There wasn't a restaurant, a grocery store, or an open business anywhere—only white, empty buildings. I glanced up Dreary Creek Drive at more white buildings, all sitting dead and empty. No people. No gas station. Perhaps just on the outside of town there'd be one, I hoped. I thought that blue highway sign back there said gas was at this exit. Must've been wrong.

In the ghostly emptiness of Pokeville, I couldn't ignore that weird feeling that people were watching me. People inside all those white one and two story buildings bordering the street. Eyes peering out through dirty gray, broken glass, staring, glaring. I looked around at the buildings again. No faces in the windows. Not a soul in sight. No reason to believe they were actually there, except that weird feeling you get when you're alone in a strange place.

I accelerated through the intersection, and before you could say Stephen King, the strangely empty town of Pokeville was behind me. I exhaled slowly. Abbeyville was several miles ahead, and it could only be an improvement, I hoped… that is, if I could get there on the little gasoline left in the tank.

The road tiptoed away from Pokeville over a shallow, stony brook and crept past a sagging, disheveled graveyard where crooked tombstones protruded from the dirt on a treeless hillside, like sprouts budding on an aged potato. A dilapidated building just outside Pokeville's limits rested unassumingly across the road from the unkempt graveyard. This elongated shack turned out to be a combination post-office, general store, and gas station, all packed into a rickety, doublewide trailer-sized building. I noticed the structure was the first one in the area that wasn't painted white. The outside walls were the color of ashes, except for the white rectangular sign with blue letters that spelled “Mobil Oil.”

My black radials crunched slowly across the gray, dusty gravel towards the single gas pump. It was one of those old fashioned pumps with rotating dials. No digital readouts, no credit card slot for “pay at the pump.” A small sign over the machine boasted “Full Service,” a kind of tease because, by all appearances, it seemed that I was the only one there.

After killing the engine, I glanced around for an attendant to pump gasoline, or for a sign indicating the place was even open. I began thinking how I was such an idiot for not stopping somewhere outside of Albany. Plus there was that town called Lake Henry forty minutes back where I could’ve filled the tank. *This* place was dead, just like the rest of Pokeville. I considered attempting to drive the remaining fourteen miles to Abbeyville on fumes.

At least that eerie feeling that eyes were watching me had gone away. Downtown Pokeville was just too weird.

Jinx! Things got creepy again quickly when the rickety, wooden-framed screen door on the building suddenly swung open and the stringy, gray head of a terribly sad-looking old woman poked out. The homely dame seemed to exert all her facial muscles to raise her droopy eyebrows and gaze sharply in my direction. I felt like a penguin on a Texas ranch by the way she stared at me, plus I really had to urinate. She glared at me like I was doing it right there in the car.

I stepped out onto the gravel and circled to the front of my Mustang. As casually as possible, I finger-combed my hair and crammed my car keys into the front pocket of my blue jeans. I figured I looked enough like the friendly suburban boy next door who would offer to mow the lawn for his elderly neighbor. With my all-American appearance, I hoped I could put the hideous old woman at ease. But she kept staring at me like I was a ghost.

“Is there a restroom here, ma’am?” I asked as kindly as I could.

The sagging skin around the eyes of the woman twitched when she saw me stand in full view. She stared quizzically at me a brief moment before she answered in a brutish, Maine dialect, “Ya mus’ puhchase sahm’n ta use eht.”

I sensed her initial inhibition fading ever so slightly. “Oh, I will. Can you fill’er up?”

She paused again, squinted her eyes, and peered at me with tenacious scrutiny. “Ya mus’ pay ‘far I pahmp,” she cackled.

“Pardon?” It was hard to understand her scratchy voice and dialect.

The woman raised her voice. “I said, ya mus’ pay a’far I pahmp.”

It still felt like she was staring at me because little monkeys were crawling out of my ears or something. I slid my wallet from my back pocket and stepped toward the woman, handing her a crisp twenty-dollar bill. She snatched the bill without looking at it, studying my face instead. I felt more like a criminal than a customer.

"Ya mus' get the key from Harold," she grumbled.

"Pardon?" I said again.

"I said, ya mus' get the key to the waash room from Harold." She gestured over her right shoulder with her flabby, spotted right arm. With her other limb she held open the screen door. "Harriup. Don' wahn' them harse flies ta get en."

I entered reluctantly.

The inside of the building was dark and oily. The left wall was a framework of post office boxes, whose miniature brass doors formed an even grid of eight high and twenty across. The wall on the near right was covered by a faded collage of outdated advertisements, legal notices, job postings, and several pieces of ruled paper torn from a spiral-bound notebook with phrases such as "Fridge for Sale" written in black ink from a cheap pen. Under the waist-high window in the front of the room leaned a small table, covered with cracked and peeling, red-and-white plaid vinyl. Two olive-green vinyl-covered stools, also cracked and peeling, kept the lopsided table company. The pathetic dinette set served as the only furniture in the room except for the narrow, splintery, wood-topped counter that divided the entire room, separating the customers from the staff.

Displayed on the back wall behind the counter were packaged foods and merchandise that must have sat for years on the dusty, wooden shelves. Everything from M&M's and Skoal chewing tobacco to Off bug repellant and fingernail clippers. Some of the wrappers and labels on the products were faded and yellowing. A glass-door cooler faced the end of the counter, sitting dark, quiet, and empty, despite its charge to "Enjoy Coca-Cola."

A man around sixty—he must be Harold—teetered on the hind legs of a wooden chair behind the long counter. He had greasy, black, slicked-back hair and was reading a newspaper.

"I need the key to the restroom," I said to him apologetically. He was concentrating on his newspaper.

He looked up and gave me the same queer stare like the old woman had. He reached under the counter and took out a block of wood the size of a brick, all the while staring at me as if I had done something terribly wrong. A piece of twine was tied to the wooden block, and dangling from the twine was the single brass key to the restroom. "Tahlet's 'round the side beyand the icebox," Harold directed, in the same Maine accent as the ugly, old woman. While I wondered if they were married or had fallen out of the same petrified crabapple tree, he continued to curiously examine my face.

I had never felt so uncomfortable in all my life. I wanted desperately to get to a mirror and see what must be wrong with my face. Why were they staring at me like this?

When I creaked open the wooden door to go back outside, the ugly woman gave me another weird stare while she pumped gasoline into my car. I circled around to the side of the decrepit shack where a beat up, rust-spotted ice machine rattled under the eave of the rusted aluminum roof.

I unlocked the dented bathroom door found that the facility wasn't fit for rats. No surprise. I emptied my bladder in the rusty commode, but I didn't dare touch the filthy knobs of the sink's corroded faucet. The black-spotted, cracked mirror above the rotting sink showed nothing apparently wrong with my face or any other part of my body.

What were those creeps staring at?

I wished I didn't have to return the key. I would've let the old woman keep the change for the gasoline and just dash to my car and drive away.

When I returned to the counter inside, the piercing stares from the old couple churned my stomach. The woman had finished at the gas pump and was behind the counter ringing up my change. I handed the wooden block with the dangling, brass key back to Harold. He took it and tossed it on a shelf somewhere under the counter, and the loud thump made the old woman jump. I sensed that he and the old lady had been talking about me while I was in the restroom. Harold held the newspaper in his lap and stared at me again.

"See ya from Ohi'a," he said, nodding towards my car parked outside.

"Yes sir. Left there early this morning." I could fake a friendly tone rather well.

"Ya las' name wouldn' be Grandstaff, would it?"

"No, sir. It's Barrett."

The greasy-haired man crooked his black eyebrows. "Barrett, eh?" Harold stood to his feet and placed the newspaper on the countertop. "Well, my soul. When Gretta and I fahst fexed our eyes upon ya, we could'ah swarn dat yar the wahkin' image of that Grandstaff boy. You shu'ah ya naht his cousin or sahm'n?"

I was amused—and thankful—to learn that my identity had been mistaken. This was why they stared at me so peculiarly.

"No. My name's Jody Barrett," I answered, truly relieved.

Both Harold and Gretta continued to study my face. "I jus' swea'ah by the dickens ya look jus' like that Grandstaff boy," Harold again contended. Gretta remained quiet.

"Is he from Ohio?" I asked, faking interest.

"Nah. He's from right 'roun this area. Er ah' leas' he was. He died this pas' Se'tembah." Harold carefully studied my features as he spoke. "Strange thing is, they'ahs an ah'ticle in smornin's papah sayin' t'was a murdah." Harold spun the newspaper around for me to see.

I hesitated before leaning over to read the headline on the front page. Bold-faced, black letters above the lead article spelled, "POLICE REINVESTIGATE SIGHT OF SMOOTH ROCK ACCIDENT." Grabbing my attention like a flashing red, neon light was the one-inch by one-and-a-half inch, black-and-white photograph, the sight of which caused me to pitch the same expression of disbelief that Harold and Gretta wore when they first saw me.

I was staring at a picture of myself!

The image was spellbinding, sending chills up my spine. The face I had just inspected in the restroom mirror was now staring straight back at me in ghostly black and white.

"Ya reca'nize that fellah?" Harold asked.

My eyes remained fixed on the photograph. "You're... you're right. He looks just like me." I could barely speak. A distant, misty memory floated in my mind and vanished.

"To say th' least!" Harold roared. "You shu'ah ya don't have a long lahst cousin or sahm'n?"

Gretta jabbed Harold with her plump finger. "Ah, Harold! It's jus' one of those ca'incidences." Her interjection surprised me, and I noticed the thin lips above her flabby chin spread open to reveal a crooked row of yellow teeth. Her demeanor had suddenly changed, and I appreciated her attempt at friendliness, although it didn't work to soothe my nerves very much.

"He'yahs ya change, honey, an' welcome to th' Adirondacks!" she said in a crackly voice, her yellow teeth poking out from behind her thin-lipped grin.

I stuffed the money in my pocket without looking at it and shifted my eyes back to the newspaper. The caption under the photograph said "JAMES GRANDSTAFF, 1980-1997."

"So how'd he die?" I asked, my voice still quaking.

"Na one knows fa shu'ah," Harold answered. "Some say he fell from the cleff, others say he gaht pahshed."

Gretta interjected, "Ah Harold, ya don' know that fa shu'ah!"

Bewildered and horrified, I kept staring at my printed likeness. I began wondering how many other local people I had never met would mistake me for the dead Jim Grandstaff. For a fleeting moment, I wondered if maybe it was a mistake to leave home. Quickly gathering myself, I thought, "No, Jody, trust yourself: you can control this." In moments, I had convinced myself that Gretta was right; it was just a coincidence.

"So what ya doin' in these pahts all by yahself, boy?" Harold asked, yanking the paper away when he noticed I was beginning to read the article.

"I'm, uh, working at the Brown Swan Club for the summer."

"Heh, ain't that som'n'!" Harold snickered as he tossed the paper to the shelf underneath. "That's whe'ah ol' Jimmy was wahkin' a'far he died… er at least a'far he was killed, as they'ah sayin' now."

Gretta glared at Harold. "It's all jus' a ca'incidence," she repeated.

"She's right!" I averred in a bold tone. "It's just a coincidence. I've never worked at the Brown Swan Club before, and I've never known anyone named Jim Grandstaff. It's all kind of funny if you ask me." I offered an affected smile.

Harold silently glared at me with eyes that seemed to say, "Come on now, tell the truth, boy." Then, for some strange reason, I started feeling guilty, like I had been lying to them about my own identity—like this Jim Grandstaff was actually a relative of mine whom I didn't know. It was like the truth as I had known it had suddenly changed under the spell of this old couple. Keep in control: trust yourself, I reminded my psyche.

"Well, I better get on," I announced, turning towards the screen door. "How far is it to the Brown Swan Club from here?" I already knew.

Gretta answered, "Fah'teen miles up Route 7. Ya can't mess't."

In a half a minute I was back in my Mustang speeding north. I hoped that my arrival at the Club would make me forget the eerie gas station experience. I desperately wanted to forget all about Pokeville, Harold and Gretta, and the chilling newspaper article.

I flipped on the radio in search of musical therapy, but all I could find was the same static I heard when I hit the mountains an hour ago. "Radios don't even work this far up in the boonies!" I mumbled angrily. I pushed the A.M. button and finally found one clear-sounding station out of Lake Henry. But with uncanny timing, the station delivered a most unwanted news report:

*Yesterday, Huron County police reinvestigated the scene of a nine-month old accident at Smooth Rock Falls where, last September, seventeen-year-old Jim Grandstaff of Pokeville fell sixty feet to his death.*

Curious, I turned up the volume. As much as I didn't want to, I had to hear this.

*An anonymous tipster, calling himself John Doe, sent a letter to the police alleging that evidence still remains at the falls. According to the police, the letter states that the evidence, if found, would prove that the late Jim Grandstaff's death was not accidental. Investigators spent several hours this morning at Smooth Rock Falls searching for the undisclosed evidence. But according to Huron County Sheriff Clive Slater, they did not find what they were looking for.*

A deep, confident voice from the sheriff proclaimed over the airwaves,

*"We have received an anonymous tip from this so-called John Doe. We followed up on it and found nothing. This area was thoroughly scoured for three days after the accident, and while the case remains open to the possibility of homicide, the lack of evidence here leaves us with very little to go on. At this point, I'm sorry to say that the only way we can know the truth about this tragic death is to hear from the ghost of Jim Grandstaff himself."*

*Stephen Hampton reporting near Abbeyville. In other news, local merchants....*

"That's just great!" I cried out loud, silencing the radio, almost snapping off the knob. "I've left home and turned into a ghost!"

# CHAPTER 2

## *The Brown Swan Club*

Fourteen miles later, I almost died—she was that gorgeous.

She was standing on the porch of the main building at the Brown Swan Club when I arrived at the top of the hill, and as soon as she came into view, everything that happened in Pokeville with Harold and Gretta vanished.

When a girl comes into your world like this, there should be a train of limousines and bodyguards paving the way for her arrival. Trumpets should sound, light bulbs should flash, and red carpets should roll in heraldry. Paparazzi should swarm, and fanatics should push and shove for autographs. Paramedics should be ready to aid the weak of heart who faint in the presence of this angel. This is how she was—I'm not exaggerating. She was that beautiful.

She was wearing a white, loose-fitting sleeveless blouse, light-gray denim shorts that wrapped firmly around her thighs, and white tennis shoes that capped her lightly sun-browned legs. Add to that her golden, wavy hair, blue eyes, and a sparkling smile—she had it all. She was Shakespeare's Hero, Fielding's Sophia, and Twain's Becky Thatcher, composed into one singular entity of human perfection. It would take a novel to explain what I mean.

Bedazzled, I stepped out of my car while she bounced amiably down the porch steps, holding a clipboard under her bare arm. "Hi there! Welcome to the Brown Swan Club!" she said in a sprightly, angelic voice. "My name's Kristel. Are you Jody?"

The very first girl I met this summer made me melt like ice cream.

She had been expecting me. My name was on her clipboard, listed among the other summer staff. Somehow, she knew I would be arriving a day earlier than everyone else.

Our first conversation was like a symphony. I was a broken oboe, but Kristel carried the show. It was as though I evolved closer to perfection every minute I stood in her presence. She had that way—she just made you want to be better. We discussed where I was from and how my trip went, and the more we talked, the more I regained composure, abating my melting and strengthening my resolve that I would befriend this princess forever. Soon I was restored, although fully enamored with the angel.

We walked together towards the large, open porch of the Club building. It was furnished with high-backed wicker chairs and cushioned love seats that overlooked the grassy, shaded hillside. From the porch we admired Lake Marilee at the base of the hill, glimmering through the pines.

I had first caught several glimpses of the lake after leaving Pokeville. The sparkling blue body of water was decked with colorful sailboats and ski boats that, from a distance, looked like flower petals sprinkled over a fishpond. The far shore, about a mile across the fourteen-mile long, narrow lake, was bordered by rocky banks where several homes and cabins peeked through the trees above the water. Beyond the Lake Marilee I could see the continuance of the Adirondack Mountains rolling eastward into Vermont, covered by the thick, green, shag carpet of pine trees. The scenery was grand and captivating, and, best of all, quiet and peaceful.

"This place is beautiful," I said to Kristel, believing that everything truly beautiful resided in the girl standing next to me.

She turned and looked at me curiously, and for a fleeting, blood-rushing moment, I believed that the only right thing I could ever do in my life was to kiss her right there and then.

But the pestering realities of the day stormed back into focus. I felt her eyes studying my facial lineaments as though she was trying to remember someone. It was then that I recalled Jim Grandstaff, my dead likeness who had invaded my world no less than twenty minutes before. I needed to get the mistaken identity out in the open and dash it as quickly as possible.

"You must think I look…" I stuttered.

Her seraphim voice interceded, "You're one of the first staff-members here. Do you know your job assignment?"

"Uh, yeah. I'm going to be waiting tables."

"Really? Then you'll be working right in here in the dining room. I'll take you through there after you meet Daddy. He's been looking forward to your arrival."

Ah ha! The beautiful princess was the daughter of George Schuple, the owner of the Club and friend of my mother. This was good news! —A connection, though Mom never told me he had a daughter. I stayed out on the porch while Kristel went inside to see if her father was available.

So strange are the things you remember about particular moments in life. I remember her hair was down that day, brushing lightly over her shoulders. She wore it the rest of the summer tied back in a ponytail. And I remember the clipboard she held with the printout of the summer staff members on it, and I remember her carefully marking over my name with a yellow highlighter. The day was bright, full of blue sky as we stood in the shade of the towering poplars—it was breezy, about seventy degrees that late afternoon. I remember the puissant scent of pine, just like the first day you bring a fresh Christmas tree into your house. What I remember most about that moment was when Kristel came back after a minute and said my name: "Jody," she called from behind me. I was still admiring the lake through the gap in the pines.

It was the way my name came out of her mouth that I remember so distinctly—like she was hesitant to interrupt my enjoyment of the view. It sounded like she had called for me a thousand times before, like we had known each other as best friends, or even family. She said it as sweetly and as kindly as I have ever heard anyone say my name.

"My father's in his office. Come on back."

We walked through a blue-carpeted lobby where the trickling sound of an indoor fountain complemented the mood set by the leafy-green wallpaper under the thick wooden beams of the ceiling.

I said to Kristel, "I really don't know your dad that well, except that he knows my mom and that he arranged for my job here."

"Daddy talks about your mom all the time," she said as we approached a door at the back of the lobby. "You'll like him. He's friendly—not intimidating at all."

A tall, plump man, not obese, but with chipmunk cheeks and a round belly greeted us in a small, windowless office. His warm, relaxed smile was not unlike that of his daughter. Thick, dark eyebrows, salted with specks of gray, arched high on his forehead as he greeted me.

"Hey there, Jody! Welcome!" George Schuple gripped my hand firmly and shook it with great gusto. "It's been a long time! Look at how you've grown up!"

I noticed that Mr. Schuple studied my features in the same recollecting way that Kristel had, yet not in the queer, eerie manner that Harold and Gretta had. From what he said, I presumed I had met this man before. Mom never told me we had visited the Club a long time ago. I thought it strange she never said anything about it.

"It's nice to meet you again, Mr. Schuple," I replied, "although I don't remember ever meeting you before." My hand remained in the firm grip of my new boss, the father of the most beautiful girl on earth.

"I think you were only three years old when your family last visited," Schuple recalled. "How are your folks doing?"

He finally let go of my hand.

"Fine," I lied.

"How was your trip? Any problems?"

I hesitated a bit. "Oh it was fine, no problem at all until... well, uh, Pokeville was a little interesting."

"What happened in Pokeville?"

"Oh, I just stopped at this gas station there, and I think I'll try to avoid that place from now on."

Schuple laughed and held his belly. I noticed how it made Kristel smile widely. "Ah, you must have met old Harold and Gretta," the Club owner chuckled.

Kristel, who had stood silently in the office doorway while she watched her father and me talk, finally joined the conversation. "I wouldn't ever stop there either, Jody! I know just what you mean. Harold and Gretta are weird!"

I was glad I could laugh with someone about my recent experience there.

"Yeah, I met them both," I continued. "The strangest thing was, they said I looked just like a guy whose picture was in today's newspaper. It was someone from Pokeville who was killed."

Schuple and his daughter immediately dropped their smiles and exchanged glances.

I noticed this but continued talking. "They said he was a guy who used to work here and they thought I must be related to him."

The warm, friendly faces once worn by Kristel and her father turned into grim stares. Discomfiting silence filled the room for several seconds before Schuple finally interrupted it. "Yes, that was Jim Grandstaff. He did work here for several years before he died at the end of last summer. It's been very troubling, especially lately, now that his accident is rumored to have been a murder."

I regretted bringing such an unpleasant subject into our happy meeting. "I'm sorry," I muttered, not knowing what to else say.

"Jimmy's death hit us all very hard," Schuple explained. His voice trembled slightly. "And you do resemble Jimmy somewhat, Jody. Old Harold and Gretta tend to get carried away, though. They have wild imaginations and they love spreading rumors. The worst place those gossipers could work is at that

Pokeville post-office."

"I'm sorry I brought it up."

Schuple regained his upbeat demeanor after a deep sigh. "Hey, *you* didn't bring it up. It's right there on the front page of the *Gazette*." He pointed to a folded newspaper on his desk. "It's not your fault there seems to be a bit of a resemblance. Now, why don't you check into your lodge and get all settled in. Then you can come up for dinner?"

"Sure thing, Mr. Schuple."

I turned towards my car outside and then realized something.

"Uh, where am I supposed to go?"

Kristel answered, her voice sounding not nearly as perky as it did when I met her five minutes ago. "Just drive around the back side of this building and down the hill. Keep going past the pool area and you'll see a field at the bottom of the hill with a softball diamond. On the far side of the field you'll see several cabins in the woods. Those are all for the staff. You're in the cabin called Saranac. It's easy to find."

She said it so dryly. Something wasn't right.

She searched through a nearby drawer and handed me a key, completely avoiding eye contact. What was wrong with her, I assumed, was the talk about Jim Grandstaff. She must have been friends with him.

So much for her giving me a tour of the dining room.

In a few minutes I was in a shaded grove surrounded by six small cabins, one of which displayed name "Saranac" painted in yellow letters across the top of the door. The names of the other cabins in the grove included "Mousetrap," "Birds Nest," "Paradox," "Hay Loft," and "Hawkeye." The paved roadway had disappeared back near the softball field, and I had driven up a dirt trail along the right-field foul line towards the wooded area where the six cabins were peacefully resting. The grounds around the cabins, including the wooden steps under each door, were carpeted with brown, pencil-long pine needles. Three picnic tables sat in the center of the grove, also blanketed with needles. It appeared that no one had been in this part of the Club property for many months, probably not since the end of last summer. I parked my car alongside Saranac and grabbed one of the large, bulging, nylon gym bags, my copies of *Gatsby* and *The Deerslayer,* and a pillow from the back seat. After searching my pocket for the key Kristel gave me, I entered my new home for the summer, my "lodge," as Mr. Schuple called it.

The place smelled and looked like an attic. Four sets of bunk beds, two on the left wall and two on the right, created a wide-open space in the middle of the cabin in which a rusty-orange easy chair rested. The chair was of garage-sale quality at best. Upon each bunk, ugly, gray pinstriped mattresses rested upright on their sides, leaning against the wall. Behind each of the eight mattresses was a window where sunlight was trying to sneak through. I found a light switch near the door and flipped it on, causing one set of fluorescent lights above me to flicker before producing a dim, yellow glow and a soft, buzzing hum. The lights were suspended from the rafters and were not very effective in brightening the room. "So this is it," I said to myself out loud. "Looks comfortable enough."

Had my spirits not been energized by the beautiful Kristel Schuple and the sight of the magnificent facilities of the Brown Swan Club, such meager accommodations might have been more disappointing to a new staff member. As for me, this was my new home, and I took to it easy enough.

I flopped the mattress down onto the link-springs of a bottom bunk, revealing a little screen-protected window made of six panes of glass that opened like the air-conditioning vents in my car's dashboard. I rotated the squeaky crank to let some air in, and the scent of Christmas trees again filled my nostrils, replacing the musty attic smell.

Graffiti scribed in small letters covered the paneled wall around the window frame, and I perused the many inscriptions from summers' past. "Girls must have used this cabin once," I said out loud to myself, noting phrases like "I love Tim" and "Lisa + Bill 4ever" written with red, pink, blue, and green ink in neat, plump, round letters with little valentines drawn to dot the i's. Graffiti of male origin was mixed in, too. Phrases such as "Red Sox Rule" and "JOANNA' GOT BIG BOOBS" were scratched in sloppy, singular letters.

"I'll bet Joanna has never seen this wall," I said with a chuckle.

My heart skipped a beat when I read the haunting words, "Jimmy G. slept here, 1995."

"So this was Jim Grandstaff's bunk three years ago," I muttered. "I guess it's fate. I was supposed to pick this bunk."

I hastily dusted off the ugly, pinstriped mattress and dropped myself down upon it, tucking my pillow behind my head. I was determined to overcome this predicament of being mistaken for a dead person. It was my bunk now, not Jimmy's.

I stared up at the rafters through the link springs of the upper bunk, took a deep breath of the pine-scented breeze wafting through my little window, and rehashed the most recent events of my life. Just last night, packing my belongings in my bedroom back home. Early this morning, hugging my mother good-bye. Eating lunch at the rest area on Interstate 90. Harold and Gretta. The picture of Jim Grandstaff. The news report on the radio. Beautiful Lake Marilee. The Goddess Kristel Schuple. Her friendly father, my new boss. These thoughts flashed through my mind like a slide show while I reclined on my newly claimed bunk. Anticipation turned to anger when I started thinking about my parents.

It had been a few months back that I seriously began hating my parents, especially Wesley. Although he's my stepfather, he's the only father figure I have really ever known. Even though he's my legal father and I'm his legally adopted son, I always called him by his first name ever since I could talk.

My greatest fear in life was that I'd turn out to be just like Wesley. The man drove an Acura Legend to work everyday, and I couldn't stand to see him in it. I never wanted to be like him, no matter how successful he looked on the outside. Frankly, he treated my mother and me like crap, and I hated him for it.

On the weekends, he would always romp around in his white Suzuki Sidekick. That really ticked me off, because when he wasn't on the job or building an addition onto our four-bedroom house, he was on a hunting trip or at the races. I never rode in that Sidekick with him. Not once.

Wesley raked in about ninety grand a year from his job at Keystone Insurance. He spent most of it on himself. He won countless trophies in sharp-shooting tournaments, and he would buy himself a new crossbow, hunting rifle, fishing pole, or some other must-have item he'd see in his *Outdoorsman* magazine. He had more stuff than he could keep in the garage, and despite all his material possessions, he had mega money problems. It didn't make sense to me, his being that wealthy and whining about money all the time.

He was also an elder at our church, Riverside Unity. Old ladies would always come up to me and say things like, "Oh, you're Wesley Barrett's son. My, you're the striking image of Wesley!" I hated that! Not only because those idiotic women didn't know there was no blood relation, but because of all people in the world, I didn't want to be compared to my stepfather at all. Ever. When those idiots praised him like that, I would try to think of something intellectual to say, like one of Mr. Gray's axioms, but I could never think of one on the spot. "He's a jerk," I'd end up saying under my breath, when the ladies were through with their blubbering.

My mother, in too many ways, was just like Wesley, and although I loved her, I never wanted to turn out to be anything like her either. She drove a Volvo to work, got her hair done every week by some lady who spoke French, and I swear she had a wardrobe that could reel in a fortune if she would ever break a sweat long enough to set up a yard sale. That's why she insisted that Wesley add on to the house, which only increased their financial stress. She complained incessantly that she didn't have enough closet space. Five bedrooms for a family of three. Go figure.

Although she could be pretty mean at times, I felt sorry for Mom a little. She was, at least, nice to me, and I thought if her husband weren't such a jerk, she'd be a much better person.

Anyhow, my parents gave me everything a person could ever want or need growing up. My own room in a big house, food and clothing, Christmas presents and birthday presents, and spending cash whenever I asked for it. The morning of my sixteenth birthday I woke up to find a brand new Mustang in the driveway, but Wesley stayed in bed when I drove it for the first time. Regardless of that, any kid my age would think I had the best parents in America. But they never saw them fight every day like I did, especially the really bad fights I had witnessed during the spring. They never knew what it was really like in the Barrett household.

When I was born, I went from the hospital to the day care center. My mother worked at a bridal shop and Wesley was busting his butt selling insurance policies. Every morning at 8:30, Monday through Saturday, I was dropped off at the Wee-Grow Family Center. That routine was just slightly altered when I started kindergarten. By the time I was in the fifth grade, I was old enough to become a latchkey kid.

Sometime during my childhood, my parents went from lower to middle class, and finally to upper middle class, but that's when, ironically, the problems really started getting bad. It was like when the money started coming in, they suddenly started hating each other. Wesley had been working for Keystone Insurance for a while and had finally become a bigwig with the company. He had a nice office, so I heard; I never actually saw it. I don't think my mother ever did either.

Mom started her own business as a wedding coordinator six years before. Eventually, we moved into a beautiful home with a three-car garage, two lifetime memberships at Countryside Athletic Club (for Mom and Wesley only), a fishing boat (we kept it on the Scioto River), and I went to a private high school. But my parents hated each other, and it was all about money. I often wondered who would get the house when they divorced.

Well, things were getting pretty bad after the holidays, and it lasted all winter and spring. I never heard a nice conversation between my parents during that time. It was always an argument about who owed what, how much this cost and who wanted to buy that. Two or three times a week the argument would turn into a scene from Jerry Springer, only Mom wasn't throwing punches—she was throwing shoes and candlesticks and coffee mugs, anything within arm's reach. One day she heaved the portable TV from the kitchen counter at him. It left a big dent in the dishwasher.

It was one night in May, one of the rare, peaceful nights—only because Wesley wasn't home, when my mom came into my room with an old photo album.

"I want to show you where I worked in the summer when I was your age," she said, opening up the thick album full of plastic pages that were turning yellow.

At first, I thought it was strange that she came in to talk to me. I looked curiously at the pages full of small, fuzzy, fading color photographs of my mother's younger days. Most of the pictures were of people—young people—strangers to me, but not to my mother who gazed at them, smiling.

"This is where I worked," she said fondly, pointing at a picture of a building that looked like a snow lodge surrounded by flowers and posh landscaping. "It's a mountain resort called the Brown Swan Club. I spent many, many summers there." She began flipping through the pages, grinning at some of the photos.

I didn't say anything.

"I thought maybe *you* might want to work there this summer. I know you could make a lot of money serving tables. The people who go there are very wealthy, and they give you generous tips if you do a good job. I know you could make at least five thousand, Jody, and probably a lot more before the summer ends."

I looked closely at the photographs, mostly of people outside on a lakefront beach with mountains in the background. It certainly didn't look like Ohio.

"Where is this place?" I asked.

"Upstate New York. Way up in the Adirondack Mountains. It's so beautiful up there!" My mother sighed sentimentally. "You would love it Jody! You'd make so many friends! We had beach parties every week, and we lived in our own little cottages. We even got to meet some famous people who were guests there."

"Who?" I asked.

She listed off a few names of entertainers that she thought were famous but whom I had never heard of before. I wasn't much into movies or TV anyway.

This idea of hers that I leave home for the summer had come from nowhere. I had assumed I'd work at the water park near the zoo like I did last year. The prospect of spending my summer away from home was one I had never, ever considered. It was a lot to think about. "So you want me to go all the way to New York for a whole summer?" I asked tentatively.

Mom nodded and smiled.

"You think I can really make that much money there? Five thousand dollars?"

"Honey, the man who owned the Brown Swan Club when I was there is still the owner. I just talked to him recently and he said that last summer his servers earned over a hundred dollars a night. Sometimes they'd make a lot more than that. Many kids went home with six or seven thousand by the end of the summer."

She obviously had put a lot of thought and planning into this before she talked to me about it.

"His name is George Schuple," she added in an excited tone. "He is a wonderful man, Jody, and he said he would love to have you on staff this summer. All we have to do is call him."

I didn't make a decision until two nights later when, during another fight, Mom took a stack of dinner plates and crushed them on the back of Wesley's head as he was heading out the door. Blood was all over the kitchen—he was yelling and Mom was yelling and I came downstairs and yelled, "I'm leaving!" They seemed to ignore me. I later heard Wesley got eighteen stitches for that particular incident.

That night, I went to my friend Mark's house and stayed there—just to stay away from Mom and Wesley. About three days later, my mom was waiting for me after school at Mark's house. She had an application for the Brown Swan Club in her hand.

I filled it out.

For the three-and-a-half weeks between that day and this one, I tried to keep a clear distance from both of my parents. I never said a word to Wesley—not a single peep. And, to be honest, the only time I talked to my mother was when it was necessary to discuss my trip to New York.

Now, here I was, on my own bunk, in my own cabin, about to make my own living at a place six hundred miles away from Wesley and Mom. No screaming, no yelling. No furniture tossed about. No blood on the refrigerator. Peace at last.

So much peace, I dozed off to sleep.

I slept for about a half-hour and woke up to the sounds of footsteps outside the cabin door. The knob rattled and the door creaked open. I quickly sat up on the mattress, preparing to accost a stranger.

# CHAPTER 3

## *Finding a Friend, Riling a Witch, and Subduing an Enemy*

He was a lanky kid with dark skin and black curly hair. He stepped into Saranac wearing gray sweat pants and a bright blue tank top. Pressed under each tubular, brown arm were bulky canvas bags, shaped like engorged laundry bags, both the color of army fatigues. I was relieved to see that the stranger must be a new staff member like myself. I said hello as the door swung shut behind him.

The newcomer hurled his bags on the floor inside the door.

"Hi," he said. "I take it that's your car out here."

"Yeah, do I need to move it somewhere?" I asked him, noticing that he was familiar with the cabin. Now I began to feel like the stranger.

"Nah. You can leave it parked there tonight. Most of the staff won't be in till tomorrow. Nice set of wheels, though." The young man flopped the mattress down on the bunk directly across from mine, grabbed each bag, and swung them onto the bed with a grunt. "These were a bear carrying up from the bus stop."

"Where's the bus stop?"

"Right down in Abbeyville. You can get there in three minutes if you cut back through these woods here. It's a lot faster than the road, unless a guy's got a car, like you do."

"I guess you've worked here before."

"This is my third summer." The friendly young man extended his hand and we shook. "My name's Boonie."

His wide, charming smile was welcoming.

"Boonie?" I repeated, making sure I heard right.

"Yeah. That's what they call me around here."

"My name's Jody."

"Hi, good to meet ya'." He paused and gave me the odd, recollecting look that I had come to expect from people who probably knew Jim Grandstaff.

"You must think I look like somebody else," I remarked.

"Yeah, you do. You look like a guy who used to work here."

"I know. I found out he died last fall, and ever since I got here this afternoon, people have been mistaking me for him—like I'm Jim Grandstaff's ghost or something."

Boonie posed a devilish grin. "Man, this sounds sick. But you could play a really cruel joke on someone!"

"Yeah. It's like *I am* his ghost. Did you know him very well?"

"Yep. He and I worked in the kitchen together. I'm really going to miss him this summer. We had some good times." Boonie studied my lineaments closely. "But you know, now that I look at you, you don't look exactly like him—only at the first glance. What's your name again?"

"Jody. I'll be waiting tables this summer."

"That's good," Boonie said, sitting down on the edge of his bunk. "I'll be cooking the food you serve."

"So you're one of the cooks?"

"Yep. This summer I'm the First-Cook," he announced proudly. "I'll do all the breakfasts and lunches. So where ya from, Jody?"

"Ohio. I got in about an hour ago." I looked at my watch. A quarter to six. "I'm supposed to meet the Schuples for dinner in fifteen minutes."

"I'm from Michigan. So you know Mr. Schuple already, huh? Great man—he's done a lot for me."

I nodded in agreement. "Yeah, his daughter isn't half bad herself."

A big white smile squeezed two little dimples into Boonie's brown cheeks. "You're friends with Kristel?"

"No. I just met her today. I'd like to be friends with her, though."

Boonie smacked his knee and smiled widely with an open mouth. "Man, you've been here an hour and you already got it in for Kristel! It's the same thing every summer!"

"What? What do you mean?"

"Every guy who comes through here falls for Kristel, and I haven't known one of them to get past her parents. They're extremely protective. Especially her mother."

"Really?" I was surprised and a little embarrassed.

"I'm not kidding. Last summer Mrs. Schuple saw Kristel and a lifeguard talking alone on the beach one night, and the next day Mr. Schuple fired the lifeguard." Boonie snapped his fingers and said, "Just like that!"

"No way!" I gasped, chagrinned by this information. "But she seemed really nice. Not stuck-up or anything, like some rich kids."

Boonie kindly slapped me on the shoulder. "Take it from me. Forget about her. There's gonna be a lot more women around here than Kristel Schuple! Jus' you wait an' see! Be glad that you'll be out front waiting tables where you can see 'em and talk to 'em!"

I was beginning to like Boonie's sense of humor and the friendly manner in which he teased me. It made me feel accepted, and that's exactly what I craved in the new world I had entered.

"I thought it was policy that staff members aren't supposed to fraternize with the guests?" I asked curiously. "That's what it said in the handbook they sent me."

Boonie put on a serious, but comical, expression. "Hey, now that's just a written policy. The bottom line is that we, as staff members, are supposed accommodate the needs of the guests."

"So Mr. Schuple doesn't care then?"

"About us hangin' with the female guests? Nah. Not as long as they initiate it and we ain't out there infringing on their vacations when they don't want us to." Boonie grinned devilishly, his white teeth shining like a crescent moon. "And believe me, Jody, Brown Swan women do most of the initiating."

I thought it over a moment, not sure if I should believe my new friend entirely. So I asked, "Just how old is Kristel?"

Boonie snickered. "She's seventeen."

"I'm sixteen!"

"Hey, I'm telling you man, you're only in for a hard time if you go after her. Her mother can be a downright witch. Just stick around me and I'll get you hooked up with one of the staff women. They'll all be here tomorrow, and I know most of 'em."

"That's okay," I said. "I can handle my own. Kristel's dad and my parents have ties that go way back." I donned a proud smile.

"Really?" Boonie said, obviously impressed.

"Yeah," I responded in a serious tone. "Besides, I don't think I've ever known anyone as nice and as good-looking as Kristel. You can't just give up on someone like her without at least trying."

"That's true. But you'll be meeting a lot more babes like her, I can promise you that. Especially if you're going to be prancing around the dining room in your waiter's uniform! And with that car of yours, we could have a lot of fun together!"

"We'll see what happens." I replied, pretending to be nonchalant by looking at my watch again. "Are you coming up for dinner?"

"Nah," Boonie sighed. "You go on ahead and dine with your Schuple women—both Kristel and her mom! I'm going to get set up here." He started wrestling with the drawstring on one of his bags. Then he asked, "Hey, you wanna go into town tonight and stock up on some food and stuff?"

"Sure, I should be back in an hour or so."

I was pleased to have secured a friend.

My first meal at the Brown Swan Club was a modest gathering of several year-round staff members. George and Beverly Schuple, their daughters: Kristel and her little sister Becky, and the leaders of the grounds, maintenance, and housekeeping crews were present at the table. There was Frank Williams, an elderly white haired gentleman with a rosebud smile and dirty fingernails. He was in charge of planting all the flowers around the grounds. Sam Buell was a baritone and balding maintenance man who acted like he was in charge of just about everything. He made sure everyone knew that new air conditioning units had been installed in twelve chalets, and that he had done the entire installation of each and every single one of them, and if there was any problems with some of the remaining older units they should be reported to him immediately. Donna Weathers was a plump, middle aged lady who didn't say a single word during dinner to anyone except the person next to her, a frail, slump-shouldered little girl about fourteen years old whose name I never learned. They both worked in housekeeping, as I heard them whisper to each other something about a new brand of shampoo they would be stocking in each room and that they could take home the leftover case of the old brand. Several other adults were at the table, but their identities don't stick out in my memory.

We ate in the quiet, commodious five hundred-seat dining room that overlooked the plush, shaded front lawn. Seated near a wall-sized bay window, we could see the entire hillside rolling down to Route 7 and the glimmering surface of Lake Marilee. The hillside lawn was adorned with a fountain, a gazebo, dozens of Adirondack chairs, and thousands and thousands of colorful flowers. This was indeed a summer paradise.

The extra-long dinner table had been created by the rearrangement of several smaller ones. The rest of the dining room was dark and quiet, despite the benevolent fuss made by the group over the modest food buffet prepared by two of the cooks.

"Next week at this time, this dining room won't be so quiet," Mr. Schuple reminded his staff as he patted his round belly. "Hard to believe another season is upon us."

His wife Beverly remarked frantically, "I hope Darlene has ordered the new white linens. We just cannot continue to use those ugly mauve ones in this dining room! And the uniforms! Oh, I hope Darlene is planning to fit the staff in their uniforms as soon as possible. I remember having to help her mend pants just hours before the opening dinner last year!"

Beverly Schuple was just as Boonie described her: insistent, meddling, and rarely did she say something pleasant. She was dressed rather elegantly for such an informal occasion: pearl earrings and necklace, bracelets by the dozen, and a professional looking business suit. Her face, makeup, and hairstyle reminded me of the president's wife, and by the way she conducted herself, it is fair to say that the first lady of the Brown Swan Club was not unlike her counterpart in the White House in every way.

Having listened to her officious comments spill from her mouth during the entire meal, I fully understood how Boonie's negative opinion of the woman had developed. Nevertheless, trying to beat the odds, I kindly suggested to her, "I could be fitted for my uniform tonight, if that would be helpful."

"Oh, are you a waiter?" Mrs. Schuple asked coldly, glancing at me before she looked at her husband. "George, I thought you told me that *he* would be working in the kitchen."

Her words were like shards of ice. Boonie was not at all exaggerating when he spoke about Mrs. Schuple being a "down-right witch." How could a shrew like her have such a wonderful family?

Mr. Schuple mumbled something about a rearrangement, and I gave up right there of ever trying to win his wife's affections. There was no use. I kept my mouth shut for the next ten minutes. The two cooks cleared the buffet while everyone else sat around the table and chatted.

"So you met Boonie?" Kristel asked me, as others eventually began dismissing themselves from the table, including George Schuple. Mrs. Schuple remained seated.

"Yeah, he seems pretty nice," I answered. "He seems like a lot of fun."

"Oh, he is," Kristel said with a little sarcasm. "Though sometimes Boonie gets a little *too* friendly with the guests."

"I can tell that already."

"Do you want me to show you around the grounds now?" Kristel asked sweetly, an invitation I did not expect, especially in the presence of her mother. The invitation caught Mrs. Schuple's attention as the woman peered across the table at her daughter in silent disdain.

I responded flatly, "Uh, well, I'd like to, but I told Boonie I'd go into town with him to get some stuff." I couldn't believe I was passing on an opportunity to spend time with the gorgeous princess, but the steel eyes of the wicked queen mother confirmed it was the prudent thing to do.

"Really?" Kristel chirped. "Would you mind if I came along? I need to pick up some things."

*That* certainly wasn't expected! I glanced at her mother who, at the most opportune moment, had been distracted by a cricket, a cockroach, or some sort of a repulsive insect scampering around on the carpet.

"George! George!" she cried.

Mrs. Schuple was a real hoot. Kristel and I got up to leave unnoticed.

A quarter of a mile around the bend of the Club property sat the romantic little town of Abbeyville. Other than the two-lane Route 7 that served as the town's spinal chord, Abbeyville had absolutely no resemblance to Pokeville, its nearest neighbor fourteen miles south. As Boonie, Kristel, and I coasted through town, people were everywhere, visiting pizza restaurants, gift shops, clothing boutiques, and ice cream parlors. A small public park nestled between the town and the lake was teeming with Frisbee tossers, screaming children, and strolling couples. The small beach adjacent to the park sported early-evening swimmers and a group of volleyball players. Abbeyville was everything that Pokeville wasn't.

"This town has been buzzing ever since Memorial Day weekend," Kristel said as we rolled slowly through town.

I parked in a vacant spot along the curbside in front of Ginny's Gift Shop where Kristel went inside to look for a Father's Day card. Boonie and I walked up the sidewalk towards the grocery store.

"Man, she's gotten even better lookin' this year!" Boonie said with a whistle. "Too bad she's off limits."

I shrugged off the gibe. "Her mother doesn't bother me," I replied, sounding confident, but feeling more like I was a little rodent sneaking into Beverly Schuple's home.

The grocery store was not modernized like the new, efficient super-stores back home. The doors opened by stepping on a black rubber mat instead of by an inconspicuous motion-detector; little price tag stickers were used instead of bar codes and scanners; and fresh produce was displayed on beds of crushed ice instead of refrigerated, mist-sprayed shelving. The aisles were narrow, and the entire store was barely bigger than the bakery section of the familiar one-stop super stores I knew in Ohio. Still, it had all the necessities for cabin-life: twelve-packs of Mountain Dew and Coke, bottles of Yoo Hoo, packages of Double Stuffed Oreos, tubes of Pringles, and boxes of Cap'n Crunch and Fruity Pebbles.

Boonie and I were in line at one of the two-check out counters where I noticed a newspaper rack displaying, among several tabloids, the *Lake Henry Gazette* and its familiar front page. I picked it up and eyed the photo of myself with Jim Grandstaff's caption under it. The article described how the police received a letter from someone identifying himself as John Doe who said that Jimmy Grandstaff's accident was actually a murder and that there was evidence left at the scene that would prove it. I read the same quote from Sheriff Clive Slater that I heard on my car radio earlier that day in which he said, "I'm sorry to say that the only way we can know the truth about this tragic death is to hear it from the ghost of Jim Grandstaff himself." I wondered how the sheriff's insensitive "ghost" comment made Jimmy's parents feel. The sheriff sounded rather stupid, if you ask me.

Suddenly, a small object bounced sharply off my head.

"What was that?" I grumbled, rubbing the back of my head and noticing of a small piece of crushed ice sitting on my shoulder. Another larger chunk shattered into pieces when it collided with Boonie's arm.

The culprit tossing chunks of ice at us was some goon in the produce section. He was a tall, young man, about twenty or twenty-one, bony and knuckly, with yellow-bleached hair, and clad in a black silk button-down shirt and baggy blue jeans. He wore a gaping, crooked grin, making his eyes squint fiendishly narrow. His appearance was the epitome of defiance.

His devilish stare abated when our eyes met. Perceiving a definite lull in his mischievous expression, I realized my likeness to Jim Grandstaff had taken yet another person off guard, briefly causing the stranger's eyes to dilate widely with surprise. However, he quickly recovered and resumed his taunting stare, this time at Boonie.

"Oh, geez," Boonie moaned. "Not him!" We both ducked when the prankster tossed a third chunk of ice our way. It disintegrated into small frozen water droplets across the candy rack behind us. The ice-tosser then shook his bony fist at us, keeping his longest finger erect in the universal symbol of vulgarity. The cashier, a gum-chewing woman with red hair in a beehive, noticed the commotion and shouted an imperative that sounded like she had shouted it many times before: "Knock it off, you imbecile!" The prankster snickered and shuffled down the dairy aisle out of sight.

"Who's that idiot?" I asked, surprised just as much by the cashier's blunt comment as I was with the stranger's ice tossing.

"That's Brock Oliff," Boonie answered. "He's the town jerk."

"You know him?"

"He plays in the band in the dining room at the Club. You'll get to see a lot of him this summer. His job is to play the saxophone, entertain the guests, and make life miserable for the entire staff."

I eyeballed Brock Oliff once more as he passed between the aisles at the back of the store. I wondered why Mr. Schuple wanted a guy like that on staff.

Ten minutes later, we met Kristel at my car, and we had difficulty pulling away from the curbside because of the constant flow of traffic crawling along the two-lane Main Street. I waited a few moments and finally capitalized on a gap—a chance to pull out safely.

At that instant, an accelerating engine roared behind us. Then the sound of screeching tires caused the three of us to jerk our heads towards the rear, where a foreign-made convertible had narrowly missed slamming into my bumper.

"You moron!" the driver behind us screamed at me. It was Brock Oliff, wearing the same crooked grin and devilish squint. "Just try that again, you freakin' idiot!"

"He did that on purpose," I said, glancing in my rear-view mirror.

Kristel ducked in the back seat while Boonie poked his head out the passenger window and yelled, "Back off, Brock! You caused it yourself!"

"Oh, no," Kristel moaned. "Why does it have to be Brock?!" She leaned over my shoulder and pleaded, "Quick, Jody, don't let him follow us! Pull off down this street!"

I obediently turned left in front of oncoming traffic and accelerated down a narrow residential lane. Boonie kept shouting out the window like a maniac, unfortunately enticing Brock to make the same quick turn and follow suit. The road led to a dead-end at a small, gravel parking area near the shore of the lake, and before I could do anything, my red Mustang was trapped between the water and Brock's silver Porsche. On either side of the car was a black wall of trees. "Oh, great!" Kristel cried, crouching in the back seat to hide from our antagonist.

Through the rear-view mirror, I watched Brock Oliff step out of his convertible and plow his bony fingers through his bleach-yellow, brush cut hair.

"I should have thrown chunks of watermelon at you instead of ice!" he shouted at Boonie, whose skinny frame was still hanging halfway out the passenger window of my car.

"Stay in the car!" Kristel screamed at both of us. "Lock the door!" She grabbed Boonie's shirt and yanked violently. "Boonie! Get in here! Roll up the window!"

To my surprise, Boonie refused to obey the demands of the princess. My new friend clicked open the passenger door and stepped out of the car to face Brock Oliff head on. Kristel cried, "I can't watch!" and ducked down in the back seat. I turned around to watch through the back window.

"Brock, you haven't changed a bit!" Boonie said boldly. "Except your hair color!" The handsome-faced, brown-skinned boy commenced a verbal assault upon his enemy with a series of curse words.

Brock cocked his pale arms at his hips. "And it looks like the mulatto still thinks he's hot stuff!" He then began his own chorus of curses, sounding even more rehearsed at the trick than Boonie did.

As I watched the confrontation develop, the last thing I wanted to do was drive somebody to the hospital.

Kristel prayed out loud, "God, don't let there be a fight!"

I don't know where it came from, but a sudden and exhilarating surge of adrenaline caused me to open the car door. Undaunted and galvanized by an inexplicable passion for adventure, I stepped out of the car and stood to my feet, and with the unwavering stare of a stalwart, I glared sharply at Brock Oliff. I had no idea what I was doing at that moment.

And for the second time, Brock's intimidating eyes softened when they met mine. Then, like the previous incident in the grocery store, the antagonist quickly recovered his bullish demeanor and returned his attention to Boonie.

"You just stay out of my way, boy!" he growled, poking his knuckly finger towards Boonie. "I don't want to see your zebra hide within ten yards of me again for the rest of the summer!" Brock then scanned my vehicle with a look of disgust, avoiding eye contact with me. "And tell your new friend the same."

I was relieved that Boonie chose not to respond. Brock strutted back to his Porsche, dropping additional profane phrases over his shoulder. His tires kicked up a spray of dirt and pine needles as he peeled away.

When we got back into my car, Kristel sat up in the back seat and slapped Boonie on the back of the head, hard enough to hurt, and certainly hard enough to show her anger. "You idiot! Who do you think you are?!" she shouted.

"I don't want him intimidating me all summer!" Boonie whined. "I had to take a stand early!"

"You almost caused a fight!" Kristel snapped back.

The three of us sat silently in the car, facing the lake. I was amazed by my own audacity, knowing that had I remained in the car, Boonie would probably now be nursing a broken nose. Feeling like a hero, I knew Kristel saw none of it. I asked, "How come you hid in the back seat, Kristel?"

She sighed, and in a much calmer voice answered, "I don't know. I hate him. I really do." She paused for a long moment and sighed again. "I don't like admitting it, but we dated for a short time this past winter, and I broke up with him. It's a long story."

Boonie raised his eyebrows in shock. "You *dated* Brock Oliff?!"

I tried in vain to show no reaction and only glanced in the rearview mirror to look at Kristel.

"I'd rather not talk about it." Kristel muttered, slouching down in her seat.

I didn't know what to think of her now. She had fallen a considerable estimation in my eyes, having dated Brock Oliff, a classic jerk. How is it that girls like her and guys like him get together? And with her mother the way she is? Perhaps I should just follow Boonie's advice and forget about her.

But then I peeked in the rearview mirror again. Her pathetic pout was cute, her eyes soft and somber. A curl of her hair brushed her cheek, and I melted again.

# CHAPTER 4

## *Learning the Legend, Starting Work, and Making a Home in the Adirondacks*

I had never actually heard the sound of quiet until that night. No whooshing cars zooming along the outer belt, no rumbling trains cutting through the city. No television chatter, no humming air conditioners, no arguing parents. Only chirping crickets. Just crickets, nothing else. Maybe a few frogs. An owl or two? Whatever they were, it didn't matter. They were making quite a raucous in the woods; but to me, it was incredibly peaceful.

Suddenly, Boonie barged into Saranac, flipped on the overhead fluorescent lights, inciting their soft buzz. He had just returned from the staff shower house near the ball field.

"Man, it took forever to get hot water!" he groused, hanging his wet towel up over a rafter with single, dexterous swipe. "The gas to the water heater was shut off. I had to light the pilot and wait for it to heat up. Stood there with my hand under the shower head for twenty minutes before it even got a little bit warm."

"I know. Mine was ice cold. I was wondering what was taking you so long."

I had taken the cold shower out of half-complacency, half-apathy. Had I even known how to light the pilot light on the water heater, I probably would have shirked the responsibility of lighting it and showered in the icy water anyway. I'm kind of like that with minor, insignificant stuff: I'll take the path of least resistance, even if it means a cold shower. With major things, like life decisions, I'm as stubborn as a mule.

So there I was, fresh clean, nearly frozen, curled into a sleeping bag on my bunk, ready to fall asleep. Boonie didn't even have his bunk made up yet, so we started talking.

"So what do you think of Kristel now?" Boonie asked, wearing a smirk.

"What do you mean?"

"You know. Her saying she dated Brock Oliff this winter. That guy's an idiot. I can't believe she fell for him."

"They're not dating anymore," I answered. "She said she broke up with him."

"Yeah, but what was she thinking? I mean, it's not like she's attracted to Brock's money. The Schuples are pretty rich themselves, not as rich as the Oliffs, but Kristel's not the type to go for money anyway. I just never would have put those two together."

I remembered the silver Porsche Brock was driving. I asked, "So how old is Brock?"

"I think he's twenty-one or twenty-two. I know he's been out of high school awhile."

"He didn't go to college?"

"Not that I know of."

"If he's so rich, how come his parents didn't send him to college? Is he stupid or something?"

"He's an idiot, but he ain't stupid." Boonie shook his head. "I don't know. Prob'ly because he doesn't need a degree to make his millions. He's got his whole future laid out for him already. His father is a billionaire and owns resorts and hotels all over the world. I'm surprised he doesn't own this one yet. He's been trying to buy it off Schuple for years."

"So why does Brock work here, then, especially if his parents are so rich? Isn't the Brown Swan Club his father's competition?"

"I guess it is. I don't know why Brock works here. Prob'ly because it's the only decent place to work around here. His parents own a huge mansion a couple miles down Route 7. It sits halfway up the mountain and overlooks the whole lake. I was up there once last year for a party. Man, is that place gorgeous."

"You went to a party at his house? I thought you and he are enemies."

"That's when it started," Boonie explained sheepishly. "It was the Fourth of July last summer—a Friday night—and a bunch of us were up there having a good time—you know, beer, girls, the Jacuzzi." Boonie's charming, bright-white grin illuminated his face. I smiled and listened to his story. "It was late at night, his parents weren't there. We had all been at the fireworks down at the lake and went up there afterwards to watch the Lights. And then Brock's girlfriend gets ticked at him for some reason and starts hangin' with me. She and I were just sitting there together watching the Lights—not doing nothin'—just sitting together, you know. And then Brock comes up and punches me out. He was drunk, so I kinda understood, but he's been pretty nasty to me ever since."

"What do you mean by watching the Lights?"

"The Lights of Marilee," Boonie responded plainly.

"What's that?"

"You've never heard of the Lights of Marilee?"

"No."

"They're the part of the Legend of Marilee Manor. You've never heard of it?"

"Nope."

"Man. Where have you been? The Legend is what put Abbeyville on the map. A lot of guests come to the Club just to catch a glimpse of the Lights."

"What are they?"

"They're the weirdest thing you've ever seen. Sometime in July, for just a few weeks, but not every night, you can look across the lake and see a lantern being carried back and forth in the woods over there. According to the legend, it's the Marilee ghost coming back for his gold. It's really weird when you see it: it freaks the heck out of me. But late at night a lot of people gather down on the deck above the beach to watch. It's a big attraction."

I asked cynically, "And everyone thinks it's a ghost? No one's gone over there to find out who's carrying the lantern?"

Boonie answered, "If anyone goes near the area, the ghost never comes out. That's why in July, there's a town ordinance prohibiting anyone from going over there at night. They don't want to scare off the ghost, because if the Lights don't show, the town will lose business. Stores stay open really late during July because there's all kinds of tourists around just to see the Lights."

"It sounds like a hoax to me."

"Could be. But it's pretty freaky if you ask me."

"And it only happens in July?"

"Yeah. It's supposed to be around the anniversary of a mass murder that happened across the lake a long time ago. That property over there is called Marilee Manor, and it's where the original Marilees first settled in this area. The Legend says that a long time ago one of the Marilees wanted to lay claim to the gold that was supposedly buried in secret vaults under the property. So he killed his entire family by blowing up the house late at night while everyone was sleeping. Thing is, he was found dead in the lake a few days later. People say he drowned in the lake trying to carry bags of gold across. And according to the Legend, the Lights are carried by Mr. Marilee's ghost coming back to carry more gold out. Some say the gold is still buried over there."

Ghosts and gold. Sounds like a PG movie. I interjected, "And people believe that crap?"

Boonie nodded and went on, "There's all kinds of versions of the Legend. I've heard some say that Mr. Marilee stayed here at the Club the night before he rowed over there and murdered his family. I've also heard there was a lantern and a bag of gold found down at the Club beach a long time ago."

It sounded like a fun story to tell, and I was surprised Mom had never mentioned it. She had a penchant for ghost stories.

"Have *you* ever seen the Lights?" I asked.

"Yeah, lots of times. The last time I saw them was that night up at the Oliff mansion, the night Brock beat me up. It was really far away though, but you could see them. Most people watch them from the Club beach, or down at the town beach in Abbeyville. They come out late at night, usually before midnight, and sometimes they last for just a few minutes, and one time they lasted for over two hours. But you can see them only for a few weeks in July around the anniversary of the murders."

"Why are they called the Lights? Is there more than one?"

"Yeah. What'll happen is, you'll see a lantern get lit up and carried near the shore where it gets set down. Then you'll see another lantern get lit up and start moving back and forth from the first light to some place back in the woods. Then, when the ghost is done for the night, he puts out both lights and disappears. I heard that sometimes the first lantern will burn all night long, like the ghost got scared off or something and didn't go back to get it. I heard that when that happens, they actually find an old lantern just sitting there the next morning. There's a restaurant in town that has three of the lanterns on display. Up in the Club lobby, there's the lantern that was supposedly found at the Club beach."

"That's really wild. Who do you think is doing it? You don't really think it's a ghost, do you?"

"I don't know," answered Boonie, as he flipped off the fluorescent lights and crawled into his bunk. "I don't know if I believe in ghosts, but it's pretty spooky to watch it. Kind of makes you think twice. Why? Do you believe in ghosts?"

"No."

"Well, wait 'till *you* see the Lights," Boonie said, as he crawled into his bunk. "One thing's for sure, I'd rather talk about something besides ghosts and crap before we fall asleep."

We talked little more after that, about girls and the current Major League baseball season and how Boonie was sure the Yankees would take it all again. Boonie had something to say on just about everything, but he wasn't an authority on anything. At first he sounded like he was a huge baseball fan, but then he didn't even know that Derek Jeter played shortstop. I decided Boonie's authority on the topic of Kristel might be just as limited. Nonetheless, he was pleasant to talk to, an everlasting party full of laughter and joviality. Plus, it was easy and fun to make him laugh, and his girlish giggle is the last thing I heard before dozing off to sleep.

I woke early Wednesday morning full of hopes of spending more time with Kristel. I soon learned, however, that she would be preoccupied most of the day. Considering her mother's unceasing meddling, it was probably for the best, for now, at least. So all I could do was spend the morning just sitting around the Club until something interesting happened.

The air was chilly as I sat in a wicker rocking chair on the open porch of the Club building. Through the trees at the bottom of the hill, I watched a thin, wispy, white cloud of fog float over the waters of Marilee. By nine o'clock, the lacy blanket of soft cotton was burnt away by the sun rising over the eastern mountains. In that wicker chair, I spent most of the morning in tranquil solitude, enjoying the heavenly setting of the Club property. I read the first three chapters of *The Great Gatsby*, part of my summer reading. I didn't have to report to the dining room until noon.

People arrived throughout the day—all of them summer staff members, some dropped off by their parents, and some arriving in vehicles of their own or in car pools. The paying guests would arrive in two days, on Friday, the official opening day of the season. In the meantime, I learned that the Club staff consisted of men and women ranging in ages from fourteen to fifty and was divided into housekeeping, grounds, foodservice, maintenance, or entertainment crews. From my seat on the expansive front porch, I watched them arrive, some exhibiting inhibitions of being in a new place, others the joy of returning to their summer haven.

A couple dozen staff members arrived before noon, and in between paragraphs of Fitzgerald, I admired Kristel who stood near the lobby doors accosting each of the morning arrivals with unfailing enthusiasm. Her charm was genuine, and her beauty unmatched. I tried to picture her together with Brock Oliff, and I tried to picture her with me. It was a stretch either way, but I believed the advantage was mine, if I could ever get around her mother.

She said "Hello" to me early, but even though she was nearby for most of the morning, she didn't say anything more. I thought she might still be embarrassed about her Brock revelation, or maybe she just didn't want to disturb my reading. Anyhow, I managed to admire her from a distance for two hours.

Around eleven, George Schuple approached and gave me another hearty handshake. "Get a good night's rest, Jody?" he asked with a wide smile.

"Yes. I never slept so soundly, Mr. Schuple."

The big man sat down on the edge of a wicker love seat across from me, causing the thick, stiff cushion to rise at the corners. He spoke slowly, "Uh, Jody, I need to let you know something. There's been an unanticipated change, and, uh, we're going to have to move you to food preparation instead of the dining room. You'll be working in the kitchen along with David and Allen, the cooks you met last night."

This news took me by surprise, but I should have expected it, considering his wife's comment at the dinner table last night.

"Why?" I asked. "I thought I'd be waitering."

"I know, and I apologize. It's just that Mrs. Schuple has been wanting for years to go with an all-female dining room staff." Mr. Schuple chuckled. "It's kind of a feminist protest thing, Jody. She sees only males on the grounds and maintenance crews and thinks it's only fair... well, I figured it couldn't hurt anything. You already met Boonie, right? You'll be working with him, too."

I thought it over for a moment. What was I to do? Say no, I'm not working in the kitchen? Instead, I acceded, saying, "I was kind of counting on the tips."

Schuple patted me on the shoulder as he stood to his feet. "I understand. I'll make sure you get a fair wage. I know you'll be a good worker."

"So who do I report to?" I asked condescendingly.

"Al Dernbaugh. He's the Head Chef. He's back in the kitchen right now, so why don't you go back and meet him and he might put you to work."

I rose from the wicker chair and glanced at Kristel sitting behind the front desk, eagerly waiting for more staff to arrive. To her father I kindly remarked, "Thanks, Mr. Schuple. I'm glad to be working here in any position." Brownie points, I thought to myself, wondering at the same time what a "fair wage" for a food prepper was. I didn't think it was appropriate to inquire at the moment, because I wanted him to trust me as someone willing to do what was needed.

Darlene, the bubbly, young head-hostess of the dining room, was folding white linen napkins into fancy, half-circle fans while Beverly Schuple stood next to her, complaining incessantly about the "tacky" decor of the dining room. I walked by them on my way to the kitchen and received one of Mrs. Schuple's signature expressions, a cringing stare that contorted her face as if she was smelling a foul odor. I was positive that she had something to do with my sudden job change, and I determined that someday I'd find out just what she had against me. I really felt sorry for Darlene at that moment, who, unlike myself, was in no position to walk away from the woman's henpecking.

Chef Al Dernbaugh was a hovering man, at least six-foot-five, and his long, white stovepipe paper hat made him yet a foot taller. He wore a loose-fitting white chef's jacket and black and white, hound's-tooth plaid pants. He was somewhat slim, as far as chefs go, yet he spoke with a deep, resounding voice—even when he wasn't barking orders.

"Ever worked in a kitchen before?" the tall chef bellowed at me.

"No, sir, but I worked at a snack bar at a water park last summer."

"All right. Just go back to the pantry and see Dave. He's your supervisor and he'll get you all set up."

Within my first hour in the kitchen, I was pleased to get to know both Dave and Allen, the two very cordial cooks I had met at dinner the night before. They enjoyed flirting with Darlene, who always found reason to come in the kitchen and ask one of them for something. I wondered if it was because she was escaping the witchy Schuple woman or if she liked Dave or Allen. They both obviously had a crush on her, and Dave, the older of the two, seemed to have the advantage over his partner.

The workload for the day was light. Only a modest lunch and dinner needed to be prepared for the fifty or so staff members who were to arrive that day. Dave and Allen made the work seem like nothing, cracking jokes and bantering back and forth the whole time, all in good fun. Boonie spent several hours by himself on the dining room porch assembling the enormous, outdoor grill. I remained in the pantry and sliced cucumbers into circles, cut tomatoes into wedges, and peeled the shells off hard-boiled eggs. The carefree spirit of Dave and Allen made the job enjoyable, and if I couldn't serve tables in the dining room, I was glad to be working with them instead.

Before lunch, two younger boys arrived in the kitchen, the Needleman twins, Pete and Rodney. These odd looking boys weren't identical twins, but each had fiery red hair and a galaxy of orange and brown freckles covering his skin from head to toe. The striking difference between them was that Pete had a plump, jolly-looking face, and he always smiled handsomely. Rodney's face was gaunt, and his ever-present goofy grin displayed jumbled rows of teeth in desperate need of an orthodontist. I learned that Pete and Rodney were assigned to the area of the kitchen known as the "dish-pit," and that they also would be my roommates in Saranac.

Throughout the day, numerous returning staff members asked me if I was related to the deceased Jim Grandstaff. I didn't mind the repeated questions. In fact, I thought it compelled people to introduce themselves to me and start up a conversation, which I appreciated. Some people were shocked at my resemblance to Jim Grandstaff, and others hardly noticed. Still others seemed to wear an eerie expression when they first saw me, and this was sort of bothersome.

At lunch, I met several more arrivals: Chad Pelham and Jason Zielig, groundskeepers; Ron Lyons, a lifeguard; and Jeff Gunderson, a van driver. As usual, these returners inquired about my possible relation to the deceased former employee. All seemed to have somehow heard about his death, as the tragic news was not a surprise to anyone.

Brock Oliff arrived at lunchtime dressed in those ninety-dollar baggy jeans and a Montreal Canadians hockey jersey. He greeted several girls with cloying chivalry, and it was obvious that he intentionally ignored me completely. It was my Jim Grandstaff-like face that intimidated him. I watched him sit at a separate table, hooting and hollering with several of his male friends, all whom I assumed to be band members with Brock. It didn't take long to realize that Brock and his friends were part of an elite clique.

Several attractive girls had arrived, and they also sat at separate tables, giggling amongst themselves and talking about the events of their recent school year. Dave and Allen joined me, Chad, Jason, Ron, Pete, Rodney and Boonie at our own table.

Kristel, who had yet to say to me anything more than a shy "hello" all day, walked past our table and said nothing. I began to think that she was purposely refraining from speaking to me. I watched her sit at a separate table with her parents, and she never once looked over to me. I even considered that perhaps Kristel might actually be a bit of a snob, but I didn't want to think negatively about this beauty until I knew for sure.

"Looks like a pretty nice-looking crop this year," Dave joshed, referring to the attractive girls who had already arrived. All of the guys snickered and Boonie nudged me and said, "See, I told ya." I looked around and thought he was right, but still no one was prettier than Kristel.

Towards the end of lunch, Boonie and I were instructed to take the afternoon off and return an hour before dinner to help set up. "The real work will begin in a couple of days," Dave advised.

Back at the cabin, Boonie and I, along with the Pete and Rodney Needleman, worked together to convert Saranac into our summer home. We built shelves made out of plastic milk-crates turned sideways and stacked in two columns, five crates high. Posters of baseball players, expensive cars, and supermodels in bathing suits were tacked to the wood-paneled walls. The old garage sale easy chair was covered with a clean, pale-blue bed sheet, and a sawed tree stump was brought in from the woods for a footrest. Boonie retrieved a large window fan that he had hidden in a storage shed from last summer. He mounted it sideways between the rafters like a ceiling fan and connected it to a wall outlet with a string of extension cords draped over the rafters. Plugging it in sent a whirlwind of dust and cobwebs around the cabin, but nobody cared to ask where we might find a broom.

Pete and Rodney Needleman brought from home everything but their own beds. I would've liked to have seen the vehicle with which their parents hauled them here. It must have been a U-Haul truck, for crying out loud. Between them they had two ten-speed mountain bikes, one small refrigerator, a 19-inch color television, a Sony play-station and a Nintendo 64, two baseball bats, four ball gloves, two soccer balls, one football, a collection of weights and barbells, an ironing board and iron, a clothes drying rack, two folding patio chairs, a hot-air popcorn popper, and an electric skillet. And these were the things *not* in the boxes and suitcases they had yet to unpack.

By mid-afternoon, our milk-crate shelving, stacked next to each bunk, displayed folded blue-jeans, an assortment of shorts and T-shirts, balled up socks and underwear, and an ungodly array of junk food. The two empty sets of bunks that would go unused were shoved to the rear wall of the cabin. They would be our storage shelves for empty suitcases, cardboard packing boxes, and most of the merchandise belonging to Pete and Rodney. By the end of the day, these empty bunks also served as a piling place for dirty laundry. The mini refrigerator, provided by Pete and Rodney, hummed in the corner of the cabin. It was full of canned pop that Boonie and I had purchased the night before. Pete and Rodney insisted it wasn't called pop; it was called soda. They were from Rochester, and surprisingly, the twins had arrived lacking their own supply of canned "soda."

"I like it this way—only four to a cabin." Boonie declared. "I never thought I'd say this, but I'm glad they moved all the girls out of the grove and up to their own lodges. It gives the guys more cabins to spread out in down here."

"I can't imagine these cabins crowded with eight people," I commented.

"Well, they didn't move the girls out of the grove because of space," Boonie said. "They did it because somebody told Mrs. Schuple that we were having wild parties down here every night."

Pete Needleman, wide eyed and grinning, piped up. "Was that true?"

Boonie donned a proud expression. "Well, you know. No parties, like Mrs. Schuple thought. But we did have one of those yellow blinkers that they use around road construction, and whenever it sat in the lower left window of Mousetrap last summer, everyone knew that it meant Do Not Disturb. It was a communication system that I devised." Boonie's white teeth flashed a venal smile.

Pete looked at Boonie in awe. "So how does the system work now that the girls are gone?"

"Well, after they moved to the lodges up on the hill, we came up with our own underground railroad. When we get it all worked out for this summer, I'll let you know. It won't take long." Boonie snickered.

Pete shook his head. "I think you're all talk." His brother Rodney remained silent as always, wearing his goofy, jumbled-tooth grin.

I reclined on my newly made bunk covered with fresh, clean sheets and a blanket that smelled like home.

"That's right, Pete," I said, half grinning, tucking my hands behind my head. "From what I hear, all the girls feel the same way you do about Boonie." A retaliation pillow collided with my face, and its originator attacked us all with lighthearted insults. We all laughed.

In the Adirondacks for just twenty-four hours, and I totally felt at home.

# CHAPTER 5

## *A Corny Number, Old Whisper, and an Appointment at the Beach*

Boonie and I helped Dave and Allen serve the evening meal that night, and I met more members of the Club staff. The inquiries about my likeness to Jim Grandstaff provoked the repeated recitation of my tactful response: "No, I'm not related, and I never met him either." I hoped a week from now, no one would think any more about it.

Kristel, who had still not spoken to me since the night before when she admitted dating Brock, again sat alone with her parents during dinner and ignored me completely. I suspected her mother might have forbidden her to speak to me. But why *me*? What didn't Beverly Schuple like about *me*?

An all-staff meeting was scheduled for nine o'clock that night, and the boys of Saranac—Boonie, Pete, Rodney, and I, slightly soiled from light kitchen duty—returned to our cabin to change clothes. We were intrigued to see that the once-abandoned shady cabin grove had suddenly sprung to life. The fluorescent lights inside all six cabins glowed dimly in the darkening woods as young men moved about, in and out of doors, unpacking cars, and arranging bunks.

A quick scouting trip educated us about our new neighbors. The cabin named Mousetrap housed five other boys assigned to the kitchen: two food preppers like myself, and three dishwashers like Pete and Rodney. Four groundskeepers, including Chad Pelham and Jason Zielig, with whom I ate lunch, occupied Paradox. Bird's Nest became the summer home for Ron Lyons, the lifeguard, and Jeff Gunderson, the van driver. Two college students, who said they were on the Club's program staff, also lived in Bird's Nest. Brock Oliff and three of his band buddies had taken over Hay Loft. Brock's shiny, silver Porsche was conspicuously parked in front of the cabin steps.

The final cabin, Hawkeye, remained dark and unoccupied.

"How come no one's in that cabin?" I asked.

Boonie answered, "There's an old man who stays there that you'll hardly see all summer. He's the night watchman, and he sleeps in there all day with the door locked and the windows covered."

"And he gets the whole cabin to himself?" Pete asked.

"Yeah," Boonie continued. "And everyone here likes it that way. He's a weird old man who supposedly spent time in prison. He's got a crippled leg, and he roams these grounds all night long in a golf cart. I guess he ain't here yet 'cause his golf cart is usually parked right along side there, plugged into the wall."

"They've got a criminal with a crippled leg guarding these grounds at night?" I asked in disbelief.

Pete joked, "He's the best man for the job. I wouldn't snoop around here knowing a convict is driving around on a golf cart ready to shoot me." Pete's twin brother Rodney stood next to him in his usual silence, his mouth hanging open in a silly grin, revealing jumbled teeth.

"Somebody once told me that the old man's got twenty years worth of girly magazines inside there," Boonie said, cracking a grin. "*Playboy, Penthouse*, you name it. I've even heard he's got a T.V. and V.C.R., and stacks and stacks of porno videos."

This news intrigued us all, and after a moment of contemplation, the four of us determined that the notorious night watchman had not yet moved into his summer quarters; therefore, it would be safe to investigate.

Together we crept onto the tiny front porch of Hawkeye and peered through the window of the wooden door, hoping to confirm Boonie's report about the stacks of paraphernalia stored inside. The wooden planks creaked under our weight, and the door rattled hazardously in its loose frame when we pressed our noses against the glass. The inside of the cabin was shrouded in black shadows, and before we could survey any contents within, a sudden and unexpected voice abruptly ended our investigation.

"What are you doing up there?" called the dulcet voice of a young woman directly behind us.

It was Kristel, straddling a ten-speed bicycle, and staring at our guilty quartet like a teacher stares at disobedient children. We each spun around on the wooden steps and stood abashed in front of the beautiful girl.

"Just seeing if Whisper's here yet," Boonie lied.

Kristel ignored him. "Jody," she called, "can I talk to you?"

Alas, to my surprise and delight, the princess had finally addressed me once again, and she wanted to talk to me! —in front of all the guys, in the middle of the grove!

I stepped off the squeaky porch and approached the Brown Swan princess. She pivoted her bike around me so that her back was to my cabin mates who were watching from Hawkeye's porch. Although I had spent time with Kristel in town the night before, I felt privileged to stand next to her again twenty-four hours later. It was different now. People were watching. The staff had arrived. The annual challenge undertaken by the male staffers to befriend Kristel Schuple had begun that morning, and my standing alone with her in the center of the grove surrounded by male cabins certainly would make my peers envious. Kristel Schuple had summoned me—just me—and I had done virtually nothing to bring it on. I felt the jealous glances of my co-workers deflecting off my back.

"Are you busy tonight after the staff meeting?" she asked in a voice that would cause angels to stop and listen.

The provocative question made every hormone in my body start spinning like a thousand toy tops whose tightly wound strings had just been violently yanked.

"No, I guess not," I stammered.

Although the hormones were spinning like mad, every muscle in my body miraculously froze when Kristel locked her blue eyes to mine. Her countenance, I noticed with curiosity, appeared to be subservient, as if she were asking me a favor.

"I'd really like to talk with you tonight, if you don't mind," she humbly entreated. "It's kind of important."

"Okay." The hormones still raged like violent tornadoes in a mass of frozen muscles.

"I'll meet you down at the beach after the meeting," she said.

For me, only the words "Jody, I want to be your girl and love you forever" could have sounded better. "All right. I'll see you there," I somehow answered.

A warm smile that could thaw Alaskan glaciers set my frozen muscles free. "Thank you, Jody," Kristel replied. "I'll see you then." She pushed down on the right pedal of her bicycle and rolled away, out of the grove and down the dirt path along the fence-line of the ball field.

Everyone, in silent awe, watched her ride off, as if a legion of nymphs had just passed through the grove on horseback.

Shortly, I would get to know more about Kristel than most of the guys on staff ever would. Few males, so I had been told, ever got the chance to speak to her in private. But she wanted to talk to me—only me—and without her wicked mother around! That meant I might soon know who she really is: a rich man's spoiled daughter with beauty only skin deep? I hoped not. A tease? A flirt? I doubted it. In any case, at least, I would know what was so important that made her want to speak with me—down at the beach, under the stars, alone!

A large multi-purpose room was connected to the refreshment stand near the swimming pool. Nearly one hundred metal folding chairs were arranged in rows at one end of the room. Billiard, ping-pong, and foose-ball tables filled the room's other end, near a small kitchen that sat dark and quiet. Glass doors of the dining area at the rear of the room lead to the white concrete pool deck. This building was known as the Poolside Cafe.

It was a scene of happy reunions as returning staff members greeted each other for the first time since last Labor Day. Other young people sat quietly and watched the folks converge as a staff once again. Still others tried to fit in on that first night, gathering in circles and standing with their hands in their pockets, attempting to hide their desire to be accepted. I noticed many new faces and recognized several familiar ones belonging to people I had met earlier that day. One well-shaped girl, I noticed, whom her friends called Joanna, did indeed live up to the message scratched into the wall over my bunk. Boonie, the Needleman twins, and I found chairs in the back row to the right of the center aisle.

Kristel was preoccupied in the front of the room, assembling a microphone stand near the piano. I watched her as she sat on the piano bench, arranged sheets of music, and scanned the room to judge if any more people were still coming through the doors. For one heavenly second, her eyes connected with mine, sending the tops a-spinning inside me again. She quickly returned her eyes to the sheets of music, positioned her hands on the keys, and pounded out an opening roll that sounded like a prelude that movie companies use at the beginning of dramatic films.

The staff hushed quickly and settled into chairs as Kristel banged out the introductory number. She ended on a sustained high note, and at this precise moment, the undivided attention of the entire room was upon her. Kristel paused just long enough to create the designed effect, and then began playing again, this time a bouncy, playful little song that sounded quite comical. Some people giggled.

Now, her father appeared in a corner doorway. He was wearing a black top hat, a matching tuxedo jacket, and a big red bow tie. He skipped and hopped to the front of the stage as if he were Mickey Rooney in an old black-and-white musical, singing a happy tune as he danced. What a showman Mr. Schuple was! He sang,

*We're here together*
*It couldn't be better*
*We're gonna have a ball at the Brown Swan Club tonight!*
*Sister or brother*
*Significant other*
*We're gonna have a ball at the Brown Swan Club tonight!*
*The food is exquisite*
*Prolong your visit*
*We're gonna have a ball at the Brown Swan Club tonight!*
*Cast off your troubles*
*In Jacuzzi bubbles*
*You're gonna have a ball at the Brown Swan Club tonight!*

The staff, comprised mainly of teenagers and college students, laughed with joy at Schuple's corny number. Boonie whispered in my ear, "He does this every week for the new guests. They love it." Hearty applause, whoops and whistles saluted Schuple when his song ended.

I noticed Kristel press an embarrassed smile between her rosy lips as she stood up from the piano bench. She tiptoed to the front row and sat in a chair in the far corner, opposite the guys and me. I could see her giggling with a few of her female friends as her father bowed gracefully to the staff members who continued their sarcastic ovation to their boss.

"Be glad you only have to see that once," were the first words Schuple quipped to his staff.

A hearty, standing ovation, full of sincere whoops and whistles was the reply from the crowd, led, of course, by the returners who knew how to mock their leader in good fun.

"Thank you. I knew I'd get a standing ovation sooner or later," Schuple kidded. More whoops, cheers and applause. Finally, Schuple pronounced triumphantly, "I'd like to welcome the 1998 Brown Swan Club Summer Staff!" For a third time, the crowd offered an obstreperous response, and I knew I was part of a lively group.

As Schuple began formally addressing the staff, I scanned the crowd and again noticed Kristel sitting up front with the group of girls, each smiling brightly and listening to George Schuple. I noticed Chad Pelham and Jason Zielig sitting in the middle along the center aisle; Ron Lyons, the lifeguard, and Jeff Gunderson, the van driver, along with several other boys from the grove seated in front of me. Brock and his buddies sat together amidst a flock of pretty waitresses with whom he had been flirting ever since lunch. Many other attractive girls, whom I had not yet met, were dispersed throughout the crowd. None of them, I again determined, came close to exceeding Kristel's beauty and charm.

Schuple continued, "I'd like to introduce some of our full-time staff members." He motioned to the front row at the corner opposite Kristel. "This is Al Dernbaugh, our executive Chef... Allen Bickers, our Sous Chef... Darlene McFarland, our dining room hostess... Jerry Krandall, the head of our maintenance department...." A light round of applause was given between each name.

During the introductions, I watched a latecomer enter the door near the snack area in the rear of the room. He was an older man, limping heavily as he walked towards the back row, and he carried a worn, leather briefcase under his arm. His right leg was stiff and straight from the hip down, making a loud "clomp" when his heavy brown boot hit the tile floor. Several heads turned backward to see who the person was.

Boonie leaned forward and informed us of the man's identity. "That's Whisper—the perverted security guard who gets Hawkeye all to himself."

"What's in the briefcase?" I inquired in a soft voice.

"Pornos, probably," Boonie said with a snicker.

I watched the newcomer clomp his way to the open back row of seats across the aisle from us. He sat down in an aisle seat and placed his briefcase upright next to his chair. This man they called Whisper appeared to be near sixty years of age. His graying hair was cut flat and close to his scalp, making him look like a retired military veteran. An aura of wisdom and experience encompassed his face—sharp, level eyebrows perched studiously under rows of wrinkles that stretched across his forehead. Thin wrinkles branched out from the corner of his eyes, reaching his long, rectangular, gray side-burns. He was a lean man, wearing neat and trim clothing, a button-down white shirt tucked into gray pants. He held a worn, faded black ball cap in his lap. To me, the man called Whisper looked more like a war hero than a pervert, or more like a wise old professor than a former prison inmate.

Whisper's arrival appeared to go unnoticed by Mr. Schuple, who either overlooked his night watchman's late entrance or choose not to bring attention to him with an introduction. Whisper's presence did, however, draw the attention of Brock and his cohorts. Earlier, they had somehow managed to obtain plastic drinking straws from which they now fired spitballs at Whisper's old briefcase. When one direct hit splatted in the dead center of the leather case, a round of suppressed laughter blew out from the boys' nostrils. Although they attempted to keep their giggles soft enough to prevent a major disruption, they did manage to draw attention to themselves from the girls around them, probably to their pleasure. Brock's crooked grin told the story to all who turned their heads to see. Several eyes glanced down at Whisper's briefcase, and after detecting what they expected to find, rolled back into the sockets of their owners as if they had seen the same thing several times before.

While Brock and his buddies convulsed with internal laughter, Whisper did not bat an eye. He just stared forward at George Schuple with a flat smile and crossed his hands over his ball cap in his lap. I wondered if the man knew that spitballs were being shot in his direction. Whisper's head never moved once, although everyone else's did when Brock's gang let loose more of their mischievous snorts.

During all this, Schuple concluded his introductions: "Finally, I would like to introduce our greeter, our resident piano player, and my oldest daughter, Kristel."

Kristel remained in her seat, smiled brightly, and modestly waved her hand once at the applauding crowd. I watched a few male heads shift in order to catch a glimpse of the Brown Swan princess.

Schuple went on, "My youngest daughter, Becky, is away for the evening, but I'm sure you will all see her here on the grounds in the days to come. My wife, Beverly, is working up in the dining room, and as soon you are done with your ice cream, all dining room staff need to report there to get fitted for their uniforms tonight."

I wondered why Mrs. Schuple was working to take care of the uniforms, instead of Darlene, the head hostess, who was sitting next to Allen among the full-time staff members in the front row. And why wasn't Mrs. Schuple here at the opening staff meeting?

"Before we dismiss you to the ice cream table out on the pool deck, there are a few staff rules we must all recognize before we officially begin our 1998 season."

Schuple went on to explain several basic rules for staff life: no use of the pool during peak afternoon hours; no entering guest's rooms; no mingling, dating, and socializing with guests. Boonie poked me in the ribs and smiled when Schuple covered that one.

As the boss continued speaking, I wondered if I was supposed to stick around the pool and eat ice cream and meet other people, or if I should go straight to the beach and see Kristel. She told me to meet her after the meeting. Is ice cream part of the meeting? While I thought this over, I noticed Kristel slip out of her seat and tiptoe down the side aisle to the back entrance. Just as she opened the door, she turned backward and tossed a quick glance towards me. I knew then that I would miss ice cream that night.

# CHAPTER 6

## *The Revelation*

George Schuple hashed over staff rules for what seemed like an hour. It was actually just a few minutes after Kristel had departed, but the anticipation of meeting alone with her in the dark on the beach was like lying awake in bed all night on Christmas Eve.

We were finally dismissed to the pool deck where everyone lined up behind a folding table where individual styro-foam bowls of ice cream had been scooped by Dave Wall and two helpers during the meeting. The glassy, electric blue surface of the swimming pool shimmered under the starry sky, and several torches around the concrete deck burned orange flames, creating flickering illumination for the ice cream lovers. I left Boonie with Pete and Rodney, and they collectively chided me for passing up make-your-own-sundaes "just to meet some girl."

Alone, I climbed the steep roadway from the pool area and passed by the Club building. Hurrying past the front porch, I could see Mrs. Schuple in the dining room busily re-arranging stacks of linens on a storage shelf. I again wondered why, at this hour, she was taking upon herself a job that wasn't hers.

The long, winding, steep driveway led me down the front of the Club property. Lamps in yellow glass boxes built into the stone wall shouldering the drive illuminated my path. The lights on the beach deck could be seen glowing at the bottom of the drive across the road. I wondered if Kristel was waiting for me there, or if she would be on the darker, sandy beach below the deck, in complete seclusion.

At the base of the driveway, I reached the crosswalk that intersected the narrow Route 7, leading to a set of white-painted wooden steps that descended down the steep embankment towards the expansive beach deck.

At last, I saw Kristel leaning on a railing, gazing out over the mass of blackness where Lake Marilee serenely slept. The princess was there alone, under a glowing globe lamp. Her golden ponytail fluttered on her shoulders in the soft evening breeze. Her back was turned, and I didn't want to frighten her with a sudden entrance, so I intentionally stepped loudly down the wooden steps.

"Hi!" she said, turning around swiftly and leaning her backside against the railing. "Is the meeting already over up there?"

"Yeah. I didn't stick around for ice cream," I answered, descending the steps towards the wooden deck.

"You could have stayed," she said in her melodic voice. "I wouldn't mind. I like coming down here where it's quiet."

Stupid me. I didn't know what to say next, so I just uttered the word "Oh." I'm such a dipstick when it comes to stuff like that.

Kristel added, "But I'm glad you're here now. Do you want to sit down?"

I quietly sat next to Kristel on the wooden bench built into the railing that surrounded the entire deck. Several white, round picnic tables were scattered about, each with a closed umbrella stemming up through the center, like a flower ready to bloom. Sitting next to the princess, with her tan legs painted amber by the globe lights, and her eyes sparkling heavenly blue, and the sweet smell of her golden hair redolent of strawberries, I could not have dreamt a better scene.

"I suppose you're wondering why I needed to talk to you down here," she said, wearing a diffident smile, one that made her eyes softer, sort of apologetic.

"Yeah. I guess. I was really wondering why you seemed to ignore me all day today." I had not planned that comment at all. It came from nowhere, slipped out, and shattered on the deck. I hated myself for it. I hoped it didn't sound like I was mad at her.

"Well, that's kind of what I need to talk to you about."

She sighed and glanced at the stars overhead before continuing. "I need to apologize for my mother. She really embarrasses me for the way she treats some people."

I lied, saying, "Oh, I don't mind that. I really haven't noticed anything out of the ordinary." I swallowed hard.

"I'm really sorry, Jody." Kristel said. "She has this problem with guys I have for friends."

I nodded. "Yeah. Boonie tried to warn me about that."

"He's right. Mom really doesn't care at all for Boonie either. She doesn't like most guys around here. I hate it. It drives me so crazy!"

I tried to appear nonchalant. "Well, it doesn't bother me. I can get over it. I understand how parents can be over-protective."

"But it's a little more serious than that, Jody."

She paused. Something heavy was about to be delivered.

"I know I shouldn't be telling you this, but my mom has a special, um… a special dislike… for you specifically."

To someone like me, who had impressed every woman I had ever known—aunt, teacher, nurse, saleslady, you name it—with my innocent boyness, this comment came as a complete shock. I could no longer pretend not to be bothered by her mother's disapproval. It was personal now.

"Me? Why me?" I asked, vexation beginning to swell.

Kristel's eyes fell to the planks of the beach deck. Then they flipped up towards the starry sky again, as if their owner were at a loss for words.

I argued carefully, "She hardly knows me."

A silky, soft hand pressed gently down upon my forearm. Kristel held it there saying, "I know, Jody. It's a long story."

I was now thoroughly confused and perplexed, despite the pacifying sensation of Kristel's hand. I was sad to see her remove it to her forehead when she rubbed her brow in stressful thought.

I insisted, "Well, you've got my attention now. Why doesn't your mom like me?"

She hesitantly replied, "You see, Jody, it has to do with other people more than it has to do with you."

"Other people? You just said your mom doesn't like me specifically."

She stared for a moment up the hill at the lights of the Club flickering through the trees. Then she directed her stare into my anxious eyes as she answered, "Myself. Brock. And some other people. That's who."

"What do you mean?"

"It was all my mother's idea for Brock and me to date. She set me up with him, and expected me to fall for him."

"Why? He's such a jerk—"

"I know. But he's a rich one, and that's what's most important to my mother."

"That sucks."

"Yes, but I can get over that," she said, with a bit of rebellion in her voice. "She's not going to dictate to me whom I marry. I'm only seventeen, anyway, for heaven's sake! I think her plan for Brock was that I would be unavailable to date other guys when the summer began, because she just hates to see me with the staff guys."

"But you ended up breaking it off with Brock, right?"

"Mm hmm. And my mom was really upset when that happened. It's funny, because my dad was sort of glad. I don't think he likes Brock very much."

"So your mom has a special dislike for me because I'm the first guy on staff this summer to talk to you? Is that it?"

Kristel paused for a moment. "It's a little more complicated than that." She buried her face in her hands and mumbled to herself, "I can't believe I'm doing this." She said it loud enough for me to hear.

I tried to come up with my own explanation for all this, and the only thing I could think of was that George Schuple was a very close friend of my mother. "Does it have to do with my mom?" I asked impatiently. "Did she know my mom when she worked here?"

"No, Jody." Kristel answered, lifting her now tear-filled eyes to mine. "Before the whole Brock thing, I dated this other guy at the end of last summer. My mom didn't like him for the same reasons she doesn't like you. It had to do with his family background."

"Why, because his family wasn't as filthy rich as Brock's?" My tone of voice was becoming rather terse.

"Yes. That's part of it. My mother places a lot of stress on a good family heritage. But I think it's something more than that. She knows something about your family that makes her nervous for some reason."

I considered the suggestion. "Well, I'll admit my parents aren't the best couple in the world. I think they're going to be splitting up soon. Is that what your mother has a problem with?"

"She's wrong for judging you, Jody."

"Judging *me*?"

"Yes. She judges you because she knows your parents and she has something against them. I don't know why, but she doesn't like them. I know it for a fact, and I'm sorry about your Mom and Dad splitting up, and I know whatever they're like should not be a reflection upon you. It's just… it's… this is all so stupid!"

"They haven't split up yet. They just fight a lot."

Kristel seemed to ignore this. She sighed heavily and fought back tears as she gazed upward. Then she said, "Jody, I'm going to tell you something that might upset you, and I'll probably get into a lot of trouble for telling you."

"What? Tell me." I was ready for anything. I thought I was, at least.

"You know that other guy I dated at the end of last summer?"

"No. I don't know him. You only told me your mother didn't like him, too."

"He was Jim Grandstaff."

The name hit me like a bucket of cold water. This fully explained why Kristel was being so emotional. I muttered, "I'm sorry, Kristel."

Unwavering, Kristel continued to speak. "You know how so many people here think you look just like Jimmy?"

"Yeah. I've been hearing about it all day long."

Now she gulped. More tears swelled in her eyes. One got loose and trickled down her cheek. I had no idea where she was taking me with this discussion.

"This is probably going to come as a great shock to you," she said, returning her hand to my knee.

"What?"

And then she hit me with the most shocking news of my life.

"Jimmy Grandstaff was you brother."

# CHAPTER 7

## *Kristel's Suspicion*

Your brother.

My brain went numb.

Your brother, she had said.

My imagination, or Kristel's nonsense? Did I hear her right? A sick joke? Was she being serious? *My* brother? Questions ricocheted inside my head like wild pinballs.

Kristel's tears were now rolling down her cheeks and I could not doubt that she was being genuine. I was speechless, only able to read her eyes, and they were shouting, It's true! It's true!

She was not lying. It was not a joke. My brain repeated over and over again the phrase she had just voiced: "Jimmy Grandstaff was you brother." I couldn't believe it. The longer I sat there gaping at her pretty, tear-streaked face, the more I was assured that Kristel was being serious, yet I still couldn't believe it. But I had to respond, somehow.

"My brother? How? That's impossible," I uttered with a quivering voice.

Before Kristel answered, the possibility of it all flashed through my mind. Could it be true? It *could* be true! Visions of my mother blinked before me. My stomach twisted and went cold as my intuition shouted, It *can* be true! It *can* be true! It *is* true! My heart froze, and my face drained into paleness.

"You had an older brother, Jody, who was adopted by a family who lives near here." Kristel compassionately explained this to me as she wiped tears from her face. She repeated it and placed her hand on my arm again.

We sat there in silence and, despite the shock, I worked the whole thing out in my head—that it was entirely possible that I had a brother I never knew. I wanted to admit this to Kristel, yet I wanted to deny it at the same time.

"My mom had an abortion when she was seventeen," I said, locking my eyes to Kristel's.

She shook her head and replied calmly through her rosy lips, "My parents told me not to tell. But I had to, because… because…"

I interrupted her stumbling. "My mom had an abortion before she had me. She was just a teenager." My voice became stern and monotone.

Kristel answered firmly, "She didn't abort him, Jody. She gave birth to Jimmy and put him up for adoption. My father told me about the whole thing."

I knew she could be right. I knew she probably was right, and as the possibilities rushed through my mind again, I knew she was absolutely right. She was telling the truth. My parents had lied to me all these years! It all began to make sense now. Still, there were questions, hundreds of them.

"But Wesley, my stepfather… he told me she had an abortion. He told *me* all about it."

I stared into Kristel's eyes and decided that if there is anytime to spill my guts to someone, it was right now.

"My stepfather—Wesley. He said my mom got pregnant when she was seventeen and had an abortion, and then about a year later, the same guy got her pregnant again, but he ran off that time when she refused to abort it again. That's how I was born. And that's when Wesley married my Mom—while she was still pregnant with me. He didn't learn about the abortion of her first pregnancy until last year when my Mom finally told him. She would always get very emotional around Christmas time, because that's when her first baby would have been born. She finally told Wesley the truth last year, and ever since then my parents have had problems." I gulped hard. Kristel listened intently to every word.

"Jody, your mom gave birth to the baby. She put him up for adoption. The Grandstaffs adopted him—they're a wonderful family—and they raised him. He grew up right around here—outside of Pokeville."

I knew it to be true now. It all made sense: the endless questions about my relation to Jimmy; the picture in the newspaper; and now this sudden revelation. It all made perfect sense! Kristel couldn't be making this up. She was sharing this with me for a reason, and suddenly, amongst the shock and anger about having been lied to all my life, I started to get excited, like I had just found something that had been lost. I have a brother! But as quickly as these feelings came, they departed. I realized I would never know my brother. He's dead. It was all falling apart as quickly as I had put it together.

"It doesn't matter. He's gone now," I mumbled, trying to stuff my emotions in my back pocket. I thought of my maxim, Trust Yourself.

We sat next to each other in silence and all I could think was, why would my parents lie to me? Perhaps it was only Mom who lied—both to me and Wesley. But why? Why would anyone admit that she aborted her baby when she actually gave birth to the child and allowed it to live with a loving family? Why claim that you killed your unborn baby when you actually let it live? Why? None of it made sense, and I wanted to know the whole truth. I had to find out why.

"Jody," Kristel said softly, interrupting my thoughts with her soothing voice. "Stay here. I want to show you something."

She retrieved a large book that had been sitting on one of the patio tables. It was a photo album—one she had brought here to show me during this planned conversation. She brought it just for this moment. This monumental moment.

"These are some pictures of Jimmy. I brought them down here for you to look at tonight," she said. We shifted to the left so as to be directly under the glow of the yellow globe light. Kristel sat snugly next to me and opened the album.

A collection of photographs of the Club's grounds, guests, and staff members filled the pages. "That's Jimmy right there," Kristel said happily, pointing to a boy standing among several other young people.

For the second time in two days, I was staring at a picture of myself.

"Gosh, he looks so much like me. He has to be my brother."

"And this is him right here," Kristel continued, smiling. Her tear-tracks had almost disappeared from her cheeks.

Another photograph, this time of Jimmy sitting on the beach deck, the same one Kristel and I were sitting upon this very moment.

Together, we thumbed through the album and Kristel talked briefly about her past summers, pointing out a few current staff members that I would get to know. She gave special attention to the photographs of Jimmy. Some of them were of Jimmy and her together.

"That's the last one I have of him," Kristel said, pointing to a picture of her and Jimmy standing in front of a large, old war cannon. "We went to Fort William Henry last Labor Day."

I stared at the photograph for a long time. It was as if I had been there myself, holding Kristel's hand at Fort William Henry.

Tucked between the last page of the album and its back cover was a small, loose photograph.

"This was taken back in 1985," Kristel explained, holding it up. The photograph was of several young children and a few adults sitting around a table on the snack bar patio next to the pool. I recognized the setting, having left Boonie, Pete, and Rodney eating ice cream there before I came down to the beach to meet Kristel. I looked closely at the picture.

"Is that your dad?" I asked, pointing to a younger and slimmer George Schuple.

"Yes. And that's your mom," Kristel replied, pointing to a young woman sitting next to Mr. Schuple at the table.

I bent my head down and stared closely at the figure. "Your right, it is! Was this when she worked here?"

Kristel smiled. "No. See—there's you and there's me." She pointed out two of several toddlers in bathing suits, sitting on the cement eating Popsicles.

I chuckled and looked at Kristel, realizing we had spent time together years ago when we were little kids. I actually had been to the Brown Swan Club before!

"And see that woman back there in the pool?" she added. "The one holding the little boy?"

I looked closely and noticed the figures in the background. "Yeah."

"That's Elisa Grandstaff, and that's Jimmy."

"We were here together?"

Kristel didn't respond, and suddenly I made the connection.

"My mom knew he was here, didn't she."

"Yes," Kristel said. "She desperately wanted to know that her first son was doing well. The Grandstaffs live around here—but they hardly ever came to the Club, except when Jimmy began working here when he got older. I think Daddy did your mom a favor and invited them over for the day while your family was here on vacation."

"So my mom got to see Jimmy. Did the Grandstaffs know that Jimmy's real mother was here?"

"I don't think so. Somehow, my father worked it out so they didn't know anything. I think your mother just wanted to see Jimmy. Just see him once, you know…"

"Did my step-dad know?"

"I don't think so. If your mom told him that Jimmy was aborted, like you said, probably not. She probably kept this little reunion a secret between my dad and her."

I paused and stared intently at the photograph. I muttered, "I can't believe this."

Kristel added, "Daddy was like a big brother to your mom, almost like a father in some ways. I think he knows everything about what happened in your mother's life. He'd kill me if he knew I were telling you this, Jody."

"Why? Why did my mom say she aborted him?"

"I don't know."

"Does she know that Jimmy died?"

"I don't know."

I thought for a moment and added, "It was her idea that I should come here this summer. I thought it was because this is where she spent her summers, but if she knew Jimmy had died… maybe… I don't know. It doesn't make sense."

"It's possible she doesn't even know that he died," Kristel offered. "Maybe she saw Jimmy that one time back then, and that was enough for her. She hasn't been back here since, obviously. And that's why my father hoped that you wouldn't learn about Jimmy—so it wouldn't get things all stirred up again with your mom."

I pondered the suggestion. "I've got to find out," I said, suddenly standing up to leave. "I'm going to call her."

Kristel grabbed my arm and cried, "No, Jody, don't! I'll get in so much trouble!"

For the first time, and although I wished otherwise, I started to get a little impatient with Kristel. My mind was spinning so fast, and now she was getting in the way.

"Then why did you tell me all this?' I asked sharply.

I received only a blank stare.

"Why? Why, Kristel?" I asked again, raising my voice. "Did you really think you could tell me all this and expect me not to do anything about it?"

"No," she replied softly.

"Then, I'm going to call my Mom and find out the rest of this ridiculous story."

Kristel gripped my arm tighter and cried, "Please, Jody, don't."

"Then why did you tell me?" I snapped angrily.

"Because I was there when Jimmy died!" Kristel shrieked.

This caught me completely off guard.

She started sobbing, spewing forth words through a flow of tears. "I saw the whole thing! I saw the blood!" She wiped her eyes, but they quickly filled with more tears. "I saw him fall, I saw the whole thing!"

Now I regretted having been sharp with her. I sat down next to the sobbing princess and gently placed my hand on her shoulder. A vision flashed in my memory. Déjà vu?

The trails of salty tears caused Kristel's face to glisten under the lamplight. She sniffled and swallowed as she shared with me her terrifying story.

"We went to Smooth Rock Falls to swim. It was going to be our last swim there for the season, before the water gets too cold. It was one morning last September."

She paused, sniffled, and regrouped.

"There's this cliff that Jimmy liked to jump from—about fifty feet above a small pool near the bottom of the gorge. The water is really deep there, but you have to jump just right to land in the middle. I never did it, but Jimmy had jumped it hundreds of times. We went there together—it was actually our first date alone, with no one else. We climbed down the gorge, jumping off the smaller cliffs towards the bottom. When we reached the last pool at the bottom where the river continues on, Jimmy started climbing up the side ledge. I knew exactly where he was going—to his favorite cliff. He got to the top and disappeared, because you have to step back from the cliff and get a running leap to clear the rocks at the bottom. He said it takes three good strides—if you jump too far, you miss the pool and hit the rock wall on the other side. If you don't jump far enough—you land on the boulders directly below.

"Six years ago, a man fell from that cliff and died, but he was drunk and didn't know what he was doing. I had seen Jimmy do it a dozen times before that day—each time he landed right in the middle. He was an expert at it, and everyone knew it.

"I couldn't see him from where I was sitting at the bottom of the gorge, but I heard him shout 'Are you ready?' and I answered 'Yes,' and then… I saw him falling over the cliff. I knew something was wrong as soon as I saw him because it looked like he was diving headfirst. He had never tried to dive from there before. He said he only felt confident doing it feet first.

"And then—it was sickening, Jody! He didn't land in the water. I'll never forget that sight! I had nightmares about it for weeks. I sometimes still do."

Tears were rolling down her cheeks again. I remained quiet and listened.

"He didn't jump out far enough," she cried. "He hit the boulders head first and died on impact. They said he must have stumbled on a stone or a tree root or something during his run."

Kristel wiped the tears from her face, sniffled, and sighed. I remained speechless, picturing in my mind the scene that she had painted for me.

Moments went by as we sat there. The breeze felt cooler as clouds crept across the sky, covering the stars. The moon was now partially blocked by the silent, moving masses of dark vapor.

I finally broke the silence. "Kristel, I've really got to talk to my Mom about this."

A red-eyed, pleading look came from my companion. "No, Jody, you can't. My parents will disown me. You're not supposed to know anything about this. I shouldn't have told you—I'm sorry."

Rolling my eyes in mild disgust, I advised her, "Just tell them I figured it out all on my own. Say that I was interested to find out about Jimmy because I look so much like him."

Kristel continued to plead against my wishes. "No. Don't tell your mom. She'll call my dad right away. I know it."

I started getting angry again. "Then why did you tell me all this?"

Unbelievably, her lips slipped into a half smile, annoying me even more. Was she now going to tell me that this is all a joke? I watched her think to herself while she stared up at the now starless sky, fighting off her untimely smirk. Then she shook her head in disbelief, still smirking sheepishly.

Finally she said, "Believe it or not, Jody, there's more to this story."

I countered sarcastically, "What, you're now going to tell me that you're my sister or something? That your dad is my biological father?"

"No, Jody. Stop it. I'm being serious, and I doubt you'll believe what I'm going to say next." Her smile finally disappeared—quite abruptly—and she hesitated before continuing. The tears welled in her eyes again as she said in a shaky voice, "I told you all this because I think you have a right to know. But even more than that, I told you because I don't believe Jimmy fell from that cliff accidentally. I think he was pushed."

I paused a moment to let it sink in, staring quizzically at the girl whom I wanted to get to know so badly. But this was more complicated than I could ever have imagined.

"Are you saying that you're the John Doe who gave that tip to the police?"

She shook her head earnestly. "No, I'm not. I don't know who did that or why. But when I heard that story yesterday morning—that someone told the police it was a murder—I started thinking. I had put the whole thing out of my life for several months, but then I started remembering. I remember screaming at the top of my lungs when I saw Jimmy fall. They told me later that I went into shock. I don't remember everything, but I do remember that the first person who came to help me was Brock Oliff. He held me as I screamed into his chest, 'He fell! He fell!' Brock is the one who first went for help. Days afterwards, he was very nice to me, very supportive, if you can picture him that way. I really appreciated his kindness. He went to the funeral, too. Several months later, we started dating, much to the delight of my mother."

"You think Brock *pushed* him?" I asked bluntly.

She nodded her head. "Maybe. He hated Jimmy before then. He hated that Jimmy and I were dating. And the more I got to know Brock during the months after the accident, the more I realized how much of a jerk he really is. As sincere as he seemed in comforting me after the accident, it was as if he was glad that Jimmy was gone so that I would be with him. Then yesterday morning, I heard the rumor about the murder, and I really started hating Brock. I haven't said anything to him about it. I just have this awful feeling. I have nothing for proof. But this feeling that he did it is *so* strong. I can't explain it."

I kept quiet for a brief moment. I knew Kristel was waiting for me to say something.

Finally, I asked in frustration, "Kristel, why are you telling me all this? Do you expect me to solve this whole thing right here and now? I'm trying to get over the fact that my parents have lied to me all my life, and that the brother I never knew is dead, and now...."

I stopped when Kristel pressed her hand upon mine. "Jody, I just had to tell you. I honestly believe that Brock may have played a part in Jimmy's death, and I had to tell someone. When I saw you the first time yesterday when you arrived, I knew I couldn't keep all this inside for the whole summer. Please don't be angry with me."

This was about all I could take. I stood up and shoved my hands into my pockets, and felt tears swell in my own eyes. I didn't want Kristel to see it, so I walked towards the steps, and without turning my head toward her, I said, "The more I sit here and listen to this, the more I wish you never told me anything."

"I'm sorry, Jody!"

Tears were escaping from my eyelids now, so I started up the wooden steps, shouting to the princess as she remained on the bench, "I'm sorry too, Kristel. I have to go make a phone call." I bolted up the steps towards the road while Kristel cried in protest.

"No, please don't!"

# CHAPTER 8
## *Midnight Madness*

At the pay phone inside the lobby, I paused to catch my breath before dialing. I had run up the entire length of the Club's grassy lawn, stumbling over tree roots, and I think I trampled through a newly planted flowerbed.

I pulled out my phone card from my wallet and began dialing, expecting to hear the voice of my mother any moment.

"Hello?" a masculine voice grumbled on the other end of the line. Not the person I wanted at all. It was Wesley.

"Is Mom there?" I asked flatly.

"Jody? Where are you? It's about time you called home!"

Yeah, right, you jerk. What do you care, I thought to myself. Still catching my breath, I ignored the man's comment and asked again, "Is Mom there? I need to ask her something." I knew Mom was always home this late on a Wednesday night, even during this busy time of the year for her. It was June—wedding season.

Wesley's dry reply was startling. "She's gone, Jody."

"Where is she?"

"She wasn't here when I woke up yesterday. Most of her clothes are gone."

I didn't say anything.

Wesley went on, "She took her car and hasn't been back. I assumed she was with you."

I knew this day was coming, but I was surprised that it had happened so soon. My mother must have planned to leave the same morning that I did.

Along with the revelation I had just received from Kristel on the beach deck, this one from Wesley couldn't have been more fitting. What a turn of events! This was supposed to be my escape from home to a summer of peace and freedom, and now my world was falling apart the day after I got here.

"She left you, huh," I responded matter-of-factly.

"It appears that way," Wesley said. "You don't know where she is?"

"No."

"And where are you?"

"You don't even know where you're own kid is?" I snapped.

"It would be best for you to come home immediately, Jody."

"Forget it."

I slammed the phone into the receiver, and boy, it felt good.

But then I tried to think, and that wasn't easy. Nothing was clear. It seemed I had no other choice: I had to talk to my mother. Only she could clear this up; but she's left home. I paused, sighed, batting empty hangers on a coat rack, trying to think. I thought of Mr. Gray's "Trust yourself. You're the only one you can count on with absolute certainty," but my gut was telling me, "you need to talk to your mother—now."

Impulsively, I mentally grasped for something I could control—anything—something within my bounds of management. Then it came to me: I decided to go home and find her. I would leave the Club tonight. That was it.

I knew it was a rash and desperate decision, giving up on the summer before it got started. It was clearly a spontaneous act, but it had to be done. I had to trust my instinct, stay in control. I had to go back to Ohio and confront my mother face-to-face about the brother I never knew.

This summer was done. Finished. Over, just one day into it.

My mind was mush.

As if my slamming the receiver down on Wesley triggered an internal switch that catapulted me into madness, I dashed from the lobby and tore down the backside of the property towards the cabin grove. I'd pack my car and leave immediately. Suspecting where my mother had gone—to her best friend's apartment across town—I could be there in ten hours.

Midnight was approaching, and the pool deck was now dark and empty. I slowed to a jog when I reached the path along the softball field, and straight ahead I could see the lights of six cabins flickering in the thick woods. Four cars remained parked in the grove, including my own, as boys were still unpacking and arranging their summer quarters. I would begin to do just the opposite.

"So, how'd it go with Kristel?" Boonie asked amicably when I entered Saranac. He had his back turned, fiddling with the Needlemans' TV in an unsuccessful attempt to pick up a station. "You were down there with her a long time!" He grinned widely, and I knew it, although I couldn't see his face. He always grinned when he talked, especially about girls. Pete and Rodney were on their bunks, Rodney above mine and Pete above Boonie's, and it was obvious that they, too, wanted to hear everything that went on with me and Kristel at the beach deck.

I walked straight to my bunk, underneath Rodney's dangling, freckled legs and slid my canvas gym bags out from under the bed.

"So, how'd it go?" Boonie repeated, trying to position the antenna made out of a mangled wire coat hanger.

I finally spoke with a strained voice, as I smashed stacks of jeans and T-shirts into the bags. "I can't begin to explain to you guys what's going on. But the bottom line is that I've got to go home."

"Huh?" Boonie grunted, turning his head with a jerk.

"I have to leave tonight. Family emergency."

My three roommates stared in disbelief while I crammed belongings into the gym bags and dumped shoes and shower supplies haphazardly into a cardboard box. Minutes later, I hauled an armload out the door to my car. Boonie, Pete, and Rodney could only sit and watch, dumbfounded.

The grove was clear of people, but I could hear the cabin residents inside their dwellings, excited and boisterous young men, acting typically for a first night together. I carelessly tossed my belongings into the back seat, and then I noticed the lights inside Hawkeye cabin burning softly. A white, roofless golf cart was parked closely alongside the front end of the structure. The cabin door was hanging wide open, and a man stood on the porch, leaning against the doorframe, smoking a pipe. It was Whisper, the night watchman, whom I had last seen at the staff welcome meeting.

I looked at my watch: five minutes to twelve. I could be on the road at midnight and home by 10:00 a.m. tomorrow. I had enough adrenaline to drive all night. Hastily, I went in and out of the cabin two more times, carrying my junk and dumping it in the trunk and back seat. On my last trip inside to say goodbye, Boonie tried to reason with me.

"You should stay at least for the night, Jody. You could fall asleep on the road."

"Nah. I'll be all right. Thanks." I felt tears rushing to my eyes again, and I didn't want to stick around and let it happen in front of the guys. A new brother who's dead, and my parents had just split up. It was too much to handle.

I scampered back to the car for no other reason but to fight back the tears, and when I thought I had it under control, I returned to the door of Saranac to say goodbye again.

"See you guys. It was nice meeting you."

Pete responded, "See ya." Rodney nodded his head, indicating he meant what his brother said.

Boonie approached me at the door. "You sure there ain't anything we can do?"

Again, I felt the tears swelling, and I suspected Boonie could detect it. "No. I really gotta go. Thanks."

We shook hands and I turned towards the car. Whisper was now on his golf cart and drove silently out of the grove. He glanced at us as he passed, and Boonie commented, "What a freak. There he goes right on time—at the stroke of midnight."

I paid little attention, suddenly remembering someone who had recently become very important to me. I turned around, "Boonie, I'll be back. I've got to say goodbye to Kristel."

I was fooling myself with my own hypocrisy. I wanted to thank Kristel for telling me about my brother, but another part of me was hoping that she would talk some sense into me and convince me not to leave. I also felt guilty for being short with her down at the beach. She only did what she thought was best. Just the right word from her, and I might not go anywhere. I was sensing it now: leaving for home all of a sudden was stupid, but this drastic situation called for drastic behavior—I had to do something. I just didn't know what. There was no one else I could count on but myself, except maybe Kristel. She seemed trustworthy. I thought, hopefully, she'd say something to talk me out of this. Otherwise, I was gone.

I traversed the entire Club property again, about a five-minute walk. It had been over thirty minutes since I left her at the beach and I hoped she would still be there. I should have asked Boonie where she lived, but it was too late to go knocking on her door at that hour, especially if her mother would answer.

Finally reaching Route 7, I saw the globes around the beach deck still burning a yellow haze. I crossed the empty highway at the crosswalk and stopped at the top of the white, wooden steps, hoping to see her still sitting on the beach deck's perimeter bench.

I saw her all right, not sitting but standing. She was facing the water, her body pressed up against another body—a tall, skinny, male with blazing blonde hair. Long, pale, bony arms embraced her tightly. One knuckly hand was spread across the back of her neck, tangled with her golden hair, and the other one was spread widely and pressed firmly on the lowest part of her back, inching down slowly. Their faces were pressed together, making a violent, passionate connection.

Brock Oliff noticed my presence at the top of the steps. He quickly dropped his arms to his side. Kristel twirled around, startled.

"Jody!" she shouted.

Before I heard anything else, I dashed back across the two-lane highway and continued non-stop all the way up the hillside a second time. Madness! This was all too insane! At the top near the Club building, my face and neck were red and streaked, stained as much with sweat as with tears. I had now completely lost my mind. I didn't care. Nobody, nothing—I didn't care. I'd get in my car and drive away for good.

She was kissing Brock Oliff! The image of that demon's lips pressed tightly to hers burned into my brain. What a liar she was! Everything she told me was a lie!

I stopped in front of the porch to catch my breath, replay parts of the long conversation I had with Kristel a half-hour ago. "Jimmy was your brother… I saw him fall… Brock was there for me… I broke up with him." It was all a bunch of crap now. I didn't know what to think anymore, even how to think—I was just going to leave.

I jogged around the Club building and down the back hill, past the pool, and back to the cabin grove, where my car was waiting, packed and ready with a nearly full tank.

From nowhere, an enormous shadow emerged on the pathway in front of me, and before my tear-stricken eyes could detect what it was, a light blazed into my face, blinding me completely. I froze in my steps, surprised and annoyed.

A sick, raspy voice, spoken as if from a lacerated throat, addressed me from behind the bright light. "Who are you, and where are you going?" The scratchy voice and its message assured me that the man behind the flashlight was Whisper on his golf cart, fulfilling his duties as night watchman.

"I'm just a staff member. Or at least I was," I said between pants. "I'm on my way out this minute. My car is parked right down there." I pointed towards the cabin grove, although I couldn't see anything because the bright flashlight still blinded my eyes.

A direct, gargled reply followed. "Name?"

"Jody Barrett."

Whisper tucked the flashlight under his chin and the light beamed down his chest. I could now see that it was indeed Whisper—his narrow, rectangular face and crew cut hair under his faded black ball cap. He removed a ballpoint pen from his shirt pocket and wrote upon a small pad of paper that was taped securely to the dashboard of his golf cart.

"All right," Whisper gargled. "Go on now."

I didn't say anything more, and neither did he. But I knew he was watching my every step down the path towards the grove. In minutes, I was driving my car back up the hill, and I passed by Whisper before I circling around to the front of the Club building and down the steep driveway.

At the Brown Swan Club entranceway at Route 7, I could see on my left the crosswalk and white steps that led to the beach deck. The thought of what I just saw there made me snarl. I slammed on the gas pedal, causing the tires to squeal madly. My Mustang whipped out onto the highway, turning right with such violent force that the rear of the vehicle fishtailed across the yellow line before I adjusted the car southbound.

The tremendous lurch caused everything inside the car to tumble towards the driver's side. That's when a large, unfamiliar, manila envelope slid from the dashboard, over the steering wheel, and into my lap. Hardly outside the Club entrance, I slammed on the brakes to examine it. Across its front, written with a fat, felt-tip black marker, was the name "JODY" in capital letters. Somebody had left it in my car for me to find.

I pulled to the side of the road and shifted the gear in park. Impetuously, I ripped open the top of the envelope and removed its contents. To my amazement, I held in my hand a full-size, eight-by-ten color photograph of Jimmy Grandstaff. Attached with a paper clip was a crude note written on a brown paper towel. The note was printed in heavy black ink, in all capital letters. It read as follows:

> DEAR JODY,
>
> YOU ARE HERE FOR A REASON.
> HELP ME SOLVE YOUR BROTHER'S MURDER.
>
> AN AMBASSADOR FOR THE DEAD.

I thought of Kristel immediately. She must have placed the envelope in my car before we talked at the beach. Only *she* would have a photograph like this. *She* must have put it on my dashboard. What's this "Ambassador for the Dead" stuff? I thought of what she said about Brock. How could she be so mean? Why did she tell me that story about Brock and Jimmy's death? Is she out to get me, or what? Is she a witch like her mother? Are they in this together? Is Brock part this cruel joke? Nothing made sense now.

Mulling this over as I stared at the photograph, I felt the urge to tear the picture to pieces, throw it out the window and speed away. But I couldn't. I kept staring into the eyes of the brother I never knew.

Why? Why did Kristel say that stuff about Brock and then haul off and make out with him? Did she lie about Jimmy, too? In these fleeting moments, I began to develop the worst of opinions about the girl whom I once considered to be the prettiest creature alive. She was a liar. She led me on. She set up this cruel joke about a dead boy who she claimed was my brother.

Then the memory of Kristel's photo album hit me. Kristel and I together as toddlers on the pool deck. My young mother. Mrs. Grandstaff holding Jimmy. How could Kristel be lying about this? And why was she kissing that sleaze-ball just minutes after telling me she hated him? Who is this Kristel Schuple, the most beautiful being on the face of the earth? Uncertainty screamed in my mind like a wailing guitar. Madness. Sheer madness.

Then I froze. A movement caught my attention and I looked sideways through the driver's window. There standing next to my car was a tall, bony, figure—the same one I saw pressed so provocatively against the girl I once liked.

Brock rapped on the window with his overgrown fingernail protruding from the end of his knuckly index finger. I peered upwards. Again, that strange, quizzical look in Brock's eyes was evident. I glanced back over my shoulder and to the passenger side. He was alone. Where had Kristel gone? Brock remained at the window; he rapped again, harder this time. For a fleeting moment, I considered shifting the car into drive and flooring the gas pedal. But I wanted to confront him. I needed to confront him. He had been kissing Kristel, moments after she was emptying her heart in front of me. I had to face him. If Brock would have beaten me bald-headed and bloody at that moment, I wouldn't have cared. And if Kristel strolled up and embraced Brock after he whipped me, my life couldn't have been much worse than it already was. It's amazing all the things a brain can think when it's in overdrive.

Brock rapped a third time on the glass. I cut off the engine and rolled down the window.

"What do you want with me?" I asked in a brazen voice. "Just what are you and Kristel trying to pull?"

Brock locked his hands to his hips and chuckled spitefully before retorting, "Heh. I don't want nothin' with you—absolutely nothin'! That's all you need to know! You give me nothin', and I'll give you nothin'! You just stay clear. Stay away." He thrust his grotesque finger at my nose as he deliberately pronounced each syllable of his last command. Next, he paused and swallowed hard, and what looked like a golf ball rolled under the skin of his neck. He gulped a second time, clenched his teeth, and growled, "Stay away from me, stay away from my friends, and stay away from Kristel!"

Another painful swallow, and his voice softened, almost as though he had emptied himself of evil and was now giving me wisdom from his heart, as malicious as it was. "Follow that advice, and you'll be doing yourself a favor—all of us a favor," he said in a half whisper. "You oughta just plain leave here before I kill you."

When he finished his orders, I thought of swinging the door open and knocking him breathless. But he was now suddenly pacified, no longer pugnacious—an astonishing withdrawal of his devilish mien like I had witnessed at the grocery store and the dead-end avenue near the lake. Maybe he does know something. Maybe he has an answer to this madness.

I raised the eight-by-ten photograph of Jimmy to the window for Brock to see. Carefully affecting an amenable tone, I asked, "What do you know about this person?"

Brock was obviously taken aback by this action. His eyes widened when he glanced at the photo, and he took one step back from the car. His voice stuttered as he responded, "What? What do you mean?" He shuffled his feet in the gravel on the roadside. "Why are you bringing Jimmy into this? He's dead!"

This reaction convinced me that Brock had nothing to do with the manila envelope. His seeing the photo took him off guard too much. It shocked him. He couldn't have put it there. Perhaps, as Kristel said, he did know something about Jimmy's death. So I continued my line of questioning. "Why did you plant this in my car?"

"I didn't!" he demanded with no hesitation.

He was clearly telling the truth.

My mind accelerated into overdrive again as I reconsidered my harsh accusations against Kristel. Perhaps she left the envelope there on her own. Perhaps she had every reason to believe Brock shoved Jimmy from the cliff. But why was she kissing him?

I studied Brock's face, and it was obvious that my antagonist had lost the edge he held over me when he first arrived at my car. The photo of Jimmy is what did it.

"Why were you kissing Kristel?" It was a stupid question, and I knew it.

"That's none of your business. I told you that already. Leave her and me alone."

"Kristel hates you, Brock!" I said in a sudden burst of rage. "She told me tonight that she hates you!"

As quickly as it had disappeared, evil returned to Brock's eyes. "You're a liar," he snarled through his clenched jaw. Then he lunged toward me.

# CHAPTER 9

## *Morning Accord*

Hours later, the only thing I remembered about what happened after he called me a liar was the clenched, bony fist advancing at a high rate of speed towards my face.

A blend of chirping birds and a soft voice stirred me to consciousness in the morning. The voice was raspy and masculine, mixed with the sounds of the feathered orchestra in the trees all around. The symphony sifted down out of a deep dream, which all too quickly vanished from memory the moment I opened my eyes.

The soft, scraping voice of Whisper accompanied his gentle nudge on my shoulder. "Son. Son. Are you alright?" The old man's face was surrounded by the golden, early-morning sky behind him, and the warmth from his hand on the bare skin of my neck informed me of how cold I was. "Are you alright, son?" Whisper repeated softly.

"Yeah," I moaned.

My body was sore from my neck to my toes, and at first I didn't notice the pain in my face where the blow from Brock's fist has left a visible mark below my left eye. I arched my back and stretched my arms out over the steering wheel.

"I must have fallen asleep."

"Better here than on the highway," Whisper gargled, standing straight up next to my window. He looked behind my car and rasped loudly, "He's okay, Sheriff, everything's alright here." Through the review mirror I saw a plump, uniformed arm wave goodbye through the window of a police cruiser. The vehicle spun away from the curb and accelerated north towards town.

Whisper glanced back through my window.

Embarrassed, I explained, "I must have dozed off here when I pulled over to look at the map." A pretty good lie, I thought. Then I fumbled for the map in the passenger seat and remembered it had been sitting in the glove compartment ever since my arrival. In the seat instead was the manila envelope, the note from "the Ambassador for the Dead," and the photo of Jimmy overturned on top of it. In an awkward attempt to cover my lie, I glanced in the rear-view mirror and noticed Whisper's golf cart parked near the Club entranceway about fifty yards back. "What time is it?" I asked, trying to change the subject.

"Almost six-thirty a.m. You're Jody Barrett, aren't you?"

I was impressed with Whisper's memory. "Yes. That's right. We met last night. I told you I was headed home, and I better get going now that I've slept all this time." I reached for the keys that were still in the ignition.

"Not so fast," Whisper gargled slowly and softly. "You're not going anywhere on these tires."

I leaned my head out the window and saw that the front and rear tires on the driver's side were completely deflated.

"Looks like someone slashed them," Whisper said wryly. "All four of 'em."

I slumped back into my seat and sighed. Then I slammed the back of my head against the headrest and moaned, "Brock!"

"That kid Brock did this?" Whisper asked.

Not wanting to waste my breath answering the obvious, I looked straight ahead through the dew-covered windshield, nodded, and said nothing.

"Brock gave you that shiner, too," Whisper alleged, referring to the bruise that had developed under my left eye.

"Yeah."

At this time, although the sun had risen and the birds were singing, my life was continuing its tumble downward. I just wanted Whisper to leave me alone so I could try and gather myself together. My mother. Jimmy. Kristel. Everything had gone to crap, and now all of my tires were slashed.

Whisper wouldn't go away.

"Why don't I give you a lift back to your cabin," he rasped. "I'll get somebody to help with the car. It'll be okay here for now."

The offer sounded reasonable, and I accepted. After all, what other choice did I have? I was obviously not going to be able to drive home for a while. I grabbed a few of my belongings from the back seat.

Moments later, old Whisper dropped me off at the quiet grove of cabins and hummed away on his golf cart. Saranac was empty. Boonie, Pete, and Rodney had already left the cabin to begin the six a.m. shift at the kitchen. I knew I was supposed to be there too, working and getting trained to serve the guests who would be arriving tomorrow. But the bare mattress on my empty bunk summoned me to it, and I collapsed on top of it.

A brother I never knew. Now dead. My parents, who lied to me all these years, now split up. Mom living in another house. Her kitchen, her living room, her curtains, her plants—all left to the mercy of my negligent stepfather. The girl I admired like a precious gem, dumping her problems upon me and ending up in the arms of a brute. A black eye and four flat tires.

I was certain Hell had found me.

Just as Brock did late the night before, and just as Whisper had done early in the morning, another person appeared at the window next to my head. Now, it was the six-paned slatted window of my bunk. And this time, the figure standing there was Kristel Schuple.

Two hours had passed since I returned to the cabin and fell asleep. The sun had risen well into the cloudless sky, projecting its beams through gaps in the forest ceiling. I stared through the window at Kristel, and those irresistible eyes of hers compelled me to crank it open.

"Jody, I'm so sorry! I'm so glad you didn't leave!" she cried in her angelic voice. "Boonie told me you had gone."

I offered no response. She had an awful lot of explaining to do. I wanted to test her, and test her hard. So I just stared at her face and said nothing. I noticed it had changed since last night. She seemed real, genuine, unmasked, like she hadn't rehearsed *this* conversation. I guessed that maybe she wasn't wearing any make-up, but I couldn't tell. She seemed even prettier than before for some reason.

"Are you okay?" she asked sweetly.

Her soothing voice could melt down my stubbornness like water melts cotton candy, and I had to come up with a defense. So I rolled to my back and stared up at the bunk above me, keeping my eyes off her face. I decided I wouldn't talk to her. A dumb, childish plan. But it was all I could think of.

From the corner of my eye I saw her stand on her tiptoes to look further into the cabin through my slatted window. "Is anyone else in there?" she asked.

"No," I uttered, breaking my vow of silence just ten seconds into it.

"Do you mind if I come in?"

"You're not allowed in here."

"So what. I'm coming in anyway," she said persistently.

With that, I knew I couldn't maintain my act much longer. It would only be a matter of time before I would give in and start firing horrible accusations her way.

She disappeared from the window and seconds later the front door creaked open. I rolled over on my side to face the window again, away from her. The door shut, and I heard her step slowly across the wooden cabin floor. The soft squeak of bedsprings indicated that she was sitting on the edge of Boonie's bunk across the center space.

"Jody. I'm really sorry. This is all my fault."

Yes, you're right there, honey, I thought to myself, keeping silent.

"You probably hate me now," she added.

Right again, sweetie. I said not a word.

"Jody," she pleaded, slightly raising her voice. "I really want you to believe me when I say this. I wasn't kissing Brock when you saw us last night."

I did want to believe her so badly. I wanted the sight erased from my memory. I also wanted to turn over and look at her. But I held on, remaining still, and said nothing.

"Brock came down to the deck soon after you left. I think he saw you and me down there when we were talking. I told him to leave me alone and that I didn't want to see him. But he kept saying he needed to talk to me about something very important. So I broke down and let him say what he needed to say."

It sounded like she was going to start crying like she did last night.

She continued, "He said he was sorry for being such a jerk. He said that I was too good for him, but that he needs me because I help him become a better person. He wants me to give him another chance. And Jody, believe me. I came this close to telling him about my suspicions about him—everything I told you. I wanted to call him a murderer. I wanted to let it all out right there, but I didn't say anything, and he kept telling me how much he needs me. And then, for crying out loud, Jody, he started balling! He was crying about how rotten his life is and how I am the only good thing in his life. I just watched him cry and spill his guts to me about his family and everything."

I remained silent, motionless on the mattress, soaking in every word she spoke. I had seen a glimpse of that sensitivity in Brock myself, last night when I showed him Jimmy's picture. He wasn't as bullyish as he put on.

"He was just sobbing—pouring out his heart about how much he hates his parents. Then he stepped forward to hug me, and I let him rest his head on my shoulder while he continued to sob. I felt so weird, Jody! I didn't know what to do! And the next thing I know—he starts kissing me, and I told him to stop and he kept it up and held me tight—and that's right when you showed up at the top of the steps."

I remained still and quiet, and I hoped to heaven that she was telling the truth.

"Jody, please believe me. That's exactly how it happened."

I wanted to believe her. I wanted to believe her more than anything. I was on the verge of sitting up and telling her so, but then the memory of the manila envelope popped into my head.

So I sat up and drilled her with a series of questions: "Why did you put that picture of Jimmy in my car?" I asked tersely. "Why did you write that note? Do you think this is some sort of murder mystery game? Do you think this is another episode of *Murder She Wrote*? You call yourself this 'Ambassador for the Dead?' What the heck do you want with me?"

She wore a look of relief when I finally began speaking, but she quickly replaced it with an expression of perplexity when she heard my questions.

"What picture? What note?" she asked.

I rolled my eyes, all part of my ploy. I was pretty good at dramatizing for effect. "Ah, Kristel, don't play games. The envelope I found on my dashboard last night when I was leaving. It wasn't there yesterday and it had everything to do with our discussion last night."

"What envelope?"

"C'mon Kristel. The note said, 'Help me solve your brother's murder.' From 'An Ambassador for the Dead.' Who else but you could have written it?"

Kristel stared at me with her wide, pretty eyes. "Jody, I have no idea what you're talking about." She sounded genuinely confused and bewildered.

I stood to my feet. "You're saying that *someone else* planted an eight-by-ten portrait of Jimmy on my dashboard with a note saying that I needed to help solve his murder? This is crazy!"

Her jaw dropped open, and I sensed that she, like Brock, truly had nothing to do with the manila envelope. I began pacing back and forth, clutching the top of my head with my hands. "This is crazy! Who can I trust?" I shouted.

"You can trust me!"

"Then who planted the envelope in my car?!" I yelled in exasperation.

"I don't know, Jody! Honestly!" She stood to her feet. "You've got to believe me! You've got to trust me!" The frustration mounting in her voice was proof that that she was being honest. But should I trust her?

I stopped pacing and faced her. Tears collected in her eyes, and I finally gave in. I stood about an arm's length away from her and watched a tear break loose and roll down her cheek.

"Did he really force you to kiss him?" I asked softly.

"Yes."

"I'm sorry."

I stepped forward and embraced the princess. We stood there in each others' arms for what seemed like an hour, and I realized that as my life had hit the rock bottom with such a thud, the only direction things could go was up. Holding Kristel Schuple was like medicine for my wounded soul. Everything else went away: my mother, Wesley, Jimmy, Brock. Only Kristel mattered, this irresistible young woman in my arms.

Kristel ended the moment as she stepped back and asked, "Can we talk up at my house?

"Right now?"

"Yes."

"Why?"

"Because I'm grounded."

I laughed. "What?"

"I got grounded for coming in so late last night. My mom and I had a big argument. This morning she's on her way with my sister to Lake Henry to go shopping, and when she gets there she'll probably call to check on me to see if I'm still in the house. I'm not supposed to leave the house for *three* days."

"Won't you get in a lot more trouble if I go up there?"

"Not as much trouble for being caught with you in here."

We regarded each other with smiles and left the cabin.

The Schuple home was located on the Brown Swan Club property, but no one would have known it. Behind the Poolside Café, a gravel road crept back into the woods, up an incline and around a bend. Halfway up the winding trail, a large gate that must be manually swung open blocked wanderers and intruders. Kristel and I climbed over the gate, because it was faster than unwrapping the chain to swing it open.

Their house had been built in a small clearing deep in the woods. It was a beautiful one-story home with a wide front porch adorned with hanging plants and flowers. I noticed the two-car garage, the neatly manicured yard, and the curved, brick pathway connecting the blacktop driveway and the wooden, front porch steps. From the front porch you could just barely see over the tops of the trees and down into the valley where Lake Marilee glimmered far below. From the right side you could see the top of the main Club building emerging above the tree tops several hundred yards away.

We entered through the front door. The home's interior was much more commodious than an outside perspective allowed. A large, tile-floored foyer caused our voices to echo slightly, as if we were in a cavern.

"Are you sure it's okay for me to be here?" I asked, noting the perfectly arranged living room adjacent to the foyer. It was like a showcase of an upscale furniture store. It looked as if it had hardly ever been used—not a speck of humanity anywhere.

"Mom won't be home until later this afternoon," Kristel said, "and Daddy's busy all day with the new staff."

Just then, in the kitchen, the telephone rang.

"Oh gosh, we just made it in time!" she cried, scampering down the hallway toward the kitchen. "It's probably my mother checking up on me!"

The caller wasn't Mrs. Schuple—it was someone from the Abbeyville Garage.

"Your car is ready," she informed me after hanging up the phone.

I had almost forgotten about my car. "Whisper took it to the garage for me," I said.

"Really? I love Whisper. He's so nice. He must've told them to call here."

"He is nice. It's funny, 'cause the guys told me that he's a real creep."

"A lot of people think he's weird—just because he's different." I could sense Kristel was a little upset at the unfounded opinions of Whisper. "You just have to get to know him," she said. "Let me show you something." She walked down the hallway and returned with an object in her hand—a small figure of a swan carved out of wood. "He made this for me a couple of years ago."

I held the tiny swan in my hand. It was no bigger than my thumb, but the intricate details carved into the wood—the eyes on the small head, the individual feathers on the body, and the thin, smooth "S" shaped neck were impressive.

"This is cool. He carved this freehand?"

"He carves figures like these and paints them," Kristel answered. "For Christmas ornaments, doll houses, and things like that. When he gave me this one he told me I could paint it white, or leave it in its natural brown color. I left it brown, of course. I told him he should make them and sell them to the guests in the gift shop."

I examined the small brown swan in silence and wondered if the other guys knew about Whisper's incredible skill. Probably not.

Kristel then posed a question that she had apparently been wanting to ask all morning. "So, Jody, are you going to stay here or are you still going home? Boonie thinks you left last night."

I placed the swan on the countertop. "I don't know. I just want to think about it a little more. My head was all mixed up last night, and I acted on the spur of the moment." I hadn't thought of home since Kristel and I had embraced.

"That's understandable. I kind of dropped a bombshell on you last night. I know that Boonie will be glad if you stay."

"Well, if it wasn't for Brock slashing my tires, I'd be long gone already."

Kristel's next words tickled my insides. "*I'll* be glad if you stay, too."

A sweet, silent moment.

"This is a beautiful house," I said.

"Oh thanks. I'll be seeing a lot of it the next three days."

"You're not allowed to leave at all?"

"Only to eat at the dining room with my family, and to play the piano for Daddy on opening night."

"Then I better get out of here. I don't want to get you into more trouble." I stood up and looked down my body. "Besides, I've been in these clothes since yesterday; I feel like a mess. I'm going to go get cleaned up and then go get my car."

"Okay, but let me show you something first." Kristel grabbed me by the hand and guided me towards the front door. "This is why I brought you up here," she said, leading me outside to the front lawn. She showed me around to the left side of the house. "This is my bedroom window. You can come and talk to me while I'm grounded—day or night. Just don't get caught—tap lightly on the window and I'll hear you."

I now had an exclusive invitation for a rendezvous with a beautiful girl at her bedroom window! I felt privileged, even though it seemed like this wasn't the first time Kristel had employed such an arrangement for someone. I almost asked her how many other guys she had invited to her window, but I held my tongue.

As though she was able to read my mind, Kristel said, "Jimmy used to come up here last summer to talk to me."

For some mystical reason, that made it seem okay for me to follow suit.

# CHAPTER 10

## *Visiting the Police, Smooth Rock, and Burleighs*

In the early afternoon I retrieved my car from the garage in Abbeyville and paid the bill with Mom's credit card. She was on my mind again, and I didn't want her there. I didn't want Jimmy there either. I could care less about Wesley: he was a nobody, as far as I was concerned. I mostly wanted to get back to Kristel's window that evening. I had decided I wasn't going home after all. My parents could handle their own mess, and Kristel would help me deal with the Jimmy issue.

It's crazy how things work in your brain. Last night, I didn't give a crap about the whole stinking world. Now Kristel had come alive to me, and life was sweet again.

Having seized my car, I drove back to the Club kitchen to find Boonie before he got off duty at two o'clock. I felt guilty for not showing up for the first day of work, and I wanted to apologize to the chefs.

"You doing okay?" Boonie asked, meeting me on the loading dock. He was wearing white apron splotched with spaghetti sauce stains, and he had a pencil tucked behind his ear.

"Yeah. Better than last night, but there's still a lot of stuff going on back home." I motioned my arm towards my car parked near the loading dock. "You want to go for a ride later?"

He flashed his big white smile. "Sure! I'm getting outta here in a few minutes. We've got lunch just about cleaned up."

I shoved my hands in my pockets and told Boonie how I felt bad for not having worked that day like I was supposed to—our first full day—and especially for not telling Dave or Allen that I wouldn't be there. But Boonie said everything was cool. The work schedule wasn't even posted yet, and I had nothing to worry about.

"So you're staying for sure?" Boonie asked, untying the knot behind him in his apron strings.

"Probably," I said, knowing I was. Boonie was a friend, and like Kristel, I was beginning to feel that I could confide in him. I knew I didn't intend to leave Club anymore. I'd be a fool to go home now.

We sat down and dangled our legs off the back dock. Right there, I told everything to Boonie about what happened last night. He listened with wide eyes, fascinated with the incredible story of Jimmy being my brother, Kristel's suspicions about Brock, and the mysterious envelope in my car. I even showed him the note from "the Ambassador for the Dead" and the photo of Jimmy.

"This is a bona fide murder mystery!" Boonie declared.

It was therapeutic to share all this with him, even though I wasn't certain if Kristel would approve. But she admitted herself that she wasn't supposed to tell me what *she* told me, so my telling Boonie was no more of a crime than hers. And I made sure Boonie knew everything. It helped justify my foolish behavior last night.

I explained to him, "At first, I thought Kristel left the envelope in my car, but now I know she didn't. And when I showed it to Brock last night, his reaction made me sure that *he* didn't leave it there either. Besides, why would he write a letter asking me to find out how my brother died if he has something to do with it?"

Boonie noted the bruise under my eye. "He didn't seem to appreciate you accusing him of putting it there." He looked at Jimmy's photo again. "Maybe the person who wrote that John Doe letter to the police knows you're his brother and left this in your car. John Doe and this Ambassador for the Dead could be the same person."

"I thought of that, but how would whoever it is know *me*?"

"I dunno. You oughta take this note to the police and see if they can match the handwriting with the John Doe letter they received."

"You think so?"

"Let's go there now. The sooner the better."

Chef Al Dernbaugh poked his head out the door. We both turned around to see the towering, rectangular man holding his white chef's hat in his hand, revealing his matted, black hair.

"Boonie," he bellowed. "We got a staff member named Jody?"

"I'm Jody," I answered. Apparently, my boss didn't remember meeting me yesterday.

"You have a long distance phone call in my office," he announced, holding the door open for me to enter.

Nerves fluttered in my stomach as I rushed into the kitchen office and picked up the phone on Chef Al's desk.

"Hello?"

"Jody, sweetie, this is Mom."

"Mom!"

This turned out to be an abnormal and awkward conversation. We first talked about the stuff that one would expect to talk about with his mother—whether I was warm enough at night, did I have enough money to do laundry, etc. etc. Finally, we got around to talking about the more important things of life—like why she left her husband the same morning I departed for Abbeyville.

"Honey, I've got some bad news. I have left your father," she said, thinking it would be shocking news to me.

"I know," I replied with as much nonchalance as I possibly could pack into two words.

She responded, "Did your father call you?"

"No. I called home last night and he told me that you were gone."

She tried her best to explain her reasons for leaving the man, but I hardly paid attention to her drivel. I wanted to talk about something much more important—my brother.

"Mom, I need to ask you something," I interrupted.

"Okay, sweetie."

I knew I was about to blow her socks off. "Do I have a brother?"

A pause. A very long, revealing pause.

"What?" she finally said nervously.

"Do I… or did I, have a brother?"

She sighed heavily. "Jody, you know about all that. I don't want to talk about it right now. Things are bad enough."

Her avoidance of answering "yes" or "no" convinced me that she knew much more than she was telling me, and I wasn't going to let her off the hook. I sat down in the swivel chair in Chef Al's tiny office. The door was closed and most of the clatter in the kitchen was sealed off. I could see Boonie through the window waiting outside on the back dock.

Through the phone, I pressed my mother to the proverbial stove. "You never had an abortion, did you."

Another telling pause. "Jody, why are you…."

I cut her off rudely. "You gave birth to the baby and put him up for adoption, didn't you."

"Why are you talking like this? What did Wesley tell you?" This response revealed that she suspected her husband of spilling the beans.

"He didn't tell me anything. I found out myself."

"Found out what?"

I knew she was lying now. I knew it. I had heard her lie to Wesley before, and she used the same tone of voice, the same expressions of feigned ignorance in her replies. I pressed her harder.

"A kid named Jimmy Grandstaff used to work here at the Club. I look identical to him, Mom. And now I found out that he was my brother."

Her lying continued unabashed. "Did your father tell you he was your brother?"

"No. Wesley had nothing to do with it. Somebody else told me."

"Who?"

I knew she was expecting me to say the name George Schuple, but I didn't provide. "A friend that I just met who knew Jimmy told me the whole story."

Knowing my mother to be the experienced liar she was, I predicted she wouldn't give in without a good showing. On cue, she continued her dishonesty: "Jody, somebody is pulling your leg. You are my only child. When I was young and unmarried, I aborted a pregnancy that should never have happened in the first place. I was there, Jody. I felt the pain."

Nice story, I thought, but the more she continued lying, the more upset I became. My voice cracked when I said, "He died last year in an accident."

At these words she offered *no* pause, and it convinced me that the awful news wasn't news to her at all. She responded immediately, "That is very tragic, Jody, and that's why somebody is convinced you're his brother—because you *look* like him. You just happen to bring up memories for someone who must miss him terribly. And their minds are playing tricks on them, and they're making assumptions that cannot be proven because the boy is gone now."

I froze. I was losing the battle—she was wriggling free.

I almost gave up and started believing her. No, Kristel is right. Mom is lying. But I was losing control of this, so I decided to get very angry. I wanted to get off the phone, just to stop hearing her speak what at first sounded like lies, but now was beginning to sound like reason. I didn't want to hear anymore.

"Well, Mom, I gotta go," I said in a low voice, and before she could respond, I dropped the receiver to its cradle. At least, I thought, the sudden hang up let her know how upset I was.

Why would she lie to me about Jimmy for so many years? *Is* she lying? My mind replayed our conversation several times. I recalled how she lied to Wesley all those years. Yes, she is lying. Jimmy was my brother and she just doesn't want to admit it! But why? Why would she lie after hearing that I've found out about it? What's the problem with me knowing that I had a brother if he's dead already?

I couldn't figure it out. My parents were keeping something from me. Neither of them could be trusted to begin with—but *this* was strange. I didn't trust them before all this happened, and this solidified Mr. Gray's maxim in my heart: I'm the only one I can trust with absolute certainty.

While I agonized over these things in the quiet office, I perused the many items packed into the tiny room. Two tall file cabinets occupied one corner, partially blocking the single window. The desk was piled with invoices, folders, notes, and catalogues. Between the stacks of papers sat a couple of coffee mugs that were stuffed full of receipts, small hand tools, pencils and pens. Books about food preparation lined the shelves against the walls, intermixed with wobbly three ring binders of assorted thickness and colors.

I twirled around in the chair. Al Dernbaugh's certificate from the Culinary Institute of America hung on the wall, along with numerous photographs of culinary art displays: ice carvings, fruit pyramids, and lavish buffet spreads that looked very expensive. A narrow countertop lined the back wall, supported by two-drawer file cabinets at each end. Crowded on it were a computer and monitor, plastic file dividers, trays for in-going and out-going mail, and more coffee mugs filled with soda machine spigots, keys, refrigerator thermometers, and a random collection of nuts, bolts, and screws. I noticed a fat black marker sticking out of one of the mugs, and next to it sat a stack of unused, large manila envelopes.

The black marker and the manila envelope.

I went outside to report this discovery to Boonie and to tell him about my mother's phone call. We discussed everything after we got in the car.

"And your mom insisted it isn't be true?" Boonie asked.

"Yes, but I know she's lying. I can tell."

We drove slowly through downtown Abbeyville and north towards to the police station.

"Maybe your mom was so totally caught off guard at your finding out about Jimmy that she just lied out of impulse," Boonie suggested. "Maybe she'll come clean with the truth after she thinks about it for a while."

"I don't think so. When my mom lies, she never comes clean with the truth. And I don't plan on talking to my parents for a while—either of them."

Boonie said nothing.

"You know Chef Al better than I do," I said, changing the subject back to what I had found in the kitchen office. "Could he have planted the envelope in my car? Could he be the John Doe who tipped the police?"

"I don't know. That doesn't sound like Chef Al, but you never know," Boonie answered.

"How about Dave or Allen?"

"Could be one of them. Could be anybody really. There's lots of black markers and envelopes in the world."

"But those envelopes in the kitchen office were exactly the same. And the black marker sitting right next to them."

I knew the choice of supplies in the foodservice office made for a stupid discussion, and it ended when we pulled into the driveway of the Huron County Police station. The building was a small, redbrick structure that looked like it had been converted from a house. A squad car was parked in one of the three parking spaces. I pulled up to the left of it because the first space was marked for handicapped parking. I grabbed the envelope and noticed that Boonie made no motion to get out of the car.

"Aren't you coming in?"

"No."

"Then why did you want to come if you're going to stay out here in the car?"

"I only came to show you where the police station is. And you said we were going for a drive. Besides," he said, shifting his eyes away from me and onto the dashboard, "if I go in, it could ruin it for you. They know me too well in there."

"What?"

"It's a long story. Speeding… beer cans in the back seat. You know."

I shouldn't have been so surprised. Realizing I would talk to the police alone, I gathered my thoughts and entered the building.

The front room was small and sparsely furnished. An officer in uniform was sitting behind a desk just inside the door. He was a black man, rather young looking, and his friendly countenance put my nerves to rest.

"Can I help you?" he asked, sliding aside a document he had been reading on his desk.

"Yes," I replied, briefly looking around the room and down the narrow hallway that led to several closed doors. No one else seemed to be in the building, and I realized that this officer is probably the only person I would talk to here.

I explained the entire story—from Jimmy being my brother, to the fight with Brock, and to the envelopes and black marker I saw in Chef Al's office. Again, I thought about what Kristel might think of my reporting all this. She'd just have to live with it; it was now as much my business as it was hers, if not more. My story took about ten minutes and the officer listened intently without interruption. His eyes widened whenever I added more interesting information, and when I finally finished, I placed the large manila envelope on his desk.

"May I look at this?" the officer asked very politely.

"Yes, sir. Of course."

He examined the contents, and after a few moments he asked in a dubious tone of voice, "And you say you're Jimmy's *brother*?"

"Yes, sir. Jimmy was adopted by the Grandstaffs. I just found this out yesterday."

"Your mother can confirm this?"

"Yes," I lied, immediately feeling guilty for it.

The officer stood to his feet and opened the middle desk drawer in front of him. He was well over six feet tall and athletically built. He wore a medical brace on his right leg, attached over his pants from his thigh down to his calf. I noticed a gun secured in the holster at his side.

"Mr. Barrett, my name is Officer Anders." He handed me a business card that he took out of the desk drawer. "All of this is very, very interesting. Sheriff Slater has been working on this case since the accident, and he'll be better able to tell you if this letter could have come from the John Doe who sent us that tip letter on Monday. I'll leave this for him to look at when he gets in, and he'll probably give you a call tomorrow. In the meantime, if you receive any more messages, please come in or call us." Officer Anders pointed to the business card I now held in my hand.

I felt rather pleased after leaving the police station. It was as if I wasn't in this alone anymore. Sure, I had Kristel and Boonie for support, but now the police were on my side, and they would get to the bottom of this mystery much sooner than three teenagers could.

Boonie and I spent the rest of the day and early evening exploring parts of the Adirondacks. He first directed me up Route 7, north about twenty miles from Abbeyville. It was an absolutely gorgeous drive. The road followed a winding, stony river cut deep into a rocky gorge. After crossing a stone bridge, we pulled off the side of the road next to the guardrail. When I cut off the engine, we could hear the unmistakable sound of rushing water.

"This is Smooth Rock Falls," he informed me.

I was terribly curious to see the scene where Jimmy died and the spot where Kristel witnessed him tumble over the cliff. I never imagined, though, how beautiful the place truly was. It was absolutely spectacular! We hopped the guardrail and walked about twenty yards across well-trampled ground into the woods. The refreshing din of rushing, pounding water filled the air and attracted us like magnets to the precipice. A metal railing had been constructed to stop hikers from falling into the deep gorge. I leaned over it to take in the thrilling view.

The crystal-clear river flowed about three feet below us, rushing into a narrow gap before it slipped over a cliff. This waterfall supplied a large, sparkling pool twelve feet below. On the far side of this pool, the water spilled over another cliff, filling yet another sparkling pool twenty feet further down. From there, the river rushed down a steep embankment of smooth, solid rock into the third and largest pool at the bottom of the gorge.

"Over here is where Jimmy fell," Boonie said, walking left along the railing further into the woods. The railing ended deep in the thick brush, but a narrow, worn path continued past it along the cliff. We followed it into a small clearing and stood at the edge of the cliff with nothing in front of us but the open gorge. The lower pool was about fifty feet below us, shaded on all sides by the rocky walls of the canyon.

I peered over the edge just far enough to see huge, menacing boulders below. One would indeed need a running start to clear them and hit the water. And yes, the stone wall of the gorge on the other side was not that far away, certainly reachable with a long jump. Three steps seemed just about right to place the landing in the dead center of the lower pool. "It's a long way down, ain't it?" Boonie said.

"So this is where it happened." I looked down at the lip of the cliff and backwards into the woods where one would have to begin his three steps. The needle-covered ground did have numerous roots and stones protruding from the dirt.

"I jumped this *once*," Boonie said, "and I almost jumped too far. I didn't think I'd actually fly out as far as I did. I landed about ten feet away from that wall over there. That's the first and last time I jumped from here."

We both looked out over the spectacular gorge and white, falling water.

"But those upper pools are pretty fun to jump in," Boonie said. "You can just stand on the edge and step off. You can dive too. They're each about twenty or thirty feet deep. You can even sit at the top of the waterfalls and let the current take you down." He pointed towards the lower pool. "And those falls down there are just like a waterslide. You just sit there and the water takes you down the slope. It's perfectly smooth; doesn't hurt at all."

It wasn't long before Boonie and I returned to the top of the gorge and stripped down to our boxer shorts to experience everything Boonie had just described. Boonie jumped first into the upper pool and I took the ten-foot leap after him. The water was ice cold at first, but not enough to stop our adventure. We dog paddled to the far edge of the upper pool and allowed the force of the water to take us over the smooth precipice, twenty feet down into the middle pool. We hardly made a splash, as there was so much foam and bubbles caused by the falls. From this mid-level, we slid down the natural waterslide to the lower pool. Soon, we climbed back to the top of the gorge and started again.

An hour at Smooth Rock Falls turned our lips blue and made our teeth chatter, but our bodies felt brand new, like we could conquer anything. There's not a more spectacular place to swim anywhere else on the face of the earth.

Later, in the warmth of my car, Boonie directed us down a maze of winding, mountain roads as we slowly weaved our way south towards Lake Marilee. There was an old town called Roark in which Boonie pointed out a garbage dump where you can see black bears searching for dinner in the early evening. Then we passed through another small town called Whaley, which claims to be the birthplace of a famous Adirondack salad dressing. About an hour later, these back roads emptied us out onto Dreary Creek Drive, which took us into Pokeville, fourteen miles south of Abbeyville.

During our scenic adventure, Boonie and I talked very little about my recent adversity. Instead, we chatted about life at the Club, the returning staff (especially the girls), and the best places to spend a day off. Lake Henry was the most popular choice for a day off, where the closest mall and movie theater could be found about forty miles south of Abbeyville. Still, others liked to spend their days off at Smooth Rock, and some liked to take an hour trip north to Lake Placid, or the two-hour trip north to Montreal.

When we rolled quietly through Pokeville, the place hadn't changed a bit since the first time I drove through there two days earlier. No pedestrians, no traffic, no signs of life. We met up with Route 7 and turned left, northbound over the small bridge, across the stony brook and past the ugly cemetery. As I drove past the meager gas station and post office where I had met old Harold and Gretta, Boonie commented, "That's the only place around where you can buy beer and they don't card you. Only thing is, they don't keep it refrigerated there."

That figures, I thought to myself, remembering the decrepit old building and its odd inhabitants.

It was about six-thirty when we approached the Brown Swan Club entranceway. Figuring we had already missed dinner, we continued past the Club and drove the quarter mile north into Abbeyville. We stopped at a popular restaurant in town called Burleighs. The place served just about everything: pizza, subs, chicken, fish, steak, French fries, salads, and twenty-two flavors of ice cream. No waitresses—you just order at the counter and pick it up when they call your number.

The decor of Burleighs resembled that of an old ski-lodge. Large, framed photos of Adirondack scenery hung above every table, and bear skins, moose heads, and deer antlers were mounted above them like wild sentries. A large fireplace with a bulky stone hearth was built into the corner of the restaurant. The dining tables were made of solid oak, and the benches looked like logs sliced in half by a lumberjack.

Boonie pointed out three rusty lanterns displayed on the stone mantle above the fireplace. "Those are three lanterns they found on the point at Marilee Manor," he said. I recalled the Legend of Marilee Manor Boonie had described to me two nights ago.

A small wooden sign below the lanterns read, "Lights of Marilee, authentic lanterns carried by the ghost of Abbott Marilee." A large black and white photograph of Marilee Manor was mounted above the mantel. It showed an enormous mansion built near the shore of the lake. A small caption at the bottom of the photo said, "Air photo of Marilee Manor, 1938."

Boonie and I ordered a pepperoni pizza with mushrooms and devoured all eight slices between us. Afterwards, we walked through town past some shops. Crowds were everywhere, just like the first night when we were in town with Kristel. We walked to the park near the town beach to check out what was going on there.

A pick-up game of basketball was being played on one of the courts, and a couple of dudes without shirts called for us to join them. They were on vacation from Long Island and had New York accents just like you hear on TV or in the movies. I enjoyed the two-on-two, but Boonie obviously didn't.

He was absolutely the worst basketball player I have ever seen. He took a grand total of three shots, all *within the key*, and the only one to hit the rim was a granny launch that ricocheted off the *bottom* of the rim and slammed into his forehead. He was a good sport about it though, although his trademark smile had disappeared. He is much better at playing women than hoops, I can tell you that right now.

The Long Islanders thanked us after we called it quits a half-hour later. We made it back to the Club to get cleaned up in time for the nine o'clock staff meeting.

# CHAPTER 11

## *At a Window and Up a Tree*

"One hundred and thirty tomorrow afternoon, and additional one hundred and fifty on Saturday." George Schuple was addressing his staff one last time before the big opening day. "Every single one of them shall be greeted with a smile, and each shall be treated as if he or she is the most important person on earth."

I hardly heard a word that the owner and host of the Brown Swan Club spoke on that Thursday night. It had been barely twenty-four hours since a storm of events had almost institutionalized me: Jimmy, the Ambassador for the Dead, a fist in the eye, a lying mother, clues in the kitchen office, and the gorgeous heroine waiting for a rendezvous with me at her bedroom window. Now, I was thinking mostly about the latter, and I wanted to tell her about my outing with Boonie, especially our visit to Smooth Rock.

I looked at my watch—a quarter before ten. George Schuple was explaining the dress code. I glanced backwards at Brock Oliff, who was tossing sunflower seeds towards a row of waitresses, squinting his devilish eyes and grinning. We did not make eye contact. In the back of the room, leaning against the back wall, was Whisper, dressed as he was last night, in a white button-down long-sleeve shirt, gray trousers, black hiking boots, and his loose fitting ball cap shadowing his pale face and covering his gray, crew-cut hair.

I thought of Jimmy Grandstaff, and then I quickly shifted my mind back to Kristel Schuple. She was waiting for me at her window.

At last, it was time for our clandestine summit. I navigated up the black driveway and arrived at the Schuple's back yard. A flitting twinkle, my beacon in the darkness, turned out to be the light above the kitchen table shining through a large bay window of the Schuple house. Through the window I could see Beverly Schuple sitting at the dining room table with a telephone cradled next to her cheek. Along the right side of the house was the glow from the window of Kristel's room.

Feeling like a prowler, I tiptoed around the perimeter of the small back yard and up to the designated window, where a yellow light emanated brightly from behind drawn curtains. The window was open wide, and another window next to it was dark and closed tight. I hoped it didn't belong to the bedroom of George and Beverly.

I crept up to Kristel's window and tapped softly on open pane three times.

Seconds later, wearing the sweetest of smiles, she poked her face between the drawn curtains.

"Hey, kiddo!" she said. Her hair was tied back and braided, and she was dressed in the same clothing she had worn this morning—light blue denim shorts and a white, sleeveless, button down blouse with a collar. She could have been a model for a J-Crew catalogue.

She rested her elbows on the windowsill and asked, "Did you go to the staff meeting tonight?"

"Yeah. It just ended."

"Was Brock there?"

"Yeah, he was there. Why?"

"Did he say anything to you?"

"No. Not a word. He didn't even look at me."

"That's a good sign, I guess. Maybe he won't bother you anymore." Kristel paused and grazed the back of her fingers softly across my cheek. "Your eye looks a little better."

"Thanks."

Directly to the left, a rattling noise scared me so much I dropped to my knees and ducked in the shadows. The window next to Kristel's was being opened, and during this split second for decision-making, I didn't know if I should bolt for the woods or just face the fact of getting caught. I ducked and froze.

The younger Schuple daughter, Becky, poked her head out of the newly opened window. "Kristel, who are you talking to?" she asked in a curious, sixth grade voice.

Kristel leaned further out her window to see her sister. I remained crouched, feeling very guilty and hoping that Becky wasn't the type to rat.

Louder than she had been talking, Kristel ordered. "It's none of your business, Becky. Close your window, now!"

"Who is it?" Becky asked. She looked down at me with a grin. I leaned away from the light, hoping my face would be hidden by the shadows.

"I'll tell you later," Kristel hissed through her teeth. "Now get back inside!"

Becky ignored her sister and addressed me directly. "What's your name?"

I wasn't sure if I should answer. I smiled, tight-lipped, and shifted my eyes over to Kristel.

"Becky, I'll tell you who it is later! Now get back inside and close your window!"

The youngest of the Schuple clan continued to goggle at me, grinning playfully all the while. "I'm gonna go tell Mom there's a prowler outside," she threatened, mixing her threat with a giggle.

"Becky," Kristel said sternly but softly, "remember our little arrangement we had last summer?"

"No."

"Yes you do. The one with the ice cream?"

A pause, and a thinking glance upward. "Yeah."

"I'll take you to Burleighs tomorrow," Kristel bribed in a sweet voice.

"You can't. You're grounded," Becky responded flatly. She giggled again.

"Then I'll give you the money."

"How much?"

"Three dollars."

"Five."

"Four."

"Okay, but you better tell me his name tonight, or I'm going straight to Mom."

"Fine. Now close your window!"

I watched the young girl smirk as she pulled the window down and latched it. The curtains remained open and her room went dark, so I couldn't tell if she was still watching me or not. I stepped closer to Kristel's window on the opposite side and stood against the wall of the house to hide myself at an angle from Becky's view.

Kristel shook her head softly. "I went through the same thing last year when Jimmy came up here to see me," she explained.

"It seems like she enjoys blackmailing you."

"Oh, she's not blackmailing me. She just wants to know who you are. After she meets you, she'll like it when you come up here. She likes to be in on it, you know, as though she's helping me hide a boy from my Mom."

"How often did Jimmy come up here?"

"Just three or four times at the end of last summer."

I wanted to ask Kristel a lot more questions about Jimmy, about her relationship with him, and about her relationship with Brock, but I didn't know how to phrase them appropriately. So I just looked silently at her—her pretty face, her bare arms, bronzed against the contrast of her white blouse, and her soft, velvety hands folded together on the windowsill.

"Do you want to go somewhere to talk?" she asked, glancing distrustfully towards her sister's window.

"Where?"

"Hang on just a minute."

The princess disappeared behind the curtain, and a moment later she reappeared at the window wearing a gray, pullover sweatshirt, the kind with a thick, floppy hood, which was balled up under her golden braid. Before I could say anything, she climbed through her window and stood next to me at the side of the house. She took hold of my hand and commanded, "C'mon, follow me."

"Aren't you going to get in trouble?" I protested mildly.

"No. I've done this before a thousand times by myself." She pulled on my arm gently. "C'mon, it'll be fine."

Kristel was bare from her toes to her thighs, where the hem of her denim shorts just barely showed underneath the oversized sweatshirt. She guided me around to the front yard, where she let go of my hand and skipped barefoot with much agility across flowerbeds, the lawn, and the brick sidewalk. We crossed the driveway and Kristel armed her way through a crowd of six-foot tall pine trees. Bare-legs and no shoes, she plowed through with relative ease as if she could do it blindfolded.

I followed until she finally stopped. In the dim light, I could detect the outline of an enormous tree trunk. Two-by-fours cut into foot-wide steps were nailed to the tree, forming a ladder up the trunk into darkness. Some of the nails looked rusty, yet others were new and shiny when the light from the house caught them just right.

"This is our tree house," Kristel chuckled, looking upward into the black foliage and speaking at a more-normal decibel than she did at the window. "Daddy helped Becky and me build it a few years ago."

With athletic, feline-like movements, Kristel was up the tree and gone in a matter of seconds. I followed, struggling up the narrow stepladder that spiraled around to the opposite side of the huge trunk. At the top, I found myself on a wide platform surrounded by three walls and sheltered under a slanting, shingled roof. The open side of the tree house faced towards the familiar, winding, gravel driveway that led to the back of the Poolside Café.

Kristel leaned against a side wall of pine wood planks and hugged her bare legs, folding them tightly to her chest. I sat down on the edge and dangled my legs over the side. If I were to get caught up there with Kristel, I hoped my dangling legs would help legitimize my claim that we *were only talking*.

"Is this the first time you've been out of the house since this morning?" I asked.

"Yes, except for dinner. I had to wait all day for my mom to call to check up on me."

"Did she?"

"No. I thought she would for sure. She didn't get home until just before dinner."

Kristel stretched the sweatshirt over her knees and legs. The night-air was cool but comfortable. "Why weren't you at dinner tonight?" she asked. "I'd thought I'd see you there."

I explained how I was out with Boonie. I told her of our adventure to Smooth Rock Falls and taking the back roads all the way around to Pokeville. Then I told her about my mother's phone call, the stuff I saw in Chef Al's office, and the trip to the police station where I turned the manila envelope and its contents over to the police.

Kristel said she didn't mind at all that Boonie and Officer Anders had heard the entire story. Like me, it provided security, assuring her that other people were aware of this amazing information. Also like me, she was entirely miffed by the manila envelope from the "Ambassador for the Dead," especially its link to the kitchen office. She agreed with Boonie that somebody in food-service may or may not have been the one who planted the envelope in my car, but whoever it was, he or she could be the same person who sent the John Doe letter about Jimmy to the police. "It could be Chef Al, Dave, Allen, or even Darlene," she suggested. "But if the kitchen gets their office supplies from the closet in the front office, then anyone here could have written that note. We can check the supply closet tomorrow and see if they have the same envelopes. Anyone could have put that letter there Jody, even Brock."

"I don't think it was him," I maintained. "His reaction when I showed the picture to him last night was weird. I don't know. He looked genuinely shocked when he saw that photograph. If he *had* planted it there, he's a good actor. He was *stunned* by it. Not to mention, your suspicion of his involvement in Jimmy's death and his writing that note just don't go together. I told the officer at the police station that I was pretty sure Brock had nothing to do with the envelope."

"Did you tell him *I* suspected that Brock… you know… that he might have pushed Jimmy."

"No. I didn't tell him. But I told Boonie."

"Who was the officer you talked to?"

I reached for my wallet in my back pocket and pulled out the business card the police officer gave me. "Officer Raymond Anders. He seemed like a nice guy."

Kristel smiled. "Oh, he is really nice. I've baby-sat his children a few times. We go to the same church. Did he say he would do anything?"

"Well, it's the sheriff who knows most about the case. He's supposed to call me tomorrow."

"Sheriff Slater," responded Kristel with a stern face. "He's a real creep. He questioned me after the accident—right there at the falls. I remember how he showed no care for how I was feeling. He wanted me to describe in detail everything that had happened, as if it didn't matter that I had just witnessed the most horrifying thing in my life!"

I added, "You know, now that you mention that, I thought it was really odd what the sheriff said on the radio. It was in the paper, too. He said that the only way to find out about Jimmy's death would be to ask Jimmy's ghost. Think of how insensitive that was to Jimmy's parents."

Kristel nodded and huffed. "That's just the way he is. He doesn't care about people's feelings. You should have seen the way he demanded details from me, just after I had witnessed all of it."

I commented, "He must've just been doing his job, you know, trying to get information. But it's hard to believe a sheriff would be that rude."

"Someone needs teach him a lesson about being a little more sensitive during a tragedy like that."

For several minutes, she stared sorrowfully out into the night. I finally interrupted her pensive mood. "You know, Kristel, what's really weird for me about this whole thing is that I never knew that Jimmy existed for all these years."

"Your parents must have had their reasons for not telling you."

"I can understand that, sort of. But now that I've found out, I don't understand why my mother has to keep lying about it."

"Maybe she was surprised that you found out, and she didn't know what to say, so she kept lying about it because she was so used to lying about it."

"Boonie said the same thing."

Kristel exhaled a loud sigh. "Parents can be pretty dumb sometimes. And they always want to appear smarter and wiser than their kids, no matter how dumb their behavior is."

I leaned back and lay flat on the platform, staring up at the slanted roof, my legs still dangling over the side. I asked softly, "Do you and your mother fight a lot?"

"Lately we have. Last night was a doozy when I got home late. She was already mad at my sister because of some stupid thing *she* did, and she took it out on me."

For the next hour, Kristel shared with me much of her personal life. She discussed the high points and low points of being the daughter of George and Beverly Schuple and living year-round at the Brown Swan Club. She talked mostly about her mother, describing Mrs. Schuple's constant demands upon her children, her meddling in her husband's management of the Club, and her incessant desire to impress the wealthiest of guests. "My father is a saint to have stuck with her so long," Kristel said. "If it weren't for Daddy, I'd be a stuck-up little snob, probably betrothed to Brock Oliff."

Her conversation shifted to her former boyfriends—a total of only three, including Jimmy and Brock. The first was a two-week steady in the sixth grade, which Kristel thought was significant enough to include in her list. The second was Jimmy, about whom I listened to every word with the greatest interest. I was fascinated to hear that Jimmy loved sports, especially baseball, and that he loved his motorcycle more than anything. I've wanted a motorcycle all my life, but my mother wouldn't allow it.

"He was very sweet," Kristel said of Jimmy. "Very polite, too. Before he ever asked me to go out with him, even with a big group of people, he asked permission from my father first. He always opened doors for me, and the first and only time he kissed me, he asked permission from me first." Kristel giggled. "And then he kissed me on the forehead."

Right there I determined that I'd ask her before I kiss her, too, and it should at least be a kiss on the cheek, if not a peck on the lips. And, of course, Kristel will never open a door herself when I'm around.

The third boyfriend Kristel ever had was Brock, a relationship brought on by the coercion of her mother that lasted a few months until Kristel broke it off in the spring. She said she was through with stupid relationships like that. I didn't know how to take *that* message.

"I'm kind of glad I'm grounded," she said, "so I don't have to see Brock at least for a couple of days."

We both snickered.

"So, Jody, tell me more about your family," she entreated, turning things over to me.

I was now sitting against the wall adjacent to Kristel's. My legs were no longer dangling over the side. They were stretched out perpendicular over Kristel's feet, keeping her toes warm. Upon hearing her request, I took a deep breath and sighed heavily, and for next hour it was my turn to share about my life. Kristel listened carefully, maintaining unceasing eye contact.

I told her about my childhood, my having gone from the womb to childcare centers before graduating into latchkeyhood. I shared what life was like growing up as an only child in an upper-middle class home—having everything to myself, but being totally alone, mostly due to my parents' busy lives. "The good thing about it," I said, "was that I had a lot of time to read." I mentioned some of the great books I've read, a list that greatly impressed Kristel. Then I focused again on my parents and how they had virtually ignored me for most of their lives—never showing up at ballgames, school productions, or anything where I saw other kids' parents in attendance. Eventually, my story turned to how bad my parents' marriage was, which led to describing my latest phone discussion with Wesley and how my mother left him on Tuesday morning.

"What did they fight about?" Kristel asked.

I told her about my parents so-called financial problems: credit card bills, house payments, car payments, business loan payments, my private school tuition, and Wesley's gambling. "Things got really rough between them, and I was glad I got out of there and came here. It's like escaping hell. Right now, I hate my parents. I was getting along with my Mom pretty good before I left, but now I know she's been lying, and my father is just a stinking bastard."

"Jody!"

"Sorry. But you know, I thought I would be escaping from all that mess back home, but I was here less than two days and I get hit with all this crap. And it's all my parents' fault."

Kristel paused a moment before she spoke. "Your parents sound a lot like Brock's parents," she said. "Branson Oliff is the one of the richest men in this part of the country. He's unbelievable, Jody. He's a multi-millionaire. But Brock is the only child just like you, and he doesn't seem to get any more attention from his parents than you do from yours."

"When I get married and have kids, it'll be different. I won't care about money, so I can give my family all my attention."

Kristel smiled.

"Are Brock's parents still together?" I asked.

"No. Veronica Oliff died when Brock was two. He was raised by several nannies."

"Did Mr. Oliff ever re-marry?"

"Yes, twice. It's kind of sad: once he married a twenty-one year old about a year after his first wife died. They divorced, and a year later he married a twenty-three year old. They're still married, if you can call it that. Her name is Peggy, and she practically lives her own life, off of *his* fortune, of course. Branson travels all over the world overseeing his business investments. He owns several restaurants and hotels. He even owns a huge resort in Cancun. And for years, he's been trying to buy the Club from my father. Every week or so during the summer, he comes to the Club for lunch and writes a dollar amount on a napkin and asks a waitress to bring it to Daddy. Of course, Daddy refuses every time."

"Does your Dad ever tell you how much he offers?"

"He never has. But Branson Oliff hasn't made an offer in a while because he's hoping to get Marilee Manor instead."

"That haunted place across the lake?"

"Yes. It's one of the few pieces of lakeside property around here that Branson Oliff doesn't already own. If he buys it, rumor has it that he's going to build an enormous, brand new resort hotel. Daddy says it would make the Brown Swan Club look like an old roadside motel."

"Is your dad worried about that?"

"Yes. He hates the thought of having to compete against Branson Oliff."

"Has he ever thought of trying to buy that property himself?"

"Marilee Manor? No, because if he gets in a bidding war with Oliff, he'll never win."

"Who owns it now?"

"It's a long story."

"Boonie told me about it—about the guy who murdered his family and has been haunting the place ever since."

"Yep. The Legend of Marilee Manor."

"He told me about the Lights."

"The Lights of Marilee. Abbeyville's claim to fame. I did my research paper on it for English last year."

Our lengthy conversation grew even longer as Kristel described the Legend of Marilee Manor as she knew it.

# CHAPTER 12

## *The Legend of Lake Marilee*

Even though it ended in the early morning hours, Kristel's story kept me wide-awake and at full attention.

"Lake Marilee was first settled back in the eighteen-hundreds by a wealthy man named Abbott Marilee. His family lived on the piece of land across the lake that we now call Marilee Manor. The town was originally named after him—Abbottsville, but he eventually had a granddaughter named Abigail, or Abby, whom he cherished. He ordered the town to be renamed when she died of leukemia as a young child." Kristel shifted and sat cross-legged. She continued, "I saw her gravestone up at Abbeyville Cemetery ... it was so sad. She was just five years old. She died in 1836.

"Well, several generations of Marilee's came and went since then, and they all lived at the huge mansion at Marilee Manor. I've seen old pictures of the place; it was unbelievable. There were twelve bedrooms in all, servants quarters, the whole bit. Legends say that underneath the Mansion was a series of secret tunnels and vaults where the Marilee fortune was kept. Supposedly millions of dollars worth of gold and silver were hidden there.

"The Marilee's were the most prominent family in the area, even though they were somewhat secluded over there across the lake from the town. They were also a very proud family, well educated and quite religious. They played an important role in the development of the community around here. They owned most of the land around the lake until the family began to scatter, and much of the land was sold to other wealthy families like the Oliffs.

"Eventually, back before World War II, just four Marilees remained: William and Elizabeth, and their two boys Abbott the Third and his brother Zane.

"The legend says that Abbott was the heir to the Manor property, and two-thirds of the fortune buried in the vaults underneath it was his. His brother Zane was to inherit the other third of the gold. He was jealous of Abbott's larger inheritance, but in a gracious act, Abbott promised that he would split the fortune equally with his younger brother, despite their parents' will.

"Then, in 1958, a scandal erupted when a fourteen year-old girl in town turned up pregnant and named Abbott as the father, claiming he had raped her. To preserve the family name, William and Elizabeth disowned their oldest son and removed him entirely from the will. Their youngest son Zane would get it all. Abbott fled town, leaving his wife and kids behind. He was twenty-eight years old at the time.

"It was just six days later that the entire mansion at Marilee Manor was destroyed by a dynamite explosion. Abbott's parents, William and Elizabeth, and Abbott's wife and son were in the house at the time of the explosion. The remains of their bodies were retrieved, some in whole and some blown to pieces, but the body of Abbott's infant daughter was never found. To this day, nobody knows for sure if the baby was in the house, but she was never found and has been presumed dead. Some think her body was blown into the lake or into the woods and perhaps carried off by animals. Some people say it's *her* ghost that comes back to haunt the land.

"But the craziest thing is that on the night of the explosion, the body of Abbott's younger brother Zane was discovered near the water with a bullet wound in his chest. He didn't die in the explosion like the others. Police determined that the explosion was detonated by Abbott Marilee who wanted revenge against his parents for disowning him. They say Abbott must have shot Zane first and then blew his entire family to smithereens. The vaults underneath the destroyed mansion were completely empty, and Abbott supposedly had stolen the gold from the vaults over a period of several days prior to the explosion. Police determined that Zane must have discovered his older brother planting the dynamite around the house when Abbott shot and killed him.

"A nationwide warrant went out for the arrest of Abbott Marilee for the murder of his family, and for the theft of about four hundred million dollars in gold from the vaults. The dollar amount gets bigger every time the story gets told, and nobody knows for sure exactly how much it was. But about four weeks after the explosion, a local hunter found Abbott Marilee's body near the shore at Cotter's Landing. The coroner determined he had put a rifle under his chin and pulled the trigger, and that his suicide occurred the same night he blew up the mansion and shot his brother Zane.

"So the big mystery is that nobody knows where all the gold and silver ended up. Some think it's at the bottom of the lake. Others think it's still buried in other secret vaults on the property that no one has discovered. It's all part of the Legend.

"This all took place forty years ago, and since then a lot of wild stories have come up about the ghost of Abbott Marilee roaming the grounds of Marilee Manor looking for gold that he missed. You know, campfire ghost stories, and stuff like that. And then tourists started coming here just to see the Lights of Marilee."

Kristel went on to describe what Boonie had already told me.

"In July, late at night, near the same time that the explosion took place, you can look across the lake at the Manor and see lights moving along to the shore. Nobody knows what causes it, and it happens for several nights in a row, right around the anniversary of the tragedy. People come from all over to see the Lights. It's really spooky—I've seen it many times. Several years ago, *Unsolved Mysteries* did a story on it, and that brought even bigger crowds. It's really quite a spectacle now, but Daddy loves it because it brings a lot of business. Tourists crowd at the Club beach just to watch.

"It looks like a light from a lantern being carried along the shore while another light burns out on the point. It can last a few minutes, sometimes longer, depending on the night. One night it was there for several hours. You can see it moving back and forth along the shoreline and into the woods at the Manor."

I interjected in a dubious voice, "I'd be over there with a camera and a shotgun."

"People have tried that. But whenever someone else is at the Manor, the Lights don't appear. So all the locals are instructed to stay away during the month of July when the Lights are supposed to come out, so that the tourists have something to see. There was one time that someone secretly set up a camera over there, and in the film you can barely see the figure of a man carrying the lantern. That's what they showed on *Unsolved Mysteries*, and they played it up as the actual ghost of Abbott Marilee."

"It sounds like a big hoax, if you ask me."

"A lot of people think that, too, but that's what the Legend of Marilee Manor is all about. This July marks the fortieth anniversary of the explosion. And according to county law, the land still belongs to the Marilee family until a full generation passes without any family member staking claim to the property. They define a generation as forty years, and unless someone related to the Marilee family steps forward before the fortieth anniversary of the discovery of Abbott's body, Marilee Manor becomes a possession of the county, and the county can sell it to the highest bidder."

"And Mr. Oliff is the leading candidate to buy it?"

"Yeah. It looks that way. And if he builds a resort on that property, it will probably put an end to the attraction of the Lights."

"That probably bothers your Dad because there won't be a rush of business, huh."

"Not really. Daddy thinks that Oliff will exploit the Legend in his own way and somehow draw people to his resort because of it. Branson Oliff's big resort over there might actually help ours over here."

"So all these years, nobody has stepped forward claiming that they're some long lost relative of the Marilee family?"

"I haven't heard of any legitimate claims. Only a crazy local or two have attempted fraudulent claims to the property."

"You don't think there's still a vault full of gold over there, do you?"

"Not really. It's just part of the Legend. But anything's possible, I guess."

"Do people go digging around over there?"

"Yes, and as it turns out, there isn't a network of secret underground passageways like everyone claims. There was just one vault found under the house after the explosion, and it was empty."

"Have you seen it?"

"No. I just heard about it. I don't go over there at all. Marilee Manor has become a late night hangout for a lot of the local teens, except during July when nobody is allowed to go over there. Except for then, kids go there to drink, smoke, do drugs, and have sex. There's supposed to be some glory in losing you're virginity there. It's really sick—all the stuff that goes on over there. I've even heard some business owners, even people who benefit from all the tourists, say that they'll be glad when Oliff gets it all cleaned up. Daddy forbids me to go near the place. He said he heard that some satanic cults have gathered there to perform weird rituals. Oftentimes, especially during warmer months, you can see a campfire burning on the point near the shore of the Manor. Usually it's just a bunch of teens hanging out there, but once on Halloween night I saw a campfire and several torches moving around in the woods. It scared me. It looked really weird."

"I'd like to see it," I said. "The remains of the mansion and the vault, I mean."

"If you go, go during the day. It's not a very good place to be at night."

We stayed up in the tree house until just after 4:00 a.m. talking about everything and anything that came to mind. Finally, I decided I needed to put an end to our evening together, so I could at least get an hour of sleep before I had to report to the kitchen for work.

"Don't fall asleep over the meat slicer," Kristel joked as she climbed back into her bedroom window.

The metal gate that blocked off the Schuple's driveway from the rest of the Club property rattled loudly when I climbed over it. The pool deck was dark, except for the light produced by a Coke machine humming against the wall of the Café. I circled the fence around the pool deck and walked down the paved roadway towards the softball diamond at the bottom of the hill. All was quiet and peaceful. In a few hours, the place would be swarming with vacationers.

A soft whirring sound grew louder behind me and I spun around to see a golf cart wobbling down the decline from the pool deck. Old Whisper was gripping the steering wheel with both hands as the cart accelerated down the hill and squeaked to a halt no less than three yards from my feet. Again, a bright light blinded me, this time only for a second as Whisper recognized me immediately.

His raspy voice was stern and authoritative. "Mr. Barrett. You plan on making this a habit?"

"Uh, no sir. This will be the last time you see me out after hours."

Whisper slid a pen from his front shirt pocket and thumbed through the small notepad taped to the mini-dashboard of his cart. "I'm going to have to report this," he gargled.

"You are?"

"Yessir. Mrs. Schuple wants all staff members reported if they are seen anywhere outside their cabin between one and five a.m." Whisper checked his wristwatch. "It's 4:20 right now. Little too early to be going to work, Mr. Barrett."

"Uh, well, I just came from the Schuple's *house*." I pointed beyond the pool where the Schuple's driveway began.

Whisper's eyes widened with surprise and he scratched his head through his ball cap. "Oh, uh, well, I guess Beverly doesn't need a report on that," he said meekly in his soft, raspy voice. He put the cap back on the pen and returned it to his front pocket. "I didn't know they'd be up this late."

Whew! This guy had me nailed and he's letting me off the hook so easily. Is he really so gullible?

The corner of Whisper's thin lips rose slightly in a half smile. "I take it Kristel's grounded again."

Not so gullible after all. He's actually quite astute.

I smiled, half embarrassed. "Yeah, she is."

"Good night, to you." Whisper said as he turned the steering wheel of his golf cart and coasted in a half-circle before accelerating back up the hill again.

Just then, I remembered the tremendous favor the old man did for me. "By the way," I said loudly in the quiet night air. "Thanks for bringing my car to the shop!"

Whisper lifted one hand in acknowledgment as he whirred up the hill. I walked sleepily towards Saranac.

# CHAPTER 13

## *The Season Begins*

I returned to work in the kitchen on Friday morning and discovered it operating with much less levity than it did on Wednesday, my first day there. Other new staff members were being trained in the basics of hand washing, knife safety, and the like, the same lessons I received two days ago. But the tone of the place was different on this day; an excited panic had taken over. Although breakfast was a simple eggs and cereal buffet for the staff, an overwhelming mood of official business enshrouded the kitchen atmosphere. It was opening day of the summer season: practice was over, and perfection would be expected from now until Labor Day.

The work schedule took full effect now, and my absence from work yesterday went virtually unnoticed by the leadership. Allen, the young apprentice chef, supervised the morning shift and was frantically trying to find more aprons and plastic gloves for the new help. Chef Dernbaugh arrived at 7:30 a.m., in time to pile scrambled eggs onto a dinner plate, fill a gigantic ceramic mug with coffee, and strut straight to his office. Dave, the evening chef, wouldn't arrive until noon.

Boonie, I, and a third helper named Nathan arrived promptly at 6:00 a.m. The hour and a half of sleep I managed to get after my long, long talk with Kristel in the tree house felt more like one and-a-half minutes. But the bright lights of the kitchen and the sense of urgency that Allen imparted when he began giving assignments helped shrug the heaviness off my eyelids. Nevertheless, I looked forward to an afternoon nap after work.

"Boonie, go ahead and put breakfast out by 7:00," Allen said as he looked over a sheet of paper attached to a clipboard. "And you can take care of all the lunch prep, too. I'm going to take these guys and get them busy on dinner." He was referring to Nathan and me.

The hours from 6:00 to noon, except for a thirty-minute breakfast break, were spent around a stainless-steel prep table in the back corner of the kitchen.

Allen trained Nathan and me how to do various tasks such as peeling and deveining shrimp, making cocktail sauce, scoring catfish filets, slicing raw beef julienne, and mixing two gallons of beef marinade. Occasionally, Chef Al wondered out of the office and inspected our work. He said nothing to us, but he vociferously shouted an update about the expected dinner count to Allen. "We could be around 125, so you better go ahead and prep a few more shrimp cocktails," he barked. "The fresh parsley came in yesterday for the garnish."

Boonie spent the entire morning by himself up at the front line, also known as the cook's line, a long four by thirty foot stainless steel table equipped with built-in sinks at each end. It was an impressive structure—the nucleus of the kitchen. Above it dangled sauté pans, cooking pots, spoons and ladles, all within an arms reach of the cook. Drawers built under the front line held an assortment of cooking tools—more ladles, whips, spatulas, meat forks and pastry brushes. Lower shelves displayed an army of plastic containers bearing everything from exotic spices to imported cooking oils. The floor of the working aisle was covered with thick, black rubber floor mats that provided comfort for the chef's feet over the hard, tile floor below them.

An impressive row of cooking appliances lined the opposite side of the aisle: a shiny, five foot grill, pressure steam ovens, a convection oven, two steam kettles, and a three-bay fryerlator. A massive exhaust hood roofed this line of equipment, and it produced a rumbling din that drowned out much of the kitchen clatter.

All morning, Boonie never left his post at the front line, except to retrieve something from the walk-in cooler which was located halfway between the front line and the prep table where Nathan and I worked. He methodically prepared the staff's breakfast and lunch, needing only a fraction of the equipment the front line offered. He obviously liked being there, up front, where the chefs performed their magic, and most of all, where he could be seen by the waitresses who were busily preparing the dining room for the opening meal that night.

At 11:00 a.m., Pete and Rodney Needleman showed up with another newcomer, some heavy kid named Skip, and the three of them began setting up the dish-washing area, the forlorn corner of the kitchen more affectionately termed "the dish pit." Allen spent a good hour training the dish crew before Boonie strolled to the back of the kitchen from the front line. "Lunch is on," he shouted proudly with a smile. By then, my feet and legs were aching, and the lunch break was a much-needed respite.

A small staff dining room adjoined the kitchen against the rear of the guest dining room. It was where the staff convened to eat their meals, and Boonie, Nathan, myself, and the dish-pit boys sat together at a rectangular, Formica-top table. The grounds crew and maintenance crew sat together at a separate table, as well as the housekeepers, the lifeguards, and program staff. Brock and his cohorts were not present at lunch this day.

Boonie, the veteran of two summers, explained things to Nathan and me while we ate leftover baked chicken and potatoes. "The morning shift is the best shift, by far. You have to come in early, but you get off at 2:30, and you have the rest of the day to yourself. The late shift hardly gets to see the sun, unless they get up early enough in the morning, but then it's too cold to swim."

Nathan remained non-talkative, making fork tracks in his mashed potatoes.

"Do we keep the same shift all summer?" I asked.

"Yeah, unless you want to change and someone trades with you. Thursday nights you'll work late, probably. It's Beach Party Night. That day we have a brunch and then a big dinner meal down on the beach. It's lots of fun, though, 'cause some of the women come dressed to swim." Boonie flashed his charming, white-toothed grin and went on to describe an episode about a woman who came to the beach party and spilled sweet-and-sour meatballs down her white bathing suit. Boonie, of course, was obliged to help her scrub the mess out before it stained. He giggled about the story like it was the funniest thing in the world.

I stretched a wide yawn and widened my eyes to keep them open. I looked around some more.

There was this back door that allowed people to enter and exit the staff dining room in order to avoid walking through the kitchen. The door swung open with a creak, and unless it was gently closed, the spring mechanism often pulled it shut with a slam that rattled the silverware in the rack built into the wall next to it. During meals, a creak, a slam, and a jingle of silverware became so common that it went practically unnoticed when a housekeeper or grounds worker occasionally walked in late.

However, at lunch on this first day, one particular staff member drew much attention, especially from us boys of the grove, when he entered the staff dining room through this noisy door. It was old Whisper, lanky and pale-skinned, wearing his ever-present white button down shirt, gray trousers, black hiking boots, and worn ball cap.

Whisper limped past the food table and opened the lid to the ice bin. He filled a large thermos with ice and then with lemonade from the sprayer machine, twisted the thermos lid shut, and thumped loudly out the door. He was careful to close the door gently, avoiding the normal slam and jingle.

Pete Needleman made the first comment. "Guess them porno videos make him thirsty!" He snorted a laugh and his brother Rodney worked up a jumbled-toothed grin. The other boys at the table chuckled likewise.

I was quick to change the tune of the ensuing discussion. "I don't know how well you know him, but Whisper is a really nice guy."

Pete chuckled out another remark. "Why, did he give you a peek at the June Playboy or something?"

"No," I said sternly. "After Brock slashed my tires, he towed my car to the garage for me, and he had to put two spares on the back end to do it. I didn't even ask him to. And last night, he could have reported me to Mrs. Schuple when he found me walking back to the cabin at 4:30 in the morning, but he let me off."

The guys were more impressed with my late-hour escapade than with Whisper's acts of service.

Boonie piped up, "What were you doing out at that hour?"

I didn't get a chance to answer him. Allen came into the room and shouted, "Phone call for Jody Barrett." He held up the receiver of a cordless phone.

Thinking it was my mother calling the kitchen for a second time in as many days, I glanced at Boonie and mumbled, "Here we go again. Maybe she's ready to confess this time." I took the phone outside, the door slammed behind me, and the silverware jingled.

The caller wasn't my mother; it was Wesley instead.

"Yeah," I blurted in a disgusted tone when I learned who it was.

"You need to come home, Jody," said the man who was legally my father but had hardly played the part for years. I wondered why he sounded so urgent. What was going on now?

"No. I'm staying here," I insisted.

"I think it's best you come home. Your mother is very upset."

This worried me a little, but I tried not to let on. I balked, "I talked with her. She's fine. I'm fine, and I'm staying here."

"Your mother told me she talked with you. She told me about some story about a boy who was killed. What can you tell me about that?"

Whoa, I wasn't expecting this. Where did this come from? Ideas bombarded my head. Does he know about Jimmy? Did he *ever* know about Jimmy? Why is he bringing it up all of the sudden?

"Who was he?" Wesley asked.

"Jimmy Grandstaff," I answered in haste. "He was a kid who used to work here who was killed last summer."

"Uh, huh."

Silence. I wasn't sure what to say, so nothing came out of my mouth.

My stepfather asked again, "Uh, well, what about him?"

I thought, why is he asking about Jimmy? What answer is he looking for? "You tell me," I retorted boldly.

"Huh?"

Suddenly, words erupted from my heart like a volcano. "Wesley, you know... tell me about Mom's first child, my brother, the one who was supposedly aborted. Or did Mom lie to you about it, too?"

I heard him sigh heavily over the phone.

"Uh, Jody. There are reasons why we never told you about Jimmy. There are good reasons... trust me."

Finally! At least one of my parents was admitting they lied to me for sixteen years. I pressed him, "Why did you lie about it! Why couldn't I know?" My voice increased in volume, so I walked further away from the staff dining-room door.

"There are reasons, Jody. Trust me."

"*Trust* you? Trust *you*? How the heck am I supposed to trust *you*?" I was practically yelling now, and I wondered if the kids inside the dining room could hear. "I don't trust anybody," I blurted, thinking of my history teacher.

"Jody, I think it's best if you come home now and we can talk about it. Your mother wants you home, too."

I was angry now. Not because they wanted me home, but because I just *felt* like being angry at them, and this phone call gave me a good reason. "Forget it," I said.

I pushed the hang-up button on the phone with as much vengeance as a thumb could possible exert. It was the third time I had hung up on one of my parents in two days, and this time it didn't feel as satisfying as slamming the receiver down in its cradle. Stupid cordless phones.

Creak, slam, jingle. I was back in the dining room and the guys had heard part of my end of the volatile conversation. I quickly summarized the whole of it to Boonie before we went back to work and finished off our shift.

At last, two-thirty arrived, and a much-needed afternoon nap was beckoning. The morning kitchen crew gathered around the time clock to punch-out and Allen met us there with some final words.

"6:00 a.m. tomorrow, fellas. It's the real thing," he said, referring to the guests who were already arriving.

I could only think about the relief I would give my aching feet and about the pillow on which I would lay my tired head. I couldn't care less if I didn't see any of the guests until tomorrow morning. Boonie, on the other hand, had different ideas.

"Let's go down to the boat dock," he said with a smirk, "to see if any guests need help with their life jackets."

"Sorry, I've gotta hit the sack for a couple of hours."

Boonie shrugged his shoulders and headed towards the main dining room where several waitresses were continuing their busy preparations. I walked out the back door of the kitchen and onto the back dock where young Becky Schuple sat alone, working on a Popsicle.

"You're Jody… right?" she asked, grinning that familiar grin that I saw her wear at bedroom window the night before.

"Yes."

"You have mail!" she squealed. Her lips squeezed tight, trying to suppress a giant smile. She trotted away, joyfully calling over her shoulder, "It's up at the staff lounge."

The staff lounge was a comfortable room furnished with sofas, love seats, and game tables. A television was mounted in the upper corner of the room and a wall of mailboxes labeled A to Z divided the common area from a small office. Most of the boxes were empty, except for the B box, which contained two envelopes.

My name was written on each, one inscribed in beautiful, flowing script, the other in block, capital letters. I opened the script one first.

*Jody,*

*How was work today? My day was pretty boring.*
*Only one more day confined to this house!*
*If you can, come see me after dinner tonight.*

*Kristel*

This was the letter that Becky must have been referring to. She probably delivered it and thought it was pretty exciting to serve in the capacity of messenger for her big sister.

But the other letter—the one in a business sized envelope with a stamp and a postmark from Pokeville, N.Y—was quite intriguing. I tucked Kristel's note in my back pocket and quickly opened this one. It read,

> JODY,
>
> YOU ARE THE KEY TO REDEEMING JIMMY. I WILL HELP.
>
> AN AMBASSADOR FOR THE DEAD.

I read the words at least five times. They injected into my mind a plethora of feelings: ridicule, doubt, sadness, anger, and crazily enough—excitement. Above all else, I enjoyed getting another letter like this. It was mysterious. It cried for a solution. And even if it was just a joke and had nothing to do with solving a murder mystery, it was, in the very least, a challenge for me to solve the mystery of who was sending the notes. More compelling to me than the contents of the letter was the question of who sent it. I couldn't wait to show it to Kristel and Boonie.

Who? Who? Who could have sent this letter? On my way back to Saranac, my brain was in hyper-drive. The letter was post-marked from Pokeville, so it could have come from anyone around here. The first letter—the manila envelope with the photo of Jimmy—someone *placed* that one in my car. But who?

I noticed some gray-haired guests who were already enjoying the swimming pool. Several others of various ages walked about admiring the beautifully landscaped grounds, some driving their vehicles down secluded roads towards their private chalets. Despite the Club springing to life on that Friday afternoon, and despite the nice little note from Kristel, all I could think about now was who was calling himself the "Ambassador for the Dead."

I fell asleep on my bunk thinking about it.

I awoke in time to join the staff for dinner in the small dining room. It was five-thirty, and normally most of the work crews would be finished for the day. But this day was different—everyone was busy well into the evening, doing last minute chores that couldn't go another day undone. Seeing all the hustle and bustle, I was glad my shift was out of the way. Only half of the staff who were present at lunch even had time to stop for dinner.

Boonie and I sat together again for the meal and I informed him about the latest Ambassador letter. We discussed it—how the Ambassador could be anyone in the kitchen, even Chef Al. It could be anyone on staff, and even anyone who lives in the area.

When the Needleman twins arrived at the table, we switched subjects and Boonie described some of the babes he saw at the beach, enticing Pete and Rodney to grin in awe the whole time.

Unexpectedly, George Schuple, wearing a blue suit-jacket and bright yellow tie, entered through the creaky wooden door. Slam, jingle.

"I could use some volunteers to carry luggage," he announced to the few of us who were there eating.

Boonie immediately stood up and offered his services. He nudged me and I stood as well. A few more boys, knowledgeable about the tips that bell hopping could earn, volunteered also.

Schuple smiled. "Wonderful, you boys get dressed in dark slacks and a white button down shirt, and meet me in the lobby."

Four of us exited the room hastily. Mr. Schuple intercepted me on my way out the door. "Jody, I need to talk with you a moment," he said in a serious tone.

"Sure, Mr. Schuple." My heart jumped. What was this about? Missing work yesterday? Visiting Kristel late at night? Did Whisper turn me in after all?

"Your mom called me this morning and she was quite concerned for you."

"Uh, huh," I said, half relieved and half upset my mother had called him.

"I guess you've learned about Jimmy Grandstaff being your brother."

"Uh, huh."

"How did you find out, may I ask?"

"Oh, I figured it out. You know—our similar looks. And I knew Mom had been pregnant before me. I just put two and two together and asked my mom about it." I wondered if Schuple suspected that his daughter had spilled the beans.

"Well, you're mother was quite surprised. She thought I must have told you, because she made me promise never to tell you about Jimmy before she did."

"She was never going to tell me," I replied bluntly. "She even lied about it to me yesterday on the phone when I asked her. She still hasn't told me the truth about it."

Schuple's thick, peppery eyebrows slanted down in concern. "Well, she's going through a lot right now, having left your father and all. She called me to make sure that you are doing okay. She had heard you were on your way home."

"Where did she hear that?"

"From your father, I suppose."

"So she *doesn't* want me to come home right away?" I asked, remembering how Wesley had told me she did.

"No. She said she's glad that you're up here, away from all the mess of the separation. But now she's worried about how this news about Jimmy Grandstaff is affecting you. She just wants to know that you're all right."

"I am."

"Good, that's good. And if you ever need anything Jody, just ask. I know how rough this must be for you."

"I'm fine."

"Good." Schuple patted me on the back turned toward the door. "Oh," he said, stopping in his steps. "Another thing. I heard that your car had been vandalized."

"Uh, huh. All four tires slashed."

"Do you have any idea who did it?"

"It was Brock Oliff." Maybe I should have added that he knocked me out with a fist in the eye.

"Mm. That doesn't surprise me. I promise I'll deal with Brock as soon as I get a chance. I'll make sure he pays up square. Right now, I've got some guests to make happy."

"Sure thing, Mr. Schuple."

As my boss walked away, I knew one thing for sure: the truth. Jimmy *was* my brother. It *is* the truth. Schuple just confirmed it.

A huge weight fell off my shoulders, as if I had been set free from something. I can't explain it, but it was like I was free again. I trotted down to Saranac to get changed for bellboy duty.

# CHAPTER 14

## *Rothschild, Religion, and Routine*

Boonie challenged me to a bet over who could earn the most bell-hopping tips before nine o'clock. The loser would buy a milkshake for the winner, and just minutes before the deadline, I had earned fourteen dollars in tips carrying luggage. Boonie's smile had earned him thirty-three, and I was resigned to the fact that I'd be paying for his next milkshake.

"You gotta know how to charm 'em," Boonie said as we waited in the lobby.

A van from the Albany airport slowed to a stop in front of the porch steps. A well-dressed family of four disembarked, including an older daughter who looked about eighteen.

"Hoo-ee, I hope she likes the beach in the afternoon," Boonie said under his breath.

A most conspicuous elderly gentleman followed the family out of the van. He wore a bushy white beard, wire bifocals, a navy blue three-piece suit, topped with a plaid, Scottish golfers hat. He was by himself, and his mannerisms indicated he had been here before. Unlike the family of four, who were gazing at the Club's scenic lawns and cottages, this old man looked at his pocket watch, fastened the top button on his vest, and, with a bamboo cane in hand, sauntered to the lobby desk to check in.

The van driver, Jeff Gunderson, began unloading the luggage from the rear of the vehicle while the family of four meandered to the front porch.

"Take your pick," I said to Boonie, referring to the old man and the family.

His eye was on the brunette, and he replied, "No. You go ahead and choose. You're way behind anyway."

"No, you pick," I insisted. "I know whose bags you want to carry." The girl was attractive, but, in my eyes, nothing like Kristel.

Boonie shrugged his shoulders and grinned. "Whatever you say. I'll take the fam', and you take Santa Claus."

He was absolutely unstoppable, but admirable nonetheless. After they checked in, Boonie was down the hall with the family, leading them toward a suite located on the second floor of the lodge. He pushed a cart-full of their luggage in front of him, and before he turned the corner near the elevator, he already knew the names of all four family members, including Angela, the older daughter.

As for me, I watched the elderly man step away from the front desk with a key in his hand. "May I help you with your bags, sir?" I asked politely.

The man jerked his head and studied me through his bifocals before a wide smile emerged from the gap between his bushy, gray mustache and beard. "Excellent! Up to the Lakeview Chalets, if you don't mind!" His words were deep and robust, and I thought that if Santa Claus truly existed, he could be this man. Pack a pillow around his waste, and he could have had a December job at any mall in America.

"Name's Robert Rothschild," the old man announced, tipping his plaid golfer's hat before extending his right hand and giving me a firm shake. During our walk up the hill, I learned that Mr. Rothschild had been coming to the Brown Swan Club for thirty-eight consecutive summers. At the door of his chalet, interestingly named Tycoon's Roost, he tipped me and insisted he could take the bags through the door himself.

Returning to the lobby, I found Boonie waiting with a big white grin.

"Ten bucks and her room extension," he said proudly, bouncing his heels on the floor. "That's forty-three dollars for three hours of work!"

I acted like I didn't hear him. "I'll take a chocolate shake," I said boldly.

"What do you mean? You're buying for me!"

Into my pocket I slid my hand, and out it came holding a crisp, folded, one hundred dollar bill. I snapped it open and I held it eye-level.

"Mr. Rothschild," I said with a smirk, "turns out to be Santa Claus after all!"

It was easy to settle into life at the Club, especially as each night promised more time with Kristel. After Boonie bought me a chocolate shake at Burleighs, I met Kristel in the tree house around ten o'clock. I wasn't going to stay late this time because I didn't want another near-sleepless night, but I did want to fill her in on the events of the day.

I offered her the remaining half of the milkshake, and when I told her about the enormous tip Mr. Rothschild gave me, Kristel informed me that

Robert Rothschild had more money than he knew what to do with. She was surprised Boonie had no idea who he was and didn't choose to take his bags.

"Well, he did get some girl's phone number," I said.

"Just one girl?" she joked.

We ended up talking for a while, and one thing I was learning about Kristel over the last few days was that she took her religion quite seriously. She very active in her youth group at church, and she knew way more about the Bible than your average person. And she was pretty firm about her Christian beliefs, especially as it pertained to her morals.

I wasn't exactly sure how I felt about this. As I said before, I wasn't an atheist or anything, but there wasn't a whole lot that I liked, or respected, about my parents' church, and I had pretty much come to the conclusion that religion worked for some people and not for others. It apparently worked well for Kristel, and perhaps it's what made her the person she was. Maybe, too, her family's religion was the reason behind her mother's stern over-protection.

Anyway, during that second night in the tree house, Kristel was describing to me her youth group and how some friends of hers had been punished for drinking at a party that Kristel refused to attend. Then, she comes right out of the blue and asks me this question:

"Jody, are you a Christian?"

More concerned with the answer she wanted to hear than the truth, I replied, "Yes, I go to church and all."

She smiled, but shook her head slightly as she responded, "But that doesn't make you a Christian."

I was quick to answer, "Yeah, but I believe in God and all that. I just don't like my church very much and the way people are there."

"You mean your parents?" she said. She was incredibly perceptive.

"Yes, exactly. They're such hypocrites, and so are a lot of other people at that church." It seemed safe to be honest with her, so I continued, "A lot of people who call themselves Christians are such fakes. I'm not saying that you are, Kristel, but I believe that religion works for some people and not for others."

Then she said something that tugged at my insides. "You're right, Jody, it must be hard to trust in God if you don't trust your parents."

I thought about that for a second; she was a sharp one, and maybe her psychoanalysis was right, in a way. I answered, "Yeah, I don't trust my parents, but I do believe in God. But I believe in *myself*, too."

"So you *do* believe in God? What do you believe about him?"

She was rather persistent with this topic, so I answered promptly, "I believe him… for lots of things. But you can't see God, so you don't really know if he's there for sure. But you *can* trust yourself. I'm the only person I can count on with absolute certainty." There was my maxim, the first time I quoted it to anyone in a conversation. I said it to her again for effect, "I trust *myself*. I'm the only one I can count on with absolute certainty."

Kristel astutely replied with, "Just like Descartes said, 'I think, therefore I am?'"

This girl was amazing. Absolutely amazing. "Yes!" I said excitedly. "That's right. My history teacher taught us about him."

Kristel added, "I believe Descartes was right—he makes sense. But he didn't stop with just proving his own existence. His goal was to be certain that he could actually know that *other* things existed too."

I was so excited to tell her about Mr. Gray that I hardly paid attention to her last comment. "Yes, my history teacher, Mr. Gray, teaches all about that kind of stuff—philosophy and logic and things. It's my favorite class, because he really gets us to think about deep stuff."

"Is he a Christian?"

"No. He's an atheist. But what he says makes perfect sense. It's all perfectly logical, just like Descartes."

Kristel proclaimed abruptly, "Your teacher's not an atheist." Her words sounded a bit arrogant.

So I sounded a bit incredulous: "What do you mean? Do you know him? He tells every class that he's an atheist, and he says we all have the right to believe what we want."

"But he's not an *atheist*," Kristel asserted. "He can't be one, especially if he's teaching logic."

"What do you mean? He can be an atheist if he wants to."

"He can't teach logic and say he's an atheist. It's logically impossible to be an atheist."

"How so?"

"What's an atheist?" she asked.

"Someone who doesn't believe in God."

"Not quite. By definition, an atheist is someone who denies the existence of God. An atheist claims that God doesn't exist."

"What's the difference?"

Kristel articulated, "To claim that something doesn't exist requires knowledge about *all* the possibilities where it *might* exist. It requires omniscience, on his part, to claim that God doesn't exist."

I silently conceded that Kristel was smarter than me. I didn't know if this was something I liked or not, especially concerning the topic at hand. "I don't follow what you're saying," I admitted.

"It's like this," she explained. "Say, for example, that I claimed that life on other planets doesn't exist. For me to make that claim, I would have had to explore every inch of every planet in the universe. Otherwise, I'm just making an assumption based on limited knowledge. To claim it as fact would require my being knowledgeable of everything about the universe—and that's called omniscience. So, your teacher needs to be omniscient to honestly claim there is no God. And if he is omniscient, then there is a god, and it's him!"

I understood what she meant now, as funny as it sounded. I replied, "But Mr. Gray doesn't claim to be omniscient about the universe. He just doesn't believe that God exists."

"Does he believe that God *might* exist, but from his limited knowledge of the universe, he can't believe in God *for sure*?"

"I guess so, that sounds reasonable. Mr. Gray is a reasonable man."

"Then he's not an atheist. He's an agnostic. An agonistic doesn't deny that God exists; he just thinks that there is no way he can know for sure, and some agnostics then assume there isn't one based on what they do know."

She hit the nail on the head. "That's it. That's what Mr. Gray thinks. That's what I think, too."

"But you said you believed in God."

She was frustrating, but she was good.

I amended, "I do believe in God, but you just can't know for sure."

"That's where faith comes in, Jody. Everybody has faith in something."

In over my head, I wanted to get off the topic all together, so I threw up a red herring. "Do you have faith in your parents?" I asked.

She was ready with an answer. "I do, but I know that they'll let me down on occasion. They're human like the rest of us."

"I guess that's why I believe the way I do," I said, and before she could respond, I furthered my distraction by informing her about how her mother was now asking Whisper for a report on any staff members that are out after hours. I told her how Whisper let me off the hook for being out at 4:30 a.m. the night before. Kristel was miffed about her mother's nosiness, and I had successfully led her away from the religion topic. For now, at least.

I then talked some more about Whisper and about the nasty rumors concerning the peculiar night watchman's viewing habits. Angrily, Kristel flatly denied the possibility of Whisper being such a creep, claiming that there is no other man as sweet and as caring as old Whisper. I believed she was right.

It was nearly eleven before I left her window, and the last thing we talked about was my phone conversation with Wesley and about what Kristel's father had to say concerning my mother and Jimmy. Kristel was relieved that her father didn't suspect her of telling me the secret.

Lastly, I showed Kristel the note I received along with hers—the second Ambassador note.

"And it was in your box today?" she asked inquisitively, studying it in her hands.

"Yeah, it must have been mailed yesterday."

She was as curious as I was to find out who the Ambassador might be, and she was very suspicious that it could be the same person who sent the John Doe letter to the police. We decided I should also turn this second letter into the police tomorrow.

Back on my bunk in Saranac, I thought about Kristel, her parents, my parents, Boonie, Whisper, my one hundred bucks from Mr. Rothschild, and about Mr. Gray. I wondered if Mr. Gray knew the difference between an atheist and an agnostic. I determined I would ask him when I got back to school in September.

Saturday at work was much like Friday, only the kitchen was busier and I was more attuned to my job responsibilities. Nathan opened up a little bit and started talking, making the peeling and de-veining of shrimp a little less monotonous. My feet ached less, and the workday went much faster, especially during the breakfast and lunch rushes in which I got called to the front line to help Boonie. I worked the fryerlator, cooking hash browns in the morning and chicken strips and French fries at noon. The waitresses, who seemed to be in a bit of panic yesterday, hustled in and out of the kitchen with trays of beverages skillfully balanced on their hands as if they had been doing it all their lives. Allen kept active, instructing the salad bar girls on the best way to peel and slice hard boiled eggs, advising the dish crew about water temperature, and creating a bald eagle out of a carved honeydew melon for the fresh fruit table at dinner. Dave worked with Chef Al in preparing a cardinal sauce that was to be served on the seafood buffet.

The three-page production sheet, a list of food preparation jobs that needed to be completed each day, seemed overwhelming to the morning crew at six a.m. But by two that afternoon, the daily production list was nearly complete as Chef Dernbaugh, Dave, and the evening crew worked on final preparations for the Saturday evening meal.

Outside the kitchen, all morning long, droves of guests arrived, most of whom I never saw but knew were there, because Chef Dernbaugh shouted out a meal count update every hour. When Boonie and I got off at two-thirty, we headed for the beach to catch a few hours by the lake under the warm sun.

The wooden beach deck, with its chaise lounges and umbrella-covered tables, had come alive with sunbathers and lake-gazers. Jet-skiers kept the water near the shore choppier than usual. Scattered across the beach in front of the deck were plastic folding chairs whose extra short legs were designed especially for sun-worshippers. Boonie and I relaxed in these chairs when we weren't bopping a volleyball or swimming forty yards out to the floating dock where the diving board gently teetered. The staff rules prohibited us from loitering on the beach deck or the pool deck. But the sandy, man-made beach down below served us just fine.

As if she were under Boonie's spell, on this first Saturday of the summer season, fifteen minutes after our arrival at the beach, Angela, whose luggage Boonie carried last night, placed a chair next to him and reclined alongside him. Her glistening legs donned a striking early-summer tan, meaning that she was either from the South or she sprayed her legs golden brown before coming to the beach. "Tanning salon," she explained in her high voice, after telling us she was from New Hampshire.

I didn't know how Boonie did it. But I did know that he had never tried his magic on Kristel. He couldn't have. She's too smart for him.

The following days went much like this: a six to two-thirty breakfast and lunch shift in the kitchen, followed by relaxation at the beach until dinner. Angela joined Boonie at the beach every afternoon, and with her grounding finally over, Kristel met us there too. All week, the four of us together either rode the giant, inflatable torpedo towed behind a ski-boat, played volleyball, or just sat in the short-legged plastic chairs on the beach and talked until dinnertime.

As for Jimmy and the Ambassador-for-the-Dead, they both became a foregone conclusion ever since I brought that second note to Officer Anders. The mystery of the letters' origin, like the brother I never knew, was absent from my mind. Only Kristel mattered to me now.

In the evenings, Kristel was required to attend dinner with her parents, play the piano for the talent show, mingle with a well-to-do family, or occasionally give tennis lessons to aging couples who were helpless without her. All of these tasks were at the request, or orders, of her mother, and because of the woman's seemingly ubiquitous involvement in her daughter's life, Kristel and I thought it best that our time together be limited to the beach or the tree house.

I often chose to nap during the early-evening hours after dinner because many late nights were spent in the tree house, including another near all-nighter on Wednesday, the day before my regular day off. We talked about everything, including religion, and Kristel never ceased in her attempts at evangelism. I proudly defended my position, especially knowing that I was now officially an agnostic. But most of the time, I was able to get her off that topic and onto something more manageable, like baseball. She had it all, Kristel did. She was even a baseball fan, albeit an unfortunate Red Sox one.

Every night without fail, after leaving the tree house or the bedroom window, I would get stopped by the Club's night watchman. Whisper would catch me on my way back to Saranac after hours, and every time he told me it was his duty to report me, but he would "let it go this one time." Old Whisper was a good guy.

Boonie spent his evenings in the staff lounge flirting with waitresses or off-duty housekeepers. Angela was his girl for the afternoons, and it was always somebody else at night. Angela didn't know this because she was usually with her parents or little sister at some activity after dinner. Boonie had a knack for keeping his life segregated in such ways. He had girls falling for him every week, and when Angela would leave in two weeks, he was sure to have another mate for afternoons at the beach in no time.

He never took a break from flirting, even during work. A waitress rarely passed by the front line without a comment from Boonie like, "Keep that gorgeous smile on," or "You can let your pretty hair down soon." None of the girls seemed to mind his comments, and many fell for them. It was unbelievable to watch.

A hot topic among the waiters and waitresses that first week was who would get to serve Robert Rothschild's table. The wealthy, elderly gentleman attended only a few meals a week in the dining room, and no matter if he had only a cup of coffee or a full lobster platter, he always left a fifty-dollar tip for the server. The dining room staff decided to follow a rotating schedule for serving Mr. Rothschild, and I figured I could have earned an extra couple hundred dollars by the end of the summer on Mr. Rothschild alone if I had remained a waiter. But I was beginning to like the kitchen, and at least I received a bigger tip from the rich old man than anyone else would receive in one shot. On a related note, I eagerly anticipated my first paycheck on Friday so I could learn what Mr. Schuple's definition of a fair wage was.

Thankfully, during this first week, Brock Oliff kept his distance from me. I had absolutely no contact with him since the night he landed his fist in my eye at the roadside. In fact, he didn't even live in the cabin grove anymore. He spent one night there and decided to live at home for the summer. Who could blame him—a mansion with servants vs. a cramped, old cabin? His band-playing duty began at dinnertime and sometimes lasted well into the evening when dances were held on the pool deck. He and his friends kept to themselves, which, to Kristel and Boonie especially, was quite unexpected.

This enemy, who looked like he would be a summer-long antagonist early on, seemed to have been sedated, and I knew it all had something to do with me and Jimmy Grandstaff.

But that wasn't necessarily the whole story. What helped keep Brock away from us was that he had won the heart of a gullible waitress named Mandi. She spent every waking hour with him when she wasn't working. And although we were glad that this relationship helped keep Brock from tossing us his dirty looks and crooked grins, Kristel, Boonie, and I felt sorry for Mandi.

The second week went much like the first, except for one thing. The Ambassador for the Dead came back to life and was trying to keep Jimmy alive and well in my mind.

Beginning on that second Friday, June the nineteenth, I retrieved from the B box a letter written in block capital letters in an envelope postmarked from Pokeville. From then on, the arrival of letters continued on a daily basis. The messages were all just one line or two, saying things like "YOU ARE JIMMY'S REDEEMER," or "YOU MUST SOLVE THE MURDER," and all were signed by "AN AMBASSADOR FOR THE DEAD." I showed each letter to Kristel and Boonie, and every other day or so I would bring the letters to Officer Anders at the police station.

My visits there became routine, and sometimes I just ran in and dropped them on the officer's desk if he was on the phone. Other times I stayed and talked with him for a while, and strangely, I had yet to see Sheriff Clive

Slater, except for catching a glimpse of his arm waving from the window of his cruiser that morning I woke up in a painful daze with a black eye. Officer Anders told me Sheriff Salter was very busy man. I was still waiting for him to call me or at least for him to relay a message through Officer Anders, but his only message was that he would contact me personally in a few days.

I was getting rather anxious to hear what Sheriff Slater thought of the Ambassador letters, and if there was any similarity between them and that original John Doe letter. But most of all, I wanted it all out of my life completely. I had grown apathetic about Jimmy, and this stupid Ambassador was getting rather annoying.

At last, Sheriff Clive Slater did get in touch with me by phone through the kitchen extension and informed me that neither the envelopes nor the handwriting matched their John Doe letter. He instructed me to bring in any additional letters, and I continued to do so every other day, dropping them off as usual with Officer Anders.

Anders shook his head with disbelief after seeing each letter, saying, "This is really bizarre. I'll pass it on to Sheriff Slater." Even though I had yet to meet the elusive sheriff face to face, I was glad to have become quite familiar with the amiable Officer Anders. He was stuck to office duty for several weeks until his injured leg healed. He had hurt it in a fishing accident when he fell down in the Hudson River and snapped his right femur between two boulders. He was stranded there for almost twelve hours before he was rescued.

Officer Anders and I talked a lot about baseball, as we both were Indians fans, Anders being originally from Buffalo. Sometimes we talked about Jimmy, but not much, because I didn't really like the topic. We both agreed that the Ambassador letters were probably somebody's form of a joke, just as the John Doe letter probably was. But we both understood the necessity for me to bring in every single letter, as the case was still open.

By the last weekend in June, I had not heard from my mother or Wesley since those phone calls and my rude hang-ups during staff training. That changed on Friday the twenty-sixth, when I returned to Saranac after work and discovered the man I despised most in the world sitting on the porch steps. It was Wesley.

# CHAPTER 15

## *A Visitor Comes and Goes, Goin' Out Kristel Style, and Settling In*

"The front desk clerk said I might find you down here," Wesley explained, as though I was expecting to see him.

I hardly had time to think of a response, not just in words, but also in the attitude I wanted to convey.

"What are you doing here?" I uttered, managing a feigned, disgusted tone.

Wesley slid his hands in his pockets. His typical dark business suit was gone, replaced by casual khaki shorts and a dark polo shirt. He leaned against the porch railing to appear nonchalant, and I could tell by his voice that he was a little nervous.

"I thought I owed it to you to come up and see you," he said, struggling make eye contact while he spoke. "Your mother and I have had a difficult time since you've been gone, to say the least."

I didn't say anything.

"Well, I'm taking a few weeks off work just to get away for awhile," he said meekly, staring beyond me across the cabin grove. "You know, to take some time and think things over." He stopped talking, and when he noticed I had nothing to say, he continued, "Actually, I've got the Sidekick parked up the hill with all my camping gear, and I thought maybe you'd like to spend some time camping and fishing around these parts."

This was the first time he had ever invited me to camp or fish, or do anything with him. Nevertheless, I responded flatly, "I've got to work. I have a job here."

"Yes, well, actually I thought you'd maybe want to spend a couple of days camping and then head home. I think it'd be better if you were home instead of here. Your mother really needs you."

"She didn't say that when I spoke to her last. Besides, it was her idea that I come here."

"You know how proud she is, Jody. She's trying to handle this like nothing is bothering her. But she really needs you. If you come home, I'd move out for a while to let you and your mother live at the house. That apartment where she is now is no place for her."

"I'd prefer to stay here. I don't want to be involved in your mess."

"I don't blame you."

Again, silence. I just wanted him to leave. It bothered me that he might be hanging around the area in a tent for the next couple of days.

Then Wesley suddenly asked, "Do you know I never knew your mother had a child before she had you?"

I stared at him, offering no reply, although I was learning this information for the first time.

He continued, "I didn't know about her first child until your mother found out that he died last fall. I believed all these years what she said about aborting her first pregnancy. Then last fall when she learned about his death, she finally told me, and… well, things between us haven't been good ever since. That kind of started it all."

Crap story. Their marriage had been nothing but a waste for years.

"Anyway, Jody, I'm sorry you had to learn about your brother the way you did. Your mother should have told us both the truth a long time ago."

"She still hasn't told me the truth," I blurted.

"I know. That doesn't surprise me."

More silence.

Wesley finally said, "So you're sure you don't want to take off for a few days? Cooperstown isn't too far away. We could go down there and check out the Hall of Fame."

Cooperstown sounded really good with anyone else but Wesley. Maybe something for Kristel and me to do sometime. "No," I answered stubbornly, "I've got to stay here and work."

"Okay," he said, stepping away from the cabin. "I'm going to be a wilderness man for awhile. If you get the urge to join me, you know my cell phone number, right?"

I didn't say anything, which prompted Wesley to take out his wallet and scratch his cellular number on the back of his business card. "Call me anytime," he said, handing me the card as though I was another client of his. "Or call my office. I'll be checking in there for messages everyday."

I took the card and held it at my thigh.

"Take care, Jody," he said as he walked off up the hill.

"See ya," I managed to mutter. I went inside Saranac to change into beachwear. Kristel, Boonie, and Angela would be down at the lake shortly.

Before I left the cabin, I ripped Wesley's business card into pieces and dropped them into an empty Mountain Dew can sitting on the floor next to my bunk.

I didn't hear from either of my parents for weeks after Wesley's surprise visit, and I was content with that. I hardly even thought of either of them. I was settling quite nicely into my life at the Brown Swan Club, and nothing else mattered.

By the end of that second week, it was well known amongst the staff that Kristel and I were spending a lot of time together, and this fact granted me a wealth of popularity among other staff members. Additionally, the staff was well aware of Mrs. Schuple's stinginess concerning her daughter; therefore, many cooperative staffers did their best to conceal from the nosy woman the relationship developing between Kristel and me. Some of Kristel's friends actually lied to Mrs. Schuple to cover up her daughter's whereabouts during our late-afternoon beach hours. One bold, naughty housekeeper even told such a lie as, "Oh, I think she and Brock went into town together," drawing a wide smile of approval from the tyrannical mother. One night at dinner, Boonie and Nathan stood near Mrs. Schuple at the salad buffet and commented out loud about how Jody has the hots for such-and-such lifeguard. With all this, combined with Whisper's help in covering up my late-night visits at the tree house, Mrs. Schuple was absolutely clueless about the secret social life of her eldest daughter. Kristel and I, with a little help from our friends, were accomplishing what was previously deemed impossible. This left many young males jealous, but they enjoyed playing a part in befuddling Mrs. Schuple.

It was strange, however, the extremes we were going through to cover up our unique relationship. It wasn't like we were having sex in secluded places, like some other couples did. We hadn't even kissed—not once. And to top that, Kristel and I hadn't even officially committed ourselves to each other in a bona fide boyfriend-girlfriend thing. Although others thought we had, Kristel and I hadn't "signed the papers" declaring ourselves an "item," even though oftentimes I thought it would be nice to make it official.

That would have gone directly against Kristel's conservative dating philosophies, especially the shape they had taken after her break up with Brock. She asserted there shouldn't be anything official between a guy and a girl until engagement. It was about the wackiest philosophy I had ever heard, but the more I thought about it, and the more I actually experienced our "just good friends" relationship, the more I understood the value of it. Kristel and I went to extremes to see each other—not because we're expected to as boyfriend and girlfriend—but because we simply enjoyed being together. There was no requirement to follow those adolescent rules of guy-girl commitments, no social code-of-dating conduct, no pressure, and no expectations. We were free of all that, being, she insisted, "just friends." And it was actually kind of nice.

As a pupil to Kristel's philosophy, I started scrutinizing the way other guys and girls behaved as "official" couples, and I could see exactly what Kristel was talking about. Those couples hung around each other all the time—at meals, at meetings, during free time, and right up until curfew. They were with each other and no one else. Not that they didn't really like each other, but they had all those immature social rules to follow—unspoken dating expectations—like if Johnny, who's dating Suzie, gets caught talking to Mary, then Johnny is up the creek with Suzie. Or if Suzie says Freddy is cute, she's now being unfaithful to Johnny. It was all rather childish and stupid when you think about it, as if they were in some quasi-marriage relationship. As for Kristel and me, we were free to be ourselves.

That doesn't mean that a big part of me didn't want, at times, to ignore Kristel's philosophy, so I could secure her as my official girlfriend. I would have liked to make her mine—all mine, if I could have. But Kristel said people only feel that way because they are insecure about the relationship to begin with—and she was right. And she said the only time to make someone "mine—all mine" is when you pop the marriage question.

She told me all this one night in the tree house when I foolishly "popped the question" on her. Not a marriage proposal, of course—it was that "steady" relationship thing I was after. I said something moronic like, "Kristel, what do you say we start goin' out." It was stupid, I know that now, but it had worked the winter before with Bridget McDermott, and I didn't know of any other way to say it to Kristel.

Her reaction was classic—typically Kristel. She said, "Go out where?"

I said, "You know. You and me."

She said, "You mean, start a commitment?"

"Yes."

"For how long?"

She was phenomenal. Simply phenomenal.

"What do you mean for how long?"

She didn't bat an eye. She said, "How long do you want to be committed to me?"

"I don't know... What are you talking about?!" (I was embarrassed by this point).

"How long will this commitment last? A couple of weeks? Until the end of the summer?"

"I don't know! How does anybody know?"

"You mean you want it to last until we break up sometime? We'll be committed to each other until one of us gets tired of it and we break it up?"

I slowly was beginning to see what she was getting at. "I guess that's what happens," I muttered.

"So you're asking me to be committed to you until I get tired of it, or until you get tired of it? That's stupid, Jody. Why can't we just be friends for always? Friends don't break up."

I liked the sound of that, but I thought I'd stump her with my next comment. "Are you going to be like this one day to the poor guy who asks you to marry him?"

She smiled and said, "Yes, exactly, I'll say the same thing to him."

"What's that?"

"I'll ask him for how long, and he better say forever, because that's how long it should be. A commitment isn't a commitment if it has an escape clause, Jody. These immature guy-girl relationships you see all over the place, especially in the summer around here, all have an unspoken escape clause called breaking up. But friends and spouses are supposed to be committed forever, and I hope one day my best friend will say he'll love me forever and we'll get married. So, the best way to go is to stay friends. It's a lot less complicated that way. Believe me—I learned a lot from Brock in this regard."

She was right. She was absolutely right. It all made perfect, logical sense, but it certainly went against the grain of the modern dating culture. And that's what I liked about Kristel—she wasn't typical. She didn't sleep around (I would have put money down that she'd be a virgin until marriage), she stuck to her guns, and she earned respect from her peers. There were not very many kids around my age that could say the same about themselves.

An example of this was Boonie. He and most other kids simply couldn't believe that Kristel and I had not made out—not even kissed once. And we hadn't. That didn't mean I didn't want to. There were times when we were together up in that tree house when all I wanted to do was to lean over and give her a big juicy kiss on the lips.

A girl like Kristel should be kissed and kissed often, and I thought when the time was right, I would kiss her. Just a kiss, though—I would never touch her inappropriately. She demanded too much respect for me to even think about that. But I hoped the perfect time would come when I could follow Jimmy's example and ask permission for a kiss. Then I'd lean over, pucker up, and experience the kiss of a lifetime, even if it lasted only a second or two. I wondered if that moment would ever present itself before the summer ended.

There was something rather confusing about Kristel, though. As extraordinary a girl that she was, I found it very odd that her mother had so little trust in her. It didn't seem right. Just the fact that I had to visit Kristel at the tree house was peculiar enough. What had happened that caused Mrs. Schuple not to trust her wonderful daughter, I couldn't tell. Kristel insisted that her mother was still hung up on Brock, but it had to be something more than that.

I never actually spoke with Mrs. Schuple during those first weeks of the summer. Occasionally, we made eye contact, and that's about the extent our communication. Her face said: "Stay away from my daughter, you poor, miserable worm." It was nerve-racking sometimes, being around her. I hoped my demeanor conveyed to her, "Hey, I'm a fine, upstanding, innocent, young man. You would really like me if you gave me a chance." But she never softened up. No telling what her problem was.

George Schuple, on the other hand, was considerate enough to check in on me every so often, usually during one of his strolls through the kitchen. He never talked to me about Kristel, and I assumed that he was as clueless about his daughter's relationship with me as his wife was.

During one of those kitchen visits, Mr. Schuple informed me that he had confronted Brock about slashing my tires. He said Brock outright denied it and there was nothing he could do without any evidence or a testimony from somebody who saw it. I was somewhat relieved that nothing more would come of the situation, especially since Brock had been keeping his distance from all of us. His mysterious alienation was sufficient cause to ignore him altogether, and I preferred to keep it that way.

But he was always a factor in my thoughts—not because he was playing in the band every night, and not because he was seen with his new girlfriend Mandi in places where they should not have been alone together, and not because he had gotten away with slashing my tires. Everyday I got a new letter from the Ambassador for the Dead, who kept urging me to find Jimmy's murderer. After opening every letter, I thought of Brock.

Kristel hadn't spoken much about her suspicion of him lately, and I was just as content to let things rest. But Brock was always there, lurking near my conscience, each afternoon, after every trip to the mailroom, and during those routine visits to Officer Anders to drop off more Ambassador letters.

To shut Brock out of mind, I had to shut out Jimmy and the Ambassador, too. And that's what I did, or tried to do. But it was that third week of the summer, as June drifted into July, that management of my own mental inventory—in other words: trusting only in myself—became more challenging than it had ever been since I had adopted Mr. Gray's quote as my life motto.

# CHAPTER 16

## *A Beach Party in Paradise and the Devil's Dedication of Marilee Manor*

It was one of those delightful summer evenings when it seemed like life couldn't get any better—but the pessimist in me insisted that it wouldn't last forever. If life is indeed a roller coaster, tonight I was nearing the top of the hill.

My behind was suspended just inches above the sand while my legs stretched straight out from the beach chair's yellow plastic straps. As I sank down and leaned back, the flimsy, lightweight chair felt more comfortable than the leather recliner in the staff lounge. My bare heels bulldozed a miniature valley under my weary legs, and the cooler, moister sand below the crusty top layer felt like a massage on my tired toes. The lapping waters on the lake's shoreline invited me in for a dip, as did other members of the Club staff who were already enjoying the water when they noticed my late arrival. I assured my friends I'd be in after a few minutes. For now, I needed a moment of quiet relaxation in the fresh open air of the early evening, after twelve strenuous hours of clamoring, steamy-hot, hectic kitchen duty. I had been asked to pull an extra half shift today.

The sun was now kissing the horizon behind the Club. In about twenty minutes, the Adirondack Mountains would invite it in for the night, but before then, the sinking sun would paint the pale-blue sky orange and would transform the silvery-green lake waters into gold. As the sun settled down from its long day, so did the sleepy lake waters, except for the rippling rings created by the splashes of my frolicking friends. Then the *Ski Nautique* agitated the languid surface of the lake when it zoomed past the beach dock, dragging a quintet of riders who, like rodeo cowboys, clutched the hand-ropes on the back of the inflatable blue torpedo. A sudden, sharp turn dumped the five riders all at once into the water, but they all bobbed up laughing and screaming, struggling to climb back onto the floating torpedo, wanting to ride again. The sinking sun, golden waters, and orange sky above the green mountain horizon could not have been a more beautiful back-drop for the Brown Swan Club's first staff beach party of the summer.

I could have sat in that chair by the lake on this piece of paradise for hours. Suddenly, a getaway volleyball bounded over my legs and into the water. I looked back over my shoulder to see five waitresses in long T-shirts and four bare-chested groundskeepers. Being the closest person to the vagabond volleyball, it was my duty to toss it back to the players. I creaked and squeaked out of my aluminum and plastic chair and retrieved the ball from the water. Soon it was covered with sand like cinnamon covers a donut, and every bop sprinkled granules into the bopper's face. I didn't care; I wasn't playing, but I was now on my feet in an inch of cool, messaging, lapping lake water.

This was all it took to get me going. Off went my stinky shirt, and with three ker-plunk steps and a bellyflop dive, sweat, grit, and kitchen grime washed clean off my body. I swam out deeper, closer to the others with a gliding, relaxed backstroke. I decided to pass on an offer for a night ride on the wild, wet torpedo when I arrived at the wooden dock. I would just play there for now, lying flat out on the dock in the middle of paradise, staring up at the new evening stars with my friends.

Boonie climbed up and sat next to me on the floating dock. We both worked extra hours in the kitchen that day because three members of the evening crew, including Dave Wall the chef, got stuck in Lake Henry when their car broke down. Boonie and I had the "pleasure" of staying in the kitchen through dinner and helping Chef Al put the meal out. It was hectic and tiring, but the time went fast, and we got to the party just a little late.

"This is Angela's last night here," Boonie said as he lay down next to me, dripping wet. It sounded like he was actually going to miss her.

"There'll be more girls, won't there?" I asked in a not too serious tone.

"Yeah, but I kind of like Angela. She said she'd like to come work here next year."

We talked for a while on the floating dock until the lifeguards whistled for everyone to come out of the water because of darkness. The *Ski Nautique* drove off towards the town beach, the canoes were hauled in and turned upside down on the holding rack, and soon everyone was circled around a newly built campfire in the sand.

Saturday night was the typical night for staff get-togethers such as this one. Nothing was specifically planned for the guests on Saturday nights except for the dinner buffet. Many would arrive or depart on the weekends, so most of the guest activities were scheduled to take place during the week. For this reason, I wasn't surprised to see Kristel arrive on the beach deck that night with nothing to do. Burdened by no talent show, tennis lessons, or mingling duties, Kristel was free to spend the evening as she pleased.

She asked if I'd like to take a walk into town, and we agreed to meet on the Club porch after I showered and changed. It was unusual that she was willing to walk with me into town—just the two of us. We hadn't been alone together, at least out in the open where people could see us, since she dropped the news about Jimmy on me seventeen days ago. Since then, all of our public moments together were spent in the presence of Boonie and Angela.

So around ten o'clock, Kristel and I were in town, strolling along Route 7. Burleighs was just across the street and I suggested we go there for ice cream. Kristel wished we would walk down to the park instead.

We wandered around the park together, sat in the gazebo for a few minutes, moseyed over to the swings and then to the seesaw, talking about everything from our parents to the monsters who scared us the most when we were kids.

With the lake rippling softly nearby, and the blackening, star-specked sky above, I wondered if this was the time to give Kristel that kiss she so much deserved.

"Wanna go sit on the beach next to the water?" I suggested, preferring the darker seclusion of the shore to the lamp-lit park and gazebo.

Soon, our shoes sat empty in the sand as we reclined in large Adirondack chairs, soaking our bare legs and feet in inches of cool water.

The romantic scene didn't last long, being rudely interrupted by a loud racket behind us. We looked back us to see a section of wood lattice under the gazebo shake and rattle before falling flat in the grass. From the dark, square hole under the deck emerged two heads, one darker than the other. Boonie and Angela crawled out from under the gazebo, brushed the dirt off their backs, and walked towards us at the beach hand in hand.

"Hi guys!" Boonie said proudly.

"Sorry to bother you guys," Angela said, embarrassed.

Kristel stood to her feet with a look of shock. I just snickered. Typical of Boonie. Under the gazebo, of all places.

Boonie eyeballed me and grinned. "Uh, sorry to interrupt you two. We'll leave you alone."

What Kristel said next ruined everything. "Oh, you don't have to go. Stay down here with us. Pull up some chairs. The water feels nice on your feet."

She just kissed the potential kiss goodbye, and as Boonie and Angela arranged chairs and took off their shoes, I considered Kristel's actions. I thought of three possibilities: first, she didn't want to be alone with me here anymore because she thought I was going to kiss her and she didn't want me to. Second, she did indeed want to kiss, but she was nervous about it and Boonie and Angela were a way of escape. Third, she did want to kiss but was embarrassed to be seen alone with me, so she wanted Boonie and Angela to think they weren't interrupting anything. Whatever the case, I knew a kiss for the princess would not happen tonight. Despite it all, the evening turned out to be more interesting than I projected.

The four of us sat at the water's edge and watched a half moon slowly rise above black eastern mountains. "Guess what I heard at the beach party," Boonie said, adjusting his chair closer to the water. "Brock and Mandi are going to Marilee Manor tonight."

"You're kidding!" Kristel groaned.

"They're going alone?" Angela asked.

"No. There's supposed to be a campfire that some of the townies are having. I heard it's gonna be pretty wild over there."

Angela asked, "Kristel, didn't you say you knew about occult rituals being held there?"

I had heard the same thing from Kristel.

"All kind of weird stuff happens at the Manor," she confirmed. "Drinking, drugs, sex, weird rituals. Almost anything. I can't believe Brock is bringing Mandi. She doesn't seem like that type."

The four of us stared over at the dark shore of the Manor.

"Check it out," Boonie advised, "they've got the campfire going already." He pointed across the lake in a southerly direction where the dim glow of a campfire could clearly be seen on the far shore.

"Sshh! Listen!" he hushed.

In the silence we could hear the soft lapping of the lake water at our feet, and, occasionally, from across the lake, the distinct sound of young voices laughing and shouting. In between the whoops and hollers, indistinguishable voices, both male and female, carried fragmented conversation across the water.

"That's them all right," Boonie confirmed. "I'd like to see what they're up to."

Kristel agreed. "I'd like to see, too. Brock told me once that he never drinks, smokes, or anything like that. I'd just like to go over there and prove that he's a liar."

"Let's go then," I suggested. Thinking of Brock, both Jimmy and the Ambassador twirled in my mind. "Let's take canoes across and take a look."

Kristel and Angela objected in unison: "They'll see us!"

"No they won't," I insisted. "It's pitch black out on the water, and the canoes don't make a sound."

Boonie, liking the idea, chirped in, "The campfire is out on the point, which means we can come in close to the shoreline from behind. We'll just sit out in the water and see what we can see or hear. They'll never know it's us, even if they see us. It's too dark for them to recognize us. If we get spotted, we'll just paddle away into the darkness."

It sounded like the perfect adventure, and, with some contrived reluctance, the girls got up from their chairs and followed Boonie and me up to Route 7. We walked ten minutes south to the Club beach, which was now entirely empty of staff members. Boonie and I unloaded two canoes from the rack.

Several minutes later we were out on the black water under the star-lit sky, Boonie and Angela in one canoe, Kristel and I in the other.

"Be careful not to bang the paddle on the sides," Kristel whispered, "or they'll hear us."

It took about fifteen minutes to cross the mile-wide lake. As we neared the eastern shore, about a hundred yards north of the point, we could clearly see human shadows hovering around the campfire that flickered near the rocky banks. Several other canoes, rowboats, and rubber rafts, all water crafts used by the gang of teens to get to the Manor, were resting on the stony shore.

"This whole area is part of Marilee Manor," Kristel whispered. "The mansion was built straight back from that point where the campfire is. If you row past the it in the daytime, you can see the ruins from the shore."

"Let's get up closer, very slowly," I said in a soft voice. "Make sure the canoes don't bang together."

In the dark silence, we created only the slightest of sounds with the oars patting the surface of the water. The voices around the campfire were dominant. Our canoes glided stealthily up the shoreline and entered a small bay, bordered by the smooth-rock peninsula where the campfire burned. We drifted out into the center of the bay, about fifty yards from the fire, and from there we could count the bodies around it, some sitting, some standing, others lying down.

There were nearly thirty people, and their voices were clearly distinguishable. Cuss words accounted for much of the dialogue, and their silhouetted movements complemented their vulgar talk. Beer cans were tilted above chins; puffs of smoke were emitted from faces; girls hung onto the necks of boys. Other bodies lay horizontally, entangled with each other on the smooth, rock surface. Cackling laughter, whoops, and screams filled the air as a boy hoisted a girl up to his shoulders and threatened, while laughing, to toss her in the lake.

The entire scene was not a display of occult behavior like we had heard rumors about; it was no more than a bunch of teenagers with nothing better to do in their tiny lakeside town than to hold a drunken revel on the haunted property.

A female voice suddenly shrieked, "I see him! I see him! It's Abbott Marilee!" Several heads turned towards the woods, and a roar of mocking laughter followed. A male voice hollered, "Nah, that's just Freddy Krueger!" Another roar of unconfined laughter, then a male figure came stumbling out of the woods with a can of beer in one hand. With the other hand he pulled a rubber Halloween mask off his head and then fell to his knees laughing.

Silhouettes shifted as bodies assembled closely together around the fire, blocking it from our sight. "Anybody got a light?" someone said. "Use the fire, ya dork!" grunted a respondent.

As the group crowded tightly together around the crackling fire, the laughter and hollers gradually subsided. Then an unusual sound was heard. It at first sounded like a disgruntled goose's honk, but soon, as the notes grew clearer and flowed with regularity, it was obvious that the noise was produced by a wind instrument—a saxophone.

"That's Brock," Kristel whispered as the silhouette of a tall, lanky figure holding a saxophone stood to his feet near the fire.

"Let's go closer," I said. "The light from the fire is blocked, and nobody's looking this way anyway."

With a few strokes of the paddles, Boonie and I guided both crafts closer to the rocky peninsula. We drifted into the propinquity of the shoreline where we could detect the colors of some of the clothing worn by the partiers. Some boys were shirtless, others were wearing long-sleeved flannel shirts, unbuttoned and hanging open. Some girls wore heavy sweatshirts, and some wore only a string bikini top and a pair of skimpy, cut-off blue jean shorts.

Brock could be seen blowing into his saxophone, wearing a light pair of chinos and a dark polo shirt, somewhat of a nice outfit for the occasion. Mandi could be seen sitting cross-legged at his feet, wearing a white tank top. She appeared to be smoking a small cigarette, maybe something else.

The saxophone number sounded like a Kenny G. song that had gone sour. However, when Brock was finished and lowered his instrument, he received a soft round of applause and a few whistles of approval.

"Give me a break," Kristel whispered, looking back at me and rolling her eyes. She and Angela were holding the sides of the canoes so they wouldn't bang together as we floated side by side.

Boonie stared wide-eyed and open mouthed. The whites of his eyes against his dark face glowed like two moons. "Shh," he hissed softly. "Listen."

Brock, still on his feet, began to address the ring of juveniles sitting around him. The fire cracked and flashed brightly in front of him, causing the brass instrument in his hands to shine illustriously.

"We gather here tonight to celebrate!" he said in authoritative, but slurred, speech. It was obvious he had been drinking.

A second deep male voice from the crowd grunted in response, "Yeah!" The speaker lifted a can of beer over his head in a triumphant pose. A few giggles followed.

The tall, bony saxophone player continued his address. "We're here to celebrate Marilee Manor—what she has been, and what she'll soon become." Brock bent over and placed the instrument at his feet. Mandi picked it up and held it in her lap. "For forty years, this legendary property has been the sight of some wild times for the youth of Pokeville and Abbeyville."

"Whoo whoo!" two girls yelped in unison. More laughter and soft applause.

"It has served us well," Brock proclaimed, undaunted by the levity of some of his addressees, even though his own words were slurred by his inebriated condition. "For many a young boy, including myself, this property has served as the stage for earning his manhood." He paused, shifting his eyes around the crowd. "And for many a young virgin, her womanhood."

A plethora of whoops and whistles filled the air.

Boonie and I softly maneuvered our adjoined canoes to fight against the gentle current that was nudging us towards the shore. Like four spies, we listened with the keenest of interest.

Brock, acting like a lord of a sacred order, continued his formal address. "And tonight we celebrate these last forty years at Marilee Manor, not forgetting the centuries that preceded us, when fortune and glory were the Marilee tradition. It is the rich history of this property that has brought us here tonight, so that—" he belched softly, "so that we can celebrate a new era, when wealth and pleasure will again reside on these very banks!" Brock raised his voice and began speaking more quickly. "Ladies and gentlemen of Abbeyville, on behalf of my father, I declare the beginning of a new day for Marilee Manor and for all of the Adirondacks. On August first, the ground will be broken here, and the new sixty million dollar Marilee Hotel will be built upon this very point where we are gathered!"

Oohs and aahs filled the air, some of them in jest, some genuine.

"My father promises me full management of the facility," Brock continued. "Which means that the next beer you drink on this property will not be from a six pack around a campfire—it will be served in a chilled mug with a cocktail napkin while you sit at a cherry-wood bar." Laughter preceded light applause. "And the next virgin to realize her womanhood will do so not on the rocky, mossy surface of this point, but upon a king-size canopy waterbed in a master suite!" Louder whoops, laughter, and applause. Brock finished his speech in a triumphant shout: "Rest assured mates! Any friend of mine will find his or her pleasure at no expense, here at my Marilee Hotel!"

With that, the crowd stood to their feet and gathered around young Oliff, hoisting him on their shoulders. They danced around the fire, chanting praises for Brock Oliff and the glorious new age for Marilee Manor. The scene was both freaky and exciting, but most of all, down right silly.

"Lets get out of here," Kristel said without whispering. Nobody in the rambunctious crowd could hear us now anyway.

Boonie and I steered the canoes away from the point, and fifteen minutes later we skidded onto the coarse surface of the Brown Swan Club's beachfront.

I helped Kristel out of the canoe and muttered, "I guess Mr. Oliff is pretty sure he's going to buy that property, huh."

Kristel sighed. "It looks that way. I just can't imagine Brock running a place like that. He'll turn it into Sodom and Gomorrah."

Boonie tried to lighten the mood. "I'm hungry. You all want to go back to Burleighs or something?"

We did, and around a large pepperoni pizza we discussed the ungodly scene we had just witnessed at Marilee Manor, not knowing that next month, two of us would return to the Manor for reasons beyond our wildest imaginations.

# CHAPTER 17

## *Proving Absolutes, Puckish Amusements and a Pool Attack*

After a hectic Sunday lunch, Kristel burst into the kitchen to see me. "Come into the cooler, I've got to tell you something."

The walk-in cooler was a great place to take a break and talk with someone. It was private, quiet, and the forty-degree temperature was a nice relief from the steamy kitchen.

Inside the cooler, Kristel crossed her bare arms in front of her to fend off the chill. She announced regretfully, "Somebody told my mother we were at Burleighs together last night."

"Who told her?" I asked, trying not to sound too disgusted with the news.

"One of the guests—a friend of my mother's. She was mad at me, my mother was, but she was trying to hide it. She asked if I went there with you."

"Did you tell her?"

Kristel frowned. "No. I lied. I told her I was there with Angela, and then you and Boonie came in together later and sat with us."

"Why doesn't she like me?" I asked, remembering that the woman's inexplicable dislike for my parents was part of the reason.

"I don't know. I still think it has to do with Brock. She's so hung up on him."

"Did you tell her where he was last night? Did you tell her what he was doing?"

"No."

"You should've."

"Well, we didn't really see him doing anything. I didn't see him drink or smoke, did you?"

"Kristel! You know he was obviously drunk, and he admitted to everyone that he had had sex there at least once before. Isn't that enough for your mother?"

"She'll never believe anything I have to say bad about him. She thinks he's the greatest guy on earth."

"Your Dad doesn't."

"True."

"So who do you listen to, your mom or your dad?"

"My mother wears the pants in the family."

I chuckled and shook my head, knowing this conversation was going nowhere because I had experienced it several times before in the tree house.

"Well, I better get out there and help clean up lunch," I said. "I'll see you in about an hour."

Kristel extended her arm in front of the door to keep me from leaving the cooler. "Hang on, there's one more thing I need to tell you."

"What?"

"I'm going to be gone all next week."

"Where?"

"On a missions trip. My youth group is going to Boston to work with an inner-city church there. We're leaving tomorrow."

"Tomorrow! For how long?"

Kristel answered dejectedly, "Six days. We'll be back on Saturday. That's the Fourth of July. At least I'll be back for the fireworks."

I was clearly disappointed with the news. I muttered, "So you're leaving tomorrow… for Boston?"

"It's in Massachusetts," she said with a grin, but her voice lacked its regular chirpy tone.

"Don't be a jerk. It sounds like you're really excited about going," I said sarcastically.

"My mom told me last night that I had to go. I went the last two years, and I liked it and all, but I wasn't planning on going this year. I think my mother wants me away from here for a while."

"Just because someone told her you were with me?"

"Maybe, I don't know."

"That's stupid."

"I know it is."

"And you're going to go just because your mother wants you to?"

"Yes. It's not worth fighting it."

I shook my head. "I can't believe this!"

"Trust me, Jody. It's for the best. I have to go shopping with my mother this afternoon, so just come to the tree house tonight, okay?"

"I'll be there."

Six days without Kristel. I didn't know what I would do.

Things didn't get better that night. Our talk in the tree house was shorter than usual, and for a while the conversation centered on Brock.

"My mom finally told me today that she likes Brock because he and his family are Christians," Kristel explained.

"Christian!" I protested. "Brock?"

"Yes, believe it or not. He was a lot different when he was younger, but over the past few years he has really backslidden. My mom thinks that if he just gets with the right girl, he'll turn around. But I don't want to be that girl."

As crazy as her mother's idea sounded, there was some truth to it, and I looked at myself as a prime example. Just being with Kristel made me a better person. Her attitude, her boldness, her beliefs, they were all catchy, and even though I didn't see myself to be like Brock as far as moral behavior goes, Kristel's character was definitely having a positive impact on me.

I asked, "Does your mom know anything at all about what he's like now, I mean like what he does with Mandi, and all that stuff?"

"She might, but she seems to ignore it. I don't know for sure, Jody. I think she just got a picture of me and Brock stuck in her brain, and she won't let it go."

"Did you ever tell her that you think he might have had something to do with Jimmy's death?"

"No. I've never said anything about that to anyone but you, and Boonie."

I philosophized, "You just never know for sure about people, do you. She sees Brock one way, and we see him another."

"Yes, but God knows his heart."

There it was again, Kristel's religion. It was something I both liked and didn't like about her. I liked it because it played a large part in the special person that she was, but I didn't like it because I didn't buy into it entirely like she did. What was worse, though, was that her beliefs were pecking away at my own conscience, and the irritation just wouldn't go away.

"Kristel," I said. "How are you so sure God exists?"

"The same way I know for sure that the earth is round."

"But science has already proven that. We have pictures. But nobody has proven God exists."

"Do you believe everything you read in the science books?" she asked smartly.

"Most, but not everything, I guess."

"But you believe what the scientists have written about the shape of the earth, and you believe the pictures of the earth are genuine, and so you know for sure that the earth is round, right?"

"Yes, of course."

"But you've never actually gone out in space to see it for yourself, have you?"

"No, but others have."

"And you put your faith in their eyewitness accounts. You believe that what they *say* they saw is true. You put your faith in the science books, and now you claim you know the truth about the shape of the earth."

"Yes…"

"Well, that's one way how I know God exists. I trust in what eyewitnesses have written. I also consider all the evidence around us, and so I *know* that God exists."

"But you don't really know *for sure*. There's a chance the Bible could be wrong, and that evolution…"

"There's a chance that the science books could be wrong, too. In fact, scientists have to revise them all the time. But the Bible, as far as I know, has never been wrong, and it has always said the same thing. I think it takes more faith for you to believe in what scientists, whom you don't know personally, have to say, than it takes for me to believe in a personal God and the word He has written."

Kristel was clever like that in her arguing. I tried to find a crack in her armor by asking, "Okay, but can't you admit that there's a small chance you could be wrong, that no one can know absolutely for sure about God?"

She was ready. "Would you admit that we all could be wrong about the earth, or about history, or about science, and that no one can know absolutely sure about anything?"

"I guess so. We can't know with absolute certainty about anything. Wait a minute… We can know for sure that we exist, like Descartes said, 'I think, therefore I am.' Okay, that's why I say that the only person you can count on with absolute certainty is yourself."

"So you're saying that there is no other absolute out there, nothing that you can know for sure, except your own existence, your own thinking?"

"Yes, that's right. Like you said, everything else is just faith, believing in what we can't know absolutely for sure."

"So there are no absolutes—no absolute facts, no absolute truth? Everything is relative to how an individual person sees it?"

I remembered having a discussion like this in Mr. Gray's class, and I was sure I could win *this* argument. "Yes," I averred. "There is no absolute truth. Everything is just a personal belief in the unknowable."

Then she got me again. "Are you absolutely sure there is no absolute truth? Is it absolutely, positively true that absolute truth doesn't exist?"

I had to concede, "Well, the only absolute is that there is no absolute truth."

Kristel grinned and she said, "That's a logical contradiction."

"It might sound like it, but that's the way it is."

"What about mathematics? Won't two plus two always equal four? Aren't there absolute truths in mathematics?"

"Math is just a technology that man has devised," I said, thinking my response sounded pretty clever, albeit fallacious.

Kristel went on, "What about physics… the law of gravity, the law of thermodynamics. Aren't those absolute truths?"

"Again, that's just the way man sees things; it's how we arrange things in our minds so we can survive better." That sounded more reasonable, I thought.

"What about murder, and rape, and stealing. We see those as wrong. Aren't those examples moral laws that are absolutely true?"

I had her now. "Once again, Kristel, that's just how man sees it. We apply those morals to help us survive and prosper."

"So you're saying that what we refer to as "truth" is really just the way we see things, and if the way we see things changes, then "truth" changes along with it?"

"Yes, that's right."

"So then the world was flat five hundred years ago, because that's the way we saw it back then. But then it went from flat to round when we started to see it differently?"

"No. It was always round, we just didn't know it."

"So the truth about the shape of the earth never changed, only our thinking about it did."

"That's right."

"Then isn't that an absolute truth, that the earth has always been round? It didn't matter how mankind saw it, because the truth about the shape of the earth was always there, always constant?"

"Yes." I sensed the foundation of my argument crumbling beneath me.

Kristel continued, "How about morality. Hasn't something, say, like slavery, always been wrong? Hasn't slavery always been an evil institution throughout history?"

"Yes."

"But it wasn't that long ago that we had laws supporting slavery in this country. Was it morally right then, when many people believed in it? Or were they wrong all along? Hasn't the evil of slavery always been an absolute moral truth of the universe that people were simply wrong about?"

"Yes." She was right, and I was losing once again.

"Just think about it Jody," Kristel said gently, being the gracious winner that she was. "If absolute truth doesn't exist, then think about all the other things that can't exist, like justice and knowledge and wisdom. All those things would just be personal opinions. I believe that God is absolute, He is the source of all truth, and He has been constant and never changing. It's us stupid humans who waver back and forth, trying to do things on our own. If we would only seek the truth, and find it, and trust in it, then we'd all be a lot better off."

I remained silent.

She concluded, "You know with absolute certainty that the earth is round, and that fact is true all by itself; it doesn't depend on people thinking about it to make it true. It was true, it is true, and it will always be true, no matter how people, or how many of them think about it. We *discover* truth; we don't create it in our minds."

After that conversation, the one thing I knew for sure was that if you trust only in yourself, and you're wrong, then you're really in bad shape. I didn't know how to attack Kristel's position. I needed to think about it more and come up with a better argument.

I blamed my disinterest in furthering the discussion on my getting sleepy, and Kristel promised me she'd come to see me in the morning at the kitchen before she left for Boston.

When I climbed out of the tree house, it felt like I was leaving on rather dubious terms with her, as though this stupid religion thing was becoming a divisive issue.

On my way back to Saranac, as usual, I was stopped by Whisper on his golf cart, who without fail gargled, "I'll let it go this time." Now there was an absolute you could truly count on: old Whisper.

The next morning, in the privacy of the walk-in cooler, for two whole exhilarating seconds, surrounded by stacks of produce, crates of milk, pounds of beef and pork, and pans piled with leftovers, Kristel and I hugged each other goodbye. We didn't have time to talk, and as she walked out of the kitchen, it felt like I was losing her. No, that wasn't it. It felt like it was me who was lost.

I returned to the front line and distracted myself by volunteering to clean the grill, a less than desirable task normally assigned for punishment.

It was just three hours after Kristel departed, during the lunch rush, that Brock Oliff waltzed into the kitchen, sneaked up behind the waitress Mandi, his girlfriend, and pinched her on the rear end. She squealed a high-pitched yelp, spun around bright-eyed, and seeing Brock standing there with a crooked grin, she giggled and embraced him. Other waitresses hurried past the sappy couple and rolled their eyes. Boonie and I watched from behind the front line and snickered.

"I can't believe Mandi fell for that idiot," I grumbled.

Boonie smirked, and with one hand he rubbed his thumb on the inside of his fingers, signifying that Mandi was after Brock for his money.

"Probably," I said. "She's just gullible, though. I feel sorry for her. She seems like she could be a nice girl if she hung around the right crowd."

"Yeah," said Boonie, shaking his head as he stirred New England clam chowder in the steam kettle. "The good ones always fall for the jerks. I mean look at Kristel!" His flat smirk turned into a wide-mouthed, knee-slapping hoot.

I simply grinned and added, "Hey, watch it now."

Brock and Mandi continued their mushy embrace until Mandi broke free and filled her tray with several glasses of iced tea. "I'll be right back," she squeaked in her southern accent. Brock smiled, strutted over to a supply shelf, and fiddled mindlessly with the glass salt and peppershakers, ketchup bottles, A-1 sauce, and miniature bottles of Tabasco sauce.

From behind the front line, where I was layering breaded chicken strips neatly into a two-inch hotel pan, I glanced at him periodically. Unexpectedly, for a brief instant, and for the first time since our confrontation on the roadside when he gave me a black eye, our eyes connected. It was a brief but significant stare, and we both looked away immediately.

As the lunch rush advanced past noon, the heat from the fryerlators, grill, and steam equipment produced a sauna-like effect for the front-line cooks.

Boonie and I often kept a glass of Coke or lemonade near the sink at the edge of the front line for a quick refresher during the busy mealtime. We usually finished off two or three glasses during a single meal.

Crowds of guests were lining up at the buffet lines in the dining room, and Brock was still hanging around the kitchen for no reason but to be near Mandi. He had moved to the ice machine where he was less in the way of the waitresses who were hurrying in and out of the kitchen.

When the first ice cube caromed off the exhaust hood above our heads with a clang, Boonie shouted with resounding authority, "Get out of the kitchen, Oliff!" Brock cackled like a happy witch and scuttled towards the dish-pit area behind the wall and out of sight.

After sliding a pan of rice pilaf into the steam chest, Boonie walked to the end of the line and looked around the corner to see Brock talking with one of the dish-pit boys. Satisfied that the menace was at least out of the front-line area, Boonie picked up his glass of Coke from the edge of the counter. After a big, long gulp, the glass dropped from his hands and a heavy spray of Coca-cola spewed from his mouth.

From around the corner, Brock screamed with laughter, crouching over, holding his gut, and slapping his leg. His laugh could be heard throughout the kitchen and even into the dining room. A hoard of workers gathered to see the commotion.

The glass from Boonie's hand fell safely onto the black rubber floor mat. While clutching his throat, Boonie picked it up and hastily rinsed it out in the sink, filled it with cold water, and took several long gulps. Tears gathered in his eyes, and a trickle leaked down his cheek. Brock continued to belch out his echoing laugh, causing others to start giggling with him, although they weren't sure exactly what had happened.

"I put half a bottle of Tabasco sauce in that Coke!" Brock screamed, bending over again while he held his gut and roared. Others broke into laughter when they were enlightened with what had happened.

Boonie guzzled down a second glass of water and wiped the tears from his eyes. Meanwhile, I stood at the fryerlator and tried to keep a straight face. I didn't want to embarrass my friend more than he already was. It *was* a funny moment.

"We'll get him back," I said later, after the commotion died down. Boonie could hardly talk. It was hours before he had full feeling back in his lips and tongue.

Kristel's departure created a void in our ability to think clearly and maturely, resulting in Boonie and I planning a revenge on Brock during dinner that Monday night. We managed to sneak into the dining room before the meal and pour a full twelve ounce bottle of egg shade, a rich yellow food coloring, all over Brock's saxophone. The liquid soaked into the spongy lining of the case, and the instrument sat in the yellow liquid until it dried. When Brock picked it up at dinnertime, the yellow coloring on the brass instrument was virtually undetectable, especially under the dim lights of the dining room.

After five minutes of playing the instrument, Brock's lips were bright yellow, as if he had been sucking on a highlighter marker. His fingers and hands were also deeply stained, and he didn't realize any of it until he took a break in the restroom a full hour after dinner began. He refused to return to the stage with bright yellow lips and hands, and the rest of the band played without their sax player for the remainder of the evening. The worst part of it was only that Boonie and I weren't around to see it. We heard about the hilarity of the successful prank from some waitresses.

Not to be outdone, Brock, still yellow lipped and yellow handed, and with the help of his alliance of band members, stormed into Saranac after midnight and dragged Boonie out of his bed.

"Get out here, ya punk!" snorted Brock as Boonie squirmed and contorted his body. A band member tightly gripped each of his limbs while Brock directed orders. "Take him behind the cabin!"

The Needleman twins and I awoke from our sleep, and before we knew what was happening, the gang was out the door with the Boonie. Tossing off my blanket, I scampered outside and found Boonie pinned down to the ground by four guys while Brock pressed his foot firmly into Boonie's stomach.

"You think you're funny, huh!? You think you're funny!?" Brock growled through his teeth. His yellow lips glowed under the dim moonlight.

It was the first time I had seen the results of our prank, and I almost laughed.

Boonie, in his helpless position in the dirt, said nothing. He had stopped resisting against the stronghold of Brock's men.

"You idiot mulatto! I oughta crack your skull!" Brock screamed, forcing his shoe deeper into Boonie's stomach. My friend winced in pain.

"Knock it off, Brock!" I shouted, and at once five faces turned and glared at me. "He didn't do it. I put the stuff on your sax. Boonie only gave me the bottle."

"I should have known," Brock snarled. He targeted me with an evil stare, and like an owner calling to his attack dogs, he commanded, "Let's get the loverboy, fellas."

Five band members, one with yellow hands and lips, lunged simultaneously in my direction. Like a scared rabbit, I bolted around the front of the cabin and up the path along the softball diamond. Feeling the dirt and pine needles under my feet, I realized I was wearing nothing but a pair of boxer shorts. The thumping of shoes worn by my pursuers closed in behind me. At the clearing around the ball diamond, I turned left up the paved, driveway and I could sense at least two of the pursuers gaining on me.

A strategy crossed my mind when I saw the lights of the pool deck on my right, and without time to contemplate its worth, I gracefully leapt the three-foot fence at the pool deck's perimeter. My followers didn't lose a length, leaping the fence with as much agility, if not more. I dove headlong into the swimming pool, not expecting the band members, stiffly dressed in suit jackets and ties, to follow.

But I was wrong. I out-swam two of them to the other side of the pool, only to find the other three waiting for me at the edge of the shallow end. These three jumped in on top of me, and in a torrent of splashing and clawing, each of my limbs was soon in the firm grasp of the enemy.

Brock clutched my wet head and forced my face under water, holding it there for several seconds before yanking it back up again.

"You think you're funny?!" he screamed as I gasped for air. My face was forced into the water again, and after several seconds, Brock jerked it back out.

"You think you're hot stuff?!"

Into the water—and finally out again, repeatedly. I squeezed my eyes shut and gasped for air whenever given the chance.

Into the water, and out. My skull ached as Brock clutched a fistful of my wet follicles.

"You're dating a freakin' slut!" Brock screamed.

The dunking and screaming continued, each time with greater force and harsher words—either about me, Kristel, or Boonie. Brock then held my head under for what seemed like minutes, and I started praying that he would either deliver another blow to my face and stop the water torture, or that my friend Boonie could muster up enough help for a rescue. Something had to happen before I swallowed too much water.

# CHAPTER 18

## Chlorine Eyes, Hawkeye, and Making Eyes

I was desperate the next time my face went under water. Brock was holding me there longer and longer each time, and my remaining strength, which I used only to breathe deeply when I could, was rapidly depleting. I was completely at his mercy. At first, I could wriggle an arm free from the strong grasp for a second or two, but then I no longer had the energy to try anymore. I could only wait for Brock's merciful yank upward—when I could at last refill my lungs with oxygen.

My head was jerked up again and I gasped.

"Yer a freak!" Brock screamed in my face.

I opened my eyes for the first time since the initial dunking, hoping my mercy-pleading gaze might help stop the torture. Through the sting of the chlorine I saw Brock's bulging eyes, his crooked, extruding jaw, and his thin, bright yellow lips. I smelled the stench of alcohol on his breath when he screamed. Water covered my face again as I was forced downward, and through the bluish liquid I could see Brock's white, button-down dress shirt rippling underwater and his tie swirling from his neck like a snake.

The painful clench of Brock's hands on my skull was remorseless, and as the seconds underwater felt more like minutes, my lungs ached like never before. The fatal thought of inhaling water flashed through my mind, and I thought I actually might drown. I needed to suck in; I couldn't hold back much longer.

Then, a cracking report, as though a cherry bomb had exploded, resounded above the surface of the water. At that instant, the bony hands of my enemy released their excruciating grasp, and my limbs were simultaneously released from the bruising clutches of Brock's cohorts. I shot upwards and sucked in the precious air.

Wiping the water from my eyes, I found myself surrounded by my enemies in their soaking wet dress suits, standing in the four-foot end of the swimming pool. They all wore a look of shock on their faces, each staring in the same direction across the pool towards the deep end.

Standing on the pool's edge next to the diving board was Whisper. His white-sleeved right arm held a 22-caliber pistol over his head. He stood there motionless, his pale face paralyzed and expressionless.

Panicked, the five band members sloshed to the edge of the pool and lunged for the surface. Some cursing, some laughing, they scampered around the cafe building and out of sight, their shoes squishing up the hillside along the woods towards the end of the Club building. Soon they were gone, leaving only a drippy track of water behind. Exhausted, I lingered in the shallow end, wearing ripped boxer shorts.

Whisper lowered the pistol from above his head and tucked it into his belt. He slowly circled around the pool, limping on his right leg, his boot producing a definable "thump" on the cement of the pool deck. As many times as I had seen him during the early morning hours over the past two weeks, Whisper had always been sitting in his golf cart, and I had forgotten about his crippled leg until now.

I hoisted myself up onto the pool deck and sat with my lower limbs in the water, rubbing my eyes and inhaling the sweet Adirondack air.

Whisper limped along the edge of the pool, passed behind me, and approached the café building. He said nothing. I heard the dangling of keys and a door to the café being opened. A moment later, the thumping boot returned to the pool deck. Then, like a mother tucking a baby into bed, a towel was placed gently over my wet shoulders. I glanced behind and saw Whisper's kind stare.

"You better get warmed up. The night's kind of chilly," mumbled the old man softly.

I stood to my feet at the edge of the pool. Cold water trickled down my legs. "Thanks," I offered, pulling the warm towel tightly around my upper body.

Whisper gargled his familiar words as he looked at his watch. "It's late, and I'm supposed to report your being out here. But I'll let it go this time."

The old man turned and limped back around the pool towards the gate behind the diving board. I watched him board his golf cart and whir up the hill towards the Club building.

A minute later, Boonie came running up the road from the softball diamond. I explained what happened as we walked back to our cabin, both of us laughing out loud about the bright yellow color of Brock's lips and hands.

During the week of Kristel's absence, the Ambassador letters continued to arrive in the B box every day, just like they had for the past nineteen days, except Sundays. Each letter was printed in block, capital letters, and each contained one or two phrases about the importance of discovering the murderer of Jim Grandstaff. The latest one said, "I NEED YOUR HELP. PLEASE BELIEVE IN ME." The plea became trite and annoying. I even tossed one of them in the mailroom trashcan, even though I knew Officer Anders wanted me to bring them all in.

I thought about another letter that said, "THE TRUTH IS WAITING FOR YOU. PLEASE CARE," and I couldn't help thinking about what Kristel and I had talked about the night before she left. It crossed my mind that maybe she was the source of the letters. But she was now in Boston, and the envelopes were still postmarked from Pokeville.

Nevertheless, I was inclined to continue delivering the letters to Officer Anders at the police station every other day or so. I started wondering if it was even worth my time, because I had heard practically nothing from this Sheriff Slater who was in charge of the investigation. His only input was that the handwriting didn't match to anything on the John Doe letter.

His lack of communication really didn't bother me that much at all. I had other things on my mind, none of them having to do with my family or its screwy past. I honestly didn't want anything to do with Jimmy Grandstaff anymore. I practically stopped caring about this brother I never knew. If the relentless letters from the Ambassador would have ceased, I probably could've put the whole thing entirely out of mind. I had found peace and happiness with Kristel and my other friends at the Club, and I was content enough not to worry about a long, lost brother and the teasing notes from his "Ambassador." Still, I was anxious to find out who the prankster was, and the sooner the better.

With Kristel gone, I found myself after work with nothing to do. Boonie was always off who-knows-where with some girl, a new one now that Angela was gone. So the day after the late-night chase into the swimming pool, I felt I owed a personal word of thanks to my rescuer.

No one was in the grove when I stepped up to the porch of the eerie cabin called Hawkeye. The golf cart sat empty alongside the wall, plugged into an outdoor electrical outlet. I had no idea what time a man who works all night gets his sleep. It was four in the afternoon, eight hours after Whisper's shift ended, and eight hours before it would begin again. Now was as good a time as any.

I stepped onto the creaking porch steps and knocked on the door. A loose pane of glass in the window rattled. I rapped clamorously several times, surely waking anyone who might have been sleeping inside. Soon, a distinguishable thump was heard inside the cabin. The rusty doorknob rotated with a squeak, and the door cracked open towards the outside. There, standing behind the wooden doorpost, was the old, pale Whisper, fully uniformed in his black boots and signature worn-out ball cap pulled tightly over his brow.

"Hello. I hope I haven't awoken you," I said politely. I stepped back away from the door so that Whisper had room to swing it further. He chose to hold it about six inches open.

His voice was hoarse and gentle. "You didn't wake me."

"Oh, good. Well, um, I just wanted to thank you for helping me last night… you know…at the pool."

Whisper stood still and expressionless.

"And, um, I want to thank you also for not reporting me to Mrs. Schuple all these times."

A smile twitched on his pale lips.

I figured I had said all I needed to say, so I set one foot behind me on the step.

"Will you come in?" Whisper suddenly gargled.

"Huh?"

"Come in? Will you?"

I had not at all expected the invitation, and my curiosity to see whether or not stacks of pornographic videos and magazines lined the walls of Whisper's cabin canceled any initial inhibitions about entering.

"Sure," I answered, stepping towards the door.

He pushed the door further open for me to enter, and his twitching smile fixed itself steady on his face.

The room inside Hawkeye had the exact dimensions of Saranac. A single set of bunks stood against the back wall next to an old avocado-green painted dresser. The windows in the sidewalls were covered with faded orange curtains with little orange pom poms dangling at the fringes. Against the left wall was a countertop constructed out of a wooden door sitting on sawhorse legs. The hole for the doorknob had a white rag tucked through it, kind of like a dishtowel holder. A small two-foot high refrigerator, a little microwave, and an electric griddle helped convert the left wall into a kitchenette. A single shelf built above the appliances held an assortment of boxed cereal and canned soup, cooking utensils, and stacks of paper cups and plates. Against the right wall of the cabin was a rather new looking beige sofa. Above it hung several framed pictures of large farmhouses and outdoor scenes of horses and barns.

Along the front wall, to the left of the doorway, was a workbench. Upon it was scattered an assortment of chisels, knives, and hammers, all covered in a dusting of wood shavings. Narrow shelves above the workbench displayed a menagerie of carved wooden figures of various sizes: giraffes, elephants, monkeys, penguins, and ducks, to name a few.

On the floor in front of the workbench was a sawed-off tree stump, big enough to sit upon. The front section of the stump had been whittled away, and the rough dimensions of what looked to be some sort of tall, upright animal had been formed. An oval, woven, pea-green carpet filled the center of the wooden floor, extending from underneath the bunk at the back wall to the front edge of the sofa. The floor in the front third of the room was covered with wood chips and curled shavings.

Whisper limped to the workbench and grabbed a broom from the corner.

"Excuse this mess," he gargled, as swept up the wood shavings. "I don't have visitors very often."

"Don't mind me," I said, both surprised and impressed with the little pad in which the old man dwelt. No girly magazines were in sight, nor a TV or VCR.

I pointed at the large tree stump on the floor. "What are you making?"

Whisper stopped sweeping. "Uh, that's going to be a swan."

I could detect the rough outline of a swan emerging from the carved facade of the stump.

The old man continued in his soft, airy voice, "I've never carved anything that big before." He pointed to the display shelf above the workbench. "I usually make miniature figures."

"They're incredible," I said of the wooden menagerie.

Whisper said nothing and resumed sweeping.

"What made you decide to work on such a big one?"

"Saw a fella down at the county fair carve grizzly bears and Indian heads out of huge tree stumps like that one. He used a chain saw to do the bulk of his work. Me, I prefer the hand-held chisel and carving knife. Chain saw's too noisy."

I lifted a five-inch tall giraffe from the shelf, noticing the minute details of nostrils, eyes, and even the giraffe's spots indented into the wood.

"This is incredible," I said again. "How do you do it?"

Another smile slipped between Whisper's pressed lips. He looked at his wristwatch and said, "I'll tell you what. You go find yourself a nice little piece of wood… any piece of wood you can find laying around somewhere. Come back tomorrow, and I'll show you how it's done."

Whisper took the giraffe from my hand and placed it back on the shelf. Then he picked up a tiny, wooden swan and placed it in my hand. The swan was identical to the one Kristel showed me, only slightly bigger, with every detail in place, from feathers to eyelashes.

"You take this, and try to picture that swan in the piece of wood you select."

"Thank you," I said. "I'll come back tomorrow."

Whisper resumed sweeping, inquiring as he stared at the floor, "Won't I see you later tonight when I'm on duty?"

I chuckled as I open the door. "Uh, no, not tonight. Kristel's gone for the week."

The old man paused pensively for a moment before he continued sweeping. "Tomorrow then, right here," he gargled, looking at the half-carved tree stump.

I decided never to tell a soul about my visit to Hawkeye cabin, at least not until Kristel got back.

The Needleman twins stormed into Saranac on that Tuesday afternoon with four wide eyes and two gaping jaws.

"Ya won't believe what happened!" Pete roared as he bounced onto Boonie's bunk, followed closely by his brother who leaped up to his.

Boonie and I paid little attention to them. We were in the second quarter of a PlayStation football game.

"Donnie Lisko got fired!"

Pete was extremely proud his having been the first to deliver the news to us. He beamed sardonically at Boonie and me while Rodney sat above him with his goofy, jumbled-toothed grin.

"What'd you say?" Boonie asked, turning away from the TV.

"Lisko got fired! Schuple kicked him out today!"

"What for?" I asked, pushing the pause button.

"He got caught with Sandi Ramey in one of the rooms!"

"Who's she?"

"A housekeeper. They were doing it on a bed when her supervisor caught 'em. They both got fired this morning!"

Boonie's eyes widened and he let out a long whistling sigh through his puckered lips.

I drilled Pete with several questions to make sure he was telling the truth. As it turned out, he was. Donnie Lisko was one of the cooks for the dinner shift, and Boonie and I recalled that he had not shown up for work at noon today like he was supposed to.

It was no coincidence that, while we were discussing it, Allen, in his hat and apron, came to our door and asked Boonie to come back and help out at dinner to cover for Donnie's absence.

"Can't." Boonie said bluntly. "Got a hot date. Can't break it."

I knew that Boonie had no date scheduled, but in ten minutes he could line one up if he had to. Allen knew it, too.

"How 'bout you Jody," Allen said. "Can you work the grill tonight?"

I thought for a moment. With Kristel away, I had lots of time on my hands.

In less than an hour, I was back in the kitchen, ready to work my first dinner meal without Boonie. The evening shift was very similar to the lunch shift, only it lasted longer and the temperature of the work space between the front steam line and the hot cooking appliances was much greater than during the lunch shift hours. They said it got hotter than 110 degrees sometimes. There were more waitresses scheduled and they were busier, too, for nearly twice as many guests attended dinner than lunch.

I spent three uninterrupted hours that Tuesday night at the grill, cooking fillets of rainbow trout and beef and broccoli stir-fry. When the rush finally subsided and it was time to clean the grill, I was caught off guard when a cute waitress looked at me with a pair of incredibly stunning eyes.

The eyes belonged to Mandi, Brock's girlfriend, and although I had seen this girl often enough, I never quite noticed the lure of her eyes as I did at that moment. They were the kind of eyes around which you would construct a perfect face—much like beautiful resort towns are built around beach-lined, sparkling blue bays. These eyes sparkled like diamonds, and I have to admit they were down right mesmerizing. Electric blue they were, and the eye shadow she had on made them all the more dazzling.

Mandi's nose, however, was a different sort of nose—not pretty, but not ugly in the least. It looked like a nose that would belong to a Muppet—lacking a distinguishable bridge, more cartilage than bone, which gave it a succinct, puffy roundness. It was as though the nose had been haphazardly selected from a large bin of assorted noses and glued to the middle of her face.

The rest of her face was virtually flawless. No blemish was detectable, and her visage would be deemed decidedly perfect by most admirers if her beautiful eyes could overpower her spongy nose. Her bleach-blonde, wavy hair bobbed playfully behind her neck in a ponytail, and when her hair and her round, spongy nose joined efforts with those glamorous, sparkling blue eyes, the result was a well-balanced cuteness in the face of this waitress.

But it was when her eyes appeared above the top shelf of the juice bar, and all I could see were those deeply set, electric blue eyes, I became a hostage for a brief yet truly significant moment.

I had never before "made eyes" with someone, and I thought it funny, at first, that it was happening in such a glaringly obvious manner. I just looked up and there they were, a good forty or fifty feet away, ogling at me from behind the juice bar.

The dinner rush had died down and I was rinsing off the knives I used to score the trout filets. Mandi had been standing behind that juice bar at for almost the entire meal, a good three hours, keeping glasses of iced tea, lemonade, and various soda pops ready to be taken by other waitresses who had no time to scoop ice and fill glasses during the rush.

Her job was the easiest—simply to keep those beverage glasses full and lined up on the refrigerated shelf with lemon wedges secured to the rims. When a waitress rushed by and loaded a serving tray, the beverage girl would just slide the remaining glasses forward and would fill more glasses to replace the ones taken. This was what the dining staff called "kitchen duty," and the girl who was lucky enough to have it for the evening hardly had to break a sweat like the rest.

Keeping those beverages ready and waiting on that juice bar gave Mandi plenty of time to watch the chefs and cooks working on the hot, steamy front line where dinner plates were filled in artful and expedient fashion. I didn't notice her there during the rush, but when the action slowed and I finally had time to look around, my eyes accidentally got stuck on hers.

It wasn't intentional, and that's the honest truth. I had been seeing Kristel regularly for almost three weeks now, and despite her unorthodox dating philosophy, I wasn't up for flirting with my Number One Enemy's girlfriend, especially in such a classic bar-scene fashion which, in fact, this very much felt like. But for some reason, my eyes just stuck on hers for a moment longer than I would have intentionally directed them. Maybe it was because

I had been staring at nothing else but sizzling trout filets and beef strips for the previous three hours, and when the image of her beautiful blue eyes registered in my brain, I reacted first with admiration and then with compassion. This cute little girl had fallen for the Club jerk, and nobody, especially her, deserved someone like him.

The extended eye contact we shared, whether or not it was intentional on my part, but obviously on hers, sent a message that at the time I didn't know exactly how to interpret. What was significant about the message was not *what* it said, but *that* it said, indeed, something.

It was I who lost the staring contest. As soon as I realized what was happening—due to the coy smile she offered upon receiving my undivided attention—my eyes darted back into the sink where the blade of the knife I was rinsing carelessly dangled from my fingers. My first thought was a ridiculous one: Is that girl staring at me? The answer was all too obvious, but I stupidly felt the need to confirm my suspicion, so without thought my eyes met hers again, this time for a mere split-second.

Yes, she was staring at me, and still is. So now I had, not once, but twice, given her the satisfaction of knowing that I had noticed. What should I do now? She is a pretty one. No, she is more than just pretty... In that hot, humid kitchen, where deep fat fryers, sizzling grills, and steam ovens had been blasting all night, she was defiantly beautiful.

I could not see her round, spongy nose from where I stood, yet I knew it to be there, as I had seen it rubbed playfully against Brock's bony little snout in days past. But it was those eyes of hers that had grabbed me, almost seductively, and had her nose been visible to hush her seductive stare, I probably would have been thinking nothing of her little game.

Having learned from my mistake, I knew it would be foolish to look up a third time to see if she was still eyeing me from across the kitchen. So I turned away and strutted nonchalantly towards the back of the pantry, where I tossed my sweat-soaked paper cook's hat into a garbage barrel before escaping to the seclusion of the air-conditioned chef's office.

"Thanks for getting us out of a bind tonight, Jody," Dave said to me in the office. "You can go ahead and sign out now."

I got out of there fast. While trying to squelch my guilty feelings, I wished to heaven that I had a picture of Kristel to look at. But I didn't.

# CHAPTER 19

## *The Day After, Avoiding Trouble, and an Invitation*

It was Wednesday morning, July 1st. Kristel had been gone for barely forty-eight hours, and I was back in the kitchen, the scene of my crime.

No, it wasn't a crime, I assured myself. Kristel had insisted we were just friends. I thought if news got around to her about my eye contact with another girl, we'd see if Kristel extemporized on her philosophy—we'd see for sure if friends are really friends forever. Still, I wished Mandi had never looked at me. No, that's not true either. I wished *I* hadn't looked back—twice.

One by one, drops of thick batter plopped onto the shiny, hot grill. I performed this chore meticulously, holding the batter dispenser just inches above the grill's surface and pushing the trigger to release a four-inch portion of pancake batter. To start, I made a column of five pancakes, beginning at the left side of the grill and copying my work to the right. By the time nine columns of five were dropped, filling the entire grill, the raw sides of the pancakes in the first column were bubbling, meaning they were ready to be flipped.

I placed the batter dispenser on the front line and pick up a thick-bladed spatula, one especially designed for flipping pancakes. I turned them in the same order that I dropped them, careful to make sure they landed in their exact spots. I did perfect work—not a drop of batter went astray like Boonie always allowed. Bits of his batter always dribbled between the pancakes and formed crusty little droplets that he had to scrape off the grill.

"Man, you're such a perfectionist," Boonie said, looking over my shoulder at the grill full of forty-five perfectly round four-inch pancakes.

I smiled and said nothing. I was very tired from double duty yesterday, and my eyes were beginning to burn from the heat radiating from the hot grill.

Boonie opened the double doors of a convection oven to check on the bacon he had been cooking on sheet trays. A blast of hot air caused him to throw his head back. "Daggone!" he said about the wave of heat. He commonly did that whenever he opened an oven. He was extra careful about getting burned; a burn injury was his biggest fear, ever since he splashed grease on his forearm early last summer and suffered a third degree burn.

"About two more minutes," he said, closing the oven doors again.

I was finished flipping the first batch of pancakes, so I went back to the first column and layered them in perfect rows into a shallow pan for the buffet line.

It was an odd morning, and I didn't feel like talking much. Sleep came hard for me last night; I missed Kristel something awful, and I still couldn't get Mandi's eyes out of my head. It was as though she had put a spell on me. In truth, I wasn't sure what I would do if I looked over to the juice bar and saw those eyes again. Thankfully, a different girl was pouring orange juice over there this morning.

Boonie, on the other hand, was his usual talkative self.

"Mr. Schuple wants breakfast out there a half-hour early," he chirped. "He said a group is leaving at seven to visit Montreal, so we've gotta hurry."

"I've got a batch just about ready here," I said, breaking my silence.

As we prepared the hot breakfast, a small crew of waitresses hurried in and out of the kitchen due to the earlier-than-normal breakfast. Getting the coffee machines going was a critical, first-thing-in-the-morning task.

"Boonie!" the girl hollered from behind the juice bar. "The coffee machine won't heat up!"

The breakfast cook sauntered over to the stainless steel urn to rescue the waitresses in distress. Meanwhile, the trays of bacon remained in the oven, and I had to stop pancake production to remove the bacon before it burned.

I was on the lookout for Mandi's arrival, and I tried to devise a plan on what I'd do if our eyes met again. Should I talk to her? Should I ignore her? Was Kristel really serious about what she said about relationships? Or was it her way of testing me?

Thankfully, Mandi never entered the kitchen. Maybe it's her day off, I wondered.

I drained the grease from the sheet trays and piled the bacon strips into a two-inch buffet pan. Boonie was still helping a growing number of waitresses at the coffee machine, so I placed the pan of bacon under a heat lamp next to the first pan of pancakes. I popped a perforated tray full of eggs into the steam oven for hard boiling, stacked a pyramid of warm blueberry muffins on a fancy silver platter, and prepared a pot of boiling water for the instant grits. This morning's breakfast would be all my doing I presumed, seeing Boonie engaged more in flirting than fixing the coffee machine.

I hustled out to the dining room to make sure the heating units on the buffet line were on. To my surprise, they were already hot, an uncommon occurrence because I was usually the one to turn them on every morning.

"I already did that for you," the sweet southern voice of a young woman announced.

Mandi stood near the hostess counter filling out the electric menu board with a special felt-tip green marker.

"Oh, thanks," I said, trying to keep under control. I forced my eyeballs onto the menu board, noticing the elaborate design Mandi had drawn. Loopy flowers and cartoon birds singing "Good Morning! Today's menu is..." That's all she had finished so far.

Pretending to be in a mad rush, I scampered back into the kitchen. Out I came again with a pan of bacon in one hand and pancakes in the other. I inserted them into the buffet unit, flipped on the warming lamps above, and noticed Mandi continuing her menu-board artwork: "Hotcakes, Bacon..." written in frilly, script writing.

"Jody" she said in her southern drawl, not looking at me, but carefully writing out "Blueberry Muffins" as she spoke. "Y'all gonna be ready early this mornin'?" Her Dixie accent was nurturing and hospitable. She was the perfect southern belle—missing only the poofy dress and parasol. Why was she wasting herself on Brock Oliff?

"Yeah, we're on top of it," I answered confidently. "You can open up in about five minutes."

I hustled back into the kitchen and in three minutes, the breakfast buffet was ready. Boonie was still tinkering at the coffee machine with four waitresses; I wondered what the head breakfast cook would have done without me.

At exactly six-thirty, the early rush surrounded the buffet line and I kept up like a pro. Boonie finally finished his "duty" at the coffee machine and ended up behind the grill flipping pancakes while I kept the line full of food. Allen arrived at seven, surprised to find half of the breakfast crowd already eating.

"Good job, Boonie, with the early breakfast." Allen said, patting him on the back. "Don't know what I'd do without ya."

I could only shake my head in mild disgust. When Allen walked out into the dining room to check the crowd, Boonie strolled over to me and patted me on the back the same way Allen did to him. "Good job, Jody," he said, imitating Allen's voice. "Don't know what I'd do without ya." We both laughed.

Around nine-thirty we sat down to eat breakfast in the staff dining room. "Lunch is going to be really slow today," Boonie said, pouring milk into a bowl of Raisin Bran. "Half the guests are in Montreal, and the other half won't even eat here."

"That's good, 'cause I'm tired," I said.

"You ought to ask Dave or Allen if you can take a half-day today because you worked the extra shift yesterday."

"That's a good idea. I could use a nap."

"Besides, you won't want to be near the front line during lunch today."

"Why?"

A mischievous smile slipped across Boonie's face. "Because."

"Why?"

Boonie's smirk grew larger and his big white teeth flashed. "Because a particular person is going to be working at the juice bar again."

Instantaneously, my eyes widened and my mouth dropped open. "What?! Did she say something to you?"

"No."

"Did you talk to her?"

"No." He giggled like a girl.

"Yes you did! Then why'd you say that?"

Boonie shook his head and grinned. "I can't get over it! A guy who has Kristel Schuple in the palm of his hand is making goo-goo eyes over another girl the day after she leaves!"

"I was not! She was staring at me!" I glanced around the room at the other people eating breakfast and toned down my voice. I griped softly, "I looked up, and she was staring at me! I didn't do anything."

"That's not what I heard."

"What'd you hear? Who told you?"

"I was out with Jennifer last night, and she told me about how Mandi dumped Brock two nights ago. They're no longer goin' out. Must've been after he got me with the Tabasco sauce and before we got him with the food coloring. It's probably why Brock was so ticked off that night. Anyway, it's not a minute after Jennifer tells me about their breakup when Mandi's bunk mate Wendy joins us. Wendy had just got off work and she told us about you and Mandi in the kitchen last night."

"What *about* me and Mandi?! There's nothing there! Nothing happened!"

"Well, according to Wendy, Mandi thinks there is. And Mandi knows about Kristel's non-committal thing with you, and Mandi is planning on asking you to come with me, Jennifer, and Wendy to Smooth Rock today."

"Oh, crap!" I said, shaking my head and looking down at the table. "No way! No way am I getting into this business. Brock will kill me if he finds out. First Kristel, and now Mandi! No way!"

"C'mon Jody, Mandi's a nice girl. And you know she at least has some senses about her now that she's dumped ol' Brocko. Just come with us tonight. The girls all have dinner off. We're planning on going to Smooth Rock until dark, and then we'll come back and go to Burleighs."

"No way."

"C'mon. Kristel even told you it's okay to spend time with other girls. What are you going to do, hibernate all week until she gets back?"

"No way. Not Mandi. Any other girl—maybe. But not two former girlfriends of Brock's in a row. No way."

"C'mon, Jody. You don't know what you're missing. Mandi's a nice girl. And who knows? It might lead to something."

"I don't want it to lead to anything."

"Then what are you afraid of?"

"My health—if Brock finds out."

"You survived stealing Kristel from him."

"I didn't steal her. He never had her. And besides—I *did* get a black eye, four flat tires, and I almost drowned in the swimming pool because of him."

"So then why were you looking at Mandi last night?"

"I wasn't looking at her! I just happened to see her staring at *me!* It lasted a couple of seconds and I was wondering what she was staring at."

"That's not what she thinks. She thought you were flirting with her."

"I wasn't."

"So you're saying that you're not interested?"

"In her? No."

"Just because of Brock?"

"Yep." I folded my arms confidently and leaned back in my chair.

"You're crazy. Mandi's gorgeous. And that accent of hers—it's like honey on a biscuit!" He giggled.

"Shut up, Boonie. She is pretty, I admit that. But I'm not getting into it with Brock again."

"But *she* broke up with *him*, and besides, he'll never know. Listen, it's not like we'll be going out on a double date. Wendy's coming with us, so it'll be five of us. Just a group outing."

"Whose car?"

Boonie didn't answer. He only grinned, and that was answer enough.

"Ah, I get it. This has nothing to do with me, or Mandi, or anyone, but that you and Jennifer need a back seat."

Boonie laughed. "No, that's not it. Wendy really wants Mandi to go out with someone to help her put Brock behind her. Wendy's hoping Mandi will spend some time with a nice guy like you to maybe help raise her spirits. I guess Brock tried to take advantage of her a few times."

"That's not surprising."

"So come with us. You'll be helping a nice girl get back on her feet. Kristel will never know a thing."

"I don't care if she knows." That wasn't necessarily true, and Boonie knew it, too.

"Then come."

I was on the verge of giving in when Allen entered the staff dining room in search of the two of us.

"Nice job on breakfast again, Boonie." Allen said.

"Thanks," he replied, smirking at me.

"You too, Jody," Allen said unexpectedly. "I heard you did most of the work while Boonie was flirting with the girls. The hostess told me you put the whole meal out."

"Mandi?"

"I think that's her name. Brock's girlfriend."

"His X," Boonie said.

"Whatever," Allen replied. "By the way, Jody, Dave wants to know if you'd be interested in working a split shift. He appreciated your help in filling in for Lisko last night. Looks like we need to replace him permanently."

I asked, "Do you mean doing a split shift from now on?"

Allen nodded. "Yeah. You'd work six to ten-thirty and then come back at four and work 'til seven-thirty."

I looked at Boonie and said, "Guess you'll have to find another ride to Smooth Rock." I then turned to Allen and announced, "I'll do it."

"Good." Allen looked at his watch. "Then you can punch out in about an hour and come back at four. Just check in with Dave or Chef Al this afternoon."

I returned to Saranac and slept until noon, putting Mandi and Boonie and all that nonsense out of mind. When I awoke, four hours remained until I had to be back at work. What should I do? The beach? Laundry? Suddenly it struck me to find block of wood and visit Whisper for my first woodcarving lesson.

I procured a six-inch piece of two-by-four pine from behind the maintenance shed. It was filthy gray and I shaved a corner of it off with a Ginzu knife Pete Needleman kept under his bunk. The inside was clean and new, and I tried to imagine this block of wood turning into a swan.

The steps to Hawkeye squeaked as usual when I approached the door. The panes of glass rattled loudly when I knocked, and unlike yesterday, I heard no movement inside. He must be sleeping, or maybe he's not in there. Without thinking I grabbed the rusty doorknob and turned it. It was unlocked, and the door creaked open.

In a normal voice that I hoped wouldn't scare a sleeping old man, I spoke through the opening, "Hello, Sir? Are you here?" No response. I pushed the door further open and poked my head inside. The bunk was empty. The kitchenette, the sofa, the shelves, and the workbench all appeared the same as they had two days before. The half-swan carved out of the large stump on the floor looked unchanged, and there were no new wood shavings on the floor that Whisper had swept when I left. Probably out fishing or something, I thought, while closing the door and stepping down from the porch.

Nobody was in the grove to see me coming out of Hawkeye cabin.

From there, I walked up to the post office in the staff lounge. In the B box was the typical Ambassador letter postmarked from Pokeville. Same style envelope, same type of paper, same block capital letters. Only this one said something different. The message wasn't the same old "help me redeem Jimmy" language. It was an invitation, and I sat down on a couch in the lounge and read it over and over again.

# CHAPTER 20

## *Ten O'clock at the Dock*

Dear Jody,

It is time for us to meet. Thursday night, July 2, 10:00 p.m. At the end of the Club dock. Please be alone, or I won't show.

An Ambassador for the Dead.

I read it at least a dozen times to let it sink in. All the possibilities raced through my mind again and again. A joke? Who? Brock? No. I must tell Officer Anders. I've gotta tell Kristel. Good, she said she would call me tonight. Should I tell Boonie? Of course.

The letters I had been receiving before this one had been no more than a nuisance. Now, I wasn't sure what to think. The confusion from those first few days of my summer at the Club came rushing back. That which I had previously suppressed was now pounding at my head for attention.

What if Jimmy Grandstaff *had* been murdered? What if Kristel was right about Brock? No. This is a joke. Some idiot is going to be waiting for me at the dock laughing his head off at me. Probably Brock himself. I looked at my watch and left immediately for the police station.

Officer Anders seemed more amused than impressed.

"So you think we ought to bug you, or should we use our high-tech surveillance cameras?" he joked, studying the sixteenth letter I had brought to him.

It was kind of funny, and kind of not.

Anders added, "I was just talking with Sheriff Slater yesterday and he's convinced somebody's just pulling your leg. Maybe it's a girl who likes you, or something like that."

At that suggestion, which I had considered beforehand, the first person to cross my mind this time was Mandi. I quickly dispelled the thought of her. Then Kristel crossed my mind again. No, couldn't be.

"So the sheriff hasn't been taking these letters seriously?" I asked.

"Oh, he most certainly is," Anders ensured. "The case is still open, you know. But all we have are these letters you've been bringing us and that John Doe letter from June 8$^{th}$. Until something breaks ..."

I cut him off. "I know, but this letter is different. I know it could be a joke, or a girl or something, but what if it's not? What if it's really the John Doe who sent you guys the first letter? What if it's the *murderer*? It could be anybody. And this person wants to meet me tomorrow night—alone."

Officer Anders paper-clipped the letter to its envelope like he had with all the others. "I understand. It's only rudimentary. All these letters you've received don't compare at all with the original John Doe letter we got. That letter was typed on a laser printer and the envelope is a different style than these. Sheriff Slater is convinced that the news reports about the original letter spawned some prankster to toy around with you because they found out you're Jimmy's brother."

Now Kristel popped into my mind again. She is the only one who knows of my relationship to Jimmy, except for her parents, and Boonie. No way—she's not sending these notes. She couldn't be; she's in Boston. Except for Boonie and the police, I haven't told anyone that Jimmy was my brother.

"Well, I'd like to talk with the Sheriff sometime," I meekly insisted. "I still haven't met him."

Officer Anders stood to his feet and said gently, "I know. He's anxious to meet you as well. He's been quite busy, you know. This brace is coming off soon, and I can get away from this desk, the Sheriff will be able to spend a little more time here at headquarters." Anders walked gingerly over to the coffee machine and poured a mug full of the steamy black brew.

I glanced at the letter on the desk. "So what do you think I should do tomorrow night?"

"Show up to meet the Ambassador, if you want to. But be careful, and don't be too disappointed if it's some secret admirer with long blonde hair and blue eyes." He smiled and sipped his coffee. "The truth about these Ambassador letters was going to come out sooner or later, and it's up to you now. It looks like the ball's in your court."

"Should I take a friend?" I asked.

"Well, the note says to be alone. Maybe you could have someone watch you close by—out of sight."

And that's exactly what I determined to do. I raced back to the Club and caught Boonie just as he was leaving work. I told him all about the latest letter, and we came up with a plan for my Thursday night appointment with the Ambassador.

In the kitchen that Wednesday night, I found myself behind the fryerlator for two solid hours. Clam strips, breaded butterfly shrimp, and hushpuppies kept me hopping, as did redressing the cold shrimp platters that came in empty from the buffet line. Mandi was off for this meal, and her replacement at the juice bar showed no interest in the action occurring at the front line. I was glad; I had enough problems with girls for the time being. I wondered if Mandi went with Boonie, Jennifer, and Wendy to Smooth Rock without me.

At eight o'clock, Kristel was supposed to call me on the pay phone in the staff lounge. I sat on the couch, tired, still smelling of fried seafood because I hadn't had time to shower after getting off work. I thumbed through a two-week old issue of *Sports Illustrated* while I waited for the phone to ring. Normally, other staff members would occupy the pay phone at this hour. But tonight, most of the staff was at the pool for an ice cream party, except for me, because I longed to talk with my friend and tell her about the most recent letter from the Ambassador.

But the phone never rang. Eight o'clock came and went, and by eight-thirty I was sure that Kristel's activities in Boston must have preoccupied her. I left the lounge quite disappointed, wondering what might have happened. Did she just forget?

I arrived at the pool too late for ice cream, so I went to the shower house and cleaned up. I thought maybe I'll catch up with Boonie and the girls at Burleighs. Maybe the only way I can deal with my curious feelings about Mandi is to face them straight on. Would I be doing this if Kristel had called? I didn't know. I just didn't know.

To my surprise, disappointment, and relief, all rolled up into a strange concoction of emotions, Mandi wasn't with the group when I found them at Burleighs. She had decided to go to bed early, Wendy informed me, as I sat down at the table.

"So how's Kristel?" Jennifer asked, knowing I would be talking to her that night.

"She didn't call. She must have been too busy or something."

I noticed a pleased look emerge on everyone's face, especially Wendy's.

We all knew full well about the topic that wasn't being spoken. Now I really wished Mandi *was* there so that no one would have asked about Kristel.

I realized the only way out of this curious mess was to talk to Mandi and get it over with—to see what she was like and get it all out in the open. So I decided to tackle the issue head on right there at the table, with or without her.

I announced, "Look, I know what you're all thinking, and listen: I'll talk to Mandi at breakfast tomorrow, if that's what you all want. I hardly even know her—but you all think that I ought to spend some time with her—so I will… tomorrow. Maybe that will help you all to shut up about it."

Boonie laughed. "I knew it! You get stood up at the pay phone and now you're willing to talk to Mandi. Just this morning 'No way! No way!'" Boonie said, mocking me in a funny voice.

The group laughed, including me, although I wasn't sure exactly what I was feeling. Part of me was glad that Kristel was gone and Mandi was interested in me, and another part of me wanted to crawl up into the tree house and talk to Kristel into the wee hours of the morning.

To be honest, a girl like Mandi was more attainable for me in some ways. Kristel, at times, seemed out of my league. Our long conversations proved that she was smarter and more mature than I was about stuff, especially in the area of religion. It was quite humbling, and a little embarrassing, too. Not that I didn't really, really like Kristel, because I did. I guess it was her religion and her mother that was a dividing wall that just wouldn't go away. For crying out loud, it had been three weeks and I hadn't even kissed her!

Now, I didn't know Mandi hardly at all, but clearly she was interested, and what would be the harm in talking to her? I didn't know… it was like I was stuck, and I knew that if Kristel had been there, none of this Mandi business would've taken place.

But my problems were all over with by Thursday morning. Mandi didn't show up at all, neither for work, nor for breakfast in the staff dining room.

It was my day off, and her bunkmate Wendy told me that Brock had approached Mandi last night and kept her out late. Apparently, they had a serious talk and Mandi didn't get back to her room until three a.m. No one knew for sure, but the consensus was that she and Brock were back together. Wendy told Darlene at the hostess station that Mandi was sick and wouldn't be in.

I was relieved, for the most part. It was a little nerve-racking to think about talking with Mandi, especially after telling the gang that I would. But now that she was supposedly back with Brock, the whole issue was dead. It looked like Mandi had no sense after all, having fallen for Brock Oliff not once, but twice. As for me, only two more days until Kristel comes back.

I ended up spending most of my day off at the beach, reading *The Great Gatsby*, yesterday's *USA Today*, and a copy of the *Wall Street Journal* that someone had pitched in the trash can at the beach deck.

I got about halfway through *Gatsby*, empathizing with Nick Carraway for unexpectedly getting tangled into a bunch of crap one summer in New York. Then I empathized with old Gatsby. It had been five years for him and Daisy; it was only three *days* so far for me and Kristel, but it felt like five years.

At dinner, Mandi didn't show again, and Wendy confirmed that Brock did indeed convince her last night to make up and get back together with him.

What a desperate case Mandi must be! Wendy was quite upset that they were back together, and she wished that *I* would do something about it.

"I don't want to get in the middle of it," I said to Wendy. "Not with Brock."

She wheedled, "Jody, I'm not asking you to sweep her off her feet or rescue her from some villain, although Brock is a jerk." Wendy had a whiny voice, but I could detect the sincerity of her heart.

"No. I can't," I said stubbornly. "Too much has gone on already. Brock's been leaving me alone, and I like it that way."

Wendy crossed her arms in front of her, spun around with a braid-whipping torque, and mumbled something evil about boys as she marched into the dining room with an empty tray.

As ten o'clock approached on that Thursday night, the second of July, according to our plan, Boonie perched himself on the hillside above Route 7, overlooking Lake Marilee. His view included the entire beach deck, part of the sand, and the dock that extended thirty yards out into the dark water. Lights partially illuminated the dock, which looked like a rickety runway ending in a T formation. This was where I would go and wait for the Ambassador.

Boonie sported a pair of binoculars he borrowed from Pete Needleman. "I'll be watching the whole time," he assured me, "in case you need any help."

For three weeks, I had put Jimmy and the Ambassador out of mind, and I wasn't sure if I wanted to let them back in. Especially Jimmy. It was all a mess I wanted cleaned up. The larger part of me hoped the Ambassador would be a prankster, even if it turned out to be Brock.

I took a deep breath and walked down the steps from the lawn towards the highway. Nervous, I crossed the pavement and stopped at the top of the white wooden steps that led down to the beach deck. Focusing my eyes on the end of the dimly lit dock, I didn't see anyone out there yet. I would just go there and wait.

At 9:51 I sat down on the wooden bench at the end of the dock where people usually sit with a fishing pole on quiet evenings like this one. But tonight, no one was there but me. I faced the dark waters and watched the moon slowly rise over the black mountains on the east side of Marilee. Noticing there was no campfire burning over on the Manor, I realized that this was the second day of July—the town ordinance bans visitors to the Manor this month. I wondered when those infamous Lights would show up.

I glanced backwards up the steep hillside of the Club property. Halfway up, among the dark trees, Boonie was watching with a pair of binoculars. I would have waved, but the Ambassador might be watching.

Minutes passed by. The scene was tranquil, but my heart was beating furiously. I noticed the lights of a boat floating out in the water about a half-mile away, and I could hear voices from the direction of the stationary craft. They sounded like older people laughing and having a good time. The air was warm, but I felt cold—almost naked—thinking that I was on a stage with eyes watching me. I was wearing a pair of beige chino shorts and a blue knit shirt. A wave of goose bumps rolled up my thighs.

More minutes passed by. I looked at my watch. 9:56. I glanced backwards again, expecting to see a figure somewhere, either on the beach, up on the large deck, or above on the roadside. But there was nobody. I waited and listened to the laughter of the adults out on the boat. Water lapped lightly under the dock, and to my left I heard the distant sound of a car horn honking in downtown Abbeyville, probably someone pulling out of Burleighs.

Then I heard footsteps on the dock. Someone was coming. Should I turn and look? Shoes clacked on the wood planks. I turned my head and saw a single figure stepping gracefully towards me. Under the dim light, our eyes connected and gripped each other like magnets. It was the unforgettable face of Mandi.

My stomach twisted as I thought about it: Mandi?! *Her*? Mandi?! What does this mean? She authored all those notes? She's the Ambassador? Is this a joke? Is this some plan of hers to meet me? Did she even know Jimmy? Or is she here by coincidence, and the Ambassador is still yet to arrive?

I remained seated as she drew nearer, keeping my eyes locked on hers. They sparkled under the lights, and she wore a shy smile, as though she was embarrassed for being there.

"Are you the Ambassador?" I asked bluntly.

"Yes," she said in her soft, southern voice. The coy smile went away, and an audacious one replaced it.

"You've been writing all those letters?"

"Yes," she said again, blinking slowly. She sat down on the bench next to me, and I noticed she was wearing an oversized tank top that left the side straps of her bra visible under her arms. Her hair was undone from its usual waitress-style ponytail, and her large blonde curls brushed lightly over her nearly bare shoulders. The excess material of her loose fitting tank top mostly covered her very short khaki shorts, and when she sat down she folded one bare leg over the other and clasped her hand on her knee. A white sandal dangled provocatively from her toes. I already knew she was pretty, and now she was sexy. I completely forgot about the round spongy nose that added a homey look to an otherwise glamorous face.

I wasn't sure what to say. My head was full of a million questions.

"So it was you? You knew Jimmy?" I finally asked.

She didn't answer. Her eyes remained locked on mine, and her face slowly leaned forward. Her deliberate motion accelerated, and in an instant her lips pressed onto mine.

I kept my eyes open while she closed hers; I was too shocked to know how to react. I pressed my lips shut, and while my racing hormones shouted for me to open my mouth and close my eyes and let the passion run wild, I somehow resisted. I tried leaning back to lessen the force of her kiss, but if I tipped back any further, I would tumble backwards into the water.

Mandi did her best to make the kiss as passionate as possible, and just before I was about to succumb to the power of those hormones, she withdrew and opened her eyes again. Her stare was seductive and alluring, and I felt my heart racing faster than it ever had before. My flesh yearned for her to repeat the action, but my mind felt like mush.

I was both disappointed and relieved to see her stand to her feet and turn to face the water. Before I could think of anything to say, I watched her step to the edge of the dock. Her hair blocked my view of her face as she stood there silently looking out over the dark water. Should I say something?

My muscles froze as I watched Mandi cross her bare arms in front of her waist, grab the bottom edge of her loose tank-top and pull it up over her head. She dropped the garment on the dock behind her and then casually slipped her shorts down to her ankles. In the swiftest of motions she stepped out of her sandals that were hidden under her ankle high shorts.

Honestly, I'm not making this up.

She stood there with her back towards me, wearing nothing but her white bra and underwear. I was schizophrenic now, hoping that she both would and wouldn't undress any further. My conscience and my flesh were at war. I thought of Kristel: I need her here right now! She would *never* do this.

And that's what kept me right: keeping my mind on Kristel, and not on this girl standing half-naked in front of me. In the strangest of ways, Kristel was right there for me at that moment, serving as my soul's reinforcement brigade.

Mandi suddenly dove headlong into the water with a loud splash. She swam several yards out and turned around to face me—her eyes glowed and her smile stretched from ear to ear.

"C'mon in! The water's so warm!" she said, waving her arms as she treaded water.

I remained seated, dumbfounded and silent. I only shook my head "no" while my mouth hung wide open. I heard Kristel telling me to run, just turn and get out of there, flee like a scared little boy. But I didn't.

Mandi giggled and used a backstroke to glide further out into the water, where the lights from the dock barely stretched. Then she took a breath and tumbled forward underwater, and all was quiet again. She was now somewhere underneath the black surface, presumably swimming out further from the dock. I remained seated, wishing she would get a hold of herself and stop her provocative game. I wondered if we'd ever talk tonight about the Ambassador letters, about Jimmy.

She stayed underwater longer than I expected. Perhaps she was swimming out even deeper and her plan was to pretend she needed me to come out there and rescue her. I wondered if I would.

Suddenly, she burst out of the water behind me, grabbed my shirt at its collar and pulled me backwards down into the water with her.

The splash and submersion doused what was left of my raging hormones, and my only thought now was to get away from her. Mandi popped her head out of the water next to me with a devilish grin, and despite her glimmering wet eyes, her smooth, wet hair, and the soaked straps of her bra on her shoulders, she no longer looked beautiful to me. Now she was a menace.

"Isn't the water great," she crooned seductively, waving her arms at her side to keep afloat.

I didn't answer. I reached my hands down to my feet and pulled off my Docksiders. "Look what you did to my shoes! These are leather," I retorted. Honestly, I could have cared less about getting my shoes wet. I just needed to find something to object to.

Mandi playfully slithered forward and grabbed the wet shoes from my hands. She tossed them above my head and they landed on the dock behind me with two thumps.

I paddled around to the front end of the dock where the stepladder was. Mandi followed, not stopping at the steps, but swimming further out. When she saw me climbing out, she cried, "Don't get out now. You're wet. You might as well swim for a while."

"I'd rather not," I said, knowing we would never get around to talking about Jimmy until much later, if at all. I climbed up to the dock and glared at her, twisting the front of my shirt to wring the water out of it.

Mandi swam toward the steps and grabbed each side of the ladder railing with her hands. She was directly underneath me, staring up at me with pleading eyes. "Come back in. Please!"

I stared down at her, knowing full well that if she pulled her body up the ladder any further, I'd catch an eyeful. I backed away and sat down on the bench and said nothing.

Mandi took one step up the ladder so she could see my face, her body blocked from the neck down. We both knew that a wet bra and underpants did not function like a bathing suit.

"If you don't want to swim with me, can you give me my shirt please?" she said dejectedly.

Thankful she had finally decided to be decent now. I reached down and tossed her shirt at her, but she didn't let go of the railing to grab it, and the garment hit her in the face and tumbled down her front and into the water.

"Now my shirt's wet!" she whined, sounding more amused than upset. "And I don't have a towel."

I was livid. "Well, if you had kept your clothes on and stayed out of the water, you wouldn't be stuck there dripping wet in your underwear!" I shocked myself with my own frankness, but I thought she deserved it.

Mandi reached down in the water and tossed the soaking wet shirt to the dock. It certainly wouldn't serve well as a body covering now.

"You'll have to let me use your shirt," she said, holding onto the railing.

I considered leaving her there, stripped-down and soaking wet with nothing to cover her. But I knew that if I left, she might just up and follow me, and I didn't want to be seen walking up the hill with a soaked, half-naked, tenacious young woman trying to hide behind me. So I pulled off my drenched shirt and tossed it at her.

This time she let go of the railing with one hand and grabbed the heavy garment before it fell.

I picked up my wet Docksiders and began walking away.

"Wait a minute," she said. "I need to talk to you."

I stopped and turned around, seeing her sink back down into the water to wrestle herself into my shirt. Finally, she climbed up to the dock, dripping, but now covered from shoulder to thighs in my drenched blue T-shirt.

I stood an arm's length in front of her, shirtless, in dripping wet chinos. "Why did you want to meet me down here?" I asked in a disgruntled voice.

She said nothing.

I was about to demand an answer but was prevented by the sound of a boat's motor approaching from the lake. We watched the lights of a pontoon boat glide closer, the treble of its motor deepening as the craft slowed down to dock.

I was trying to determine who the passengers were. But suddenly, Mandi embraced me and locked her arms around my midsection. In one swift motion she pushed me sideways and we both fell into the water again with a splash.

We each bobbed out of the water at the end of the T-shaped dock as the pontoon boat glided toward us. The boat decelerated, approaching the dock, and I raised my arms out of the water to signal the driver that we were in the way.

As the craft glided into the glimmer of the dock lamps, I didn't recognize the driver, a tall man in a sports jacket. There were four other adults standing at the railing of the boat, staring at Mandi and me in the water. A young, unfamiliar lady had one hand on the driver's shoulder. The third person was Brock Oliff, and I assumed the driver and the lady were his parents.

Then I recognized the other two riders: George and Beverly Schuple, each staring in disbelief when they saw the moonlight swimmers.

Brock looked at me with a devilish, crooked grin, as if he wasn't surprised at all to see me and Mandi in the water at the end of the dock.

The craft glided in idle as Branson Oliff maneuvered it sideways, parallel to the T-end of the dock, about twenty feet away from us. Mandi and I bobbed up and down in the now choppy water, staring abashed at the riders on the craft.

George Schuple gripped the boat's railing with both hands. His wife covered her lips with three fingers, wearing a look of horror.

I stared at my onlookers, speechless. Mandi, having forced me into the water twice now, bobbed behind me.

"What in heaven's name?" George Schuple blurted, staring wide-eyed at Mandi and then at me.

The expression on Brock's face was puzzling. I expected him to be raging with anger to find me swimming in the lake with his girlfriend. But he was grinning, shifting his eyes back and forth between me and Mandi, as if he was tickled with what he saw.

I turned around to look at Mandi. There was something different about her. That seductive facial expression was gone, replaced by a different one I didn't understand at first.

"Oh, I'm so embarrassed," Mrs. Schuple cried. "Branson and Peggy, we're so sorry that you have to see this."

Suddenly, it occurred to me what was different about Mandi. I looked back at her again, and sure enough, her shoulders were completely bare. I saw my blue T-shirt sitting in a wet pile on the edge of the dock above her. On top of it was a pile of wet, white material.

Mandi was treading water five feet away from me, her naked body concealed from her shoulders down by nothing but the dark lake water. Branson and Peggy Oliff looked on with puzzled faces. George and Beverly Schuple were sickened.

Brock stared at us with a fiendish grin, and I realized that I had been set up.

# CHAPTER 21

## *A Desperate Case of Proving the Unseen*

The first thing I could do was show was that *I* wasn't naked, so I swam to the ladder and hoisted myself up the steps. Beverly Schuple gasped when I lunged out of the water, fearing she'd see my nude rear end, but instead she saw a soaking wet pair of tan chino shorts. She and the other adults on the pontoon boat all breathed a sigh of relief.

"Jody," George Schuple commanded in a stern, deep voice. "Go up to the bathhouse and get a towel for this young lady."

"Yes sir," I said, jogging down the dock in my bare feet.

I considered lashing out at Mandi and Brock when I returned, right there in front of everybody. I knew they planned the whole scene, but no one would believe anything I had to say during this precarious moment. I would have to explain it all later to Mr. Schuple. But I knew one thing: I had Boonie watching the whole episode with the binoculars, and he would be my witness.

I returned to the end of the dock with two towels. Branson Oliff had maneuvered the boat alongside the dock and Mandi remained in the water at the bow of the boat. I handed the towels to Mr. Schuple who gave me a crossed glare.

"I think it's best if you head on back to your cabin," Mr. Schuple said loudly, no doubt so everyone present could hear his directive. "I'll speak with you later."

Brock was smirking as though he has just pulled off the greatest of stunts. I grabbed my shoes and was about to pick up my wet shirt when I noticed Mandi's wet undergarments sitting on top of it, so I just left the shirt behind. I walked briskly down the dock, jogged up the steps towards the road, and went into a full sprint across the highway and up the driveway of the Brown Swan Club. I ran all the way to Saranac, not bothering to stop and check with Boonie on the hillside.

I had never been so angry with any one person as I was then, including my parents, and I actually envisioned myself grabbing Brock Oliff around the neck and strangling him.

The thought of Mandi conspiring with Brock enraged me even more. Is she really that wicked? Or did Brock coerce her into the evil, whorish deed? I hoped I would never see the face of Mandi again. As for Brock, I yearned for a chance at revenge.

I ran into Saranac and slammed the door, my body almost dry by now, except for sweat beading at my brow. After stripping off my shorts and changing into boxers, I pounced backwards onto my bunk and stared up at Rodney's mattress.

They had planned it perfectly. Brock lingered close by out on the boat with the adults, knowing full well what Mandi was doing at the end of the dock with me. Mandi manipulated me into the water (she forced me actually), conned my shirt off my back, and stripped down when the boat approached. I had been framed!

Beautiful Mandi, nothing but a slut, working for Brock like he's her pimp! And all the letters—they were nothing but a cruel joke! Whether Brock had anything to do with Jimmy's death or not—I now considered him the embodiment of deceit.

I slammed the wall next to my bunk with my fist, causing Rodney's framed autographed picture of Pamela Lee to fall to the floor and shatter.

About ten minutes later, Boonie barged into the cabin with eyes as wide and white as golf balls, holding the binoculars in his hands.

"Did you die and go to heaven, or what?" he sang, grinning with a wide-open mouth.

I sat up in my bunk. "What? Didn't you see what happened?"

"I saw enough!" he said, still grinning. "But then a minute ago I saw you streaking by the Club building. What'd she do? Scare you away?"

"What were you doing at the Club building?! You were supposed to be watching me!"

"I was. But when I saw Mandi strip down in front of you, I put the binoculars down and went up to the porch and sat with Jennifer and Wendy. I didn't want to be a peeping Tom."

I was furious. "What?! You didn't see what just happened?!"

Boonie was still smirking. "I saw her pull her shirt off, and at that point I said to myself, 'I can't spy on my friend while he skinny dips with that babe.'"

I clutched my head with both of my hands. "Oh, God, I can't believe this."

"What? What'd she do?"

"Like it matters now! You were supposed to be my eye witness!"

"What happened?"

"I was framed! It was all a trap! Brock and Mandi set it all up!"

"What?"

"Brock, his parents, and Kristel's parents were out on the lake in a pontoon boat, and they drove to the dock when Mandi and I were there."

"They found you skinny dipping?" Boonie's eyes nearly bulged out of their sockets.

I growled through clenched teeth, "I wasn't skinny dipping! The whole thing was planned by Brock and Mandi to make it look like we were. But I wasn't. I had my shorts on the whole time."

"Was *she* naked?" Boonie tried to suppress a smile, but he failed. He thought this whole thing was funny.

"Eventually she was! But I didn't know it until the Oliffs and the Schuples discovered us. I turned around and she had stripped everything off after she saw the boat coming. And that's just it—she *wanted* to get caught naked with me!"

"Did you see her?"

"God, Boonie! Is that all you can think about? I was framed! And I didn't see her! I gave her my blue shirt to wear so she could cover up. I didn't want to be there with her like that! I thought she was crazy! I'm completely innocent! She stripped everything off when they showed up!"

Boonie was a little more serious now. "Man, what did Mr. Schuple say?"

"Not much. He ordered me to get a towel for Mandi. Mrs. Schuple was in shock. Mr. and Mrs. Oliff just looked embarrassed. And Brock was grinning from ear to ear. Mandi had done her job, and Brock looked pleased."

"I can't believe she did that! I was surprised when I saw her kiss you, and then when she started stripping—man, I didn't know she was like that."

"Or you would've hit on her first, huh?"

"Hey man, I don't play on easy street. I just can't believe Mandi is like that. She seems so innocent."

"That's what I thought. But before I knew better, she was kissing me and swimming half-naked, and then she actually pulled me into the water—twice! I almost got out of there before the boat arrived. I had given her my shirt because she let her own shirt fall in the water. She had nothing left to cover up with, and she put mine on before getting out of the water. Then we heard the boat coming and she grabbed me and pulled us both into the water again. And by the time the boat came in and I saw who was in it, she had stripped everything off and was completely naked next to me."

After I precisely recounted the incident, I shook my head and pounded my fist into the mattress. "And you would have been my witness! Do you think anyone's going to believe me now?"

"I don't know," Boonie said, not smiling anymore. "All you can do is either tell the truth or come up with a really good lie."

"What do you think will happen to me?"

"Don't know."

"Look at what happened to Donnie Lisko. You think Mr. Schuple will fire me?"

"Possibly. But Lisko was actually caught in the act. At least you had your pants on."

At that moment Pete and Rodney stormed into the cabin.

"Hey, Jody!" Pete roared. "We heard you got caught skinny dipping with Mandi Winters! Dude, I can't believe you! You're such a stud!" Rodney stood next to him with a dumb grin, not yet noticing his framed picture of Pamela Lee busted on the floor.

"Who told you that?" I asked.

"One of the guys in the band just told us. You actually saw her naked?!"

A look of disgust crossed my face as I groaned, "Brock! I can't believe this!" I stormed outside, slamming the door behind me. I heard Boonie tell Pete and Rodney to shut up about the whole thing before he walked outside after me.

He and I sat on the porch steps and discussed what happened. All the letters, the setup, and now the lies being spread by Brock and his guys. I couldn't believe what was happening to me. It was the most humiliating moment of my life.

The Needleman twins left the cabin, and when they got halfway up the hill, I could hear them talk about the skinny-dipping story to another group of kids. Pete just couldn't shut up about it.

I was getting cold sitting on the porch steps, wearing only a pair of boxer shorts, but I didn't feel like going back in the cabin. I expected Mr. Schuple to come down to the grove at any time to fire me.

We sat out there for almost an hour, talking and watching other staff members periodically enter their cabins. Schuple never showed.

Eventually, Whisper emerged from Hawkeye, his cabin door rattling shut behind him. It was the first time I had seen the old man since visiting him in his cabin two days ago. It was just a little past eleven o'clock, a little early for his midnight shift.

Whisper unplugged his golf cart, tossed the electric wire over the porch railing in front of his cabin and boarded his vehicle. The cart whirred toward us and Whisper hit the brakes when he noticed Boonie and me out in front of Saranac. He stayed in his cart and looked at us, saying nothing.

I rose and walked over to him, leaving Boonie behind on the steps.

"Hi," I greeted him. "I stopped to see you yesterday, but you weren't in."

Whisper gargled, "Yes, my grandkids made a surprise visit. Been spending the afternoons with them."

"That's nice. Bet you haven't got much sleep during the day then."

"Ah, I get caught up easy enough. Couple hours in the morning, couple in the evening. Just woke up from a nap as a matter of fact. I can give you a carving lesson anytime. You name the time."

I suspected that Boonie couldn't hear what we were talking about because of Whisper's soft voice, so I kept mine low as well. Although it was obvious that I was acquainted with the old man, I still didn't want anyone to know I had actually been in his hovel or that I had planned to learn the craft of woodcarving from the strange night watchman.

I told him, "I don't know if I'm even going to be around much longer."

"Eh?" The concern on Whisper's face was comforting.

"I kinda got into trouble tonight. A lot of trouble, actually."

"Trouble with a gal?"

"Yeah, you could say that. How'd you guess?"

"Oh, I've seen young men get into trouble over pretty, young gals before."

I quickly added, "It wasn't Kristel, she's not even here."

"I know it mustn't be Kristel. She's not the kind of gal that causes trouble for a guy—even if she keeps him up late at night." The corner of Whisper's mouth twitched a slight smile.

"Yeah, well, Kristel's parents are pretty ticked at me right now."

"Well, I'm sure the best'll work out for you. The truth always will prevail."

"Thanks."

Whisper whirred away on his cart, out of the grove and beyond the ball field. I felt encouraged by the old man.

By now I figured it was too late for Mr. Schuple to come speak with me tonight, so I followed Boonie into the cabin and went to bed.

We must have been asleep for about twenty minutes when Pete and Rodney barged in and flipped the light on.

"Hey guys! Guys! The Lights are out! The Lights of Marilee are out! Boonie, where are my binoculars?"

Boonie squinted and sat up. The binoculars were sitting under his bed.

"C'mon guys!" Pete continued, "You've got to see them! The whole staff is headed down there."

Pete grabbed the binoculars and he and Rodney bolted out the door.

Boonie asked, "You comin'?"

"No," I groaned, too tired, and too embarrassed to go back down to the Club beach. I rolled back over in my bunk and noted the time on my clock, 11:52.

I heard Boonie get dressed and leave the cabin, flipping off the florescent lights as he left.

The next morning was the first time I had been in Schuple's office since the day I arrived at the Brown Swan Club. Then, we had talked about starting my job. Now, we would discuss terminating it.

"Have a seat," Schuple said, motioning to one of the twin leather cushioned chairs in front of his desk. He lumbered around to the other side of his desk and sat down in a swivel high-backed chair. The chair squeaked as he perched himself on the front edge of it and rested his elbows on the mahogany desk.

It was nine-thirty Friday morning, less than twelve hours after Schuple discovered me swimming next to a naked girl in the lake. His face was plastered with anxiety as he began speaking. "Branson and Peggy Oliff have insisted that an apology from you and Miss Winters isn't necessary."

"I'm sorry, Mr. Schuple," I said with a tone of desperation.

"I don't doubt that you are, after being caught in that situation. I'm surprised at you, Jody. In fact, I'm shocked."

"I can explain everything," I countered in a pleading voice. Mr. Schuple didn't seem to listen.

"Let me say I never expected this out of you. Someone else—yes, I've dealt with things worse than this before."

The telephone on Schuple's desk chirped loudly. "Excuse me, one minute," he said as he picked up the receiver.

Before entering the office, I had decided to tell the truth to Mr. Schuple.

I planned to describe how the whole thing was a set up. I would tell about the mysterious Ambassador letters I had been receiving, and I would explain Brock's motive for pulling such a prank. But one thing I knew I would never tell Mr. Schuple, even if it left a gaping whole in my story, was the suspicion Kristel and I shared about Brock's involvement with Jimmy's death. I wouldn't and couldn't betray Kristel's trust to save my job. I hoped I wouldn't have to go that far to explain my story.

Mr. Schuple hung up the phone and resumed speaking to me as if there were no interruption.

"I'm going to get right to the point, Jody. I met with Miss Winters first thing this morning. I explained to her the strict code of conduct that our staff is expected to follow, and because she violated that code, it was necessary for me to terminate her employment here at the Club. It hurts me to say this, son, but I'm afraid we're going to have to deal with you in the same manner."

"Mr. Schuple, I can explain!" I sat up straight in my chair, both of my hands gripping the armrest.

"I think I heard enough about it from Miss Winters. I'd rather not hear the embarrassing details all over again."

"But I was framed! It was all a set up! I'm completely innocent of everything!"

"What?"

"I was set up!"

"Are trying to tell me that you're innocent of skinny dipping because she *seduced* you?"

"No! I was framed!" I nearly shouted my response. Quickly, I regained composure and toned down my voice. "I didn't do anything wrong. I'm completely innocent. My shorts were on, remember?"

"Yes, but Mandi, uh, Miss Winters said you put them back on when you saw us approaching in the pontoon boat."

"She's lying. I don't know what story she told you this morning, Mr. Schuple. But I'll bet my life that it's all a lie."

Schuple leaned back in his chair, forcing a loud creak in its springs. He rubbed his forehead, sighed heavily, and rested his hands on his lap. "Then go ahead and tell me your version of the incident," he said. "And, son, this better be the truth."

I told everything. The Ambassador letters. The police station. The confrontations with Brock, including the flat tires, black eye, Tabasco sauce, yellow food coloring, and the fight in the pool. I described Mandi eyeballing me in the kitchen, and the rumors that she had broken up with Brock and that they got back together soon after. I recounted in detail her meeting me at the end of the dock last night, her forceful kiss, her stripping down, and her twice pulling me into the water. Then I described the look of pleasure on Brock's face when I would have expected one of anger when he saw Mandi with me in the water.

In about twenty-five minutes, I covered just about everything, leaving out Brock's drunken antics at Marilee Manor and my shared suspicion with Kristel that Brock may be involved in the death of my brother. I felt my story was sufficient and truthful enough without those parts.

Schuple soaked it all in, and afterwards he thought silently for several moments. He closed his eyes, rubbed his forehead, and exhaled an enormous sigh.

"I must say, Jody, that I hope your story is true. Obviously, however, someone is lying—either you, Miss Winters, or both of you."

"I'm telling the *truth,* Mr. Schuple." I thought of Kristel. My story *was* true, even if no one believed it.

"And you've been going to Sheriff Slater with the letters everyday?"

"Yes," I replied in a hopeful tone. "Well, I haven't actually met Sheriff Slater. I've been delivering them to Officer Anders who has been working at the office every day because he's got an injured leg."

"And you think Brock and Miss Winters have been writing those letters?"

"That's my guess. I had strongly suspected it was all Brock's doing. I was surprised to find out that Mandi was involved."

"And you're saying this whole scheme is Brock's way of revenge?"

"I think so."

"For your befriending Kristel?"

"That, and the prank with the food coloring. And I'm sure he heard about everyone trying to get Mandi and me together."

I sensed Schuple was considering my story carefully. "Mmm. Brock was very insistent last night that we drop him off at the Club dock at a quarter past ten."

At that auspicious moment the office door opened without a knock and the contorted face of Mrs. Schuple poked in. She glared at me disgustedly, flaring her nostrils. "George, I need to speak with you," she said sharply. "This is urgent!" Without waiting for a response, she pulled her face back out and shut the door again.

I noticed a twitch in Schuple's stoic eyes, as though he wanted to roll them in a sarcastic response to his wife's sudden entry, demand, and departure.

"Excuse me, again, Jody. I'll just be a moment."

He walked to the door and opened it. I saw Mrs. Schuple waiting just outside the office with her arms crossed and her lips pressed together in a firm frown. Her husband stepped out and shut the door behind him, leaving me in the office alone.

Fifteen minutes passed before Mr. Schuple came back in. He closed the door and stood by it, choosing not to return to his chair. I had to turn around to face him as he spoke.

"An unfortunate incident has just occurred, Jody. I will have to delay my inquiry into the events of last night for the time being. My wife has just informed me that Brock Oliff is on the way to the hospital in Lake Henry. Apparently, he tried to kill himself this morning."

# CHAPTER 22

## *Aftershocks, Un-solving a Mystery, and Re-solving It Again*

The rest of that morning was spent in Saranac on Rodney's PlayStation. It was my half-day and I was not scheduled to work until 4:00 p.m., so there was plenty of time to wait and hear whether I was fired or not.

Mr. Schuple was, no doubt, preoccupied with the news about Brock. I hoped that once he had time to consider my story, the truth would save me.

The truth… the absolute truth which *did* exist. Kristel was right—absolute truth exists no matter how we see it. It's our job to discover it and know it and believe it. Schuple had to believe the truth in this case, or I'd be gone.

I tried reading more of *Gatsby*, but there was too much on my mind, so I went back to the video games.

Brock attempted suicide this morning. It was hard to believe. Just twelve hours ago he was laughing at me from his father's pontoon boat. What happened? What a turn of events in one night! Why did he do it? What was he thinking?

The news had already spread throughout the kitchen by the time I went to the staff dining room for lunch.

"Suicide attempt." "Brock Oliff." The words were mumbled across the room. "Typical of a spoiled rich kid," someone said. "He was probably high on crack," quipped another. I overheard Pete Needleman claiming that Brock wanted to kill himself after discovering his girlfriend skinny-dipping with Jody Barrett.

I was sick of the talk and went straight back to Saranac without eating to escape to the video games and await Mr. Schuple's decision.

Boonie came down to see me during his lunch break. "So how'd it go with Schuple?" he asked.

I stared at the animated racecar I was controlling on the TV screen. "I guess it went okay," I answered. "I was explaining to him my story when the news broke about Brock. He said he'd get back with me."

"Does he believe you?"

"I hope so. Mandi gave him a completely different story earlier this morning. I don't know everything she said, but Mr. Schuple was shocked when I tried to tell him I was framed."

"So are you fired or not?"

"I don't know. I am if Mrs. Schuple has her way. You should have seen the look she gave me this morning."

"Did you hear that Mandi's outta here?"

"Yeah. Schuple told me. He was just about to do the same to me when I told him the truth about being framed. Then the news about Brock came down."

Boonie nodded, stepped next to the TV where I could see him, and scratched the back of his neck. I could tell he had something important to say.

"Jody, while you were in his office, I was talking with Wendy in the kitchen. This was before the news about Brock came out." He stopped, winced, then continued. "You know them Ambassador letters? Wendy said that neither Mandi or Brock had anything to do with them."

This couldn't be true. I shook my head in disagreement. "What makes her say that? Mandi herself told me she was the one. And how does Wendy even know about the letters?"

Boonie shamefully confessed. "Well, you know that night you came down to join us at Burleighs?" he said, fiddling with the knot in the string of his apron.

"Yeah." I set down the controller and crossed my arms in front of my chest.

"Before you got there, Jennifer, Wendy, and I were talking about Mandi and how we could get her set up with you before Kristel gets back. Well, I kind of let it slip that you've been getting anonymous notes from someone."

"You're kidding."

"No… but I didn't say anything about what the letters were about. I didn't say anything about Jimmy. In fact, I was stretching the truth to make the girls think the letters were love notes from someone. You know—like you and I talked about how they might be from some secret admirer of yours. But I never let on that they had anything to do with Jimmy. Nobody knows about that but me, you, and Kristel."

"But last night I asked Mandi if she was the Ambassador and she said yes."

"Well, I did tell them that the letters were signed 'the Ambassador of Love.'"

I groaned, and Boonie went on. "Honestly, Jody. All I told the girls was that you're getting these notes and that the latest one asked you to be at the dock last night. Well, you know Wendy. She goes off tells Mandi about it. Wendy told her she ought to get there early before the real secret admirer shows up. Honestly, Jody. I didn't know it would be Mandi there last night. That was all her and Wendy's doing. Wendy just told me all this at breakfast this morning."

"So Mandi never knew about the letters until Wendy told her about them on Wednesday night?"

"Yep. And that was the same night that Brock came to her room and took her out so late. Remember—she missed work yesterday. That's when Brock and Mandi made up."

"So she and Brock must have talked about me getting the letters, and then they came up with a plan to frame me?"

"Well, there's more. Mandi spilled her guts to Wendy this morning after Schuple fired her. Mandi told her that when she was out with Brock so late Wednesday night, Brock told her he loved her and couldn't live without her and all that kind of crap. So she fell for Brock again and said she'd do anything for him.

"So Brock tells her how bad he wants to get back at you for accusing him of vandalizing your car, and for the food coloring and Kristel and all that. And then Mandi also tells Brock how we were trying to get her and you together. So Brock gets jealous and wants Mandi to prove that she's got nothing for you and that she's devoted fully to him. So then Mandi says she'll do anything to prove it and she tells him how you're expecting to meet an admirer at the dock. And that's how they came up with the plan to frame you."

"Didn't Mandi care that she'd get in trouble for what she did?"

"Nope. Brock promised her that if she did it and got fired for it, she could live at his house the rest of the summer and drive his Porsche around town. So Mandi bought into his bait."

"But then Brock goes and tries to kill himself this morning. What happened?"

"Well, Wendy said that Mandi dumped Brock again late last night after the skinny-dipping. That's probably why Brock went off his rocker. But who knows? It's all pretty crazy."

"No kidding."

I thought for a minute.

"So you're telling me that Wendy knows for sure that Brock and Mandi planned their whole scheme just two nights ago?"

"Yep. Wednesday night, after we were at Burleighs and after I told them you were getting letters from the Ambassador of Love."

"Neither of them knew anything about the letters before then?"

"Nope."

"So there's still no explanation for the Ambassador letters. The Ambassador is still out there."

"That's the way it looks. And we know at least who the Ambassador is not. It's not Mandi, and it's not Brock. The only reason Brock knew anything about the letters is because I told Wendy you've been getting them. Wendy goes and blabs to Mandi, and Mandi tells Brock. But nobody knows what those letters are really about except for you, me, Kristel, and the police."

"And whoever the Ambassador is," I added, shaking my head in disbelief over all that I had just heard. The once-solved Ambassador mystery was now unsolved.

I pondered, "So when Mandi showed up at the dock, the real Ambassador probably didn't come out. He's still out there."

Boonie could tell I was ticked at him. "I'm sorry, Jody. I had no idea all this would happen. I should have kept my mouth shut."

I accepted Boonie's apology before he went back to the kitchen, but I was doubtful how much I could trust him anymore.

I was sick of hiding out in the cabin, plus I was hungry, so I hopped in my Mustang and drove off the property, stopping first at the deli in Abbeyville for a sub sandwich and a bottle of Minute Maid soda. I consumed each at a picnic table down at the town beach. Afterwards, I drove three miles north of town to the Huron County Police Station.

Officer Anders was in his usual spot behind the desk.

"Jody, I'm glad to see you. I was going to try to contact you this morning," he announced eagerly as I entered the station. "Did you hear about Brock Oliff?"

"Yeah, and rumor has it that I'm partially to blame."

"I was just going to call you to see if you could shed any light on it."

"I might know some things," I said. "Have you heard how he's doing?"

"Well, I heard through our dispatcher that Brock didn't try very hard if he was intending to kill himself. He cut one wrist with a razor blade, deep enough to draw blood, but not deep enough to do any major harm. His father walked in on him and flipped out—called 911 and the whole bit. Brock was fully conscious when they brought him to the hospital this morning. He was treated at the emergency room and released with two stitches."

"That's it?" I said. "Word around the Club is that he was found on the brink of death on the floor this morning in a pool of blood."

"Well, you know how rumors fly."

"I know first hand," I said with a tone of sarcasm.

"Just two stitches took care of it," Anders continued. "But he's required to go to the mental health center in Lake Henry for an evaluation. Standard procedure."

I sat down in the familiar chair next to the desk.

"So you might know something about what led up to it?" Anders inquired.

"Maybe. You know—he and I have had some run-ins."

The officer slapped his desk lightly with his palm. "Hey, I almost forgot. How did your meeting turn out? Did you meet the Ambassador?"

"I thought I did. But now I'm clueless."

I went on to explain the entire story of Mandi's arrival at the dock and getting caught in the water by the Schuples and Oliffs, including Brock. I then explained the events that transpired this morning—my meeting with Schuple, the news of Brock, all the rumors, and then Boonie's explanation of what Wendy had told him—that Brock and Mandi had nothing whatsoever to do with the letters except capitalizing on the opportunity to frame me at the dock.

Anders listened carefully and even took notes on a legal pad. I was glad to see him do it. It meant someone important was taking me seriously. Someone cared about my side of the story.

The officer studied his notes and said, "So then it's possible that whoever the Ambassador is might have seen you at the dock with Mandi, and because you weren't alone, he or she decided to leave."

"Mm hmm. Like I said, I still have no idea who the Ambassador is. Last night I thought I did, but Boonie's conversation with Wendy unsolved the mystery."

"Did Boonie see anyone around—on the road, near the beach, anywhere?"

"He said he stopped watching when Mandi, you know, took her shirt off. He said he didn't want to be a peeping Tom."

"Not many American males would stop watching a scene like that."

"Well, Boonie's seen his share. Believe me."

We both chuckled briefly before Anders asked, "Have you received any more letters? Since the last one you got on Wednesday?"

"Since the one inviting me to the dock? No. Nothing came yesterday. I haven't checked yet today."

"You might start getting more."

"Maybe, if the Ambassador isn't too upset at me for not being alone on the dock."

"I'll bet you'll start getting more letters any day now."

"In a way, I hope you're right. But I also wish it would all just go away."

"But then you'll never know who's writing them, or more importantly—*why* they're writing them."

I sat up in my chair. "Do you think that this Ambassador person actually knows something about the death of my brother? Do you really think it could have been a murder?"

"You never know. Investigations involve anonymous tips all the time from crazy wackos who just want to stir up trouble. In this case, the Ambassador is either one of those wackos, a secret admirer, or he or she could actually be someone who knows something about Jimmy's death. The same could be said for the John Doe letter. So don't give up on it, Jody. Keep us updated."

"I will. But I wish it would just all go away. It's pretty annoying. Have you heard anything more from Sheriff Slater?"

"Nothing new."

After a silent moment, Anders hopped to his feet and slapped his right thigh. "Doc says I can go back on regular duty starting Monday. So next time you come in, I might not be here."

"Then I'll actually get to meet the Sheriff?"

"Either him or his sister-in-law who fills in here at the desk. My bum leg has kept her out of work for six weeks now. Hey, you might be able to catch him tonight. He'll be a the Brown Swan Club this evening."

"What for?"

"The Lights appeared last night for the first time this season. Usually that draws a big crowd the following night. The Sheriff will be there at the beach just to keep an eye on things."

"I missed them last night. I was already asleep." I rose and headed for the door. "I have to get to work pretty soon, that is, if I still have a job."

Anders smiled. "Good luck. Let me know what happens."

Here we go again.

Upon returning to the Club, I found one piece of mail waiting for me in the staff lounge—the all-too-familiar envelope with my name printed in large capital letters. Same old handwriting. Same old black ink pen. I shook my head and took a breath before I read it. This message was much longer than any of the others.

DEAR JODY,

I ASKED YOU TO BE ALONE AND YOU WEREN'T. DON'T WORRY, I FORGIVE YOU, AND SO WILL GEORGE SCHUPLE. MEET ME IN THE PRODUCE AISLE AT THE SUPERMARKET SATURDAY NIGHT AT 7:00 P.M. SHARP. YOUR WORK SCHEDULE HAS BEEN CHANGED. BRING KRISTEL WITH YOU THIS TIME, AND DON'T TELL ANYONE ABOUT THIS LETTER EXCEPT FOR BOONIE. I'LL SEE YOU THEN.

AN AMBASSADOR FOR THE DEAD.

Like the last letter, I read this one repeatedly until I almost knew it by heart. The words kept my mind spinning for hours.

The fascinating aspect of this letter was all the extra information it included—mentioning the names of Kristel and Boonie, and that George Schuple would forgive me, and that my work schedule had been changed.

And something else was interesting. Unlike all the others, this letter had no stamp or postmark. It had been hand delivered to my box today.

The first thing I did was go to the kitchen and check the work schedule. Yes, Chef Al had changed my split shift for tomorrow to a breakfast-lunch shift. Saturday was Boonie's day off and Chef Al needed me to cover lunch. The same for Sunday too. Monday through Wednesday I'd work a split. Thursday remained my day off, and Friday a half day.

Somehow, the Ambassador knew about the work schedule changes before I did. The Ambassador also knew Schuple was going to forgive me for the skinny-dipping incident.

I immediately showed the letter to Boonie at the front line, and he joked that Mandi might show up at the produce aisle half naked. I didn't think he was funny, but we didn't have the chance to discuss all the implications of the letter because there were too many people in the kitchen.

Minutes later, Schuple stopped me as I was passing through the dining room.

"Mr. Barrett," he said, placing his hand on my shoulder and leading me to a corner to converse with me privately. "I'm need some time to work on your situation. Miss Winters is staying with a friend in town, and I will meet with her again tomorrow. I may have to meet with the both of you together. Until then, please continue to do your work as Chef Al needs you, and please—stay out of trouble, son."

"Yes, sir."

"I'll get back with you as soon as I can," he said sternly, but kindly.

I felt relieved, yet I was amazed at how this conversation was a near-fulfillment of the Ambassador's prophecy. The Ambassador is someone close by, someone who knows about things around here.

I wanted to call Officer Anders, but the letter said not to tell anyone about its contents except for Kristel or Boonie. I read the note over and over again, *I asked you to be alone and you weren't. Don't worry, I forgive you and so will George Schuple. Meet me in the produce aisle at the supermarket Saturday night at 7:00 p.m. sharp. Your work schedule has been changed. Bring Kristel with you this time, and don't tell anyone about this letter except for Boonie. I'll see you then.*

There was so much that this letter revealed, and I wanted to tell Officer Anders about it so badly. But I wanted to follow its instructions precisely. There was the fact that the Ambassador knew Mr. Schuple would not fire me even though he hasn't made a decision yet. There was the missing postmark, meaning the letter was hand-delivered to my box. There was the fact that the Ambassador knew that I've been sharing all the letters with Boonie and Kristel. The Ambassador also knew that Kristel would be back from camp in time to join me at the supermarket Saturday night.

Also, there was the sense that the Ambassador knew I was familiar with the produce aisle at the supermarket. I had been there only once, when Brock tossed ice at Boonie and me. That was my first day in the Adirondacks, just moments before a near fight with Brock at the dead-end road near the lake. Why does he want to meet at the supermarket?

With everything considered, I could not ignore the evidence shouting out that the Ambassador was someone who had been watching me closely every day. I determined it must be a staff member who is very familiar with me and my friends. All the previous letters never revealed such familiarity. They were distant and I thought they could have been written by anybody—a local, a guest, anyone. But now I was convinced that the person I will hopefully meet on Saturday night is someone I already know, and know well.

Who could it be?

Boonie and I talked it over during dinner. I made him swear by his life that he wouldn't say a word to anyone this time, and that he should keep his distance from the supermarket tomorrow.

Tomorrow was Saturday! I could hardly wait! Not only would I finally—hopefully—meet the Ambassador, but Kristel will be back!

In light of Brock, and in light of Mandi, I tried to keep a low profile after work that night, so I hung out by the fireplace in the lobby reading *Gatsby*. The rumors about my supposed skinny-dipping episode with Brock's girlfriend were common news, no thanks to Pete Needleman, who loved telling the story as he imagined it. Boonie promised to do his best to counteract the rumors, but I believed my vindication was dependent on Mr. Schuple's meeting with Mandi again. If the truth prevailed, then Mandi would be fired and I wouldn't be. Unbelievably, it was the prophetic letter from the Ambassador that gave me the greatest hope that Mr. Schuple would make the right decision.

Then it hit me.

All at once, I knew who the Ambassador was: he's Whisper. That's it! Whisper is the Ambassador! It all made perfect sense!

How could I have been so stupid?

Why I had never seriously considered him, I don't know, but he was the best and obvious candidate: Whisper knew me personally—he had seen me almost every night of the summer; he had the ability to check my work schedule; and he's the hermit type who would resort to writing such letters. *It has to be him!*

All at once, the Ambassador for the Dead came alive to me. I wanted to go back to Officer Anders and look over all the letters again and read them through Whisper's eyes.

Whisper has been sending me those letters! He knows something about Jimmy, about his death, and maybe about Brock. A guy like Whisper would know stuff like this!

As quickly as the Ambassador came alive, Jimmy came alive, too. Maybe, as his brother, I *can* do something for him. Maybe I *can* solve the supposed mystery of his death. Maybe he *is* crying out from his grave through the person of Whisper.

I thought it over more and more, and my curiosity overcame me. I decided to go straight to Whisper's cabin and confront him. Forget this Saturday night in the supermarket stuff.

I scampered down to the cabin grove and knocked on the door of Hawkeye, causing the loud rattle. Again, no answer. It was after nine o'clock. He was probably napping before his midnight shift. The door was still unlocked, and again I peeked inside. No sign of him. Everything looked the same as I had seen it three days ago.

Still curious, I stepped completely into the cabin, shut the door behind me, and flipped on the overhead lights. I thought maybe I'd find a box of manila envelopes and a black pen to confirm my suspicion. There was the shelf displaying miniature wooden figurines above the workbench. The enormous half-carved swan sat on the floor untouched. I saw the makeshift kitchenette countertop, the fridge, and the microwave, and I wondered what he did for running water. Probably used a big thermos jug. I noticed the neatly made bunk and the avocado green carpet rolled out from under the bed. The upper bunk was piled with a stack of cardboard boxes and an old leather briefcase.

The briefcase—a place to keep paper, envelopes, and a pen.

I stepped carefully across the creaky floor to the top bunk and laid the briefcase flat. The buckles flipped open easily. I opened it. Nothing. Absolutely nothing inside.

Still in my irrational super-sleuth mode, I peeked over the tops of the cardboard boxes. One was full of an assortment of old ball caps, working gloves, and a pair of black leather boots. Another box held a rusty lantern.

An old lantern, almost identical to the three lanterns on display on the fireplace mantel at Burleighs.

A wave of goose bumps rolled down my chest. My mind went spinning.

Without a hesitation, and without a bit of thinking, I unwisely snatched the lantern, bolted for the door, flipped off the light, and scampered out of Hawkeye and across the grove into Saranac.

I had just committed theft, but I was sure I had discovered the secret of the Legend of Lake Marilee. Not only is Whisper the Ambassador, but he's also the ghost of Marilee Manor!

# CHAPTER 23

## *Lantern, Lights, Lunacy, and Logic*

Boonie was in Saranac when I tumbled inside with the lantern. I showed him my discovery, and he, too, was sold: the night watchman of the Brown Swan Club was the ghost of Marilee Manor, and Boonie and I were the only mortals who knew it!

Together, we imagined how Whisper could have pulled it off: some say he was a Vietnam vet, and with the correct training, he could pull a stunt like that; he also worked at night; he was a loner; and he lived here only in the summertime. We were convinced that we had uncovered the great hoax.

Boonie rather astutely wondered, "If this guy is also the one sending you all those letters, then maybe that's a big hoax, too. Maybe he doesn't know anything about Jimmy, he's just trying to stir up another legend."

"That could be," I replied. "I could care less really. But maybe he *does* know something. Maybe he knows something about Brock's involvement. He did rescue me from Brock that night at the pool. And maybe he's also the John Doe the police are looking for. He's just the type."

"I can't believe you actually snuck into his cabin and swiped that lantern!"

I admitted my crime, and then I tried to rationalize it by revealing to Boonie my previous visit with Whisper in his cabin. I described how Whisper has his living quarters set up in there and how he spends his time carving wood, not watching pornos.

Boonie at first didn't believe me, but then he looked closely at the lantern and couldn't deny my story. "This is just like the lanterns they have at Burleighs," he confirmed.

"I know. There's another one up in the lobby that looks just like it."

"Maybe he's just a collector. Maybe he just found it over there like they got all those other ones."

"That could be, but think about it. Remember when we saw Whisper leave his cabin last night? Remember… 'cause I talked to him, right?"

"Yeah."

"That was just after eleven o'clock. It was about forty minutes later that the Lights showed up at the Manor."

Boonie speculated, "That would give him enough time to get over there. And now that you mention it, there were only a few people down at the beach last night to see the Lights, and Whisper wasn't one of them. Practically everyone who was still awake was there. And I didn't see him anywhere on his golf cart on my way there or back."

I added, "There's supposed to be a big crowd down there tonight. He's not in his cabin now, and I'll bet he won't be at the beach if the Lights show up!"

Boonie and I hid the lantern in one of my suitcases and we hustled down to the Club beach. A crowd had already gathered there, consisting of much of the staff, nearly a hundred Club guests, and even some local people congregating on the beach deck and the sand below.

I recognized Branson and Peggy Oliff who were sitting at a round table with another couple; I tried to avoid eye contact with them. Very odd—their son had just tried to commit suicide this morning. How can they be here tonight? Even old Robert Rothschild was there, speaking with another guest, pointing his cane out over the lake in the direction where the Lights normally appeared. I also saw old Harold and Gretta from Pokeville sitting in lawn chairs down on the beach, each with binoculars. And sure enough, Whisper was nowhere around.

The scene reminded me of the masses that gather in anticipation of a fireworks show, and this being July third, such a show would actually be put on display from the town beach tomorrow night. But here at the Club's beach deck, people gathered to see if two little lights would flicker silently on the opposite shore. They said the show last night was a brief one, only about twenty minutes, and it was an exceptionally late one, too. I glanced at my watch. It was 9:47.

It was getting crowded on the beach deck, so Boonie and I moved down to the sand where most of the staff members lingered, laying on blankets, playing cards, eating caramel corn and sipping from cans of soda pop, all waiting for the mysterious Lights of Marilee to appear a mile across the lake. 10:00 p.m. came and went, a common time for the ghost to come out, witnesses said.

I watched Harold and Gretta peer through their binoculars into the darkness. They kept watch nonstop while Boonie and I got in on a game of

Uno with Jennifer and Wendy.

Time waltzed silently by, and no Lights appeared. By eleven o'clock, some guests lost patience and left. I was glad to see Branson and Peggy Oliff leave early. Maybe they should go attend to their son, I criticized. One by one and in small groups, other locals and guests eventually wandered off, discouraged but determined to come back another night.

By eleven thirty, only a few dozen watchers remained. Harold and Gretta were still there on their lawn chairs, binoculars ready. Most of the guests, including Robert Rothschild, had departed long ago, leaving only a family of five, an elderly couple, and a young honeymoon couple snuggling on a chaise lounge on the deck above.

I was ready to return to Saranac and hit the sack when a shout from the mouth of Gretta captivated the sparse crowd. "There he is!" she cackled, as she pointed her flabby arm in the direction of the Manor.

At once, all attention was focused across the black water. People stood to their feet and gazed in silent awe. Indeed, the yellow flicker of what looked like a lantern wobbled slowly along the shoreline. It crawled to the stony point where campfires had burned earlier in the summer.

As expected, the light suddenly stopped moving, as if the ghost had set it down near the stony point. Another light soon appeared to the left on the shoreline. It crept slowly into the woods, flickering behind trees and brush.

Low, mumbling voices filled the air around the Club's beachfront.

"That is so freaky!" a girl behind me whispered.

Boonie and I exchanged glances, and I thought of the stolen lantern in my suitcase in Saranac. We were convinced that all this was the work of the Club's night watchman.

The second light continued to move through the woods along the shore. Then it reversed direction and appeared to head deeper into the trees before it worked its way closer to the shore again.

Harold and Gretta were on their feet with their binoculars focused on the eerie glow. I looked around at my fellow staff members who were staring in disbelief. Up on the deck behind me I saw the honeymoon couple gazing out into the darkness, pointing and whispering to each other. Others stood near the rail: children on their tip-toes gaping and pointing, the elderly couple oohing and aahing, and another man operating a video camera.

Among the onlookers on the deck above I saw a newcomer standing in the shadows. It was the unmistakable figure of Whisper looking out over the water.

I felt the blood rush from my face, my jaw dropped open, and I yanked on Boonie's sleeve, gesturing up to the deck. Boonie's eyes nearly popped out, and his mouth dropped open like mine.

"Let's go!" I whispered.

We scampered up the steps, past the deck, up to the road, and all the way up the hill. I wanted to return the lantern to Whisper's cabin before he came back to get ready for his nightly rounds. He probably wouldn't notice it missing, but I wanted to reverse my stupid accusation about the man as quickly and as thoroughly as possible.

It was ten minutes before midnight, and the grove was empty when I stormed into Saranac to retrieve the stolen lantern. Nearly out of breath, I ran up to Hawkeye and entered without knocking while Boonie remained on watch in the grove.

The cabin was dark inside and I crashed to my elbows when I tripped over the half-carved tree stump on the floor. Thank goodness the glass in the lantern didn't break! After placing it safely back in its box, I dashed out the door, and Boonie and I scurried to Saranac's porch.

"We're a couple of idiots!" Boonie huffed, trying to catch his breath.

"I'm the idiot! I stole the lantern!"

I couldn't believe my stupidity.

We sat down on the front porch to catch our breath.

In about five minutes, two lifeguards strolled into Bird's Nest. The pool must be closed now. Some of the staff members who were down at the beach began to return to their cabins, including the Needleman twins.

A few minutes later we heard the whir of a golf cart coming down the hill near the pool and then the crumble of gravel on the path along the ball diamond. Whisper entered the grove, his golf cart in full throttle. He didn't see us when he parked his cart in front of Hawkeye. He climbed out and limped up the steps and into his cabin.

We saw the glow of lights flick on inside his hovel. Two minutes later they flicked off, and Whisper came out the door, still wearing his standard uniform. He boarded his golf cart again and put it in gear. This time, he saw us and stopped, looking across the grove in our direction.

Like last night, I left Boonie on Saranac's porch and approached Whisper.

"Hey," I said coolly.

"So, did you get out of your pickle?" he asked in his raspy voice.

"Huh?"

"The trouble you were in with the gal. How'd that turn out?"

"Oh. I don't know yet. Mr. Schuple hasn't made a final decision yet."

I noticed the notepad taped to the little dashboard of the golf cart. I wanted to look at the handwriting to see if it was written in large block, Ambassador-style letters. If Whisper wasn't the ghost of Marilee, he still could be the Ambassador.

"Did you tell him the truth?" Whisper asked softly.

"Huh?" I was distracted by the notepad and the thought of the old lantern.

"The truth. Did you tell him the truth?"

"Yeah."

"Then that's all you can do."

"I know."

"Thought I saw you and you're friend down at the beach. Was that you to who ran up the stairs in such a hurry?"

"Yeah." I was embarrassed for the reason we ran, and I hoped Whisper wouldn't ask.

"Did you see the Lights of Marilee?"

"Yeah."

"First time?"

"Yeah. For me. Boonie's seen them before."

Whisper had never been this talkative, and I had never been so reticent. I thought he had talked up a storm last night when we met here in this same spot. But tonight he was really coming out of his shell.

Although I was dead wrong about the ghost, I was still convinced that he was the Ambassador, and his gregariousness tonight supported my hypothesis. I still wanted to flip open the notepad and look at the handwriting.

"So what did you think?" Whisper gargled.

"Huh?"

"About the Lights? You think it's really a ghost?"

"I don't know."

Whisper huffed and smiled. "You must think something about them. What do you think?"

"I thought they were kind of creepy."

"Do you believe in ghosts?"

"No. Yeah, maybe. I don't know."

"What about your friend?" Whisper asked.

"Boonie? I don't know what he thinks about it."

Whisper sighed and then said, "It's amazing, isn't it."

"What? The Legend?"

"No. The way the people around here think."

"Think about what?"

"About the truth behind those Lights. Everyone is indifferent about the truth."

"What do you mean?"

"The Lights. For years people have gathered along the shore to look across the lake at those mysterious Lights of Marilee. Either they believe in ghosts, like something supernatural or unexplainable, or they believe it's a hoax. You have to choose one or the other. But what I find amazing is that most people are indifferent about the truth. In fact, there's a law here that prohibits people from trying to discover the truth."

"You mean not being allowed to go to the Manor during July?"

"Exactly. Do you know why they made that law?" Whisper asked.

"So people won't scare off the ghost?"

"You think it's a ghost then?"

"No. I don't know."

"You see, that's exactly what I'm talking about."

He was right. It had to be one or the other. A ghost or a hoax, and up until a few minutes ago, I thought I had it solved.

"So what do you believe?" I asked him, turning the tables.

"I believe it's a hoax."

"Why?"

"I've searched for the truth. I know."

"How do you know for sure?"

"Evidence. I've examined evidence and I am compelled believe what I believe."

"Who is it then? Who's pretending to be the ghost of Marilee?"

"I haven't quite figured that part out. I just know it's not a ghost. The town ordinance makes it difficult for me to investigate further."

Curious, I asked him, "Have you snooped around the Manor at night when the Lights were out?"

"Yep. I've scared whoever it is a few times. That's how several of those lanterns have been retrieved from the point. Happen to have one of them myself."

What a coincidence that he would mention that lantern. It made me nervous.

"Say," Whisper rasped, as he looked at his watch, "when are we going to get together for that wood carving lesson?"

"I'll be busy tomorrow. Kristel's coming back, and I'm supposed to meet someone tomorrow night." I watched his reaction closely. "I get off at two-thirty on Sunday, though."

Whisper's expression remained consistent. "Sunday then. Come over Sunday, and while we carve, I'll tell you about Marilee Manor and how you might be able to help me find out who the ghost is."

"You want to ruin the Legend of Marilee Manner for everyone?" I thought of George Schuple and the business the Legend brings.

"If the truth ruins the legend for you, would you be disappointed?"

"Not for me, but maybe for others."

Whisper nodded and looked at his watch again. "I'm late. I've got some rounds to get to."

My curiosity had the best of me now. "Hey, one thing," I said. I unloaded an impulsive question on Whisper: "Do you know who the Ambassador is?"

"The Ambassador?"

"Yes. Someone around here who calls himself the Ambassador for the Dead."

"No, not anyone I know."

He sounded sincere. I didn't know whether to believe him or not. Then again…. "See you on Sunday," I said.

Whisper drove out of the grove and I watched him whir up the hill toward the pool and out of sight.

# CHAPTER 24

## *Kristel's Back, the Fruit Aisle, and a Drive to the Nether Regions*

The busiest breakfast day of the week was Saturday. The guests who were checking out made sure to get a good morning meal for their day of travel. Consequently (and thankfully for us cooks), this made Saturday the least busy day for lunch. Most of the guests were gone before noon, and those coming for the new week wouldn't arrive until the afternoon and evening. So by ten o'clock that morning, I knew the majority of my work for the day was behind me, and the next four hours would be a breeze. Best of all, Kristel was coming back today.

For reasons obvious to some of us, the kitchen seemed to run more efficiently when the veteran Boonie wasn't there. Today was his day off, and, coincidentally, the breakfast buffet was set up and maintained in a timely, orderly fashion. Waitresses weren't distracted, vociferous comments meant to be funny weren't shouted across the kitchen, and the front line wasn't a disaster by the time the morning rush was over.

In my first few weeks in the kitchen, I had assumed a great deal of responsibility. And on this Saturday, the fourth of July, when Boonie was off and Allen granted me the task of putting two meals out, I fulfilled my duties aptly. Although the morning atmosphere lacked its usual levity created by a personality like Boonie's, the kitchen was improved by my orderliness and sophistication.

Darlene, the head hostess in the dining room, noticed the difference. "It's nice to have the buffet open on time for a change," she said to Allen. "I hope Mr. Schuple doesn't send Jody home."

By eleven o'clock, the lunch preparation was complete, and Allen invited me into the chef's office. "Take a break for a little while, kiddo. Saturday's are nice, aren't they? Here, try some of this new cheesecake we're going to run tonight."

I obeyed my supervisor and enjoyed ten minutes of relaxation in the air-conditioned office, eating a deluxe chocolate cheesecake and looking through the window at old Mr. Williams of the grounds crew primping up a flower bed near the side patio. Allen was about to ask me about the skinny-dipping incident when he was interrupted.

George Schuple had arrived at the office door.

Allen rose to his feet as if he was busy at work. "G'morning, Mr. Schuple."

"Hello, Allen. Busy morning for you?"

"Yessir."

I remained seated, holding a half of a piece of cheesecake on a plate in my lap. I wondered if I should follow Allen's lead and pretend that I, too, was busy. But the presence of the cheesecake made it seem like a futile act.

Mr. Schuple didn't seem to care, saying, "Allen, would you excuse me. I hate to send you out of your own office, but I need to talk with Jody for a moment."

"Sure thing." Allen grabbed a clipboard that he probably never intended to look at until his break was cut short. He walked out the door and began giving orders to two of the pantry girls.

Schuple sat down in the swivel computer chair and commented, "Darlene said you did a fine job this morning. Boonie ought to shape up or you'll run him out from under that chef's hat of his!"

I smiled and thanked him for the compliment.

He continued, "I wanted to get back with you about the incident that took place Thursday night."

"Did you talk to Mandi again?" I asked.

"Yes I did. And, by the way, I talked to Mr. Oliff yesterday, and Brock is going to be fine. It wasn't as serious as we thought, but there are obviously some emotional problems going on there."

"I heard he would be okay. I saw his parents down at the beach last night waiting for the Lights."

"Yes, they had stopped by to reassure us about their son."

I was uncertain about my own sincerity over the well being of Brock Oliff, so I redirected the conversation to its origin. "So what did Mandi say?"

"Well, Jody, you were absolutely right. Miss Winters finally broke down and told me the truth. She said that it was, indeed, a plan for revenge upon you that Brock had worked out, and she helped him pull it off. She's sorry she ever listened to Brock, she told him afterwards she never wanted to see him again, and she feels guilty for hurting you."

The Ambassador's prophecy was right; Mandi came clean and Schuple was forgiving me. I asked, "Do you think that's why Brock tried to hurt himself—because she broke up with him again?"

Schuple pressed his lips tightly together and considered it for a moment. "Well, that might have triggered it, I suppose. But Brock's got a long history of problems with his family—his father especially. I guess they had a nasty fight later that night after our boat ride. But I'm not one to say why Brock did what he did."

"So Mandi's still fired then?"

"Uh, well, I offered her a chance to stay after she decided to be truthful with me, but she refused. She said she needs to go home and get her life back in order. Her parents will be in tonight to pick her up."

I shook my head, unsure about how to respond.

Schuple smiled, saying. "You were put in quiet a precarious predicament, son." He chucked. "I'd have to say you handled it better than most men would have. You were kind of like Joseph when he fled Potiphar's wife after she ripped the shirt right off his back."

I smiled, knowing inside that I had Schuple's beautiful daughter to thank for my uprightness. Being pedantic with the little Bible I knew, I said to him, "Yeah, and wasn't Joseph put in charge of all of Egypt?"

Schuple laughed. "Yes he was, son. And let me tell you—if you flee youthful lusts like you tried to do the other night, and if you resist the temptation of short-lived pleasures, I wouldn't be surprised to see you running this place, or something like it, in a few years." He sounded like a preacher.

"Thanks!" I grinned widely, feeling for the first time a special attachment to Mr. Schuple—like a boy to his father. Never before had Wesley ever offered such an encouraging word to me.

I was now off the hook with Brock and Mandi; and later today Kristel would be home. Whew! What a week it had been!

Little did I know what the next one would bring.

I didn't plan on falling asleep after getting off work at two-thirty, but that's what happened. And when I awoke, the most beautiful face in the world was outside my little bunk-side window. Her gentle tap awoke me, and her perfect smile was like a warm, soft blanket in a chilly room. I enthusiastically cranked open the windowpanes.

"Kristel! I'm so glad you're back!"

Her smile brightened and she said, "So am I! I heard a lot happened to you since I've been gone!"

"Boy, you're not kidding."

"My mother told me her version on the way home. I'm glad I had already heard Daddy's version of it last night on the phone!"

"Which one do you believe?"

"Whose do you think?" she said with a sarcastic grin.

"Did your mom tell you about Mandi finally confessing the truth to your dad?"

"Yes, and I could tell Mom was giving her own version of that, too. She made it sound like Mandi had planned the whole thing and that Brock just made a poor decision about the girl he chose to spend time with. Mom said he'd be better off with a nice girl like me."

"That figures. What will Brock have to do to make your mom believe that he truly is a jerk?"

"Maybe get convicted of murder?" Kristel's suggestion was facetious, but we both knew the irony of her statement.

"Did you hear about his suicide attempt?"

"Yes. I told you that boy has some serious problems."

The conversation continued after we skulked up to Kristel's tree house and talked right up until dinnertime. I shared every detail of the week, especially the facts of the latest Ambassador note, my suspicion of him being Whisper, and that I hoped she could be with me at the grocery store's produce aisle at seven o'clock tonight like the letter requested.

"I'll be there," she said. "Even if I have to lie to my mom. I'll tell her I'm going to the fireworks with some friends."

Kristel agreed with my theory about Whisper being the Ambassador, as she had begun to suspect the exact same thing when she was gone. She knew Whisper to be a rather intelligent man and the type to do most of his communicating in private—like through written letters. She said that whenever Whisper has to report something to Mr. Schuple, he always did so by sliding a hand-written note under his office door. When I told her how Whisper had become rather talkative with me, especially last night, it made Kristel even more certain that Whisper is the Ambassador.

I also described how Whisper had done his own sleuthing to try to solve the mystery of Marilee Manor.

Kristel questioned, "I wonder if Daddy knows he's been doing that. He could get into trouble, you know."

"Does your dad think the Lights are a hoax?"

"He never says either way. He's just happy about the business the Lights bring."

I thought, in Mr. Schuples' case, it paid for him keep the truth covered. I wondered what Whisper would say about that. Perhaps I could ask him if he's the one who shows up at the supermarket tonight.

In the hours leading up to seven o'clock, my nerves were pecking away at my stomach like the world was about to end. It wasn't just finding out who the Ambassador was that made this meeting so nerve-racking, but it was the possibility of coming face to face with the truth about Jimmy—the reality that he was really my brother, my own flesh and blood, and the possibility that someone, maybe Brock, murdered him. My intuition grew increasingly stronger, and I was nearly convinced that the Ambassador was no prankster, and that Jimmy was posthumously going to become a big part of my life. I didn't go to dinner, I was so nervous.

Kristel and I arrived at the supermarket at 6:50. I had said almost nothing during our walk down there. When we stepped on the black rubber floor mat that triggered the automatic door, Kristel attempted to alleviate the tension.

"I promise not to start taking off my clothes," she whispered into my ear with a grin.

"Very funny!"

The first person we saw in the produce aisle was Boonie.

"What are you doing here?" I asked, quite upset to see him.

Boonie ignored me, choosing instead to greet Kristel. "Hey, Kristel, welcome back."

"Thanks, Boonie. I'm glad to be home."

He looked backwards over his shoulder as he answered my question. "I'm here with Jennifer. She's down the aisle back there. I just wanted to see if the Ambassador is Whisper or not."

I looked at my watch. 6:52. "Well, you better get out of sight, because the letter said that only Kristel and I could be here." I was clearly annoyed with him. "I told you that already. In fact, you better just leave, 'cause whoever it is could be watching us right now."

Boonie retorted, "Well, whoever it is wasn't on time last time, so I doubt he's watching us now." He began walking down the aisle. "I'll be in the back of the store just in case something happens."

Kristel asked, "What might happen?"

I shrugged my shoulders, and Boonie stopped and turned to answer. "You never know. It could be some wacko, remember, Jody? What if Whisper pulls his gun on you? I'll be back there just in case." He pointed towards the back of the store and walked in the same direction.

He was trying to be funny, but he was more like a jerk, just showing off for Jennifer.

"You better not let him see you," I ordered. The tension in my voice was clearly noticeable. I knew Boonie was feeling guilty for blowing it the last time, but with Kristel here with me, I didn't need Boonie around. It was hard to trust him anymore.

I looked at my watch again. Same time—6:52.

Kristel and I stood and waited, perusing the produce section as if we were interested shoppers. I picked up two kiwi fruits and shuffled them over each other repeatedly in my hand. My stomach was swirling with apprehension. I put the kiwis down and looked at my watch again—probably the twentieth time in the last eight minutes.

Quietly, Kristel announced, "Look—there's Mr. Rothschild."

We watched the elderly man with the full white beard enter the store and stroll casually past the rows of shopping carts. He was sharply dressed—as usual—in his dark three-piece suit that he wore to every meal. On his head he donned the same Scottish plaid golfer's hat he wore when I helped him take his luggage from the van to his chalet three weeks ago.

Robert Rothschild made eye contact with Kristel. He smiled and nodded a greeting. He then looked at me and offered the same gesture. He walked casually around the far checkout aisle to the seasonal section stocked with two-liter bottles of Pepsi products, chips, and paper cups, plates, and napkins, everything you need for a July 4th picnic by the lake. When Mr. Rothschild turned the corner, he rapped his fingers on the dome of a small barbecue grill. He then began walking towards us near the fresh fruit, and he again made eye contact with us as he approached.

Kristel, who had known the Brown Swan Club regular all her life, greeted him. "Hello, Mr. Rothschild. What brings you to the supermarket? Did you miss dinner tonight?"

The elderly man smiled and patted his button-down vest that fit firmly around his plump tummy. "Oh, I had a grand meal tonight. I thought I saw *you* there at the head table, if my eyes weren't deceiving me."

"Yes, I was there. We ate early. I wanted to come into town for the fireworks."

"Oh, yes. What time do they start?" he asked politely.

Kristel answered, "Nine-fifteen. They're launching them from the town beach."

I remained silent, attempting to maintain a pleasant expression, but hoping at the same time that the gentleman would be on his way, so as not to distract the Ambassador who should be arriving anytime. I looked at my watch again. Now 6:57. I wished that Kristel, despite her knack for being friendly and social, would bring an end to the conversation and direct Mr. Rothschild down an aisle towards whatever item he had come to purchase.

But I noticed that she wasn't talking anymore; instead, she was looking at me with eyes wider than normal, as if she were trying to tell me something. Mr. Rothschild stood before us, his hands clasped under his belly, smiling politely. He really did look like Santa Claus wearing a navy blue three-piece suit and a plaid golfer's hat.

I finally spoke to the old man. "Are you shopping for something specific, sir?" I sounded like a store employee.

Mr. Rothschild chuckled and shifted his feet. He adjusted the wire-rimmed glasses on his nose as he responded. "Oh, no, no. Chef Dernbaugh feeds me quite well enough. I'm actually here to meet someone."

I held my breath and glanced at Kristel, Her eyes bulged even wider.

"You're here to meet someone?" My stomach twisted inside me.

Rothschild stood there before us as his smile widened beneath his bushy white mustache. His eyes twinkled from behind his bifocals, and he answered my question as he hopped lightly on his heels. "Yes, Mr. Barrett and Miss Schuple. I'm here to meet someone at seven o'clock sharp."

He pulled from his jacket a gold watch on a chain. He examined its face, nodded to himself, and focused again on Kristel and me while each of our mouths hung wide open.

As we stared at the old gentleman, the smile behind his bushy whiskers remained gleefully firm, and his eyes glistened as if they were filled with tears.

Finally, I asked, "Are you the Ambassador?"

Rothschild sighed deeply, nodding his head slowly, and he answered. "Yes, it is I."

"The Ambassador for what?" I asked impudently.

"For the Dead," the old man emotionally replied, his voice cracking ever so slightly. He rubbed his finger in the corner of his eye where a tear was swelling. He kept smiling: it was a happy tear.

Neither Kristel nor I could respond. We simply stared at him.

"Would you and your lady friend care to join me for a ride?" he said to me in a quaking, but amicable, voice, as he motioned toward the doorway beyond the two checkout aisles.

Kristel looked at me. Her lips parted and her eyes emanated an expression of joy and surprise. I glanced at her and then at Rothschild, who continued to stand prominently before us.

I answered his invitation hesitantly. "Um, yes. I guess so,"

Rothschild turned towards the door before stopping abruptly. "Uh, you are alone, aren't you? We can't have anyone following us."

Kristel and I again exchanged glances, each knowing the other was thinking the same thing—that Boonie was watching from the back of the store with Jennifer.

"Yes, we're alone," I lied, returning my eyes to Rothschild. "We won't be followed." I affirmed this, hoping—just hoping—that Boonie wouldn't do anything stupid.

"Very well," said the gentleman. "My car is parked out front."

Subdued like sheep, we followed the shepherd through the parking lot to a silver Mercedes, with plates indicating it was a rental. Rothschild opened the back door of the car and Kristel crawled inside. I stooped to do the same when the old man said, "You may sit up front if you like."

"Um, I'd rather sit back here with Kristel."

The old man's mustache quivered with delight. "I don't blame you, young fellow," he said softly, patting me on the shoulder.

Now I was with Kristel in the back seat of a Mercedes with the beloved Mr. Robert Rothschild at the wheel. Where was he taking us? *He* is the Ambassador! The letters. Jimmy. Boy, was I wrong about Whisper. All of it was mind-boggling.

We headed south down Route 7, out of town, beyond the entrance to the Brown Swan Club, and past the green highway sign that said, "Pokeville 14. Lake Henry 46."

For the first few miles of the drive, nobody said a word. To our left, an army of floating vessels was gathering in the north end of the lake, to secure a good view for the fireworks that would be launched in a couple of hours from the town beach. Hundreds of boats—sail boats, pontoon boats, ski boats, and fishing boats filled up Lake Marilee's north end like a parking lot. On the highway, cars passed us on the left, all headed north towards town. We were the only car heading southbound out of town.

Kristel sat next to me on the passenger side and had a better angle on

Rothschild's face than I did. She leaned forward and politely asked her longtime acquaintance, "Where are we going, Mr. Rothschild?"

The old man leaned the back of his gray head on the headrest. His hat lay in the passenger seat next to him, and he casually held one hand on the steering wheel.

"We're going to meet someone. Someone you'll be very interested to get to know."

I leaned forward and asked, "Does this person know anything about Jimmy Grandstaff and how he died?"

"That's what this is all about, isn't it?" the old man replied kindly. "You did read the letters you've been receiving from me?"

Fully subdued, I managed an affirmative "uh, huh." Kristel and I glanced at each other and remained quiet for the rest of the ride. Neither of us was sure what to say, but we knew we were each thinking the same thing—that Mr. Rothschild was the last person we ever expected to meet at the supermarket, and riding in a Mercedes, heading somewhere to meet another unknown person was the last thing we expected to be doing at this moment.

We quietly rode southward down the winding highway along the narrow, fourteen-mile lake. As the sun began its gradual spill over the western horizon, the sky above the hillside on our right was fading into an orange glow. On our left, the shimmering lake waters reflected the changing daylight. Meanwhile, seemingly every watercraft that had been docked along its shores was migrating northward.

Eventually, we passed by the Pokeville Mobil and post office. I saw old Gretta sitting on the front porch, looking out across the highway at the disheveled graveyard. I noticed her head follow us as she watched our car go past. I wondered where old Harold was.

Then we crossed over the little brook and into Pokeville, where white paint on all the buildings was cracked and peeling, and no one was around to care. Just before passing the little church with the sagging roof and leaning steeple, Rothschild took an unexpected left turn down a two-lane road that was much narrower than Route 7. It squiggled though a cluster of tall pines before eventually working its way eastward around the southern edge of Lake Marilee.

On the left we passed a boat ramp where two fishermen stood at the end of a concrete dock, casting their lines into the lake. The road continued its winding trek eastward and eventually came to a T at another road named Marilee Trail. It was a narrow, undivided, paved road that ran north and south. Rothschild turned left and drove north up the dark, tree-covered passage.

Through the pines on my left I could see the sun dipping into the western mountains. The clouds above it were a brilliant orange, and the waters of Marilee were reflecting the sky's colorful array. I realized we were now on the opposite side of the southern end of the lake. I glanced at Kristel who was gazing forward through the windshield with great curiosity about where the old man was taking us. Does she know these roads? I didn't ask.

About two miles up the snaky, hilly passage, the pavement on the ground disappeared into gravel. Rothschild slowed the car to twenty miles per hour. The gravel kicked up into the wheel wells, killing the silence that had subdued us back in Abbeyville. The gravel road became rather tortuous as it hugged the eastern, serpentine banks of the lake.

We passed by summer homes that were built into the cleft of the hill between the road and the lake's rocky shore. Many of these gorgeous, waterfront houses had sport-utility vehicles parked in their steep driveways. Nearly all of the homes boasted long, wooden docks that shot out over the water, most of them empty of a watercraft that was now, most likely, sitting in the north end of the lake near the fireworks.

We crept on for twenty more minutes. The sun dipped behind the western mountains, causing the sky to glow in a brilliant gold. The trees around us faded into black silhouettes against the blazing background.

Occasionally, the road curved farther inland where the woods loomed much darker, hidden from the golden, western sky. Then we would emerge out on the open banks under the gold canopy again. The gravel roadway tiptoed up and down the hilly terrain, and Rothschild now maintained a snail's pace at less than ten miles per hour. The shiny, silver Mercedes was not the ideal car to take wherever we were going.

I figured that at any moment we would come to a stop in back of one of the lakeside homes—a house belonging to the unknown person Rothschild wanted us to meet. I wondered what this person knew about Jimmy and if this person had employed Mr. Rothschild to send the letters to me. Then I remembered that Rothschild was too rich of a man to be doing someone else's work, so I figured that this unknown person we were about to meet was probably some rich friend of Rothschild who lived in one of these fancy, waterfront summer home and knew something about the death of my brother. Otherwise, this precarious drive was inexplicable.

After a few miles there were no more homes to pass. The gravel leveled out, and as we approached a glimmering bay, half-enclosed by a point jutting out into the lake, I could see that no more houses existed along the lakeshore for the next few miles. At this moment Kristel clutched my hand.

I looked at her, noticing how her curiosity and wonder had faded from her visage. Now her demeanor was one of ominous apprehension. She leaned to my ear whispered, "That point up ahead is Marilee Manor!"

I looked forward through the front windshield as the car entered a clearing. Looming before us was the smooth, rocky point of Marilee Manor, the one that we visited via canoe that night during which we witnessed Brock perform his sadistic commemoration ceremony. I glanced at Kristel, who was now trembling.

The road bent to the right, following the bay. The trees hovering above were black statues, while the western sky darkened into a rich amber. On the passenger side, the eastern sky was deepening in its blue hue, and the mountains below it were turning from forest green to black. The once-noisy gravel underneath the car gradually petered away into quiet dust, and the road was now nothing but hard dirt with a strip of weedy grass tracing down its spine.

Rothschild slowed to barely five miles per hour as darkness seeped into the surrounding forest. He didn't have his headlights on, which made the journey all the more perilous. The lake disappeared from sight as the woods on our left grew thicker. The sky continued to provide just enough light to see, but eventually it would be necessary to turn on the headlights to keep from going off the path.

Kristel whispered into my ear again and delivered a daunting message. "This road ends at Marilee Manor. It doesn't go any farther." I felt her arm tremble as I held her hand. She prophesied, "He's taking us to Marilee Manor!"

We both peered forward to catch a glance of Rothschild's face in the rearview mirror. The twinkle in his eyes had abated as he strained to follow the darkening terrain. He seemed to be searching for a particular spot in the woods.

Wild thoughts raced through my mind. Why is he taking us here? Is this guy a satanic priest? Is his cult assembling at the Manor tonight? Are Kristel and I going to be the human sacrifices? Or is this rich old man an axe murderer who needs to fill his summer quota? Will we be shot? Knifed? Tied to a stake and burnt? Who awaits us at the Manor? Why is he taking us *here*? I thought of the horror movie *I Know What You Did Last Summer*. This *is* the Fourth of July!

It was all too crazy, and I knew it, but Kristel's expression screamed that she was thinking similar horror-filled thoughts. Perhaps we had watched too much television and seen too many movies. But *this* was far too weird. Too, too weird.

Kristel eyeballed me as if to say, "What's going to happen?" I considered telling her to click open our doors and jump out. The car was certainly going slow enough and we could run for it. The nearest house was only a mile or two back. Or should we remain in the car and trust this old man? He certainly seemed harmless enough.

Before I did anything hasty, Robert Rothschild suddenly stopped the car.

I looked out my window and saw two square, four-foot stone pillars, each surrounded by tall weeds and covered in snake-like vines. Two gothic, black iron gates hung limply from the aging pillars, sagging inward so feebly that one could probably drive a truck up and over them. A weedy path led westward from the gates through acres of thick, black woods towards the shore. Somewhere, beyond the shelter of the trees, was the smooth, rocky point. As I realized we had stopped next to the dilapidated entrance of Marilee Manor, Rothschild killed the engine.

Again, I considered telling Kristel to open the door and run for it, but the kind voice of the old man dissuaded me.

"Well, we're here," he said cheerily. "Sorry about the bumpy ride."

I glanced at Kristel. The look of trepidation and uncertainty in her eyes caused me to fire a question at Rothschild: "Just who are we supposed to meet *here*?" I snapped sharply.

As Rothschild clicked open his door, he turned sideways in his seat and looked at Kristel and me over his headrest. "Why, there's no one else here but us." The old man slowly crawled out of his seat and stood on the ground outside the car. Then he clicked the handle and pulled my door open, but I made no motion to get out.

I objected, "But you said we were going to meet someone—someone very interesting. You said … "

A puzzled look crossed Rothschild's face while he leaned down into my doorway. "Oh, yes… I'm sorry. I did say that. Yes, you're right… I nearly forgot. Yes. You're going to meet Mr. Marilee tonight."

"*Who*?" I asked.

Kristel leaned over on my lap so she could see Rothschild's face. "Did you say Mr. *Marilee*?"

Rothschild's mustache twitched and his eyes twinkled again. "Yes. Mr.

Abbott Marilee himself. Come out of the car. Don't be afraid."

Kristel and I held onto our seats, staring up at Rothschild with disbelief. *Abbot Marilee* he had said. The man behind the legend; the man who killed his family for the gold; the man whose ghost supposedly still haunts these grounds.

Rothschild urged us, "Come now. There's no reason to fear. Don't be afraid. My aging body can't do much harm to you two youngsters. Come on out of the car now so you can meet Mr. Marilee." His voice was sweet and kind, like Santa asking a shy child to climb on his lap.

"You just said no one else is here," I sternly reminded him. I wondered if the old man would say next that we would meet Abbott Marilee's ghost or something crazy like that. I wanted to say something to that effect, sharp and sarcastic, but the kindred spirit of the old man persuaded me otherwise.

Rothschild stepped away from the car and held out his arms. "Why, you're absolutely right, Mr. Barrett. No one else is here but the three of us." He dropped his arms down on his sides, turned away, and walked between the stone pillars and through the narrow gap between the sagging, black iron gates. "We're here alone," he called over his shoulder as he ambled down the path away from the open car. "But those crazy kids from town might be here soon, I'm sure. They can get a good look at the fireworks from the shore over there." He pointed his arm in the direction of the point and continued walking as he added, "So we must hurry,"

Kristel leaned over my legs and cried out through the open door. "What did you mean about Abbott Marilee?" she hollered.

Rothschild stopped and turned around. He was about twenty yards away from us on the weedy path, standing between the vine-covered stone pillars. "Both of you have certainly heard about the Legend of Lake Marilee, haven't you? Well, I'm going to show you the truth tonight. Abbott Marilee is alive and well."

The old man thrust his index finger into his plump belly and bounced it repeatedly as he emphatically declared, "I am Abbott Marilee!"

# CHAPTER 25

## *A Buried Testimony*

Kristel leaned back into the car and vented softly, "Heaven help us; he's gone crazy."

The old man stood on the weedy pathway, his silhouette bleeding into the blackening woods.

Poking his finger into his vest, Rothschild proclaimed again, "Abbott Marilee is alive, and I am he!"

I didn't know whether to feel sorry for him or just laugh at his joke. "Maybe he's senile—Alzheimer's or something," I whispered to Kristel,

"Please come!" Rothschild urged, waving his right arm for us to follow. "Come now, while we're alone. This is *very* important. And there's not much time."

He did sound genuine—so if he was joking, he was really good at it. In any case, we *were* parked next to the hallowed gates of Marilee Manor. All this was just too weird.

Rothschild ranted on: "I know, children, that you must think I'm just a crazy old man. But I am telling the truth. I am Abbott Marilee. Please give me the opportunity to prove it to you. We've come this far."

"Abbott Marilee has been dead for forty years," Kristel asserted, almost shouting through the window.

"No, no. That's what you've been led to believe. That is *not* true. I am Abbott Marilee, and as you can see, I am alive and well."

I got a bit cocky. "If you're Abbott Marilee, then I'm Jesus Christ." With that, Kristel nearly cracked one of my ribs with a sharp jab of her elbow followed by a hard scowl. I didn't know if it was for making fun of the old man, or for using the Lord's name in a joke.

Rothschild only huffed and shook his head.

Trying to atone for my remark, I appended, "If you're Abbott Marilee, then you're wanted for murder."

Rothschild's eyes softened as he folded his hands limply under his belly. He remorsefully replied, "I am not a murderer, but I am a fugitive. An innocent one. I did not destroy the mansion here forty years ago. I did not murder my family, and as you can see," he declared, raising his arms from his sides, "I did not blow my head off with a shotgun!"

He spoke confidently as we listened. He, indeed, sounded authentic and sincere, and I was gradually getting more curious.

He spoke like prophet crying for the obedience of his auditors, pleading, "Come now, let me prove to you my true identity."

"Why are you telling *us* this?" Kristel asked. "We're just a couple of kids. Why us?"

"I've brought you here, Miss Schuple, because I trust you. And because you are a friend of Jody Barrett. It is Jody here who must know and accept the truth of these matters."

"Why me?" I asked.

"Because it was your brother, Jimmy Grandstaff, who was murdered last September."

I said nothing, only sharing a brief glance with Kristel.

Rothschild took one step towards the car and pleaded, "Please come! Let me show you! I will not harm you!" He sounded as though he was about to cry. "Please! I need your help."

Whether I believed him or not didn't seem to matter now, but he definitely had me listening.

"Please," Rothschild begged. He reached to the inside pocket of his jacket with his right arm. "I will reward you for your time with me tonight." He pulled out a thick stack of bills. "Here, this is yours, Jody, if you come with me now. One thousand dollars." He fanned out the stack of bills in his right hand.

This was serious. Rothschild was known to give large tips, but nothing like this.

I nudged Kristel and whispered, "Holy cow! What do you wanna do?"

Kristel whispered back, "Don't take the money. It might get us in trouble. But maybe we should go ahead and let him show us what he wants to show us. Even if he's a crazy lunatic who thinks he's Abbott Marilee, I can't imagine this sweet old man harming anyone. But don't take the money."

Kristel was just too wise for her years, and I knew it. Don't take the money—only Kristel would say that!

But I knew she was right. If the guy was a lunatic, it would be loony for *me* to take the money. And if he was being serious, well, this encounter could be worth thousands in itself.

I replied to Rothschild, "We'll listen to whatever you have to say about Jimmy, but we won't take any money." I couldn't believe I just refused one thousand dollars, and I secretly hoped he'd offer it again.

"Very well," Rothschild said, returning the cash to the inside pocket of his jacket. "Please follow me."

In an act of faith, Kristel and I stepped out of the car. Rothschild beamed with pleasure and turned toward the dark woods.

It wouldn't be long before the sky would be entirely black and we wouldn't be able to see anything. I wondered how far into the woods we'd have to go, and if we could get back without a flashlight. But I didn't say anything. Not now. Kristel and I were at the old man's mercy.

Rothschild walked about ten yards in front of us down the weedy path. We could see the lake through the trees and the evening lights of Abbeyville twinkling gently above the water across the lake. The herd of watercraft gathered on the north end was also well illuminated, honking and tooting in the distance like a floating traffic jam.

We arrived at a clearing in the woods. The old gentleman stopped and announced, "This is where my mansion once stood." He pointed to an enormous rectangular perimeter of stone that looked to have, in ages past, outlined the foundation of a very large structure.

Kristel had seen this once, years ago, in broad daylight, when she explored the banks of the property during a canoe ride with her friends. Then, it scared her. Now, in the darkness, with no way of escape but to trust this old man who claimed to be Abbott Marilee, I wondered what she was thinking. The sequence of events since we had spoken to Boonie at the supermarket was enough to make us both crazy.

Boonie! When we left, I had hoped he didn't follow us, but now I wished he had.

Rothschild walked up to the stone foundation. He stood at one corner, faced north, and then with a militaristic spin, he twirled to the south and planted his heels squarely against the cornerstone. He began pacing, counting his carefully measured steps out loud. He counted all the way to sixty before he suddenly stopped, about half a football field's length from the stone foundation.

He pounded his right heel into the dirt several times. I held Kristel's hand tightly and we walked toward him, while he stamped out a small circle with his shoe. He gradually extended the circle wider until the dull sound of his shoe changed to a hollow thumping sound.

The old man had found what he was looking for. He crouched to his knees and clawed with both hands through leaves, foot-long pine needles, and black dirt. Then he stood to his feet and pulled the ground toward him—a rectangular section of dirt and grass opened up like a door in the earth. It was a wooden door on hinges, and as Rothschild allowed it to fall open, the dirt and grass that had covered it crumbled loosely away. Rothschild stood by the open underground passageway and motioned for Kristel and me to come closer.

We cautiously stepped toward the rectangular opening in the ground and observed limestone steps leading downward into darkness.

"Is this one of the secret vaults?" I asked.

Rothschild audaciously descended to the bottom of the steps. "Yes. Come, follow me."

"It's pretty dark down there."

Kristel was now painfully gripping my hand.

"There's a light down here somewhere," the old man answered matter-of-factly. We heard the jingle of keys. Completely enshrouded in darkness, he was unlocking something.

The we heard the rattle of metal followed by the scrape of wood against limestone. Now a light flicked on and a vertical wooden door became visible at the bottom of the newly illuminated steps. Rothschild had stepped into a lighted room when he called, "Come now, the light still works."

We carefully descended the steps to the underground doorway and ducked into a cool, musty room where the old man was waiting.

"Please close the door behind you so that the light doesn't shine up the steps." He spoke as if he had visited the vault many times.

Kristel and I took in our surroundings with amazement. The room was about eight by ten feet, illuminated by a rather modern looking battery powered camping lantern sitting on the ground next to the doorframe. The floor was nothing but dirt and loose gravel, and the walls were red brick. Huge wooden beams crossed the ceiling above, supporting slabs of sheet rock. Thick, white cobwebs covered nearly every corner and crevice. No other doors were in the room, except for the one we entered. I reluctantly closed it, not tight, but enough to keep the light contained within. The place smelled wet and earthy.

"Is this where Marilees' gold was hidden?" I asked.

"No, not in this particular room," Rothschild answered.

Kristel spoke. "Is this the vault they discovered after the explosion?"

Rothschild smiled. "Yes, they found this one back then," he said. His mustache twitched and his eyes gleamed as he stepped toward the front wall near the doorway. "But they never found the rooms that are connected to this one."

With that said, the old man faced the wall and traced his fingers over the crevices in the brick, causing dirt to fall from between the bricks to the floor. He formed a jagged track from floor to ceiling, forming an outline of two interlocking columns of bricks. The dirt packed between the bricks crumbled away with ease, and soon a half-inch gap was dug between them. Rothschild then inserted his eight fingers into the gap halfway up the wall and pulled to his right.

The sound of squeaky wheels filled the room as the wall of brick began sliding sideways. Rothschild pulled it with relative ease as the pocket door rolled into the perpendicular wall. A dark tunnel was revealed.

"They never found this," he said, slapping his dirt-caked fingers into the palms of his hands. He picked up the battery powered lantern, stepped into the new passageway, and repeated a phrase that had become familiar, "Come now, follow me."

I kept a firm hold of Kristel's hand as we stepped behind him. The air in the newly revealed tunnel was chilly, and its walls, ceiling, and floor looked like the room we had just left. Rothschild batted away cobwebs as he walked. On our left we passed several wooden doors, each like the first one at the bottom of the limestone steps.

The tunnel led directly east for almost fifty yards, away from the shore and towards the road where the car was parked. I estimated that we would be under the road itself if the tunnel continued much farther. But it ended at another doorway, one that Rothschild opened easily by lifting an iron latch hook. The door creaked as it opened and Kristel and I, like amateur explorers, followed in utter amazement.

The room was just like the first, only lined at each wall with large wooden shelves. Each shelf was about two feet deep and braced underneath by four-by-four beams. Four shelves horizontally divided the walls evenly from floor to ceiling all the way around the room, with about two feet of space between each. All the shelves were empty, except for a small one-by-two-foot wooden crate sitting on the bottom shelf on the back wall. The floor in this room was not dirt and gravel, but limestone.

A second battery-powered camping lantern sat on one of the shelves next to the doorway. Rothschild turned it on and placed the first lantern on a shelf in the opposite corner. The second light swallowed up the long shadows that the first lamp had produced.

We watched the old man lift the third board from the shelf on the right wall out of its frame and stand it up lengthwise against the back wall. Then he dusted off the shelf below, swiping cobwebs away from the corners.

"Here, sit here. It's as good a bench as it is a shelf. Come, sit down."

We obediently perched ourselves upon the planks, and my toes barely touched the limestone floor beneath. Kristel's legs dangled freely. We exchanged glances, still holding hands, and then we watched Rothschild drag the wooden crate from the lower shelf on the back wall forward to the ground. He brushed it off with his hand and sat gently upon it, facing us.

"There now, this is comfortable enough, eh?"

Both Kristel and I were wearing shorts and T-shirts. The air was damp and chilly, and Kristel let go of my hand and crossed her arms in front of her to try to warm them. I knew she was cold and I thought of putting my arm around her shoulder, but I didn't.

"Was gold kept in *here*?" I asked, clasping my hands in my lap.

"Yes, there was gold in here at one time," Rothschild answered, his eyes gleaming. "All the rooms we just passed once housed a great fortune in gold bullion."

I remained unconvinced, but very intrigued. "And you're saying that you are *the* Abbott Marilee?"

Rothschild sat up straight on the wooden crate and smiled. "Yes, I am he."

Kristel and I again exchanged quick glances. In this underground setting, his claim seemed more credible now.

"But you're supposed to be dead," Kristel said.

"And what does all this have to do with my brother Jimmy?" I added.

"Ah, we'll get to that. But first I must explain how I'm alive and why I have lived by the name of Robert Rothschild all these years."

The old man unbuttoned his vest, allowing him the freedom to lean his elbows on his knees, a more comfortable position for sitting on the wooden crate.

"I imagine," he said, "that both of you know everything about the Legend of Lake Marilee?"

I looked at Kristel, who knew the Legend much better than I did, having written her research paper on it last year for school.

She said to Rothschild, "I know that Abbott Marilee was disowned by his father, so he destroyed the mansion, killing his parents, his wife, and his kids. Then he shot his brother before he killed himself."

I recalled the mystery and suspense with which Kristel first told the story to me during that first long evening in the tree house. Now, in the presence of a man who claimed to be Abbott Marilee himself, she spewed forth a ten-second version of the legend like it tasted bad.

Rothschild snorted softly. "Well, as you can see, the Legend is nothing but folklore. It's not true, because here I am."

"Then tell us the real story," Kristel said skeptically. She kept her arms folded snugly across her front and gripped her biceps tightly. Then she shuddered. I knew she was both scared and cold.

Rothschild cleared his throat and rubbed the thick, white whiskers under his chin.

"I was twenty-eight years old that year," he began. "1958 it was. I had lived on this property all my life, except for my college years at Dartmouth. I had been married to a beautiful woman named Annie for six years. We had a five-year-old son and a brand new little daughter. We all lived right here in the mansion. My mother and father lived here, too. And my brother Zane had just returned home from New England.

"Zane was five years younger than I was. We were much alike in physical appearance, and both of us were the spitting image of our father. But Zane... well, he was sort of the wayward son. Our parents raised us in a very strict home. Church and school were what mattered most to the Marilee family. But Zane—he hated church, and he skipped school as often as he could get away with it. When he was a teenager, he got into trouble with the law several times. On one occasion during the winter, he stole a pickup truck with some of his friends. They drove it across the ice on the lake, and they hit a soft spot and the back end got stuck. It took a tow truck to get it out.

"Zane was always in some sort of trouble. I remember my father whipped him with a belt for every incident. The whippings became a common occurrence in our house. A couple of times, when Zane was a teenager, my father threw him out of the house and made him stay out all night. Once it was during the summer, but the next time it was during the winter and it must not have been more than ten degrees outside. So I was very glad to see Zane finally go off to college. My father hoped it would straighten him out. I hoped so, too.

"As for me, I got along much better with my parents. I studied hard and went to church. I tried my best to get Zane to do the same, but he never listened to me.

"Being the oldest, I was the heir to the property and two-thirds of the gold here in the vaults. It was an old family code that directed two-thirds of the inheritance to the oldest son. Therefore, our parents' will was always a source of contention with Zane. But here's what I did for him: I promised Zane that when my father and mother passed away, I'd split everything with him evenly, fair and square. But he didn't trust me to follow through on my promise. Zane could never trust anybody, not even his own brother.

"Anyway, in 1958, life couldn't have been grander for me. I had a wonderful family of my own. My father was preparing me to take over his banking operation in Abbeyville. I already had my own office there, as my father was getting ready to retire.

"That summer, Zane had just returned home from college, or so my parents thought. I found out that Zane had actually dropped out of school one semester into it. He stayed in New England and lied to my parents about how much he liked his classes and how well he was doing. But he actually was working several jobs—bar tending, highway construction, anything he could find to stay busy, and living a life in the fast lane with the tuition checks my father sent him. He made me swear to secrecy that I would never tell.

"So he comes home after four years, and he even brought with him a fake diploma that he had forged. He was going to work with my father and me at the bank, and I was going to do my best to train him in the business. I hoped a decent job would give him a new lease on life.

"But one day that summer, everything changed. It was a few weeks after Zane came home that some young woman in Pokeville turned up pregnant. She claimed she was raped—and she pointed her finger at *me*.

"I didn't know what to say or do, except to be sure as the sun rises everyday that I didn't do it. I hoped my reputation would speak for itself. I loved my wife; I had two beautiful children— everything a man could ask for. But the young woman insisted that I did it. She came up with a story that put me at the scene, and I had no alibi.

"My wife stood by me, and so did my brother Zane—at least he seemed to at first. But my father—he didn't believe me; he believed the victim instead. And, you're right, Miss Schuple, my father disowned me; he kicked me and my family right out of the house. He cut me out of the inheritance entirely, fired me from the bank, banned me from the property here, and said he never wanted to see me again.

"I was in a panic because the young woman had taken her story to the police. I didn't want to be arrested, and I was scared, let alone homeless now, so I took my wife and kids and went south. We didn't get very far because I had no plan and nowhere to go. We all lived out of my car down in Lake Henry for three days.

"During that time, my wife urged me to try to talk sense into the young woman, the girl who said I raped her. Well, that was good advice, because after things calmed down a bit, we drove up to her father's place in Pokeville, and lo and behold, she admitted to me right there before my wife and children that the person who had impregnated her wasn't me—it was my brother Zane.

"He had gotten drunk one night at the bar in Pokeville where he met her. He took her out, and, well, he got her pregnant. Not rape—it was consensual. She said that when she learned she was pregnant a few weeks later, she informed Zane that she was carrying his child.

"Well, my brother goes off and pays her thirty thousand dollars in cash to blame it on me. She even showed me the wad of cash he had given her. She hadn't spent a dime of it because she grew to feel so guilty about it. She had no idea who I was at the time she blamed me. She didn't know I was a man with a family of my own. She just thought I was as low as the man who had impregnated her.

"So when she told us the truth… heaven's sake, I never even found out what her first name was, and I still don't. We just called her Miss Emory. All I knew about her was that she was the daughter of Nathaniel Emory, the owner of the bar in Pokeville.

"Well, when she confessed the truth to my wife and me, I was entirely overjoyed, obviously. So right there we convinced her to get into the car and come back home with us so she could tell it straight to my father and to the police. And, praise God, she was perfectly willing! She said she had just been born again that very week… you see, made things right with God, and she needed to make this right, too.

"So we got back here to the house—the five of us—myself, my wife, our children, and Miss Emory. My father answered the door and my brother Zane was standing right behind him. Zane took one look at Miss Emory standing amongst us there on the porch, and his eyes grew big, and he turned and ran through the house and out the back door.

"My father was shocked enough to see us all standing out on the porch there. But when he saw Zane run off like that, he allowed us to enter the house to explain what was going on. My mother joined us in the living room, and Miss Emory told the whole story—the truth about her and Zane. She confessed that Zane was the father of her unborn child.

"My father was thrilled to learn his favorite son was no longer guilty. He wept and hugged me, he apologized, and he praised God that the Lord had brought Miss Emory to tell the truth. My father had always favored me over Zane when we were growing up, mostly because Zane was always getting into trouble, and he was so happy to find out that at his favorite son wasn't a rapist. He welcomed us all back into the house, and even gave Miss Emory a room in which she could stay for the time being. He knew she was from a family of alcoholics and her home or her father's bar wasn't the best place to have a baby.

"Now, there was still a warrant out for my arrest and my father was very anxious to clear my name in town the next morning, even though it meant revealing that it was his younger son who was guilty. He knew no one would be surprised when they learned that Zane was actually the guilty one. But what was worse for Zane, everyone would find out that he had paid thirty thousand dollars to get rid of me. I knew that what my father would do to Zane would be worse than what he had done to me, if that's possible.

"So that night, we assured Miss Emory that I would press no charges against her for making the accusation against me that she did. We would go to the police the next morning, she would return the thirty thousand dollars, and my father and the police would deal with Zane as they saw fit.

"Well, that same night, about two-o'clock in the morning, Miss Emory came into our room and woke my wife and me out of bed. She said that Zane was outside the house and wanted to talk to me. Our little infant daughter, who slept next to our bed in a bassinet, woke up crying. So Miss Emory stayed in the room with my wife and the baby, while I went out to see what Zane wanted. My son was asleep in another room, and my mother and father were asleep in the back room.

"I found Zane sitting out near the shore of the lake. Back then, there was a dock that extended out into the bay out there. Zane was sitting on the edge of the dock leaning up against a small storage shed. I noticed an unfamiliar pontoon boat tied to the dock, and I assumed that's how he got there.

"He told me he needed some money. He said he wanted his half of the fortune that I had promised him, and he wanted me to help him unload his half of the vaults so he could take it right then and there.

"Now, neither of us had any right to the gold until our parents passed away. I reminded him of that, and I chose not to mention to him anything about what he had done to me. Think of it! He had the nerve to ask me for his half of the fortune, something I was going to give him out of the kindness of my heart, after he had paid somebody to accuse me of rape, just to get rid of me. But I didn't say anything about it. I just said I couldn't help him to any gold without father's permission, and I knew there was no chance of him getting that.

"But then he said something completely unexpected. He said that all he wanted to do was to present his fortune to Miss Emory and ask for her hand in marriage. He said he was sorry for what he had done and he wanted make things right and raise his son with her. He said wanted to show Miss Emory the fortune so that she might be more inclined to accept his proposal.

"Well, I told him it was a fine decision he had made about marrying her, but trying to *buy* her hand was a mistake. I told him that she had already planned on giving back the thirty thousand dollars. Then I told him that because of what he had done, he wasn't likely to see any of the fortune as long as our father was alive.

"So he asked me if I could at least help him out—you see, give him a hand financially until he and Miss Emory could get on their feet.

"Had he forgotten what he had done to me? The nerve of it! But I still held my tongue. I could picture myself helping him for Miss Emory and the baby's sake, but not for Zane's.

"I told him that he was a step ahead of himself. I advised him that he needed to ask her hand in marriage first, and then I would consider how I could help all of them. So what he did next—to prove his sincerity, I think—he asked me to go get Miss Emory so he could do it right there on the spot: ask her to marry him.

"Not seeing any harm in this, I went inside and found Miss Emory in the living room. She was feeding a bottle to my daughter as my wife had fallen back asleep in the bedroom. I took the baby in my arms as Miss Emory went outside to talk with Zane alone. She asked me to stand by because she was uneasy about it, so I sat on the front porch steps with the baby and watched Miss Emory walk down to the dock to talk with Zane.

"They talked for some time. I heard each of their voices raise occasionally, and I figured they were at least getting in some much needed discussion. She glanced up at me on the porch every once in a while. I prayed at that moment for Miss Emory, that she would make the right decision. Half of me wanted

Zane to become a responsible husband and father, and the other half of me wanted to see Miss Emory kick dirt in his face.

"They stopped talking for a few minutes, and then Zane waved at me to come down to the dock. I went down there with the baby in my arms, and I could tell that Zane was very upset. Apparently, Miss Emory had refused his proposal.

"Zane's demeanor had changed drastically from what it had been a few moments before. He was extremely frustrated, and he was getting angrier by the second. Miss Emory *had* rejected him, and he was obviously very disturbed. I tried to reason with him, and calm him down, but he kept telling me that he's just not good enough for anyone—not our father, not me, and not even Miss Emory. I tried talking sense into him, but he wouldn't listen. He told me, 'You told her to say no, didn't you Abbott. Just to get back at me, you told her to say no to me."

"I denied it, of course, but that didn't help. It just made it worse. Something had snapped in him. His eyes were ablaze with fury as he began cursing me, my father, and Miss Emory. It was as if he was losing control of himself, like a demonic force possessed him.

"He opened the door to the shed behind him and pulled out a shotgun and a detonator box. The box was connected to a wire that circled all the way around to the side of the house where the bedrooms were. He said he stole the dynamite, wires, and detonator from a mining company down in Lake Henry. I knew he had the knowledge to rig it because he had worked for a highway construction company during his time in New England. He said he had originally planned on killing only our mother and father, but now his plans had changed. He kept blaming me for Miss Emory rejecting his marriage proposal.

"I was scared to death to say the least. My wife and family were in that house, and Zane was holding the detonator. Then he put the detonator down on the dock near the grass and pointed the shotgun at me. He cocked the gun and told *me* to push the detonator.

"I said that he was making a mistake and that my wife and son were inside. I was still holding the baby. Miss Emory was standing alongside of me, shaking in terror.

"Zane said that I was getting what I deserved. He said that once my family was gone, then *I* could marry Miss Emory and start a new family, taking once again what he thought was his.

"He again commanded me to push the detonator. There was fire in his eyes, and his voice sounded like the devil's. I knew by the look in his eyes that he was serious about killing someone, maybe everyone.

"I said, 'Zane, I'll help you to all the gold you want, right now. You can take it all and get out of here tonight.' But now he was seething with anger. He didn't want the gold. He wanted revenge.

"He yelled at me to push down on the detonator or he'd shoot me and do it himself. I tried to reason with him. I said again that I'd help him take whatever gold he could fit in his boat. But he kept growling at me, saying 'Put your hand on that detonator or I'll shoot you.' He growled at me again in a demonic voice, 'Put your hand on the detonator or I'll shoot you.'

"I handed the baby to Miss Emory and knelt down at the detonator near Zane's feet. He had the barrel of the gun pointed at my face the whole time. I kept pleading that I'd help him, but he wasn't listening.

"So this is what I planned to do. I was going to put my hand on the detonator and then lunge at Zane, hoping to grab the rifle before he fired.

Zane kept growling, 'Push the detonator, or I'll shoot you.' I pleaded with him once more and he said, "Shut up or I'll blow your head off!" So I put my fingers on the handle of the detonator, and I was a split second away from lunging towards him to grab the rifle.

"But at that moment Miss Emory bolted away down the dock towards the boat. As I watched her, I felt Zane's boot press down on my fingers on the detonator. The plunger went down.

"The blast lit up the sky and echoed across the lake and against the mountains miles away. I watched in horror as debris fell down through the trees. Two-thirds of the house was completely gone—the section where my wife, son, and parents had been soundly sleeping was obliterated. I heard later that they died instantly, never felt a thing.

"I don't know how long I sat there on my knees and stared at the flaming ruins before I looked at Zane. He had stepped backwards onto the dock after the detonation. I stood to my feet and watched him raise the rifle at me as he walked backwards down the dock. Miss Emory was now holding my baby in the pontoon boat with the engine running, trying to untie the boat from the dock to escape.

"I watched Zane run to the end of the dock, lay the rifle down, and wrestle with Miss Emory, trying to keep her from leaving in the pontoon boat. I ran and tackled him down to the dock, and Miss Emory sped away in the boat with my baby girl. I was able to grab the rifle, and I shot Zane in the forehead at point blank range. He fell dead right there on the dock. I ran back up the dock toward the house and found my son's little shoe laying in the front yard near the shore. The right section of the house left standing was now on fire. I fell to the ground and wept.

"I don't know how long I wept there, but soon I realized what would happen when the authorities arrived. I knew they would have grounds to arrest me on several counts: one, for the alleged rape of Miss Emory; two for blowing up my parents house in revenge, and three for shooting Zane. The evidence was stacked against me. I was, indeed, the perfect scapegoat for Zane's crimes.

"I got scared and ran. I don't know how far I ran that night, but I remember waking up in the morning in the woods, knowing that I had to find Miss Emory. Not only did she have my baby daughter, my only living family member, but she was the only other living eyewitness who knew the truth about the explosion, and her pregnancy.

"I had no idea where she had gone in the pontoon boat. The news about the explosion had spread so fast—about how I, Abbott Marilee, had come back to kill my family who had disowned me, and how I blew up the house and shot my brother. I knew I had to find Miss Emory to reveal the truth, but I had to stay in hiding, too, in case I couldn't find her. I was terrified.

"So there I was—a condemned man, accused of rape, of blowing up a house, and of the murder of five people. Warrants were out for my arrest, and I was a fugitive. And I have been so ever since.

"Anyway, the entire Marilee fortune still remained safe in these vaults here, and I thought its secret was safe with me. However, Zane apparently let the family secret be known during those years he was in New England. He probably bragged about it to anyone who doubted his status in life, and that's how the legend started. It's true—we had millions of dollars in gold and silver down here, and when the rumor spread to the authorities, they searched and found only the entranceway to the vaults. Those imbecile investigators never got passed the first room! That secret wall had been built back in the eighteen hundreds. We rarely opened it, and whenever we did, we were always sure to pack mud into the cracks between all the bricks.

"So, one of the nights after the explosion, when the coast was clear, I sneaked inside the vaults and took enough money to get by on for a while. I got myself a motel room down in Lake Henry.

"The next morning, I woke up to find my little girl wrapped up in a blanket laying in a cardboard box outside my motel room door. I found a note stuck in the blanket that said, 'Here's your sweet baby, I'll have my own to take care of soon.' I found out from the desk clerk that Miss Emory had spent the night in that same hotel and checked out early that morning. She must have seen me the night before. I was so glad to have my baby back, but that was the last I ever heard of Miss Emory, the only hope of clearing my name of rape and murder charges.

"Now I was a fugitive with an infant daughter to take care of. We went down to New York City, and with the money from the vaults I got a place for us to live under a different identity. Over a few months I made several trips back to the property to take some of the fortune, not nearly all of it, but enough to do what I needed to do. I assumed a different identity completely. It was easy to do back then, in the days when computers weren't around to track your every move. I became Robert Rothschild. I got a job in a bank in Manhattan, bought a house on Staten Island, and hired a nanny to help care for my daughter.

"I spent the first several years trying to track down Miss Emory so that my name could be cleared and I could go back to Lake Marilee and rebuild the property. But I couldn't find her. All I was able to learn was that she had given birth to Zane's baby and then she got married to someone else and moved out of state, maybe out of the country.

"I made numerous trips back here to Abbeyville over the years. The amazing thing was that no one ever found the fortune in these vaults. It was easy for me to come onto the property unnoticed, climb down here, and take anything I wanted. I knew it was all legally mine, and I had no problem removing the entire fortune over time. I did it over several years and many, many trips—about ten years as a matter of fact. By the time these vaults were empty, the tragedy at Marilee Manor was old news and the Legend of Lake Marilee had been born.

"I put my daughter through school, I had opened my own financial business in Staten Island, and we were living rather luxuriously. Today, the Marilee fortune still exists a hundred times over, much of it in investment accounts with financial institutions all over the country.

"I had created for myself a whole new life, but it wasn't ideal. I was very sad about my family, and very bitter towards my brother. Over the years, the sadness went away but the bitterness didn't. I never remarried because I poured my time into my financial business. I wasn't the best of fathers either. My daughter was raised by various nannies, and when she was in high school, I traveled a lot. I made sure she went to a good college; she never graduated, though. Instead, she got married, and had children of her own. Quite a rift has developed between us over the years. We aren't on very good terms now. You see, it doesn't matter how much money you have if something in your heart just isn't right."

The old man spoke these words as tears again welled up in his eyes. Several moments of silence passed as Kristel and I looked on in wonder. It all sounded incredibly convincing.

Kristel finally said, "I'm so sorry, Mr. Roths--um, I mean, Mr. Marilee."

The gentleman sniffled and smiled. "Ah. I haven't been called that name in forty years."

"There's one thing I don't understand," Kristel added. Her voice was now free of trembling. "How did the story of your suicide come about? A hunter found your body, didn't he?"

Abbott Marilee removed his glasses to wipe his eyes. "Uh, yes, that's right. I left that part out. It's one part of my story I'm most ashamed of, but I must explain it to you." He settled his eyeglasses back on his nose and continued.

"A few days after the explosion, our church held a funeral service for my wife, son, mother, father, and brother. Everyone was buried next to each other in the Abbeyville Cemetery. I did not attend, for obvious reasons, but I read about it in the paper.

"At that time I was still in desperate straits. The authorities were hot after me, and I was worried I'd be found. This was before my baby had been left at my door at the motel, and I desperately needed to find Miss Emory. I needed to get the authorities off my back, so I did something horrible—I faked my own suicide.

"The night after the burial I exhumed Zane's body from the grave. I dug up the casket, pulled Zane's body out, and re-buried the casket—empty. The only things left in it were some trinkets, things like old school photos that people had placed in the open casket at the viewing. After I had replaced all the dirt and left the grave as best as I found it, I dragged the body to the woods. There, I changed the body into my clothes, put my wallet and identifications on it, even my wedding ring. I noticed that the bullet wound in Zane's forehead had been patched up nicely during the embalming, and my greatest fear was that the real identity of the body would be discovered in the autopsy. I went ahead with my plan anyway, figuring I had little to lose.

"Once I had the body dressed in my clothes, I took the rifle, the same one I had killed Zane with, and poked the barrel up under the neck of his corpse. I held it at an angle so that his face literally got blown off. I did that so the face would be unrecognizable if it was found before it decayed. I dropped the body in the lake and I threw the rifle in also. I knew the body would turn up down near the dam at Cotter's Landing.

"Amazingly, the plan worked. Zane's faceless body, with my identification on it, was discovered several days later. Investigators wrongly determined it had been in the lake since the night of the murder. They also wrongly determined that the body belonged to me and that I had fired a bullet under my chin to commit suicide seconds after killing my entire family.

"They buried me—actually Zane's body—right next to Zane's now-empty grave. To this day there's an empty coffin in Zane's grave, and his body is under the tombstone with my name on it. I had successfully faked my own death.

"I never heard anything about any strange discoveries during the autopsy of what they thought was my body. All I knew was that nobody was suspicious. Perhaps whoever performed the autopsy might have suspected something, having worked on the same body twice in a matter of days, and has kept the secret to himself to this day. I don't know, but it was a miracle I got away with it. Regardless, Abbott Marilee was officially dead and buried with the rest of his family.

"A couple of days later, I found my daughter at the motel room door, and I began a new life as Robert Rothschild. I did the best I could. The authorities were no longer chasing me, and I invested much time searching for Miss Emory to no avail. I spent many, many years in bitterness towards my brother and towards God. And now, here I am."

The old man stopped speaking and stared at the ground as he tried to fight back his emotions.

We sat there quietly for a while. As fascinating as the story was, I kept wondering: why me? He said his bringing us here had to do with Jimmy. But I didn't push the issue at the moment.

Kristel seemed to be more focused on the old man's well being. "You don't seem like a bitter person now," she said sweetly.

He spoke again. "Thank you. You see, after several years, and after my daughter had grown and moved away, I made things right with God. Remember how I said I had created a second life after the murders? Well, I learned to truly trust God since then, and I have a third life now. I thought for many years before the tragedy that God and I were on good terms because of my religious upbringing. But I was wrong. Since then, I have given my previous two lives over to God, the one as Abbot Marilee, and the one as

Robert Rothschild, and now this is the best life I've had yet, as a child of God."

Kristel smiled. "You're a very kind and generous man, and your faith in God is obvious."

"Thank you," he said in a weary voice.

Silence again filled the cold, damp underground room until our host resumed speaking.

"Well, Mr. Barrett. You're probably wondering what all this has to do with you and your brother."

I chuckled softly. "I can't imagine there's more to your story!"

"Ah, yes, there is. That is why I've brought you here tonight."

# CHAPTER 26

## *Identities, Doubt, and Inducement*

The old man rose from the crate he was sitting on and stretched his arms and legs. He leaned his backside against a support post of the wooden shelves and resumed speaking.

"Many years ago, Jody, after my daughter moved away, I became a regular guest at the Brown Swan Club, under my identity as Robert Rothschild, of course. Kind of ironic, isn't it? My coming back here as a guest? I did it because I had such an attachment to this area and this land. I'd occasionally visit these grounds after nightfall—and, well, I started scaring a few kids away who came snooping around here. That started the stories about my ghost roaming these grounds.

"I was kind of tickled with the way the Legend of Lake Marilee was developing—about the buried treasure, the ghosts, and so forth. It became somewhat of a game for me, being in Abbeyville in disguise like that. It's empowering to hear people talk about yourself in such a mythical sort of way, even though it was all terrible and false. And I don't mind the things that go on here, the wild parties and such. I've even heard that satanic cults have performed occult rituals here on the property. I don't mind that kind of stuff much—it actually helps keep greater numbers of people away from here—keeps the place kind of sacred. And that's just the way I want this place to stay—sacred, across the lake from Abbeyville, separated from the business of tourism and the like.

"So I've spent many summers as a guest at the Club, and occasionally I walk the property over here, reliving my childhood. So now you know the secret behind the mysterious Lights of Marilee that have drawn so many people to the lake's shore this time of year. Yes—that's me wondering around with a lantern, acting like a ghost."

He chuckled, and Kristel and I looked at each other, in absolute awe over this revelation. The great mystery! Its solution unfolded before us with a matter of words! We now knew that what had drawn ghost-crazy tourists and TV cameras to the lake for years was nothing more than a simple hoax performed by this kind old man. Old Whisper was right with his hunch, after all.

Rothschild continued, "Well, I've had this ghost legend going every July for some time now. But then a couple of years ago, I heard that the county is about to take over the land unless a relative of the Marilee family claims it. I figured the county would just assume rights to it, but then I heard that a local investor plans to buy the property and build a huge hotel resort right here at the Manor."

"Branson Oliff," Kristel interjected.

"Yes, that's right. He must wait until July 27th before he can purchase it. That's when a full forty years has passed without a Marilee claiming the property. Well, the last thing I ever want to see is Marilee Manor turned into some ritzy resort. I think the Brown Swan Club is enough resort for our little lakeside town here.

"When I first heard of Branson Oliff's plans, I realized there was nothing I could do to protect these grounds because I am a Rothschild and not a Marilee anymore. However, I do have the money to compete in a bidding war with Branson Oliff. Think of it—I'd be buying my own property!

Kristel huffed softly and shook her head.

"Legally the property is mine, as William Marilee's son, as it was stated on my father's will when he was killed. My own will, as Abbott Marilee, which I had drawn up when my first child was born, grants the property and the rest of the family fortune to my own children."

I interrupted. "So, since Abbott Marilee is legally dead, doesn't the property belong to your daughter? Can't she come out with her true identity, as the Marilee baby whose body was never discovered, and claim the property?"

"Yes, but she has no love for her heritage. She wants nothing to do with me, and she's not interested in the property at all. She's doing very well on her own as it is, and we rarely speak to each other. She doesn't want anything to do with being a Marilee."

"Can't she just take it anyway?" Kristel asked. "She could just keep it the way it is and pass it to her children—your grandchildren."

"Yes, she could. But she doesn't want to have to endure all the attention and publicity of revealing who she is. Plus, in any case—in order for her to get the property—I would have to reveal to the authorities my true identity and confess faking my own death. There is no other way that my daughter could prove her identity as the only living Marilee. So for me, as Robert Rothschild, to obtain this property, I would have to buy it when the county puts it up for sale, just like anybody else."

"Why can't you reveal your true identity to the public, just like you did to us?" Kristel asked.

"I've been hiding for forty years now, and that idea has eaten at me every day of those forty years. As much as I want to return to the world as Abbott Marilee, I have no alibi, except for Miss Emory, if she's even alive. I'd be convicted and sent to prison."

Kristel said, "But you know what Branson Oliff plans to do with this place, and his son is supposedly going to manage the resort."

"I know that. And that's where Jimmy Grandstaff comes in. I met Jimmy at the Club about three years ago. I enjoyed his company and spent many hours conversing with him about things, about life. It was his dream—his plan for his life—that I found to be so wonderful.

"He, as you know, was adopted, and it was his dream to someday build a home for unwed mothers that would provide them with an alternative to abortion. He wanted the home to coincide with an adoption agency for the children born to unwed mothers. Jimmy's own biological mother was unwed and chose adoption. I thought it was a wonderful dream, and I thought that Marilee Manor would be a perfect place for the home—a beautiful quiet setting. I became very excited about the prospect, and I considered strongly my options to help him.

"Jimmy was still rather young then, only sixteen. But I got to know him well, and I decided that when he turned eighteen, I would come out of hiding and reveal my identity to the public.

"It took me two years to come to that decision. I knew it would involve the authorities exhuming the graves, and the possibility of my being convicted was still very real. But even as a convicted rapist and murderer, I would have legal rights to my estate, and I would grant it all to Jimmy, who, as a legal adult, would be able to do with it as he pleased, which would be to build a home for unwed mothers and their children. And, perhaps, if I got lucky, a good lawyer would win me an acquittal in my murder trial. In any case, I'm getting old now, and spending the rest of my life in hiding didn't seem any better than going to prison, if it meant giving Jimmy a chance at his dream.

"So last summer I had resolved to do it—to reveal my identity to Jimmy. I was ready to do for him what I'm doing for you right now—take him down here and tell him my story and what I wanted to do for him. Then I'd reveal myself to the police. But a few months before he turned eighteen, Jimmy died in the diving accident. I believe it was you, Kristel, who witnessed the death?"

"Yes."

"That is so tragic, very tragic. Of course, I was extremely saddened over Jimmy's death, and I was also disappointed that his dream died with him. I was eager to see what this property might be one day, and in one tragic step, it was all gone.

"During the months since then, I resolved to come out with my true identity anyway. I'm so tired of this lifestyle. I'm too old for it. And in the back of my mind, I feel there is always a chance that the truth would prevail in the trial. I hope and pray so, anyway. I know I will have to face the likelihood of prison, but in the least, the property would never be purchased by Branson Oliff and turned into a resort. I could hire someone else to build and run the home and dedicate it to Jimmy. It will be my property again, and I can do with it as I please, even from prison.

"I had been planning on revealing my identity this month, because perhaps public sentiment would be on my side with the Branson Oliff purchase being so imminent. Perhaps the locals here would like my plans of an adoption home over Oliff's big plans.

"I knew that before I go public with my identity, I needed to contact my daughter to tell her of my plans and to promise that I would not reveal *her* identity. So I spoke with both my daughter and her husband for the first time in years several months ago, not long after Jimmy died. They both discouraged me from doing this. They thought the adoption home was a noble idea, but they didn't think it was worth it. My daughter told me I should live the rest of my life in the comforts that I have and let the property go as it might.

"I've been considering her advice ever since, even though my daughter and I still haven't reconciled. I've been praying everyday about what I should do: come clean and turn my property into an adoption home, or live the rest of my life as Robert Rothschild and see the place become a big resort.

"And one day last month my prayers were answered. At the beginning of the summer, the rumors came out about Jimmy's death being a murder. I read the article about the John Doe letter the police received. I was so intrigued by it! I loved Jimmy, you see, and to hear that he could have been murdered—well, I couldn't stop thinking about it. I felt it was God telling me to do something.

"And shortly after that John Doe letter, I saw you, Jody. You looked so much like Jimmy! I immediately talked to George Schuple about the striking likeness, and he revealed to me that you are Jimmy's brother and that you hadn't even learned yet that you had a brother. I could hardly sleep that night thinking about it!

"What an incredible collection of circumstances for you, Jody! You happen to come to work at the same summer resort that your brother worked. The day you get here, news breaks that your brother, who you never knew to begin with, may have died by murder. I found it incredibly fascinating and I couldn't stop thinking about it—how and why Jimmy died.

"And, you might think this is silly, Jody, but I think that the Lord arranged for you to come here. I think that it is God's plan for you to find out who may have killed your brother. That's why I started sending the letters—to urge you to look into it. I even faked like I had arrived in the area several days after you got my first note… you know—the one with Jimmy's photograph I put on the dashboard of your car. That way you would never think it was Robert Rothschild sending them because you received the first one days before I arrived.

My jaw dropped open. "Wait a minute," I interrupted, shaking my head. "When I first met you and carried your luggage to your chalet, you already knew who I was?"

"Yes. I came into town immediately when I learned of the John Doe letter. I happened to see you in the supermarket that night and I was shocked at your resemblance to Jimmy. I overheard you talking with your friend and I learned you were an employee at the Club. So I called George Schuple to find out more about you. Then I placed the first note, along with Jimmy's photograph, in your car the next day."

"So when you wrote that note, it was just a day after you read the newspaper article?" I asked.

"Yes. I spent all night and the next day meditating on it. And I came to the conclusion that you showed up here for a reason—a divine reason."

"But why didn't you just come right out and talk to me like you're doing now? Why all these weeks of mysterious notes and secret rendezvous?"

"That's a good question, Jody. For one, I can't live in hiding and investigate Jimmy's death at the same time, so I wrote those notes to try to get you to do it. And secondly, I wanted to test you."

"Test me?" I started to get a little ticked off—like I was being used to carry out the old man's silly quest to solve a supposed murder.

"Yes. I needed to test you first. I needed to know how much I could depend on you."

"By passing me those ridiculous Ambassador notes?"

"Yes. That's right. I wanted to test your faith in the uncertain and the unknown. Imagine, Jody, if Robert Rothschild came up to you one day and asked you to put your faith in John Doe—to believe that there was some truth behind that single John Doe letter. You see, that's what this is all about—the John Doe letter. John Doe got this started, but I don't know who or where he is. But I know that *I'm* real. *I* exist. And I wanted to see if the written words of a true-to-life Ambassador for the Dead could provoke you to action. How could I trust you to invest your faith into a single letter from the unknowable John Doe, if you couldn't be provoked to action by a series of letters from a real person?"

"I'm beginning to think I should have never taken those letters seriously," I said with a disgusted tone.

"You're right. My letters didn't work, obviously. You didn't look into Jimmy's death, and that's why I'm talking to you here tonight."

"Did you really think that a bunch of Ambassador-for-the-Dead letters would get me to take the John Doe letter seriously? The police aren't even sure about the John Doe letter themselves."

"At least it led them to investigate the scene again. You virtually ignored most of my letters."

"That's not true. I took every single one of them to the police station because I thought there might be something to them. And I did go down to the dock that night like you wanted, and I did meet you at the supermarket tonight, obviously."

"You're right, Jody, you're right. But those letters were intended to not only test your faith in the unknown, but to also test your dedication to Jimmy, your own flesh and blood."

"That's not fair! I never knew Jimmy! Are you questioning my dedication to my dead brother because I didn't respond to your stupid letters?"

"No, Jody, not at all. I was using the letters to see how much it would take for you to do something about Jimmy. Your response to those letters showed me that it would take more than my own written words to prompt you to action. I learned that I would have to go to more drastic extremes, like what we're doing here right now. My words weren't enough for you. I had to bring you here and *show* you—a miraculous action, in my view."

"Well, I'm still not convinced! What if you're lying? What if all of this is a lie? What if you're not Abbott Marilee and just some impostor instead? Or—even better—what if you are Abbott Marilee, and you really did rape that girl and kill your whole family? Aren't you just asking me to believe your *words*? You haven't offered me any real proof."

"You're absolutely right. I was hoping you would believe my letters. And now I'm hoping that you will believe me as I speak directly to you. But the choice to believe in me is entirely yours. I can't force you to believe. You're right—I can't offer any overwhelming physical evidence. And there's only one other eyewitness to the truth of the tragedies forty years ago, and I don't know if Miss Emory is alive or dead. All I'm asking of you, Jody, is to trust me. Believe that what I have said to you tonight is the truth."

I was exasperated. "I can't. I'd like to believe you, but I wasn't there. Nobody but Miss Emory was. So nobody is ever going to know for sure. You might as well start writing Ambassador notes to the authorities, because they're no more convincing than your story here tonight."

He paused and a slight sneer crossed his face. "You sound just like your mother," he grumbled.

Those words hit me like a two-by-four. "How do you know my mother?" I asked with a snobbish tone.

He stood silent for a moment. I watched his mustache quiver; his sneer turned into a smile of amusement. I could sense that Kristel was looking back and forth from him to me.

I repeated my question: "How do you know my mother?"

Then he hit me with the big one.

"I know your mother, Jody, because she is my daughter."

He paused to let it all sink in. But it didn't sink in. It was stuck in my throat and I couldn't say anything.

"Your mother was my little infant daughter who survived the explosion. She's the baby that Miss Emory took care of for those few days. I brought her to New York with me and raised her as Madeline Rothschild."

My voice cracked when I interjected, "That's not true. Her maiden name was Wallace."

"Yes. Like I said, we had a falling out when she was older, and she changed her name. In fact, it was a night very much like this one when our differences began. I had never told her about her true family heritage until she had come home from college one Christmas. I told her everything that night just like I'm telling to you here tonight. And she took it the same way—a lot harder, in fact. She *does* believe that I am Abbott Marilee, but she *doesn't* believe in my innocence. She, to this day, believes that I am a rapist and murderer."

Kristel cut in, "Why? Why did she believe part of your story but not the other part?"

"I think it's because she grew up seeing how I lived my life as Robert Rothschild—as a man in hiding, a man who disguises himself, a man who would sneak up here to these vaults to obtain the remaining fortune. But not as a family man. Not as a man who once had a wife and children. I paid an army of nannies to raise Madeline for me. What she saw of her father was only the sneaky, furtive side, not the husband and father that existed before the tragedy. I think that's why she chooses to believe the way she does. I wasn't a very good father to her at all, and I'm reaping the results of my work."

I had my voice back now. "So you're saying that you're my *grandfather*?"

He smiled and said, "Yes, I am."

"Then you were Jimmy's grandfather, too. How long did you know that?"

"Only for about three weeks now—no longer than I've known that you are my grandson—the day I learned from Mr. Schuple that you are Jimmy's brother. When I asked if you were adopted like Jimmy was, Mr. Schuple told me about your mother, and I knew that he was talking about my daughter. Your last name is Barrett, and I know my daughter's husband's name is Wesley Barrett. In one day, I learned that the person I was going to give my property to was my deceased grandson. And God saw fit for me to learn about my other grandson, the living one, on the same day. "

"Have you talked to my mother since you found out who I was?"

"I have tried to contact her, but I cannot reach her."

"That's because they're separated now. She doesn't live with Wesley anymore."

He frowned. "Hmm. That doesn't surprise me."

"So that's what this is all about, huh. You brought me here to tell me that you're my grandfather?"

"Yes, that's part of it."

I was incredulous. "Look, it's not that I don't believe you, and it's not that I do believe you. It's just that I can't believe any of this. Right now, I don't know what to believe."

"Give it time, Jody. This is a lot to take in."

"So are you still going to go public with your identity?"

"I plan on doing that shortly. I don't want Branson Oliff buying this property, and I'd still like to fulfill Jimmy's dream for him, unless, of course, you'd like to help."

"What do you mean?"

"The property is yours, son, if you want it. And if I give it to you before the 27th of this month, I won't have to buy it from the county. I'd just give it to you."

"My mother doesn't want it?"

"Not a bit of it."

"So you'd just give it to me? Just like that?"

"Well, not exactly." His mustache twitched again. "You first have to trust me, and you have to trust John Doe."

"What do you mean?"

"I want you to find John Doe."

I laughed. "You're crazy! The police can't even find him."

"Yes, but you're Jimmy's brother."

"So?"

"If I give you this property, I want you to see to it that Jimmy's legacy lives on."

"What's that got to do with John Doe?" I was getting angry again.

"John Doe obviously knows something about Jimmy's death."

"So. Maybe he does; maybe he doesn't."

I didn't like where this conversation was heading, as my mind was already in a storm. I added, "Maybe you just ought to count me out. I don't know if I want anything to do with this family."

The old man solaced, "I don't blame you. You hardly know me, and what you do know, you can't believe. And you never knew Jimmy. But, Jody, listen to me. I am convinced that John Doe is a tool in God's hands. And I need you to act on it. I can't explain everything to you right now, but I think John Doe has something more to say about Jimmy's death, and you're the perfect person to bring John Doe out of the woodwork."

"But you don't know anything more about Jimmy's death than I, or the police, do." A tone of sarcasm rang in my voice.

"I have my hunches."

I laughed again. "A hunch?" I now was very upset. "Heck, Kristel and I have our hunches! We have our suspicions! We think Brock Oliff might have pushed Jimmy. But I thought you actually *knew* something! You're saying that all those letters you sent me about Jimmy—those were all based on a hunch? They were motivated only by that John Doe crap?"

My alleged grandfather remained calm, despite my displeasure. "Jody, be patient and trust me. I don't have any solid information about your brother, but I have spent countless hours over the last few weeks developing a hypothesis."

"O, gosh! A hypothesis! I looked at Kristel and joked, "He's got a hypothesis!"

Kristel said, "Jody, just listen to him. Give him a chance to explain."

"How are we supposed to believe that what he's explained so far isn't a lie? How do we know that this guy is who he says he is?"

"Dig up my brother's grave," the old man said confidently, "and you will see I wasn't lying about that."

I snorted a mocking laugh. "Okay then, you just might be Abbott Marilee himself. Maybe you did fake your own suicide. But how do we know that everything else you've said is true? How do we know you weren't the one who raped Miss Emory? How do we know that she confessed to you and your father that it was Zane? How do we know that you didn't blow up the house in a mad act of revenge against your father?"

"Why would I kill my wife and son?"

"Maybe because you did get Miss Emory pregnant, and like your father, your wife didn't want any part of you."

The old man's chin fell to his chest and he stared at the ground.

I glanced at Kristel and I could tell she was angry with me for being so nasty.

"Jody and Kristel," the old man said suddenly, raising his head and sticking his forefinger under his glasses to rub his eyes. "I don't blame you for doubting what I've said about the Marilee legend. That's why I've never revealed my identity after all these years—I have no proof of my innocence. The evidence that does exist can only send me to prison. But if you believe anything I've said to you this evening, please, I beg of you, believe this—Jimmy Grandstaff was murdered! I'm sure of it."

I rejoined, "But you said it's only a hunch, a hypothesis that you've come up with because of one single John Doe letter."

"Yes, it is just a hypothesis. But the only way I can prove it is with you, Jody. You are the best person to go digging around for the truth. You're Jimmy's brother! Nobody would think twice about it! Me, on the other hand, what are people going to think if some rich old man makes a huge fuss over the investigation of a nine month old accident?"

"Why not just let the police handle it?"

"They are handling it. And I think they're covering it up."

"Covering what up?"

"The murder. I think the police are involved in a cover-up."

"You're crazy! What makes you think that?"

"I've got my reasons."

"You're nuts!"

"Do you trust the police?" he asked.

"Yes!"

"Why do you so easily put your faith in them and not me?"

"Because they're the *police*! You're just some crazy old man!"

"The police can be crooked."

"Some of them, sure."

"So how do you know whether to trust them or not?"

"Because! You see… it's… this is so stupid! I don't know how you can trust anybody! That's why I don't trust people—not anyone! That's the safest way to operate."

"Do you trust Kristel here?"

"Yes. Listen. You know what I mean. You have to get to know them. Then you can make a decision. I don't know you very well, all right? I know Kristel, and I know Mr. Schuple, and I know Officer Anders, and I know I can trust them."

"What about Sheriff Slater?"

"I hardly know him, so I suppose I don't trust him."

Kristel interjected. "*I* don't trust him. If there is a cover-up, I'd bet *he's* in on it."

The old man nodded and spoke to Kristel. "Okay, Kristel—so you don't trust Sheriff Slater, but you trust Officer Anders?"

Kristel answered, "Yes."

"So what's the difference between the two? Why do you trust one and not the other?"

"Roy Anders is just a great guy! He loves his wife and his kids. He's nice and considerate. Sheriff Slater is kind of a jerk. He swears a lot, and he left his wife for a younger woman, and then dumped her, too. He's just not the kind of person I would trust, even if he is the sheriff."

"So you're judging these two men based on their character, aren't you."

"I guess so," Kristel answered.

"And you could be wrong. Officer Anders could be as crooked a cop there ever was."

"He could be, but I know he isn't."

"You don't have any doubt?"

"No. I know he's an honest man."

The old man stopped and looked at me. "Jody, Kristel here claims that she knows something about Officer Anders. She can trust him and put her faith in him." He paused. "Give *me* a chance here, Jody. I just want you to *trust me*. I know things. I know things that others don't. And I know that God had John Doe mail that letter for a reason. I think there's a conspiracy centered around your brother's death, and we've got to find John Doe."

I was still pretty miffed at everything. "So what do you want me to do? Explain your hypothesis to the police and say that I dreamt it up myself?"

"No. All I want you to do is to stir up some publicity about your being Jimmy's brother and wanting to find out the truth. Just make a little noise, stir up some trouble and see who comes out of the woodwork. That, hopefully, will draw forth our John Doe. We've got to find out who he or she is. I must talk to that person."

"And you'll just stay in hiding as Robert Rothschild until John Doe reveals himself? And then you'll talk to him or her and find out whether your hypothesis is right?"

"Yes and no. We've got to find John Doe so that I can prove or disprove my hypothesis. But in the meantime, I have to disappear."

"Disappear? Why?"

"If my hypothesis is indeed correct, then I am in considerable danger. I must go into hiding, yet again."

"Why?"

"I think they're onto me. I think they know who I really am."

"But you were planning to come out of hiding anyway."

"I know. But I think they plan to eliminate me altogether. So I've got to disappear until we, I mean you, find John Doe."

Kristel looked at me and I returned a noncommittal expression.

"I don't know about all this, Mr., uh, Mr. Rothschild? Is it okay to still call you that?"

"Yes. I'm more used to it than Mr. Marilee… or grandpa." He smiled shyly.

Grandpa. I couldn't believe it.

I said, "I'm not sure I want anything to do with all this stuff—family or not. I came here to get away from my family."

"I know, Jody. I don't blame you for doubting what I've said tonight. If you doubt who I truly am, then I've done all I can do to convince you. If you doubt that my brother framed me for *his* murders, then so be it. I would probably have doubts if I were in your place.

"But please consider this: for the first time in forty years I have revealed to someone besides my daughter my true identity, and I have put the wonderful life I currently have in great jeopardy. I have chosen to do this for one reason and one reason only—to compel you, Jody Barrett, to begin making a public issue over the death of your brother. If the cause of his death isn't so important to me, then I would never have revealed to you the things I have tonight."

He sounded sincere. I replied, "I don't know. I would just rather live my life without all this."

"Please," he continued. "I have everything to lose by telling you this. And I have to leave the Club tonight."

"Aren't you going to tell us your theory—your hypothesis about Jimmy's death?" I asked.

"All I can say is, it involves a conspiracy of several individuals."

"Can you tell us any names?"

"No definite names yet. I've only been working on this for few weeks, you see. And I'm a man in hiding. It's not that easy, because now I think someone is onto my true identity."

"This is nuts!" I said. "Your hypothesis is… is that Jimmy was murdered and the police are covering it up?"

"Yes, believe it or not."

"I *can't* believe this!"

Kristel tapped my leg. "Jody, listen to him!"

The old man rubbed his beard. "I don't know the who's, the what's, or the how's, but I'm sure that Jimmy was murdered. I can feel it in my heart. And if he was murdered, then there's someone involved in the investigation that's covering something up."

I huffed mockingly again. "A police cover up. Sir, you've been watching too much TV."

Kristel was hooked on the old man's theory. She asked him, "Sheriff Slater is in charge of the investigation. Do you think he's covering up something?"

"I don't know the names of anyone. I try to keep my distance from the police for good reasons. That's why I'm trying to get Jody here to help. But if you say this sheriff is the one in charge of the investigation, I'd have to suspect him in the cover up."

"To protect Brock?" Kristel asked.

"Again, I don't know any names. I'm helpless. In fact, I'm fairly certain I'm in danger. That's why I, a man already in hiding, have to go into hiding again. And that's why it's imperative that Jody does everything he can to raise publicity and start his own investigation."

"How?" I asked in a disgruntled voice.

"Contact the media. Your story will attract much attention, Jody. Talk to people, talk to as many people in the police department as possible. The whole department can't be covering it up, for heaven's sake. Talk to other police departments, too. I'm sure they will do all they can to work with you. You're his brother, and that should mean something."

"And you're just going to disappear? How will we contact you?"

"I will contact you in due time. Do you agree to assist me in these matters?"

"I can't," I replied defiantly. "This is all too much. I came up here this summer to get away from my family, and now you want me to investigate a murder and turn my life into a big public story."

"Jody, we're dealing with a murder here. The murder of your brother."

"I didn't even have a brother until I got here! And besides—we don't even know he was murdered. He wasn't found stabbed to death! He fell from a cliff. We only have murder on our minds because of that stupid John Doe letter!"

"You don't care to find out if he was murdered or not?"

"No. I don't. I don't want any part of it."

The old man shook his head. "Then you couldn't care less about the truth. I should have known. All those letters didn't work. Why did I expect that bringing you here would make a difference?"

"I care about the truth," I responded. "I just don't want to have to deal with it. It'll turn my life upside down."

"That's exactly it. You don't want the responsibility that comes with knowing the truth," he said, raising his voice. "For you, Jody, knowing the truth will inconvenience you. You'll have to do something with it. You might have to change the way you've thought all these years—change your philosophies, your outlooks on life, your relationships with others. Right now, for you, ignorance is bliss and the truth is a heck of a lot to handle. So you prefer ignorance and avoid the truth!"

I didn't say anything.

"Indeed, Jody, the truth carries with it the responsibility to act, the responsibility to live with conviction, the responsibility to distinguish right from wrong, true from false, the responsibility to reject what's wrong and what's false and embrace what's right and true.

"But you'd rather be indifferent; what you don't know isn't your concern; all's relative in a world without truth, isn't it, Jody? People like you prefer uncertainties. That way, you never have to take sides. You never can point a finger and say 'that's wrong!' or 'that's right!' Without truth, everything is accepted, condoned, or tolerated.

"But the fact is, in this case, Jody, without knowing the truth, there's a fifty percent chance you could be tolerating an accident, and there's a fifty percent chance you could be tolerating a murder. Now do you want to live with those odds, or is tolerating murder something you normally do?"

I stared at the limestone floor as the old man's words echoed in my brain.

We all sat there in silence. Kristel said nothing. The old man shifted his weight. I kept staring at the floor.

Finally, he said, "I thought it might come to this, Jody. If the truth about Jimmy isn't enough for you, then I can resort to bribery." He reached for his pockets where his money was stashed.

"You don't have to bribe me," I said.

"Then you're willing to fulfill my request?"

"I don't know. I just don't know right now. This is a lot to dump on me all at once, you know."

"I will reward you greatly," Marilee said, "with more than I have in my pockets right now."

"How?"

The old man pointed at the wooden crate upon which he previously sat. "That crate right there contains fifty thousand dollars in twenty dollar denominations, and we're going to leave it right here tonight, unopened. I'll drive you both back to the Club and arrange for a reporter to come and talk to you in a few days. He'll want to interview you because you're Jimmy's brother. That's how you'll get started. After the interview, if you wish, you can come right back here and obtain this money. I will have a key that unlocks the padlock on the door of the vault delivered to you after your story hits the media."

"You're going to pay me fifty grand just to do an interview with a reporter?"

"You don't seem motivated otherwise."

I looked at the crate and then at Kristel. She raised her eyebrows and shook her head as if to say, "Don't look at me!" I laughed to myself, shook my own head and said, "I can't believe all this. It all sounds so crazy! We're down here in a secret vault like Indiana Jones, and you're bribing me with a supposed fifty grand in that box, just to send me out on a murder investigation as though I'm a member of the F.B.I.!"

Marilee smiled. "Believe it, please. Will you do it for me, son?"

I crossed my arms and stared at the wooden crate. I didn't care to look inside it to see if the money was there or not. It wouldn't surprise me if the crate suddenly sprouted legs and horns and started walking around the room.

"So you're the legendary Abbott Marilee, standing here as healthy as a horse." I said sarcastically.

"I'm as sure of it as I have a beating heart!"

"Did you murder your family forty years ago?"

"I've already given you my version of the story."

"Uh huh. And you're going to leave tonight to go … God knows where."

"That's right. My flight leaves Albany at 2:00 a.m. The van to the airport leaves from the Club at 11:00. So we must hurry back."

"And you're going to contact us when you see fit?"

"Yes, I will as soon as I see your story in the media. Then I'll Fed-Ex the key to this vault so you can get your money. Are you with me?"

I looked down at the wooden crate again.

"I'll do it."

# CHAPTER 27

## *Going Public, Sheriff Slater, and Mission Accomplished—Twice*

It was minutes before eleven o'clock when we returned to the Club. The fireworks had come and gone, and we didn't hear as much as a pop from our position underneath Marilee Manor.

Now we were at the porch of the Club building, where Kristel kissed me on the cheek and hurried home. She *kissed* me. *She* kissed *me*! Had it been any other night, the action would have been most significant. But this wasn't any other night. Tonight, I learned that I was a Marilee—at least that's what the old man said—and even Kristel's affection couldn't clear my brain of it.

From the porch I watched Abbott Marilee, a.k.a. Robert Rothschild, my alleged grandfather, board a van headed to the Albany airport. After he was gone, I picked up the pay phone in the lobby and called the number where my mother was staying.

"Hello," she answered. I hadn't heard her voice in weeks.

"Mom, this is Jody."

"Jody, honey! I'm so glad to finally hear from you again! How is your summer?"

"It's been rather exciting."

"I knew you'd have a wonderful time. I'm so sorry I haven't written, honey. My life has been such a mess. It's getting better, though."

"That's all right. I've received plenty of mail this summer."

After a pause, she admitted, "Jody, I've been wanting to tell you that I'm sorry about your brother. I'm sorry I never told you." She paused a moment again and continued, "I… I didn't know what to say when you confronted me like that on the phone. And I know I should have told you the truth. I did have a baby boy two years before you were born. It was a rough part of my life. I was young, just out of school …."

I appreciated that she was finally confessing what I already knew, but there was something more now. Something big. Bluntly, I interrupted her. "Your father never died, did he."

"What, honey?"

"Your father never died before I was born like you said, did he."

A long silence confirmed the allegation that I was, indeed, the grandson of Abbott Marilee.

"Mom, you just told me the truth about Jimmy, so why don't you tell me the truth about the rest of the family."

"Jody...." Another long silence.

Unsympathetically, I waited.

She finally said, "Have you met somebody—an older man up there?"

"Yes, I have."

"What did he tell you?"

"Everything."

"He told you he's my father?"

"Yes. He told me everything. How come you never told me? Why don't you want any of his estate?"

"Because he's a criminal, Jody. A murderer and a rapist. I don't want to be linked to him whatsoever."

"What makes you so certain he did it? Maybe his brother Zane did it. Maybe he's completely innocent."

"He has told me one lie after another for so many years, honey. And he's telling you the same lies. He's a man on the run—he's been in hiding for forty years. All he's got is his money, and he killed my mother and brother and my grandparents and my uncle to get it."

The more my mother tried to convince me he was guilty, the more I wanted to believe he was innocent.

"I believe his story," I fibbed, attempting a tone of confidence.

"Honey, don't. He's just a lonely, old, rich man who wants to keep his name on that property. He raped a fifteen year old girl before he killed his entire family, and he doesn't want to go to prison."

"He didn't kill *you*."

"He didn't need to. I was too young of an eyewitness."

"He could've killed you if he wanted. But he chose to raise you and give you a life."

"He didn't raise me. He hired others to raise me."

"At least he did *that*. It would have been easier, if he was a cold blooded murderer, to just drown you in the lake or something."

"Jody, you don't understand. He was never around for me. He wasn't a father to me. To him, I was an inconvenience that could be taken care of with his wallet. He was never a father to me—never there when I needed him."

"Sounds like you married someone just like him." Ooh, that was mean, and I knew it. It just popped into my head, and I said it.

Another pause.

"Have you talked to Wesley about this?" my mother asked.

"No. I haven't talked to him since he was here a few weeks ago."

"He was there? When?"

"After you left him. I only saw him for a few minutes. He wanted me to go camping with him and then come home, but I told him to forget it."

Another pause.

"Jody, is… is my father at the Club now?"

"He was. He just left tonight."

"Where did he go?"

"I don't know. He's going into hiding again."

"You see, honey. That is what my entire life was like with that man. Don't believe him, Jody. Don't trust him."

I didn't say anything. She went on, "Has he said anything to you… about what he plans to do?"

"He wants to give me the property so I can let Jimmy's dream come true—to build an adoption home, instead of letting this other guy buy it."

"And that's something you really want to get involved in?"

"I don't know. I guess. I haven't had time to think about it."

"Jody, just be careful. Don't get disappointed if they suddenly take him away in handcuffs."

"I won't."

"You're old enough to decide whether or not you want a part in his tainted estate, but I'm just telling you not to get your hopes up."

"I won't."

"You *can't* trust him."

"We'll see."

With that, the conversation ended.

That night I lay in my bunk into the early morning hours, incapable of falling asleep. How in the world was a sixteen-year-old kid expected to handle all this? Fifty thousand dollars waiting for me in a secret vault! An old man's "hunch" about conspiracies and police cover-ups? Can Officer Anders be trusted? Sheriff Slater? And then there was the story of rape, bribery, and murder, and a man claiming to be my grandfather who was blamed for it. Dynamite. Gunshots. Digging up corpses and faking a suicide. A baby delivered at a doorstep. Forty years of living in disguise and luxury. Fooling a town with a Scooby Doo-like mystery ghost. Sliding doors and underground tunnels. A confession of a lifetime. A legend, dumped in my lap, with "hoax" stamped all over it.

Why me? I had enough problems of my own at home! Now I had *two* family members haunting this lake, a dead brother and a grandfather.

And it was all because some adopted kid and I shared the same mother. That's the only reason I was tied up in this thing. Some dead kid I never knew. My brother. How did he really die? Why? Brock? Jealousy? It could be that he just tripped. An accident? No, a conspiracy. A police cover-up. A crazy old man thinking up a convoluted "hypothesis." And now I had promised him I'd go public and make a big fuss. An award of fifty thousand dollars in a crate, hidden in a legendary secret tomb, and the key to be sent in the mail. Just like the movies. I wasn't dreaming this up—I was living it.

I kept thinking: my mother says that he's a liar, that my grandfather is a rapist and a murderer. Mr. Rothschild? *Him*? It just didn't fit. I wanted to believe everything he told me, but my mother was just as convincing. It was her personal opinion vs. his personal testimony.

For now, I'm sticking with my grandfather… or I at least *want* to. See, my mother had *lived* with the man. All I know about him is that he looks like a charming old gentleman and he gives money away like it's candy. I want to believe my grandfather, and I don't want to believe my mother.

How much does *wanting* something to be true make it true? Kristel and Whisper have proven that truth is truth, and it doesn't matter what I believe or want to believe. In this case, the only certainty is that either my mother or grandfather is right, and I need to choose between the two.

At least I'm not alone. At least Kristel is back now, and I can trust her, and she is definitely on my grandfather's side. And *she* kissed *me* on the cheek tonight.

Sunday morning at work meant blueberry pancakes, and I was behind the grill performing the craft meticulously once again. It was a mad rush at first because Boonie and I woke up late. A brief power outage threw off our alarm clock in the cabin, and if it wasn't for Boonie's internal clock that got us there just thirty minutes late, breakfast would have been a complete disaster.

I stayed at the grill and flipped row after row of pancakes. The routine permitted my mind to juggle the emotions of last night. I was off in my own little world, dropping batter, sprinkling blueberries, flipping once, stacking, sugaring, over and over again, and all the time thinking, contemplating, wondering, doubting, considering. Meanwhile, the kitchen was in its regular mayhem.

Good old Boonie, after about two hours of scurrying, cooking, serving, and rushing, finally had time to come to the grill and talk to me. His first words were, "So what happened with Santa Claus last night?"

I couldn't tell him anything. I couldn't trust him with it, not yet. Not with this. So I kept my eyes on the grill and lied. "Nothing. It turned out to be nothing. I'm kind of ticked about it."

"What do you mean it was nothing? Is Mr. Rothschild the Ambassador? Is he also John Doe?"

"He's the Ambassador, but he's not John Doe."

"So what did he say? Where did he take you?"

"He just drove us around in his Mercedes so we could talk. He said that he was very fond of Jimmy and that he wants me to do all I can to find out about his death."

"That's it? That's all he said? He doesn't know anything about Jimmy being murdered?"

"No. Nothing more than you or I do."

I wanted desperately to tell Boonie the entire incredible story, but I respected Abbott Marilee's secrecy and kept silent. Boonie had already proven to me he wasn't responsible, so I answered his questions carefully.

"That sucks, man. But at least you finally know who's been sending all those stupid notes. How come he didn't just come right out and talk to you in the beginning?"

"Because he wasn't sure what I'd do. He said he heard the news about the police getting the John Doe letter and he became absolutely convinced that Jimmy was murdered. He wants Jimmy to get his justice and redemption and stuff like that, and me being his brother, he thinks I am the perfect person to do it for him. You know, go on a quest to find my brother's murderer, and all that. Mr. Rothschild admits he kind of went overboard. But it's weird, you know, 'cause he's so sure that Jimmy was murdered. And the more I talked to him, the more I began to believe it, too. So does Kristel."

I finished lifting a grill full of pancakes, and began dropping more batter in nice, neat columns for about the billionth time that morning.

Boonie continued, "But why did he have to write all those Ambassador notes?"

"He's just a private kind of person. He wanted to see if he could motivate me to look into Jimmy's death without getting involved in it himself. But when I basically ignored all his letters, he had to talk to me face to face."

"That's it? Man, he sounds like an odd ball."

"He's not. He was very fond of Jimmy, and he's convinced that he was murdered."

"Who does he think did it, then? Brock?"

"No. He has no idea. He just has this feeling it's true, like God told him or something. And because he feels so strongly about it, he thinks it's best for me to do something about it because I'm Jimmy's brother. He just wants me to make a big stink of it in the news, and maybe it'll bring out this John Doe person to give more information."

"So are you gonna tell the newspapers that you're Jimmy's brother?"

"Yeah. That's all Mr. Rothschild wanted me to do. He left last night, though."

"He left?"

"Yeah. He said he had to go somewhere—business or something. He might not be back for a while. That's why he wanted to talk to me so badly last night."

I felt incredibly guilty for lying to my friend, even though it was a pretty good lie that revealed just enough, but not too much. Boonie seemed satisfied with my story.

Just before lunch, I received a call in the kitchen office from Sam Barney of the *Lake Henry Gazette*. He said he wanted to interview the long, lost brother of the late Jimmy Grandstaff. *Boy, Rothschild works fast!* I agreed to an interview scheduled for three o'clock that afternoon at the picnic pavilion at the town beach.

Consequently, I had to cancel my wood carving session with Whisper again. I was kind of glad, because he was going to tell me about his snooping around the Manor and trying to uncover a hoax. I would have had to bite my tongue the whole time during that conversation!

Sam Barney was a recent college graduate, no more than twenty-two or twenty-three years old. He took a job with the *Gazette* in May, just after graduation, and had since written articles for public interest, covering events like craft shows, the remodeling of a local restaurant, and even the hunting accident in which a Huron County police officer named Roy Anders broke his leg and was stranded in the Hudson River for twelve hours.

I was disappointed that he had never written an article covering a murder investigation, a faked suicide, or fifty thousand dollars in cash hidden in a wooden crate. But at least Sam Barney could provide me media coverage, and that's all that mattered. That was all Rothschild asked me to do.

I answered questions about my upbringing as an only child, how I came to discover that Jimmy was my brother, and how my parents never told me the truth. Finally, Sam Barney asked me if I believed that Jimmy was pushed from the cliff. I surprised even myself with my bold answer. "I believe my brother's death might not have been an accident. Somebody out there knows something. Maybe he did fall. Maybe he didn't. But if someone out there killed my brother, I just want to know why. I'd really like to speak with the John Doe who sent that letter to the police."

That quote was the final paragraph in Sam Barney's third page article that would appear in the local section of tomorrow's *Lake Henry Gazette*, and my mission to make a big deal about the death of Jimmy Grandstaff had been accomplished.

For reasons unbeknownst to the general public, the Lights of Marilee would stop appearing at the Manor, and only Kristel, I, and the departed Robert Rothschild knew why.

Hundreds of new guests had arrived over the weekend, and many anticipated seeing them on that Sunday night, July 5th. Kristel and I gathered with dozens of others on the beach deck, just so we could hear their comments from an entirely knew perspective. Numerous regulars, including the fanatical Harold and Gretta, perched themselves down on the beach close to the shore with their binoculars. Branson and Peggy Oliff were there again, sitting casually at a table with another couple. George Schuple conversed with several men near the railing. Cliques of other staff members gathered on blankets down below on the beach again. Kristel and I stayed at a table on the deck, knowing full well there wouldn't be a show.

Around 10:30 the crowd was at its largest. Some people had their camcorders ready and waiting for the Lights to start flickering. The anticipation was exciting for even Kristel and me.

"What's everyone going to do if the Lights don't come out all week?" I asked Kristel quietly. "Who knows where Rothschild went last night."

"There's going to be a lot of disappointed guests," she muttered, looking over towards her father. "Especially my dad."

Like we expected, the Lights of Marilee never appeared. By midnight, most of the watchers had left, knowing that it wasn't uncommon for the Lights not to show on some nights. Sometimes, Kristel said, the Lights would appear once or twice and then not come out for a whole week. So the disappointment I had expected wasn't as extreme, as most of the guests were confident they'd see the Lights before the end of the week. As they were leaving, many said they'd come back tomorrow night to watch.

On Monday morning, Kristel read the page three article out loud to me in the staff lounge after I finished my breakfast shift.

"Well, how does it feel to be famous?" she asked smiling, folding the *Lake Henry Gazette* over in her lap.

"It's nothing. There's not even a picture in there," I said, trying to appear nonchalant, but smirking nonetheless.

If anything, the article had aroused the attention of a few locals, most significantly Sheriff Slater. At nine o'clock I received a call from a secretary at the police station. The sheriff had read the article this morning and wanted to meet me right away. A one o'clock meeting was scheduled.

Unlike me, Kristel was nervous about it. "Do you think Mr. Rothschild was right when he said the police might be covering something up?"

"I don't know, Kristel. How can we know something like that?"

"Your grandfather seemed convinced of it."

"Should I just come right out and ask the sheriff, 'are you covering up evidence about Jimmy?'"

"No. But it's about time Sheriff Slater finally talked to you about it."

Kristel was making a bigger deal of this than I wanted it to be. "I don't understand why you don't trust him, Kristel. He is a sheriff."

"I know. I just don't like him. Call it a woman's intuition. You'll know what I mean when you talk to him, Jody. If there's anyone down there I don't trust, it's Clive Slater. And I don't care that he's the sheriff. He's rude and obnoxious."

Her comments stuck in my mind when I visited the police station after lunch that day.

The only other time I had seen Sheriff Clive Slater was when I was half unconscious at the roadside early in the morning with a swollen left eye. Now, under the florescent lights of the sheriff's office, I saw him as a rather robust man, somewhere in his mid forties and balding on top. The hair remaining on his chunky head was thin and black, the same as his mustache under his cavernous nose. He had a bushel of black chest hair sprouting through his collar, thicker and much curlier than the flat flimsy stuff above his ears and his upper lip. He was about 5’ 10” and looked to weigh over two hundred and fifty pounds. His neatly pressed gray uniform, shiny black boots, and brass badge helped thwart his otherwise burly, country woodsman physique.

The sheriff gripped my hand tightly and challenged me with a husky shake. “It’s a pleasure to finally meet you, son,” he announced in a deep voice that echoed crisply off the tile floor and concrete walls of his office. “Anders has told me much about you. Have a seat.”

I sat on a metal folding chair near the door. Slater reclined in a swivel chair behind a gray metal desk across from me. After cursory introductions and small talk, he got right down to business.

“I read the article in the *Gazette* this morning, and I thought it’s time we finally get together. I’ve been going over these… uh… ‘Ambassador’ notes you’ve been bringing in to Anders over the past few weeks.” The Sheriff opened a manila file folder and thoughtlessly shuffled through a pile of documents with his thick, sausage-like fingers. “The last letter I have here says you were to meet this… uh… this ‘Ambassador for the Dead’ last Thursday night at the end of the dock at the Club.”

I suddenly remembered that I had forgotten to bring in the latest letter, the one that invited me to the produce section at the grocery store. He didn’t know about that one yet, and neither did Anders. Heeding Kristel’s advice, I decided to let the Sheriff do the majority of the talking. I wouldn’t say anything about Robert Rothschild—not yet anyway.

“Yes, sir.” I answered in response to his holding up the letter that invited me to the Club dock last week.

A smirk sneaked across the Sheriff’s face. “Anders told me what happened with the girl at the end of the dock.”

I wondered why the Sheriff would think my being framed like that was so funny. “Yes sir,” I said flatly. “It was a rather embarrassing situation.”

Slater’s smirk grew more devilish. “Yes, I imagine it was.” He noticed that I wasn’t offering a return smile, so his smirk disappeared, replaced immediately by a look of concern. “Anyhow, Anders told me that you think Brock Oliff was behind it—that he sent the girl to the dock to set you up.”

“That’s correct. The girl admitted…”

Slater cut me off with an unexpectedly frank question. "Do you think that Brock Oliff was involved in the death of your brother?"

His directness caught me off guard and I adjusted my legs under the metal chair.

"Um, well... we... uh... I suspect Brock knows something about it." I didn't want to bring Kristel's name in on this discussion if I didn't have to.

Slater stared at me solidly for several seconds and said, "Brock Oliff *would* be our number one suspect, that is, if Jimmy's death wasn't just an accident."

*Really!? He agrees with Kristel and me!?* I asked him eagerly, "What makes him your top suspect?"

"You mean what *would* make him a suspect? Well, he was the first to show up at the falls, for one. He also had a history with Jimmy. Jealousy over the Schuple girl. Family problems. Drug abuse. You know, most fingers point at him than anyone else. But it's all speculative."

"Did you question him?"

"Of course."

"What did he say?"

"What do you think he said, son?"

Surprised at the sheriff's insolence, I didn't answer.

Slater continued. "I told you he would be our top suspect—IF—if and only if Jimmy's death wasn't an accident. But that's what it was, and that's what it still is—an accident. There's no proof, no evidence—nothing to establish a case. We checked every angle, son. We questioned Brock, and he came clean. We questioned the Schuple girl—the only eyewitness, and she said he fell. There wasn't anyone else there. No struggle seemed to take place. All arrows point to an accident. That's all we have."

"But Kristel couldn't see who was up on the ledge. She was down at the bot..."

He cut me off again. "There was no one else on the cliff! We found Jimmy's footprints of the rubber sandals he was wearing up in the dirt near the ledge. Believe me, if anyone pushed Jimmy off that cliff, he didn't leave one speck of evidence. That's why Jimmy's death is in the books as an accident, and nothing else."

I looked at Slater silently, not certain how to respond. His eyes softened, apparently satisfied that he had made his point. Then they narrowed again as he put forth another direct, and unexpected, question.

"Let me ask you something, Jody. Do you by any chance know a Mr.

Robert Rothschild?"

*Whoa! That came out of nowhere!* My brain spun. Why is he suddenly asking me about Rothschild?! Is he onto Rothschild's true identity like the old man suspects? Why does Slater think I know him? Did he see us at the produce aisle?

I tried to remain nonchalant. "Yes," I said, clearing my throat. "He was a guest at the Club. Everyone knows him."

"Was?" Slater said with a puzzled look.

I let this information out: "He checked out and left last night."

"Is that a fact!" The sheriff scribbled a quick note on a piece of scrap paper. I knew I had made a mistake. Slater then asked cheekily, "So you must know him then, or do you keep regular tabs of the guests as they come and go?"

His tone was unsettling. I knew he must know something rather significant about Mr. Rothschild. Yet, I couldn't believe his supercilious attitude.

I carefully responded, "I just happened to be sitting on the front porch of at the Club when he got in the airport van. I was there talking to Gundy; he's the van driver. That's how I know he's gone. Why are you asking about Mr. Rothschild? Is *he* a suspect?"

"There are no suspects for an accident. You've got to understand that, son. I was just asking about Robert Rothschild because we know that your brother had a relationship with him. Some sort of business relationship that may have gone bad. Like I said, we're working on this from every angle possible."

I was startled by Slater's knowledge of Rothschild and Jimmy, so I asked for the sake of it, "Do you suspect Mr. Rothschild of pushing him?"

"No, but Rothschild's name came up during our investigation. We tried to question everyone who knew Jimmy, but we never had the chance to question him. He had already left town when the accident happened last fall. Like I keep telling you, we have uncovered every stone in this case. I was just wondering if Rothschild said anything to you about the case."

I lied: "No, he hasn't said anything to me about it."

"I see," Slater muttered. He stared at me steadily before jotting down another note.

I now knew exactly why Kristel was so uneasy about this man. We had been talking for less than ten minutes, and already I felt like I was under attack

Then he asked, "Did you ever speak with Mr. Rothschild at any time since you've been here this summer?"

I lied again. "No, sir."

It was a worse lie than the first. Rothschild was my grandfather, for crying out loud. I had been in the supermarket with him less than forty-eight hours ago, and I knew I had made a major mistake with this lie. I thought for sure that Slater's next question would be about my being seen with Rothschild on Saturday night, boarding his Mercedes in the parking lot of the grocery store in the middle of town.

"You haven't?" Slater asked, disgruntled. "Mr. Rothschild has never spoken to you, called you, written to you?"

"No sir." The lie was growing even larger, and I braced myself for the worst. Thankfully—and curiously—it never came, at least during this conversation.

"Mmm." Slater hummed, wearing a puzzled expression as he shuffled through the documents in the manila file folder. By this action, unless he was a master at bluffing, I believed that the Sheriff had no knowledge of my meeting with Rothschild. And he didn't know it was Rothschild who wrote the Ambassador letters either. At least not yet. I remembered how yesterday I told Boonie about Rothschild being the Ambassador. I was glad that Boonie and Slater don't pal around, because knowing Boonie....

Thankfully, for now at least, I seemed to have gotten away with lying to the sheriff about my grandfather. As boldness began to swell within me, I decided to fake a question in order to further authenticate my testimony.

"Is Mr. Rothschild the one who sent the John Doe letter to you guys? Do you think it was him?"

"No," Slater said sharply. He stopped shuffling documents, as he was obviously still very puzzled. "We have no idea who John Doe is. The letter was printed on a laser printer, and it's too difficult to trace."

Strengthened by Slater's puzzlement, I faked another question, one I had already asked Officer Anders. I wanted to control the direction of the conversation and steer it away from the Rothschild topic. "Did you find anything at Smooth Rock Falls like the John Doe letter said you would?"

"Just a few insignificant items." The sharpness in Sheriff Slater's voice was fading. He was still puzzled over something following his Rothschild questions, and whatever it was, he was keeping it to himself.

"Like what? What did you find?"

"A couple of empty beer bottles and cigarette butts. They were obviously dropped there months after the accident, probably more recently."

"That's it?"

He looked at me, half-annoyed, and answered, "One of our officers found a camera that had been dropped near the bottom of the gorge. We thought it might contain the so-called evidence that John Doe talked about, but it didn't."

"You found a camera where Jimmy fell?"

He sighed like he was tired of my questions. "No. Down the river a little ways, between some rocks."

The Sheriff apparently had no more questions prepared for me, now that his dead-end trail of questioning about Rothschild had seemingly baffled him. My lie had thrown him off, and I wondered how long the lie could remain intact. Although I didn't know what Slater knew about Rothschild and what answer he had hoped to get out of me, I boldly continued drilling the sheriff with my own questions.

"Was there film in the camera?"

Slater cocked his head sideways, clearly annoyed. "Yes. But the camera was busted. The lens was cracked and part of the case was broken off. We developed the pictures that were in it, hoping it might lead to something or someone—like to our John Doe. Only six pictures had been taken out of the role."

"What were the pictures of?"

I could really care less about the insignificant camera and the photos. I just wanted to bury my Rothschild lie good and deep.

The Sheriff glared at me again. "You're really bent on this murder theory, aren't you."

"And you're not?" I retorted. Now I was being the saucy one.

"I haven't ruled out anything. But we have no evidence. All I know is that the camera was all we found that day. The John Doe letter could be a fraud, you know."

"Could I see the photos?"

The Sheriff snorted and shook his head. "If you insist. They didn't lead anywhere."

He unlocked the bottom drawer of a file cabinet with small key from a loaded key ring hanging on his belt. From a file folder he removed a smaller envelope that contained several photographs.

"Here you go. Just some pretty girls that no one around here can recognize."

I looked over six color photographs of two teenage girls, maybe college students, standing near a large body of water surrounded by mountains. One girl sported a white tank top; the other a Tampa Bay Devil Rays baseball jersey. The body of water behind them looked too wide to be Lake Marilee.

"Do you know where these were taken?" I asked, still faking my interest.

"Looks like Lake Henry," Slater said, cocking his head sideways again. "Could be Champlain. Could be anywhere." His words were spoken with an I-couldn't-care less attitude, emphasizing that the pictures had led him nowhere.

I continued with my bluff, "Could the developer tell *when* these pictures were taken?"

"Yes. It was obviously during the summer. The trees in the background are all green, and the girls are wearing clothes for warm weather."

"Do you know if these were taken last summer, or early this summer, before the camera was found?"

"No telling. But does it really matter? All we know is that someone dropped their camera at Smooth Rock Falls and it fell in the water in a gap between two rocks. They either couldn't find it, or they didn't bother trying to climb down to there to get it. We found it because we searched that whole area with a fine-toothed comb after we received the John Doe letter."

"What do you think you were supposed to find there?" I asked.

"Beats the heck out of me. Like I said, that John Doe letter could be a fraud. The longer we go without a follow up letter, the more I suspect it's a fraud."

I looked again at the faces of the two pretty girls in the photographs. One of them, the one in the baseball jersey, looked vaguely familiar, but I couldn't place her. No one I knew at the Club. No one I knew at school. The face was a common face, a plain hairstyle, and I disregarded the notion that I had met the girl somewhere before. I just was glad the photographs diverted our conversation away from my big lie.

The phone on Slater's desk rang and he picked it up. "Yes ma'am... You're kidding? Are they outside?... Both of us?... Yes, I'll comment... I'll tell him now." He held the receiver in his hand and clicked the button to hang it up.

"There's a news crew outside. They want to interview both of us."

"A TV crew?"

"Yes." The sheriff's eyes softened as he rested the receiver in its cradle.

"Let me tell you something, Jody. You might get yourself into the limelight here for a few days, because people love stories like this. But it'll all go away, and in the end you'll probably know nothing more about Jimmy's death than you already do now. I hope you're aware of that."

"I just want to do all I can for Jimmy's sake."

"Then go on out there and get your face on television. Be a hero who's trying to avenge a supposed murder. But remember, we've already exhausted this investigation. We've done all we can, and there's little more to go on. And I'm going to assure the T.V. viewers of that very fact myself."

The interview with the Channel 10 Eyewitness News crew went much like the newspaper interview. My strongest comment before the camera was much like the closing paragraph of third page article. "I want to do everything possible to find out about my brother's death. I have no doubt there's a legitimate John Doe out there who knows something."

Slater also gave a confident reply to the reporter: "The department has left no stone unturned—and I mean that literally. The John Doe letter we received last month looks like a hoax at this point. I just feel bad for this young man who never got to meet his brother."

I left the police station with no further discussion with Sheriff Slater. I knew I would soon be receiving an onslaught of attention, and I prayed that my bold-faced lie about not speaking with Rothschild wouldn't come back and bite me.

When I returned to the Club, Kristel was waiting for me near the driveway.

"Did Channel 10 interview you?" she asked excitedly.

"How did you know about that?"

"They called, and I told them you were meeting with the sheriff at one o'clock. So how did it go?"

"With the news crew or with the sheriff?"

"Both."

"The TV interview went fine. I just pleaded for Jimmy's sake, just like Mr. Rothschild, er... Marilee, whatever... told me to do. But the meeting with the Sheriff was pretty intense."

"What happened?"

"He knows something about Rothschild."

Kristel's eyes widened. "What does he know?"

"I'm not sure. He said he knew that Rothschild had some sort of business relationship with Jimmy. He asked me if I have ever talked with him or if he's ever called me or written to me. I lied and said, 'No.'"

"You did?"

"Yeah. I didn't know what else to do. You're right about him, Kristel—Sheriff Slater's got a chip on his shoulder."

"Do you think he knows who Mr. Rothschild really is?"

"I don't know. I tried to get him off the subject after I lied to him."

"Your grandfather called me at home while you were gone."

"Rothschild! He did?!"

"Mm hmm. He said he saw the newspaper article in the *Gazette* on the Internet. I also told him about Channel 10. He sounded thrilled, and he said he'd overnight the key to the vault to us today."

"Did he say anything else?"

"No."

"When's he gonna call back? I've got to tell him Slater asked me about him."

"I don't know. He just said he was proud of you and he'll Fed-Ex the key today. I'm sure he'll call again."

"I hope so."

Kristel suddenly changed the subject. "Daddy told me today that Brock is in a drug rehab center down in New Jersey."

"You're kidding! How long is he going to be there?"

"It's a ten week program. It's a Christian organization."

"So what does your mother think about him now?"

Kristel snickered. "She hasn't said one word."

"Maybe she's finally getting the picture."

Kristel asked, "So do you think we ought to go to Marilee Manor tomorrow when we get the key from Mr. Rothschild?"

"I guess so. Supposedly, there's fifty thousand big-ones over there for us, isn't there?"

"It's your money, Jody. You followed through on his request."

I shrugged off her comment. "Rothschild must have money to burn if he can pay me so much to say a few words to some reporters."

"His name could be Marilee, you know, and so could yours!" Kristel poked my stomach lightly. "And you could be a rich man tomorrow night!"

I grinned. "If there's fifty thousand dollars in that wooden crate, then I'll believe anything that old man tells me." I laughed and said, "I'll even go on TV and tell the world that I'm the long lost brother of Elvis Presley, if that's what he wants."

# CHAPTER 28

## *The Lights Extinguished*

Channel 10 out of Albany ran my story during both the 6:00 and 11:00 broadcast, following a leading piece about a bombing in the parking lot of an abortion clinic in Florida, and then a story covering the President's trip to Africa. The whole segment lasted about a minute. A small screen to the left of the anchorwoman displayed a still shot of me outside the police station. The anchorwoman reported, "In September of last year, James Grandstaff of Pokeville was killed when he attempted to jump from a sixty-foot high cliff at Smooth Rock Falls in northern Huron County. Grandstaff is the fourth person to have died at the falls in the last two decades. While the three previous deaths were alcohol related, investigators determined early last fall that the seventeen-year-old tripped as he attempted his jump, causing him to fall to his death. But early last month, the police received an anonymous tip that Grandstaff may have been pushed from the cliff. No evidence, however, has substantiated the tip. But now, a young man has stepped forward claiming to be the brother of the late James Grandstaff. Sixteen-year-old Jody Barrett of Ohio claims that he is Grandstaff's younger brother, and he is convinced that his brother's death is a homicide. He wants the John Doe who tipped the police four weeks ago to come forward with more information."

The still picture to the left of the anchorwoman came to life and expanded, filling the entire screen. The words, "Jody Barrett, brother of James Grandstaff," appeared at the bottom of the screen, while my image proclaimed to upstate New York the familiar words, "I want to do everything possible to find out about my brother's death. I have no doubt there's a legitimate John Doe out there who knows something."

The image switched to Sheriff Clive Slater standing proudly and confidently in the vicinity where I had stood. The anchorwoman voiced over the video, "Huron County's Sheriff Clive Slater had this response...." and the Sheriff declared, "The department hasn't left a stone unturned—and I mean that literally. The John Doe letter we received weeks ago looks like a fraud at this point. I just feel bad for this boy who never got to meet his brother."

The picture switched to the standard view of the anchorwoman centered behind the news desk. Reading from a tele-prompter, she said, "Jody Barrett is currently employed at the Brown Swan Club at Lake Marilee and is planning to return to Ohio at the end of the summer. His late older brother had been adopted by Earl and Elisa Grandstaff of Pokeville in 1970. If anyone has any information about this case, please contact the Huron County Police Department." A new graphic of a police badge appeared on her left as the anchorwoman transitioned to the night's fourth story. "Police in Albany today..."

The eleven o'clock version of my interview was an exact replica of the six o'clock piece. Kristel and her sister Becky sat with me as we all watched in the Schuple living room. After my story, Becky gazed at me with wide eyes. "Wow, do you think you'll go on *Geraldo*? You should go on *Hard Copy* or *Dateline* or something!"

I smiled and said, "No thanks. I think the local news is enough." Indeed, it was. It was more than I had bargained for, literally. I hoped my grandfather had seen it.

Kristel added, "You're gonna be famous in Abbeyville tomorrow."

The telephone tweeted loudly and Kristel picked up the cordless receiver from the coffee table.

"Hello?... Yes... Hi... Yes, we watched it." She eyeballed me with a look of excitement, her I-told-you-so gesture. "He was there today... As a matter of fact, he's right here... Sure! Here he is. Good bye, Mr. Anders."

She handed me the phone.

"Jody, I just saw you on TV!" Officer Anders squawked through the receiver. "I didn't know you went down to the station to see Slater. Today was my first day back on regular duty."

"The sheriff's secretary called and said Mr. Slater wanted to see me. He read the newspaper article this morning."

"The paper, too? Wow, you must have found out something, huh?"

The latest information Officer Anders had from me was when I talked to him the day after the skinny-dipping incident. He, like Slater, didn't know of my appointment with the Ambassador at the supermarket, and certainly nothing about our incredible meeting with Abbott Marilee. As much as I wanted to, I couldn't tell Officer Anders the whole truth, even though Kristel thought we could trust him. I figured it would be best to talk with my grandfather first before I tell anyone else the whole story, especially a police officer. Then I remembered the lie I told Slater today about knowing Robert Rothschild.

I asked Anders, "Did the Sheriff say anything to you about my meeting with him today?"

"Not a thing." he replied.

A million thoughts rushed through my head: Kristel was right about Anders—we could trust him. But what should I tell him? Should I come clean with him now about Rothschild? I had lied already today to Slater, and another contradicting lie to Boonie. Now, as I spoke with Roy Anders, my only choice was to continue the lie or come out with the truth. I needed to buy some time to think about it. I asked him, "So you told him about my encounter with the girl at the dock?"

"Yes, I filled him in on that. Have you received any more Ambassador letters?"

"No," I said bluntly. Another quick, hold-this-over-till-tomorrow lie. "Can I call you back?"

"Sure. Is everything alright?"

"Yes."

"Has something happened?"

"No—well, yes. Can I just call you back tomorrow?"

"Sure. I'm on duty six a.m. to three. You can call me at home after three o'clock if you want, okay?"

"Okay."

I hung up the phone and promised Kristel I'd tell Anders everything, but I needed to talk to my grandfather first about several important issues: First, I had to tell him Slater was asking about him, and I wanted his permission to talk to Anders; I also wanted to hear his rebuttal to what my mother had said. I just hoped he would call again soon, and I prayed that my lie to Slater wouldn't blow up in my face before then.

It was a quarter after eleven o'clock, and Kristel suggested we go see how many people were still left at the beach waiting in vain for the Lights to come out.

The night was quiet, and the air was warm as we left her house and walked down the long, dark, gravel driveway to the back of the Poolside Café, up past the Club building, and down the front hillside. As we neared Route 7, we could see the glow of the beach deck through the trees. Just like last night, dozens of people were gathered there. But unlike last night, the crowd was gathered at the railing, binoculars glued to faces, cameras propped and running, and arms pointed eastward. Everyone was staring out across the lake.

Kristel stopped abruptly in her steps. "Oh, my gosh!" she cried, pointing out beyond the beach and across the lake. "The Lights! There they are!"

Indeed, from the Club's front lawn, we could see the glowing dot of a lantern sitting stationary near the rocky point at the Manor property. Another yellow dot flickered behind it, moving slowly along the eastern shore.

"He's here!" I exclaimed. "I'll bet that rascal never left!"

"Or he came right back here after he read your interview this morning," Kristel suggested.

"We've got to talk to him. I've got to tell him about Slater."

"Maybe he'll call us tomorrow."

"I can't wait until tomorrow. I want to take care of this now. Let's go over there and find him! We've got to talk to him!"

"We can't," Kristel objected. "We might scare him off. Besides, we'd be breaking the town ordinance if we go over there now."

I knew she was right; it was a crazy idea. But there was nothing more frustrating than needing to talk to a man so badly while watching his exhibition less than a mile away.

We sat down right there on the grass of the hillside and watched Abbott Marilee perform his ghostly ritual. I noted the crowd at the beach deck gazing at the Lights in amazement. There was old Whisper among them, using a small pair of binoculars.

Good ol' Whisper was right about the Lights—just a big hoax played on a gullible town. But in truth, he wasn't completely right. It really wasn't a hoax. True—it wasn't a ghost, but it was the real Abbott Marilee carrying those lights back and forth along the shore. Nobody was being taken, after all! They were seeing the real thing!

"I can't believe he's doing this," I muttered to Kristel. "He made it sound like he had to leave the country."

"It's his thing," Kristel said. "It's his tradition. He's been doing this for years."

"Yeah, but what if the police *are* on to him? What if Slater knows who he is and goes right over there and nabs him?"

"He's been chased before. He said he can disappear just like a ghost."

We watched the scene for quite some time, amazed by the old man's ability to put on a display of mystery and suspense, all for the sake of protecting his land and namesake. The little, yellow glowing dot seemed to dance along the shoreline, back and forth between the trees while the other lantern burned stationary near the point. It was mesmerizing.

Then, off the surface of the black water, we heard the splintering crack of gunshots echo through the valley. Two shots fired in succession, coinciding with the sudden extinguishing of Marilee's lantern. Then we heard the shouts of a male voice echoing across the water from the far shore.

"What's happening?" Kristel gasped.

The crowd below began to murmur.

I stood to my feet as two little white lights suddenly appeared on the banks of the Manor, just north of the point. They looked like flashlights moving rapidly along the shore, flickering behind trees and deeper into the woods.

"Was that a gun?" Kristel asked, rising to her feet.

The low murmur from the crowd at the beach grew into shouts and cries of astonishment.

The two flashlights could be seen wriggling and flickering madly, deeper into the woods behind the Manor. Then they suddenly stopped moving. Another shout of a male voice echoed from across the water. Its words were indistinguishable, but its tone sounded like a man on a foxhunt.

The crowd hushed. The two flashlights disappeared, and all was still and silent at the Manor. The crowd began to murmur softly again. I heard a guest mention, "Somebody fired a gun." Then somebody silenced the crowd with a large "SSSHHHHH!" Silence again. There was another faint sound of a male voice skimming across the water from the Manor. Somebody on the eastern side was yelling something.

"Oh my gosh!" Kristel yelped, grabbing my arm. "I think somebody got shot!"

The distant, echoing sound of a man yelling was heard again. A car passed below us on the highway.

One little white light reappeared above the shoreline. Then a second flashlight. They both flickered amongst the trees and quickly disappeared again. Silence. The echoing male voice went quiet. The crowd on the deck started murmuring again.

"Jody, somebody got shot over there!" She clutched my shoulder.

Together we dashed down the lawn and across the highway. We leaped down the steps, past the beach deck and down to the sand where people there were gathered in groups, gazing out across the black water. I noticed Whisper using the phone at the lifeguard station, most likely reporting the gunshots to the police.

The murmuring at the beach evolved into loud conversations. People were announcing, "he was chased... somebody fired twice... did you hear what they were yelling?"

Kristel and I stood at the edge of the water near Old Harold and Gretta, each with a set of binoculars fastened on the Manor.

I noticed Whisper hang up the phone at the lifeguard station. I ran to him and he looked at me with a worried expression. "I called 911," he gargled. Then he limped up the steps, and I rejoined Kristel at the shore.

We waited by the shoreline. There was no action at the Manor for several minutes. No lights moving. No sounds. From our position we looked left and could see the lights of the park above the Abbeyville town beach. Small crowds were beginning to gather there, all bodies facing the Manor. The news of the gunshots must have spread to Burleighs.

About two minutes passed. Then we saw the flashing blue and white lights of a police boat as it took off from its dock north of town and headed southeast across the lake towards the Manor. We watched several other boats from the town dock leave and follow behind it. Two more speedboats were now motoring up from the south.

Kristel and I shared worried looks. I glanced beyond her at the rack of canoes.

"Let's go over there," I said softly.

As crazy as it was, she didn't disagree.

In seconds we had a canoe turned upright and were dragging it across the sand towards the shore. We knew everyone on the deck was watching, but we didn't care. Old Harold warned, "Ya bettah nat go ovah they'ah, you keds! Let tha pahlice handle et!" We ignored him, and soon we were off the shoreline, gliding swiftly across the black water.

By the time we passed the diving dock, we counted seven boats arriving near the point of the Manor. A bright search lamp was shining against the trees.

"Let's row to the other side of the point and watch and listen," Kristel said. "We should stay in the canoe."

I agreed.

When we were finally close enough, a well-illuminated crowd of men could be seen huddled around something at the edge of the woods. A body, I speculated. "It looks like they're working on someone."

"Do you think it's him?" Kristel asked worriedly.

"Maybe it's one of his pursuers. Maybe he shot *them*."

"He would never shoot someone," Kristel claimed. "He's never done that."

"Then it's probably him," I said gravely.

We watched several men run back and forth from the gathering in the woods to the shoreline where their watercrafts floated just off the point. One man was ready on one of the boats to hand supplies to the other men on shore. Eventually, two men retrieved a stretcher and carried it into the woods. The voices at the scene were low and muffled.

Several minutes later the huddle of men stood upright and started moving toward the shore. Four men were carrying a body on a stretcher towards the point. Two other men were shouting commands. They scampered into the water and jumped to their crafts to prepare to hoist the stretcher into one of the boats.

Then we heard one of the men say the name George Schuple.

Another man commanded loudly, "You go and inform Mrs. Schuple and take her to the Lake Henry hospital. John, you find the kids and stay with them."

"Daddy!" Kristel shrieked, causing a dozen heads to turn in our direction. She instantly lunged into the water and began swimming frantically towards the shore. I jumped in after her, leaving the canoe floating freely in the dark water.

Kristel crawled frantically out of the water at the stony point, screaming for her father.

I was several yards behind her, just having reached the shore when several men grabbed Kristel before she got to the stretcher. She shrieked and cried and tried to twist away, but they kept her in a tight hold.

I stepped closer to the men, and there, on the stretcher, was George Schuple, laying face up, eyes closed, and an oxygen mask covering his mouth.

"He's alive," one of the crewmen assured Kristel. "We need to get to get him to the hospital."

More orders were barked while Kristel buried her face into the shoulder of a rescue worker. Nearby, I saw Roy Anders, out of uniform, saying something into a radio. Having just spoken to me on the phone less than a half an hour ago, he must have come over on one of the rescue boats. He whispered something into the ear of the man holding Kristel, and then he saw me.

"Is he going to be all right?" I asked him.

Anders leaned close to my ear and said quietly, "He took a bullet in the stomach. They say it came out of his side. He's still breathing, that's all I can say. But look at what's in his hand."

Near his hip, on the edge of the stretcher, the unconscious George Schuple was clutching an old, rusty lantern.

# Chapter 29

## *The Witch Softens and Confesses*

By Tuesday morning, the only official news was that George Schuple was listed in serious condition at Lake Henry General. At breakfast, hardly a word was spoken in the kitchen, and just a low mumble rippled softly across the dining room. Everyone had heard that George Schuple was shot at Marilee Manor last night. And now, everyone knew.

No one was talking about the weather. No one was talking about the Yankees. We could have skipped the bacon and eggs and served just cold cereal for breakfast, and no one would have said anything. No one was asking *why* George Schuple was at the Manor last night. No one was asking *who* shot him. No one was talking about the Lights of Marilee. Yet, everyone knew.

Certainly no one talked about my appearance on the news last night and in the paper yesterday. No one was talking about me or Jimmy Grandstaff.

Nobody knew what to say. But everyone knew. Everyone knew that George Schuple was the ghost of Lake Marilee.

And as for me, I now knew that Robert Rothschild was a liar. Abbott Marilee he was, maybe. My grandfather, yes—Mom had confirmed that. But he had asked me to trust him, and he had lied to me. *He* wasn't the ghost of Marilee; George Schuple was. Mom was right—my grandfather couldn't be trusted.

At dinner, the latest news was that George Schuple had been upgraded to serious but stable condition. He was on a respirator, and surgery had been scheduled for earlier that afternoon.

By now people were talking. People were asking why and how. People were talking about George Schuple being the man behind the Lights of Marilee. They were gossiping about George Schuple, a great hoaxer, getting shot during his act. People were calling him "a con-artist," "a prankster," "a showman," and "an exploiter of a horrible tragedy." While the owner of the Brown Swan Club lay in surgery, his guests and staff were boasting about the ghost of Marilee and how George Schuple had pulled off one of the biggest hoaxes in the region's history.

I was just trying to make sense of everything. Rothschild had lied about being the ghost. Did *he* know Schuple was the ghost? Who fired the gun last night? Why? There were two flashlights, so two people must've been after him. Were they after the ghost? The gold rumored to be in the vaults? Schuple? It was just yesterday that I thought I was one of two people who was privileged to keep a great secret. Now, I was more confused than anyone else. Anyone except for Kristel, that is.

Kristel had been at Lake Henry General since last night. Tonight, Boonie offered to go with me to the hospital after dinner, so I took him along for company.

Before we left, I stopped at the lounge to check the mail, and there was the expected Fed-Ex envelope waiting me. Inside was a brass key. No note, and no familiar handwriting from Rothschild. Just a key. I discarded the envelope and slid the key into my pocket, all the time suspicious of its value. I lied to Boonie, saying it was a spare key to my car my mother thought I should have.

I hated how much I had been lying of late, just to cover up the mess that the phony Robert Rothschild had gotten me into. Now I had his key to the vault, but because of the shooting, and because he had lied to me, I had no desire to go over there anytime soon. Fifty grand, my foot.

We arrived at the hospital about eight-thirty and learned that George Schuple was out of surgery and visitors were allowed in his room: friends and family only—no press. Boonie said he'd be glad to stay in the waiting room while I visited with the Schuples. Before I turned the corner in the hallway, Boonie was already conversing with a cute nurse behind the desk.

I knocked lightly on door one-twelve and gently opened it. The first thing I saw was George Schuple laying on the hospital bed, his eyes closed, wires running from under the sheets, connected to a monitor beeping softly nearby. Beverly Schuple sat vigilantly by his side. No make-up, her hair was a flat and limp: apparently, nobody to impress around here, not at a time like this. She looked at me and didn't frown or grimace in disgust. She had greater concerns than to contemn me. Then I saw Kristel on a chair in the corner, her eyes swollen; her hair pulled back in a ponytail. She rushed to me and embraced me, right there in front of her mother.

She didn't cry or speak; she just hugged me tightly. Then she released and lightly pecked my cheek with a soft kiss. She pulled over another chair next to hers, and we sat down holding hands, right there in front of her mother. I quietly asked Kristel how she was doing, and she said fine. We shared a little small talk—about how her sister was staying with her aunt and uncle, and about how Kristel slept here last night and would like for me to bring her home tonight. I was impressed with how strong she was.

Her mother said nothing as Kristel shared with me the latest information from the doctors. They had performed a successful surgery this afternoon; he's breathing on his own; and he's lucky the bullet didn't hit any vital organs.

We sat quietly for a few minutes and I felt awkward for not having said anything to Mrs. Schuple. Finally, I asked her, "Can I get you anything, Mrs. Schuple? Maybe something from the cafeteria?"

She smiled at me for the first time ever and shook her head. "No thank you, dear." Then she paused and asked, "Tell me, what's the reaction like at the Club?"

I was surprised at her sudden question. It seemed rather inappropriate, considering the circumstances. But I answered, "Everyone is terribly worried, and they're all praying for Mr. Schuple and you, Kristel, and Becky."

"Thank you," Mrs. Schuple said pleasantly. "But what I meant to ask is, how have they reacted to his finally being caught? Are they upset? Do they feel cheated?"

"What do you mean?"

"About George being the man behind the ghost of Marilee. How does everyone feel about being fooled by their own host?"

That she was asking me this now put her completely back into character. Even the health of her husband was less important than the health of her reputation.

I tried to answer the question as gently as possible. "Well, everyone is mostly very sorry about what happened. Nobody's talking much about the ghost being discovered." Not a completely honest answer, but at least a gentle one.

Mrs. Schuple grimaced. "Oh, I have a hard time believing that," she said. "He had people all over the country believing in that ghost! I'm expecting some people to even say that he deserved to get shot."

It was all coming unraveled now, straight from the ghost's wife.

Mrs. Schuple continued, "I knew it was going to happen one of these days. George found it amusing to dodge a few adventurous teenagers here and there, but then there were so many ghost fanatics out there! Crazy people who'd do anything to catch a ghost! He always said he'd be careful. Just one more summer, he told me in the spring. But it was already too far out of hand. The legend got too big. Too big for even George Schuple to handle."

She stopped talking as suddenly as she had started. Except for the soft beeps of the breathing monitor, the room was quiet.

It was fascinating to hear this confession from Beverly Schuple, as it put everything in perspective: Whisper was indeed right—a big hoax it was, after all. And now I was convinced that my new grandfather was a liar—a worse liar than anyone could accuse George Schuple of being. How could I have even believed his stupid ideas? A big conspiracy! A police cover-up! Hah! Mr. Schuple probably fed my grandfather's ego by creating the ghost of Marilee himself. My grandfather is nothing but a rich, lonely, old man running from the law, and he loves to see people get all worked up about his supposed ghost. George Schuple is a genuine entertainer, but my grandfather plays tricks with your mind. And the next big mystery to come along—the John Doe letter and my showing up the next day—that was just more fat for his ego. Get it in the news, he said! Make a big fuss over Jimmy! I felt ashamed and stupid for doing those interviews.

Yes, Mrs. Schuple was right. There are plenty of ghost fanatics out there, and my grandfather loves every one of them because they feed his demented ego. Look at old Harold and Gretta—down at the beach every night with their binoculars. And they got sucked in by that John Doe letter like my grandfather did! Maybe he wrote it himself—maybe he is John Doe! And then there's old Whisper, another fanatic, sneaking around the Marilee property collecting old lanterns. But at least he was right. At least he knew the Legend of Lake Marilee was a big hoax. Too bad he didn't uncover it sooner—before all this happened. Those stupid Ambassador letters! There's a hoax for you! I'm such an idiot.

And then I felt that brass key in my pocket. Fifty grand. For a moment I wasn't so confident.

I wondered what Kristel thought of my grandfather now. She had been staring at the floor since her mother stopped talking, just staring at something on the floor, probably not thinking at all about Robert Rothschild's stupid story. Just staring, not blinking, in a complete daze. I nudged her.

With that, Kristel suddenly lost her composure. She spilled everything, right there in the hospital room, everything about that was supposed to be a secret—she just let it all out, right there, without warning. She sat straight up and confessed, "Mom, we met Abbott Marilee. We met him Saturday night. We know who he is—he's Robert Rothschild. He's been in hiding all these years because he never killed himself. He's still alive and we met him and talked to him and he told us everything."

I was stunned.

Mrs. Schuple glared at her daughter in absolute surprise for several seconds. Then she pressed her lips tight and smiled slightly. Shaking her head, she exclaimed, "Mercy! I never would have expected it! It sounds like the truth was already out of the bag before all this happened!"

Kristel looked puzzled. I was speechless.

Mrs. Schuple looked at me and asked, "So Abbott has already made himself known to both of you?"

We both nodded.

"And he told you everything? About his brother Zane and about that Miss Emory woman?"

We nodded again.

She looked at Kristel and asked, "And how your grandfather helped him get away with faking his own suicide?"

We exchanged puzzled glances.

Her daughter answered, "No. He didn't tell us that."

Mrs. Schuple chuckled. "Ha! Well then Abbott didn't tell you *everything.*"

"What?" Kristel asked earnestly.

Her mother shifted her eyes back and forth between Kristel and me several times, seemingly holding back a haughty smile. "I suppose I can spill all the beans now. It was all going to happen soon enough."

She patted her husband's hand lightly, and then, sitting back in her chair, she proclaimed, "Yes, old Abbott Marilee is very much alive, not in ghost form, mind you. He's known today as Robert Rothschild, and he was able to fake his death forty years ago because he had some help from my father-in-law. Your grand-dad, Kristel, your dad's father, was the county coroner."

# CHAPTER 30
## What He Didn't Tell Us

Kristel and I listened in amazement as Beverly Schuple delivered a most unexpected revelation.

"Kristel, your father has known Abbott Marilee for a long, long time. In fact, I'd say he's been Abbott's best friend for the past four decades."

She paused for a second, leaned over her sleeping husband and straightened the fold in the bed sheet over his chest. "George was twelve years old in 1958 when the Marilee tragedy happened," she said, smiling kindly as she straightened her husband's thin hair above his left ear. She leaned back into her chair.

"Before we were married, he told me the story of how he attended the Marilee funeral with his parents, and how back at his home later that evening, well after midnight, he heard people talking in the living room. He said he tiptoed to the top of the stairs and listened to his parents having a serious discussion. There was a third person there with them, a man, whom he recognized to be Abbott Marilee, the man who had murdered the poor family that was buried that very day. Here was the murderer on the loose, talking with George's parents in their own living room, and little George, true to his mischievous character, spied on his parents and Mr. Marilee from the top of the stairs.

"George told me how he learned that this was not the first time that Abbott Marilee had visited his parents after the killings. On that particular night, they were telling Abbott all about that morning's funeral service. George told me how he listened to Abbott tell George's parents how he was getting along, avoiding arrest, and how he desperately needed to find that Miss Emory woman and his little baby girl."

Beverly Schuple shook her head and glared into space. She wore an expression I was familiar with when she said, "Heaven sakes, some people are just down right filthy people! Imagine that Zane Marilee and what he did to that poor young woman! And then blaming it all on Abbott!" She glanced briefly at Kristel and me, and I didn't like the insinuation. But she went on with the story.

"Well, that same night, George heard his father and Abbott leave the living room, and then he heard the back door open. Through his bedroom window, George said he watched Abbott and his father walk across the back yard towards the tool shed, and there they removed two shovels and a rake and walked down the driveway toward the street. George said that the next morning, the tools were back in the shed, caked with fresh dirt.

"He said that for the next several nights, after George was in bed, Abbott Marilee would sit up with the George's parents late in the evening and talk." Mrs. Schuple chuckled and shook her head. "At least, his parents thought he was in bed!" She sighed and said, "My husband, I tell you… Well, little George was able to learn from his eavesdropping that Abbott was actually spending nights at the house on a cot in their basement. He overheard Abbott and his parents talk about everything, such as how the body should turn up any day, how they could help him get away, and how Abbott would reward them graciously for their assistance.

"And sure enough, a few days later, the news spread all over town about Abbott's suicide and his body being found at Cotter's Landing. And little George knew Abbott was alive and well, hiding out in their basement. He also knew that his father was the county coroner and would be performing the autopsy.

"Well, one night, and mercy sakes did he deserve it, little George finally got caught eavesdropping. His mother discovered him at the top of the stairs, sound asleep, the little rascal! So the next morning, his father brought him into the basement and sat him on the cot right next to Abbott Marilee. George said that his father and Abbott explained everything—the truth about the murders—and that Abbott Marilee was absolutely innocent."

Beverly Schuple stopped talking and looked at us for a moment. "That's why…" she said to me, "that's why, Jody, I was interested in how the town has been reacting to the shooting of my husband. Abbeyville is soon going to learn the truth about Abbott Marilee, and I'm worried that they're not ready for the whole truth yet. Especially in the aftermath of learning what my husband has been doing with the Lights all these years."

I wasn't sure if I was supposed to respond to that or not, but she hardly gave me the chance. "Anyway," she said, getting back to her story, "George described how his father and Abbott told him everything, even the fact that

George's father had tampered with the autopsy records on the body, helping Abbott fake his own suicide. George said his father was ashamed for deceiving the people of Abbeyville, but it was all for the greater good—to protect an innocent man, and little George understood.

"Well, it wasn't long after that, just before Abbott was about to leave the Schuple household and go into hiding in New York City, the little Marilee daughter was found on the doorstep, secretly delivered by Miss Emory. George described how Abbott was so happy to have his daughter back, but he desperately needed to find Miss Emory because she was the only eyewitness to the crimes. He ended up staying a few days longer with George's family and his little baby girl, but he ultimately had to leave the area.

"I met George Schuple six years later, and it wasn't until after we were engaged that he told me this story. The week before we were married in 1965, I met Abbott Marilee for the first time down at Burleighs restaurant, and he's been a dear friend to me ever since.

"So all these years, Abbott would return every summer to visit George and me, wearing some clever disguise. One time, I recall, after George's father had passed away—this was when you were about two years old Kristel—old Abbott visited the Club dressed as an Army recruiter. And another time he claimed he was a golfer from Scotland on the PGA Tour!" Mrs. Schuple laughed and tossed her head back lightly. "Abbott is quite the clever man, I'd say. Maybe a genius, and a difficult old coot to keep a track of!" Mrs. Schuple chuckled some more as she continued, "Finally, he came up with the Robert Rothschild disguise, and he's been coming back here under that identity ever since. George and I have been his confidants here in Abbeyville, especially after George's parents passed away. We were the only people in the world who knew that Abbott Marilee was alive—and innocent—except for the missing Miss Emory, of course. Why that woman stayed away and kept Abbott on the run, I'll never understand it.

"But we owe Abbott much of our lives, George and I do. Most of what we have, Kristel, is because of Abbott's generosity towards George and his parents. Your grandparents became a wealthy family because Abbott shared part of his fortune with them. It's how your father was able to eventually own the Brown Swan Club."

Imagine that! The Schuple family had my grandfather to thank for their wealth. But why did Mrs. Schuple always treat me like she did? I had to find out. "Did you know," I cut in, "that I'm his grandson?"

Mrs. Schuple offered a wry smile. "Yes, I've known that, and I was wondering how that was going to all play out this summer. I know how your mother, Jody, feels about her father, and with his plans to turn himself into the authorities this month, I didn't understand how you were going to fit into all this. In fact, George and I knew you were coming here this summer before Abbott did. It worried me quite a bit. George had to tell your grandfather who you were after you got here."

I nodded and said, "My mom thinks he *is* a murderer. How are you so sure that he isn't?"

Vexation flashed in Mrs. Schuple's eyes. She exclaimed, "Why, his character says it all! That man wouldn't hurt a flea!"

I responded, "Then why did he stay in hiding all these years?"

"Oh, my child, your mother has led you astray. Your grandfather had no reason to come out of hiding for the past forty years! If he did, he'd be charged with murder, and without Miss Emory's testimony, he'd go straight to prison! Besides that, it made no difference whatsoever if Abbott lived the rest of his life under a new identity. His entire family was dead, except for his baby girl, so he had no other choice but to start a life completely over again."

Mrs. Schuple wagged her finger at me and continued her chiding. "And changing public opinion is not as easy as you think. Only Abbott's closest friends know of his real character; but in the public eye, Abbott is believed to be a cold-blooded killer and a rapist, so he was better served by starting over again under a new identity. And he still had access to all that gold without anyone knowing it."

As much as my mother was convinced one way, Mrs. Schuple believed the other way. I still had my doubts, such as why did my grandfather lie to us about being the ghost behind the Lights of Marilee? But before I could ask that question, Kristel suddenly spoke up. "So you've known who Abbott Marilee is and where he's been all this time?" she asked her mother. "Do you know where he is now?"

"Your father keeps me well informed. I've known the real identity of Robert Rothschild for years, but George says he uses several other aliases. I believe he actually has an apartment here in Lake Henry as well as several homes in other states. He's a hard man to keep track of, and I don't keep up with him as much as George does. I haven't seen or heard from him for a few days, not even after this happened." She glanced at her sleeping husband.

I interjected, "But he lied to me the other night. He said that *he* was the man behind the Lights of Marilee. He didn't say anything about Mr. Schuple."

Mrs. Schuple chuckled, and answered. “Oh, both Abbott and George have been in on it together for years! I’m sure he didn’t say anything to you about George just to protect him. But it was when Kristel was a little girl that her father and Abbott started scaring kids away from the Manor. Abbott actually did it the first time, and your father thought it was so funny that he started doing it, even when Abbott wasn’t around. Then people saw it from the shore, and the whole godforsaken “Lights of Marilee” legend started. George went a little overboard with it, I’d have to say. But he loved it—the crowds, the mystery, the excitement of a chase. He knows all those tunnels and caves and trap doors over there like the back of his hand, even better than Abbott himself.”

“So Daddy *has* been the ghost of Marilee this whole time?” Kristel asked, glancing once at me. “Abbott told us that *he’s* been the one who carries the lanterns.”

“No, it’s been your father most of the time, but every once in a while Abbott fills in for him so your father can be seen at the Club viewing the Lights himself. Ninety-five percent of the time, though, it’s your father out there, just having a ball.”

She patted her husband on his chest and added, “I was scared to death when *Unsolved Mysteries* did their piece. But George pulled it off like a pro. He always has, until… well… last night.” She gently squeezed her husband’s hand again. “This would have been his last summer playing ghost because Branson Oliff is going to have that hotel built. Your father had hoped that the town’s love for the legend would prevent it, but most people think Branson’s hotel will bring more business to Abbeyville than the ghost of Marilee does.”

Mrs. Schuple sighed heavily and smiled as she looked at her husband. “George just loves playing that ghost. I only wonder what happened last night—what crazy person wanted to hurt my husband? Lord knows, I pray the police catch whoever did this to him!”

With that, I now felt guilty for having doubted my grandfather—the real, living, breathing and innocent Abbott Marilee, a partner in “crime” with George Schuple. Now, I knew for sure that my mother was wrong about him. My grandfather—the great Abbott Marilee!

The drive back from the hospital to the Club with Kristel and Boonie was a quiet one, except for Boonie talking about two gorgeous nurses for the first fifteen minutes of the ride. Kristel and I would have a lot to discuss at a more appropriate time.

It was after midnight when we got back. I drove up the Schuple driveway to the house and walked Kristel to the door. The house was dark and empty inside. I couldn't understand why she was going to stay there by herself for the night.

"Thank you, Jody," Kristel said sweetly. "Thank you for coming to the hospital and giving me a ride home."

"Are you going to be all right here by yourself?"

"Yes. I'm fine. It's been a long twenty four hours, and I just want to sleep in my own bed."

"I'm so sorry about what happened to your dad, Kristel. You're taking it so well. So is your mom. You're both pretty strong."

"Thank you, Jody. Thank you for being here for me." She pressed her chin over my shoulder and we embraced. I don't know how long we held each other, but all I could think about the whole time was how strong she was—how strong her faith was. Anyone else, including myself, would be an emotional mess in the same situation. But not Kristel.

Wednesday morning I worked my usual breakfast shift. I wasn't surprised to see Kristel out in the dining room talking with guests, providing updates, giving and receiving hugs and reassurances. She just had that way about her. She came in the kitchen to tell me that she'd be at the hospital most of the day, but she'll be back tonight, and maybe we can go to Burleighs and get a pizza or something. That would be nice.

Around ten a.m., Darlene brought me a message from the hostess stand. She said somebody wanted me to call him at the number she wrote down—a local number. He wouldn't say his name, and he was kind of short with his words. I was sure it was my grandfather.

"This is Slater," the burly voice said after two rings.

My heart sank.

"Uh, hi. This is Jody Barrett. I got a message to call this number."

"Ah, yes. I need to fill you in on some telephone calls we received yesterday and today."

Sheriff Slater. Jimmy. John Doe. I hadn't thought much of any of them since the shooting.

"Oh, did you find out something?" I responded in a hopeful voice.

The sheriff growled, "Only that there's a lot of weirdo's out there, son.

We got a call yesterday morning from someone who said that he had a videotape of your brother's death and he'd send it to us if we first mailed two million dollars in cash to a P.O. Box in Albany. He called back later and said he'd offer it to us for one million."

"No legitimate calls?"

"We did hear from a representative from *Hard Copy* asking if there was any validity to the murder/homicide theory. We said no, not as of yet, and he asked us to contact him if any solid evidence came up."

"Really?" I said.

He didn't answer, and just went on with, "I had'ta let you know that you've stirred things up quite a bit around here, kid. You've caused a lot of phone work for my secretary. It's bad enough around here with the Marilee Manor shooting and all."

"Thanks anyway," I said. What a jerk this guy was!

Slater continued, "And like I said before, I don't want you getting your hopes up, son."

"I know."

I hung up the phone, relieved that the sheriff hadn't figured out I lied about knowing or speaking to Robert Rothschild. At least he hadn't indicated that he knew.

That night, Kristel and I decided to skip Burleighs. While she was okay visiting with the Club guests, she was uncomfortable sitting in a restaurant with Abbeyville locals and tourists pointing fingers saying, "There's the daughter of George Schuple, the hoaxer behind the Lights of Marilee." Neither of us was hungry anyway, so we just drove around a little bit before we stopped at the park and walked down to the town beach. There, we sat under the dark sky in roomy, wooden Adirondack chairs near the edge of the water.

"Daddy had his eyes open for much of the afternoon," Kristel said in a hopeful tone.

"That's great!"

"The doctor's ran tests and said his breathing will need to be monitored closely for a few days." Then she stopped and changed subjects. "Can you believe what my mom said—that Daddy is Abbott's best friend?"

"Yeah, I believe it. Your mom confirmed almost everything Abbott told us. I was having my doubts about the old guy for a while."

"I was, too. But, like my mother said, he didn't tell us about my father to protect him. I never knew my grandfather was a coroner! Daddy always told me he was just a police officer."

I changed the subject back to her father. "I don't think what your dad did is a terrible thing," I said. "The ghost, thing, I mean. Yeah, it is a big hoax, but he was doing it to help Abbott Marilee. I think if everyone knew the truth about Abbott, how could they blame your father for doing what he did?"

"I know," Kristel said. "And I know my father well. He created the ghost so the Club would have a great attraction. He would have hired the Loch Ness Monster and brought her here to Lake Marilee—just for the show."

We both laughed.

"Jody," Kristel said, shifting gears, "Now that we're both positive that your grandfather is who he said he is, and that he's also an innocent man, do you really think he might be on to something concerning your brother's death?"

There was Jimmy again. He just wouldn't go away. "I don't know," I said with a sigh. "I don't know if I want to know, the way things have gone around here."

We sat quietly for a moment, and then Kristel turned towards me with an unexpected, sly smile.

"Do you think there's money in that crate over there?"

"There's only one way to find out."

"Did you get the key?"

"It came yesterday. It's up in my cabin."

"Let's go!" Kristel said, standing to her feet as though she had been revitalized with a sudden burst of energy.

"Now? In the dark?"

"Yes! I've been at the hospital for the last two days. I've got to do something crazy or I think I'll explode. Besides, if there's fifty thousand dollars in that crate, it'll help keep our minds off things."

"Are you sure you want to go over there now?"

"Not really, so we better get going before I change my mind."

Just like that, we were off on an expedition in search of buried treasure: me, a princess, and a promise from the ghost of Lake Marilee.

# CHAPTER 31

## *Securing a Crate and an Ally*

We decided to park my car at the town beach, where the contents of the canoe could be loaded into it more conveniently, and furtively. It was after nine-thirty by the time we got the key from Saranac and arrived at the Club beach to get the canoe.

Kristel and I unloaded one from the rack and soon we were off across the water. It was impossible to keep out of our minds the last time we made this trip less than forty-eight hours ago. I perceived that Kristel's burst of energy tonight, which enticed her to suggest this trip, was beginning to waver. Nevertheless, we paddled on towards the shore of Marilee Manor, focused on one thing: what Abbott promised was in that crate.

The night sky and water were ominously black. The moon and stars were snuffed behind unseen clouds, and we could see no other watercrafts anywhere on the lake, unless like ours, they were boats without any lights, hidden in the darkness, partaking in a business no one else was meant to see. Our solitude in the middle of Lake Marilee was unsettling, especially when we felt the warm western breeze, pushing us onward, followed by the distant rumbling of thunder.

"It's going to rain," Kristel said grimly, looking behind us.

"We can get there and back in twenty minutes," I assured her, exaggerating the brevity of the trip.

"Are you sure you can find the trap door without a flashlight?"

"There's no way I'm shining a light anywhere over there. We can find it. It's exactly sixty paces directly south from the southeast cornerstone, that's exactly what he told us."

"I hope you're right."

"So do I."

We both increased the force of our rows as we glided swiftly across the black water. The rumbling thunder grew louder. Two flashes of lighting rippled across the western sky.

At last, the stony point was in sight and we guided the canoe towards the banks of the Manor, about fifty yards north of the point. Kristel reached out and grabbed one of the large stones on the steep bank and pulled us parallel to the land. Sounds of rocks scraping the canoe's belly rankled our nerves, despite a distant peal of thunder. I stepped ankle-deep into the water and reached to help Kristel climb across the rocks, but she made no motion to get out of the canoe.

"Aren't you coming?" I asked.

"No. I changed my mind."

"Kristel!"

"This is where Daddy was shot."

"You knew that before we came."

"I know, but I changed my mind. Let's go back."

I wanted to be sensitive, but we were already here. "No," I said stubbornly. This will only take a minute."

A lightning flash illuminated the entire Lake Marilee valley. It seemed as if a thousand eyeballs could see us for that split second.

"You better get out of the boat before you get electrocuted," I cautioned.

Kristel scampered to the shore, drenching her white tennis shoes. "I'm not going up there. I'll wait right here!"

Impatiently, I gave up on her. "All right, I'll be right back." I scuttled across the huge stones and up the steep, grassy embankment.

Kristel and I were separated now, on the black property of Marilee Manor. The knee-high grass brushed against my bare legs as I trotted inland towards the ruins of the mansion. My wet shoes squished with each step, and the thunder rumbled more frequently and with increasing propinquity. The swaying timber, invisible in the black sky, groaned as the wind grew more aggressive. The unyielding storm was going to hit soon.

I descried the stone foundation of the house, detectable in the darkness only by its straight lines intersecting the acres of tall grass. I circled around to the south side, butted my heels up against the southeast cornerstone just as Rothschild did, and carefully took sixty measured steps directly southward, occasionally looking back to make sure I was keeping a straight line. After the sixtieth step, I began stomping on the ground in a spiral.

An intense and slowly developing peal of thunder, like a watermelon being ripped in half, followed a blinding flash. A gust of wind shoved a shower of needles, pinecones, and small branches to the earth. I kept stomping in a wider and wider circle, and finally, I heard a hollow thump under my foot.

I fell to my knees and brushed the dirt and debris away from the wooden trap door. My heart thumped against my chest as I raised the door and looked down the cold limestone stairwell leading into utter blackness. Another flash of lightning illuminated the steps to the netherworld for a split second, followed by a crack-and-tumbling roll of thunder.

I took a breath and descended the steps as if I were going under water, reaching out in front of me to find the wooden door at the landing. Another flash of lighting helped me locate the black iron latch and padlock. I used the Fed-Ex'd key and pulled the door open, its loud scrape and creak was muffled by another clap of thunder. One more flicker of lighting helped me find the battery powered camping lantern without groping for it. I clicked it on, shut the door, and searched for the crack between the bricks in the secret wall.

It opened easier than I thought it would, sounding like a bowling ball rolling slowly down a cement sidewalk. The door settled into its pocket in the right wall, and I dashed down to the room at the end of the musty corridor. Spider webs that had been cleared during our last visit had since been spun and I batted them away with disgust.

The coveted wooden crate sat in the last room on the limestone floor where we left it only four nights ago. It was heavier than I thought, solid and bulky, about two feet long, a foot wide, and a foot tall, nailed together with extra planks reinforcing the seams and joints. It would require a crow bar to open it.

The trip back through the corridor took longer than my arrival. I had to balance the battery-powered lantern on top of the crate as I held it against my stomach with both arms. It was a relief to set the cumbersome crate to the floor when I reached the first room. I pulled the brick doorway from its wall pocket, rolled it shut, guiding the interlocking bricks into the adjoining wall. No need to pack the crevices with mud: nothing more remained in the vaults in case anyone made their way down here.

The thunder, silenced in the underground, echoed down the limestone stairwell. The steps to the earth's surface were consumed by the distinguishable fragrance of fresh rain. In the darkness I touched a step with my hand and felt rainwater collecting in its pocks. A flash illuminated the wet steps. I closed the wooden door behind me, secured the padlock, and lugged the bulky crate to the top of the steps where a heavy downpour was soaking the ground.

I frantically covered the wooden trap door with soggy leaves, grass, and pine needles, and I was soaked and muddied in seconds. With the trap door buried under a satisfactory layer of soggy debris, I hoisted the wet crate to my chest and churned my legs for the shore.

I had to stop once to set the crate down and rest my aching arms. As I scampered through the tall wet grass, its splintery surface scratched and dug into the bare skin of my biceps. Several emerging nail heads clawed through my soaked T-shirt into my stomach. As I advanced towards the water, a series of lighting flashes emblazoned the grounds. Near the shore, a figure stood facing me. Another flash of lighting revealed it to be Kristel, standing soaking wet at the top of the steep embankment.

I dropped the crate at her feet and flexed my sore arms. The canoe was resting on top of the boulders on the shoreline beneath us, collecting rainwater in its belly.

"This thing is heavy!" I moaned above the din of rain and wind, kicking the crate with my soaked sneaker. Water dripped from my eyebrows, nose, and lips. "It's definitely full of something!"

A flash of lighting coincided with a booming clap of thunder, causing Kristel and me to duck in reflex.

We both sat down on the opposite edges of the crate with our wet backs pressed against one another. In this posture we waited for the brunt of the storm to pass. The rain soaked us as if we were sitting directly under a showerhead.

I looked back over the property and imagined the Marilee mansion standing there, sheltering its family from two centuries of summer storms. I gazed out over the bank and imagined a dock extending out onto the water, with Marilee children diving from it, grandfathers and uncles sitting upon it with fishing poles. Then I imagined Abbott Marilee—a younger version of Robert Rothschild—lifting a rifle and shooting Zane Marilee in the chest. I imagined the pontoon boat with a young pregnant woman and a six-week old infant fleeing for their lives—Miss Emory and my mother.

In several minutes, the thunder and lighting petered into the eastern mountains, but the rain continued to fall steadily. Kristel and I together dragged the crate down the muddy embankment and onto the rocks. We shoved the canoe into the water, and then I hoisted the crate into the narrow craft, setting it long ways into its belly.

By now we were both covered with grass and mud, having slid down the bank with the crate, so we each submerged ourselves into the lake to wash off. The lake water felt much warmer than the rain that continued to pelt our faces. Soaked but clean, we boarded the canoe and pushed off, paddling through the abating storm towards the Abbeyville town beach where my car was parked.

Two inches of water had collected in the deepest part of the canoe by the time we reached the beach. Cautiously, we loaded the wooden crate into the trunk of my car, looking around to see if anyone was watching. The beach and the park were dark and deserted. With the crate secure, I took off in the canoe and headed south towards the Club beach while Kristel drove my car to meet me there at the crosswalk at the top of the steps.

Finally, we were together in the front seat, soaked clothing on cold, wrinkled skin, with the procured crate and its supposed contents sitting in the trunk. Rain rapped heavily on the car's roof, and we were still panting from the excruciating exercise. The task was more grueling and chilling than I had imagined.

"Where do you think we should open it?" I asked.

"Let's go see Officer Anders," Kristel suggested.

That made sense. We needed someone—an adult, an authority—a person on our side until my grandfather showed up again.

But then that conspiracy theory crossed my mind again. I cautioned, "We'd have to tell him everything we know."

"No kidding, Sherlock," Kristel huffed. "We've got to tell someone. Name someone else you can trust."

I couldn't, and although I wanted to talk to my grandfather first, I conceded. "Okay, lets go."

Kristel turned my Mustang north and drove through Abbeyville up Route 7. Just past downtown, she turned left down a residential street and parked in front of a house where a squad car sat in the driveway.

"Look's like he's home," she said.

Anders' pretty wife Michelle answered the door and insisted at once that we come in out of the rain. She ran upstairs to get towels for us as Roy Anders emerged from the living room.

"Kristel, it's so good to see you. How are you doing?" he asked compassionately.

"I'm doing okay."

"Jody, hi, my friend. Good grief, what brings you two out on a night like this?

"We need to talk to you about something," I said, "And maybe show you something, too."

Kristel interjected, "Are the kids in bed?"

"Yes. Just sent them upstairs after the storm passed over. You two look like you were out in the middle of it."

Michelle Anders returned with large, soft bath towels, and we gathered around the kitchen table while Kristel gave them an update on her father's condition. Then, with the intent of securing our adult ally, albeit one from the police department, I began sharing the incredible story.

In great detail I described our Fourth of July meeting with Robert Rothschild at the grocery store, and how he drove us to Marilee Manor and guided us down into the secret vaults. Kristel helped me recount the story that Rothschild told us that night from his perch on the wooden crate in the vault—the story of Zane, Miss Emory, William and Elizabeth Marilee, and the horrible events of the summer of 1958. We told the story about the faked suicide and the assistance from the coroner, Kristel's grandfather; the return of Abbott's little baby; his life of secrecy with a new identity for the forty years since; his friendship with Kristel's father; and finally, how George Schuple invented the Lights of Marilee with Abbott's help. We provided assurance that all of this had been known and confirmed by Kristel's mother.

Then I explained Rothschild's recent relationship with Jimmy Grandstaff and his strong suspicions that my brother was murdered. I told them, to their utter disbelief, that Abbott Marilee is my grandfather, and my mother is the missing Marilee baby. I described my assignment to go to the media and arouse speculation about the supposed murder, the murder about which my grandfather was so certain, as if he received a divine message about it. I then described tonight's procurement of the crate that supposedly contained my reward for going public.

It took nearly an hour for Kristel and me to recount the story in its completion. Roy and Michelle Anders took it in with great awe. Their eyeballs nearly popped from their sockets when I told them about the fifty thousand dollars that Abbott promised was in the crate.

"This is absolutely incredible," Michelle exclaimed in disbelief.

"So this Rothschild fellow, your grandfather, is gone now?" Roy asked, "because he thinks the police are onto his real identity?"

"Yes," I answered, explaining how I saw him leave for the airport Saturday night.

"And you now have that money from the underground vaults at Marilee Manor?"

"Yes. The crate is in the trunk of my car."

"Did you open it?"

"Not yet."

"Wow. This is unreal. Let's go open it up."

I stopped him. "But wait, there's more."

I then described my meeting with Sheriff Slater on Monday, the day of the Schuple shooting. I described the forwardness with which the Sheriff interrogated me. I told how Slater asked directly about Rothschild and that he all but ordered me to stop making a big deal out of a rumored murder theory that had been spawned by the John Doe letter. Then I described the rude call Slater made to me today in which he told me I had caused too much trouble.

Anders tried to speak for the sheriff. "I don't know why Slater would ask about Rothschild. I don't remember anybody named Rothschild being one of the suspects. I do remember him questioning Brock Oliff. Slater must know something about Rothschild, obviously. Honestly, Jody, I don't keep track of the sheriff very well, especially lately, because he's been in another world since we received the John Doe letter. And I haven't seen him since after the shooting two nights ago."

"Do you think he's trustworthy?" Kristel asked.

Michelle snickered and covered her mouth with her fingers.

Roy looked at his wife and smiled. "Well, Clive is a sly old fox. I can't pin a crime down on him, but I wouldn't use his name and the word trustworthy in the same sentence."

"Why do you say that?" I asked.

"Well, this is just between all of us. He'd have my head if he knew I was saying this, okay?"

Kristel and I nodded.

"Clive Slater isn't your typical, Andy Griffith-type sheriff. He likes to gamble, and he even goes down to New York City every so often to visit the strip clubs. He also drinks—not out of control, because I don't think he's an alcoholic—but I do know he consumes alcohol on the job, which is a *big* no-no. It's things like that that make us believe that the Sheriff of Huron County isn't the most upright individual for the position. Again, I haven't gotten to know him all that well. We just moved to Abbeyville two summers ago."

"Do you think he'd cover up a murder?" I asked.

"Gee whiz, I don't know about that! But these days, you never know what a person of prominence can get wrapped up in."

I revealed for the first time, "Abbott suspects several people may be involved in Jimmy's death, and he thinks someone with the police might be covering it up."

Anders shook his head in amazement. "Man, I never would have guessed the sheriff could be involved in something like that. It's possible I guess. Is your grandfather a prophet or something?"

"I hardly know him myself. He just says he has this really strong hunch."

"About Clive Slater?"

"He didn't say his name specifically. But my meeting with Slater makes us suspicious of him."

"And you're not suspicious of me?" Anders asked with a smile.

"We trust you," I said. "But Kristel and I both don't trust the sheriff, and... well... I might have made a mistake when I met with him on Monday."

"Why, what happened?"

My eyes fell sullenly to the table. I said, "I lied to him. When he asked me if I have ever spoken with Rothschild or received any letters from him, I told him I knew who he was but I had never spoken with him. Do you think that could get me in trouble?"

"You were protecting your grandfather." Anders said reassuringly.

"Yeah, but I didn't know what else to do. I was so surprised that he brought up Rothschild's his name out of the blue."

"I can understand why you don't trust Slater," Anders said. "But do you think he knows you lied about Rothschild?"

"I don't think so. But I'm sure he knows something about Jimmy and Rothschild that he's not saying."

"About Jimmy too?" Anders eyeballed me inquisitively. "Is this what *you* think, or is this part of your grandfather's hypothesis?"

"This is what we both think," I said, gulping. I glanced at Kristel and suddenly she took over.

She leaned forward and placed her hands flat on the table. "I've been thinking about this for a few weeks," she said, sighing heavily to gather her thoughts. "Think about this for a second. Suppose that Brock Oliff was involved in Jimmy's death. He and Jimmy weren't the best of friends, you know. Suppose that Brock caused Jimmy to fall—pushed him or tripped him or something—whether premeditated, on purpose, or by accident... whatever. And suppose somebody saw it and didn't have the guts to say anything about it at the time."

"John Doe?" Anders said.

"Yes. And suppose John Doe finally got the guts to report it, so he planted a clue or something at the scene that points the finger at Brock, and he tips the police to go and find it. Then Sheriff Slater discovers it, and he realizes it implicates Brock. So somehow Slater works out a deal with Branson Oliff to keep Branson's son from being convicted of manslaughter, or murder."

Anders slowly responded. "Well, that's quite a theory. It means that the sheriff is involved in extortion, not to mention covering up a homicide. Obstruction of justice is a pretty serious crime and it would have to have a very serious motive. It's a long shot, but it is a theory."

"Do you think it's possible?" I asked.

"Like I said, anything is possible. And with everything you've told me tonight about Abbott Marilee and your grandfather—this Rothschild guy—who knows what the truth might be?" Anders shrugged his shoulders and continued, "You might be right, Kristel. With Clive Slater, and the money Branson Oliff could afford to pay him, I wouldn't put it past anyone to cover up the crime. But I also don't want to see you two disappointed if this murder theory turns up nil."

We both nodded. Kristel said, "I guess I'm just trying to think of every conceivable possibility."

"With what you two have told us tonight, I don't blame you. Has Rothschild contacted you guys since he left?"

I answered, "Not since he phoned Kristel on Monday and said he'd send the key for the vault. Then the shooting happened that night, which I'm sure has scared him to death. I wish he would call again."

"You think he actually left you fifty grand in that crate?"

"I need a crow bar to find out."

# CHAPTER 32

## *A Grander Promise and a Grandstaff Dinner*

In the Anders' garage, Roy braced the wooden crate with his foot while I inserted a crow bar into the top seam. The wood, still wet, creaked painfully and as I applied leverage.

The top frame split open, wet shards cracking and splintering. Roy used a hammer to pull up on the ends of loosened planks, removing the lid of the crate completely. The inside was lined in black plastic—an everyday garbage bag.

Kristel stood nearby, wrapped in a towel, her golden hair still damp from the rain. Roy stood next to his wife Michelle and they all watched as I unfolded the excess plastic at the top of the crate. I pulled it down over the sides of the box, stretching and tearing the plastic on the splinters and nails. A piece of paper lay atop a dingy nylon material. On the other side of the paper was familiar handwriting.

"It's a note from him," I said, noting the block lettering that characterized Ambassador letters. This one read,

JODY,

ACT WISELY WITH THIS MONEY. DON'T FORGET YOUR BROTHER.

YOUR FRIEND AND GRANDFATHER,
THE AMBASSADOR FOR THE DEAD,
ABBOTT MARILEE

I read it out loud before handing the note to Roy. Then I pulled on the nylon cloth inside the crate and lifted out a large bag that looked like one of the laundry bags used by the housekeepers at the Club. The bag was heavy, and when it was freed from the confines of the rectangular crate, its contents separated and loosely filled the bottom of the bag. I set the bag on the floor and loosened the drawstring at its mouth.

A stack of twenty-dollar bills tumbled out its opening. Glancing at my audience, I stood up and turned the bag over, dumping stacks of currency to the garage floor. The load of cash formed a knee-high, green mountain of money.

"My Lord!" Michelle exclaimed.

Kristel's jaw dropped.

Anders bent down and picked up several stacks of cash and thumbed through the bills.

I fell to my knees and did the same.

Then we began counting. One hundred twenty-dollar bills per stack, each stack wrapped with a rubber band. Two thousand dollars per stack, and two hundred and fifty stacks in all. Total: *five hundred thousand dollars!* Ten times what the old man said!

Anders held several bills up to the light. "Gee whiz, and these are real!"

With shaky hands and a heart beating in hyper-drive, I helped Roy arrange the money neatly into twenty-five piles, ten high. "A half million bucks!" we both said in unison.

Kristel laughed and shook her head. Michelle stared in shock. Roy and I kneeled around the piled fortune.

Roy declared, "Before we do anything more, I want to meet this Robert Rothschild!"

I gazed at the small towers of cash. "What should we do with it?"

"Keep it in a safe place," Roy answered.

Michelle quipped, "We can keep it in our fireproof safe you bought, Roy. You know—the one you bought to keep all of our valuables in." She looked at her husband and laughed. "There's plenty of room in it!"

"Very funny," her husband said. "But that's not a bad idea, unless, Jody, you'd rather keep it somewhere else. This is your money, unless proven otherwise."

I thought for a moment, and I began to understand. This fortune at my fingertips was causing everything to gel: Jimmy, Rothschild, Brock, and Branson Oliff. It was making sense now.

"You know," I said, "Think of this. Imagine if sometime last year, Rothschild gave Jimmy a large amount of cash like this, and then somebody found out about it. That would give someone a solid motive to kill him."

"That's true," Roy said.

Kristel objected, "But I don't think Brock would do something like that for money. He's got plenty of it already."

"That's true, too," Roy replied. "Did Rothschild ever mention he gave Jimmy anything as remotely as valuable as this?"

"No," I said. "But if he'd give me this much so easily, he might have done the same for Jimmy. And just sitting here with all this money makes me a little nervous."

Everyone agreed.

We put the cash back in the laundry bag and went inside the house where Anders stashed it in his safe in the den. It was nearly midnight when we were ready to leave.

"You let me know the minute you hear from your grandfather," Anders ordered. "In the meantime, I'll try to look into what Slater might be involved in. I'll also do a check on Robert Rothschild and see what I can find out on him. Maybe we can locate him."

"I'm glad you can help us out, Mr. Anders," I said.

"It's my pleasure, Jody. Thanks for coming to me."

Kristel and I were both thoroughly relieved to have someone, besides us, aware of what was going on. It felt like a two-ton load had been lifted off my shoulders. Before we left, he and his wife offered best wishes to Kristel and her family.

I barely slept that night, thinking about the money, about Jimmy, Brock, Slater, Rothschild, and Mr. Schuple. Tomorrow would be Thursday, July 9, marking one month since I had arrived at the Brown Swan Club. What an amazingly unbelievable month it had been, and what the next few weeks held for me, I couldn't begin to imagine.

Thursday was my day off and I traveled with Kristel to the hospital. Her mother had rented a hotel suite nearby, where she intended to stay until her husband could come home. Becky was also staying in Lake Henry with her aunt and uncle, so Kristel had accepted the chore of public relations for the Schuple family at the Club. She would live at home and mingle with the guests, providing updates about her father's condition and making sure essential tasks were being fulfilled, as directed by her mother. But she was determined to visit her father as much as possible, especially during these first few days. While she was in Lake Henry, Darlene adequately filled the role as the official Club hostess.

I spent an hour on Thursday with Kristel in her father's hospital room. Mr. Schuple looked much better than he did Tuesday night: he was awake, but still wired to several machines, and the doctors refused to permit reporters to question him. Only the police were allowed to interview him for their investigation into the shooting. The likelihood of a full recovery was a real one, but he would be out of commission for several weeks.

Kristel and I returned to the Club around dinnertime and I ate in the staff dining room with Boonie, Pete, and Rodney. I about tackled Pete when he wouldn't stop his constant slamming of George Schuple and his ghost tricks. I couldn't stand Pete anymore.

Boonie, wearing his famous grin, privately suggested I stay at the Schuple home with Kristel while her parents were gone. I didn't think he was funny. That night's dinner wasn't a pleasant one.

Meanwhile, Kristel dined and mingled with the guests, reporting the good news of her father's recovery. She was such a pro at making people happy, even during the most stressful times.

I hadn't been getting any mail the past few days, but after dinner I checked the staff lounge anyway. There was something there for me in my box. It was a folded sheet of stationery—pretty, pastel colored paper with a faded mountain range as a backdrop. The note was written in small, narrow, script letters. It read:

> *Hi, Jody,*
>
> *My name is Elisa Grandstaff—Jimmy's adoptive mother. My husband and I would be pleased to meet you. If you would like, please call and we can arrange a visit.*

In the midst of my recent publicity, I had never before considered Jimmy's parents. They had never crossed my mind, and although I'd be a little nervous, I would certainly love to meet them. I called the number at the bottom of the note right away.

Elisa Grandstaff sounded like a very sweet lady when she invited me to her home for an early dinner Saturday afternoon. I made sure it was okay if Kristel could come, and Mrs. Grandstaff said she and her husband knew Kristel through Jimmy, and they would be delighted to see her again.

While I was at the payphone, I called Roy Anders at home. He said Sheriff Slater had been in his office all day working on the Schuple shooting—talking with investigators, making phone calls, and the like. Roy said he'd keep a close eye on him and try to find out what the sheriff might be up to, but he said it would be difficult, an officer checking up on his sheriff. I then told Anders about my dinner plans with the Grandstaffs for Saturday.

"I just thought of something," I said to him on the phone. "Could John Doe be one of the Grandstaffs?"

"Could be," Roy said. "A bitter parent unable to face the reality of their son's death. Maybe your media coverage has brought John Doe out of the woodwork."

"Did Slater talk to them after the John Doe letter?"

"I have no idea; I know he met with them several times last fall. You might want to find out what the Grandstaffs' opinion of Slater is. You know, see if they have any reason not to trust him, too."

"I'll let you know how it goes."

"Good luck."

The Grandstaffs lived about two miles south of Pokeville, down a shady country road, in a one-story home on two acres of wooded property.

Earl Grandstaff was a short man, of a muscular and stocky build. He was a foreman at a lumberyard in Cotter's Landing, and he even built his own house. He was the type of man who likes to cook his dinner outside on the grill whenever possible—which was exactly what he was doing when Kristel and I arrived.

Elisa Grandstaff came out to meet us. She was sturdily built like her husband, and even a little taller. Her face looked to be worn by over-exposure to the sun, as deep wrinkles had formed in the skin's most active areas. She loved working outdoors, and the multifarious flower and vegetable gardens around the property were evidence of her hobby.

"Kristel, it is so nice to see you again," Mrs. Grandstaff said as she gave Kristel a light hug. "We're so sorry about your father. How is he?"

Kristel gave a brief answer and Mrs. Grandstaff kindly responded.

Then she looked at me pensively, "And you must be Jody—oh, you're the striking image of your brother!" She held my hand and squeezed it.

Earl Grandstaff gave me a husky handshake and stared at me straight in the eyes. "Glad to meet you, son." He quickly shifted his eyes toward Kristel. "Kristel, it's a pleasure to see you again. Our prayers are with you and your family."

"Thank you," Kristel responded, smiling sweetly as usual.

"Hope you two like marinated pork medallions," Earl barked happily, as he stepped back onto the porch deck. 'Bout ready to throw 'em on the grill. Got myself a new Coleman this summer. My old gas grill went to the garbage dump when our Memorial Day steaks had to be brought inside and pan-fried. I said that's the last time I'm pan-fryin' a steak 'cause of that dumb old grill, so I went down to the Builder's Warehouse in Lake Henry and got me this one. Works like a charm. Whenever the weather's dry I say 'Why not cook out!' You can't beat endin' a summer's day with a picnic while the sun sets."

Earl Grandstaff was a good ol' talker.

"Can I get you some iced tea or something?" Mrs. Grandstaff asked, smiling at her husband's verbosity. "C'mon inside if you like. We're going to eat out here on the porch in a moment."

The dinner conversation around the patio table was, at first, limited to pleasant subjects—mostly Kristel's school and church activities of the past year. Earl, predictably, did a whole lot of talking about a variety of topics: gas prices, Wednesday's storm that knocked the power out in Pokeville, Sammy Sosa's sudden surge into the national spotlight. I shared a little about my high school activities in Ohio and how I liked working at the Brown Swan Club.

"I came here to get away from home for the summer," I said, about to introduce a not-so-pleasant topic. "And since I got here, my life has been a whirlwind."

"When exactly did you arrive in town?" Mrs. Grandstaff asked.

"On the ninth of June."

"The same the day the news broke about the John Doe letter," she said somberly.

"Uh huh. I got here and saw Jimmy's picture on the front page of the paper. I thought it was me at first! Here I was in a brand new place miles from home, and people thought I was his ghost or something. I didn't even know who he was at that point."

"How'd ya finally find out?" Earl asked as he picked his teeth with a toothpick. Three empty corncobs sat on his plate.

I glanced at Kristel and noticed embarrassment swarming over her face.

"Kristel told me."

Puzzlement crossed the faces of Earl and Elisa Grandstaff. "But how'd *you* know they were brothers?" Earl asked Kristel.

Kristel shifted in her chair and began explaining. "Well, it's kind of a long story, but I'll try to keep it simple. My Daddy knew Jody's mom because she used to come and work at the Club when she was younger. He was kind of like a big brother—almost like a father to her. We have pictures of her when she was on the summer staff years ago. Anyway, Daddy kept in touch with her for a while. He was aware that she had put her first child up for adoption before she got married. And Daddy knew that you were the family who adopted Jimmy."

Earl and Elisa listened with great interest. It was the longest length of time that Earl had stopped talking.

"Daddy kept in touch with Madeline, Jody's mom, and he knew that she had a second child with the same man who left her just after Jody was born. Six months later, Madeline got married to another man, and Daddy went to the wedding. I think that's when he told her he knew where her first child Jimmy was.

"A couple of years later, Madeline desperately wanted to see Jimmy, so Daddy arranged it so that she could. She only wanted to see him and the family who was raising him. That's all she wanted. So Daddy invited you to the Club when the Barrett's were here on vacation."

"Yes!" Elisa exclaimed. "That's when he gave us the free week at the Club. We hardly knew him then. We were acquaintances at church, but that was all. We thought it was a wonderful gesture."

Kristel nodded. "Yes, well, he did that so you would be at the Club with little Jimmy while Madeline and her family were there too. She got to see her first child and be comforted by knowing that he was being raised by such a nice family."

"So were you there that week, too, Jody?" Elisa asked.

"Yep. I was three years old. I don't remember, though."

"We have a picture at home," Kristel said. "It shows my Dad and Madeline sitting at a table on the pool deck, and Jody and I were sitting on the cement, eating Popsicles. In the background you can see you in the pool holding Jimmy."

"Yes!" Elisa exclaimed. "I remember! He was five years old, and that's when he learned to swim without his little arm floaties!"

"Ah hah," Earl laughed. "I remember! I remember him jumpin' off that diving board for the first time. He stood there prob'ly twenty minutes before he finally got the courage to jump. After that—that's all he did the rest of the week was jump off that diving board!"

The sad irony of Earl's comments abruptly silenced the discussion.

"Do you have that picture?" Elisa asked, reviving the conversation. "I'd love to see it."

"I'll bring it over sometime."

Elisa asked, "So you found out from your father that Jody and Jimmy were brothers?"

Kristel continued. "Yes. When I was little, I was always looking at photo albums and asking who the people in the pictures were. I asked about Madeline, and Daddy always explained that she was a good friend of his. He showed me that picture and pointed to me sitting with Madeline's little boy eating Popsicles. Then a couple of years ago when Jimmy started working at the Club, Daddy told me the whole story. He showed me the picture again and explained how he had helped Madeline get her wish—to see her first child just once. I thought it was such a neat story. Jimmy never knew that his biological mother had come to see him when he was little."

"Neither did we," Elisa added.

"Mm hmm. And that's the last time she ever saw him. It was enough to comfort her."

I began speaking on the subject. "I never knew about Jimmy all these years. I know that my legal father, Wesley Barrett, is actually my stepfather, and I know that Mom had been pregnant before me. But she always said that she had aborted that pregnancy."

"She told you she had an abortion?" Ellie asked, dumbfounded.

"Yes. That's what I've believed all these years. I guess she told me that so I wouldn't go looking for my brother or something."

"Did her husband know?"

"He said he found out just recently—last fall when my mother learned about Jimmy's death. My stepfather and I don't get along too well."

"I'm sorry," Ellie said.

"So how'd you find out, Jody?" asked Earl. "You say Kristel here told you?"

Kristel answered, "I told him the day after he got here. I saw how much he looked like Jimmy, and I couldn't keep it in. Daddy wasn't too upset that Jody found out, because he knew Jody was going to find out sooner or later, especially because of the newspaper article about the John Doe letter."

Earl didn't skip a beat. "Yeah, when we saw you on T.V. Monday night, we knew you were really his brother just by looking at ya. But this whole thing about murder and John Doe and the police investigation and all that… well, it got us all stirred up again. Rather painful, I'd say."

"Yes," Ellie said. "We discussed it for a few days and decided we ought to meet you, so I dropped you a note at the Club."

"I'm glad you did," I said.

Ellie smiled and stood to her feet. She began collecting dishes and silverware and brought them inside through the sliding glass door into the kitchen. Kristel cleared some more things and followed her.

"So what do you really think of all this," Earl asked me when his wife and Kristel were inside. "This murder stuff—you really think there's something to it?"

The face of my grandfather flashed through my mind, but I couldn't bring up that epic story at this time. I just wanted to find out what they thought of Slater, as Anders suggested.

"Well, I think it could be possible. I'd really like to meet John Doe."

"He's prob'ly just some idiot stirrin' up trouble. The police didn't find anything at the falls 'cept a busted camera."

"Did Sheriff Slater talk to you since they got the John Doe letter?"

"Yep. He came by here a couple'a weeks ago to see if we knew anyone in the pictures from that camera. All a bunch of strangers to me. It seems somebody just dropped their camera over the falls, that's all. They didn't find anything else there like John Doe said they would. And besides, what were they going to find there nine months later that would prove how someone pushed Jimmy off that cliff?"

Earl bantered on with his doubts about the case until Elisa and Kristel returned from the kitchen, the elder carrying a tray of four dessert plates towering with perfectly manicured strawberry shortcakes. Elisa caught the end of her husband's comments.

"It doesn't matter what the police were supposed to find if they didn't find it, now, does it?" Elisa said, as she placed a dessert at each person's place. "If they missed what was supposed to be there, then *of course* we would think that the John Doe letter was only a prank."

Earl shoved into his mouth a monstrous bite of strawberries covered in whipped cream. He wiped the corners of his mouth with the back of his thumb as he spoke again. "If the cops missed it, then John Doe would have told them so in another letter."

"But John Doe is probably scared," Elisa argued. "It took him nine months to write the first letter. He's probably too scared to write another. If John Doe is a phony, then he would've sent the letter soon after the accident. But he waited until June because he was probably scared to death."

I offered my theory. "What if John Doe actually witnessed the accident. What if he saw a struggle on top of the cliff and saw Jimmy fall. Kristel says that Jimmy was somewhere up on that cliff longer than normal. And John Doe might have been too scared to go to the police. I think you're right, Mrs. Grandstaff."

"So do *you* think Jimmy was pushed, Kristel?" Earl asked, digging his fork into shortcake again.

"I have reasons to suspect it," she carefully answered.

Earl nodded his head and eyeballed his shortcake.

I continued. "So imagine that John Doe saw the whole thing. He knows who did it, and because he's scared, it takes him this long to tip off the police."

"But what were they suppose to find at the falls nine months later?" Earl asked again.

"I don't know. Maybe another letter explaining exactly what he saw and exactly how it happened."

"Then why not just tell 'em in the first note?" Earl asked. "Why send them to the falls to read the explanation?"

"Well, I talked with an officer about it. He said that John Doe might have believed he would have had more credibility if he sent the police to the scene, so they could imagine first hand how it happened. You know, who was positioned where, the distance between things, and so on."

"Okay," Earl said. "So if there was another note there, or some evidence or somethin' er other, why didn't they find it?"

"Maybe they did and they haven't said anything about it."

"Why the heck wouldn't they say anything? You mean cover it up?"

I looked at Earl seriously. "Do you trust Clive Slater?"

"Sure I do! He's the sheriff!"

"Well, I don't."

Earl dropped his fork on his plate with a clank. Frustration covered his face as he said, "I think you've been watching too much television! My son fell! He tripped! He stumbled and tripped and that's all there is to it!"

Elisa laid her hand on Earl's arm. "Honey, calm down."

I glanced at Kristel.

"Did Jimmy have any enemies?" Kristel asked in her candy-sweet voice.

"Heck," Earl said angrily. "The sheriff asked us that already. Jimmy was just like any other boy his age. He and that Oliff kid had disagreements—over you, Kristel, if I remember. But nothing to entice murder! Nothing!"

"Did Jimmy ever have a large sum of money?" I asked.

"Money? No. What is this? You saying he was tied into drugs or gambling or something?"

"No. I was just wondering if a guest at the Club ever gave him some money."

"Not that we know of." Earl looked to his wife for an approving eye. She offered none.

I asked another probing question. "Did he ever talk about Robert Rothschild, a very wealthy guest at the Club?"

"Not that I know of," Earl insisted. "He didn't talk about any of the guests he knew. He had his friends on staff who he talked about—kids his age. The last three weeks before he died, all we heard about was Kristel here." Earl's forehead wrinkled tightly. "Why? Who's this Rockerfeller, or whoever you said? The Sheriff asked us about him, too."

"No one. I'm just thinking."

I looked at Kristel and became quiet. No one else around the patio table said anything for a while. Everyone got busy eating strawberry shortcake, except for Earl, who was now just staring at the remainder of his and picking it with his fork. Finally, in a low, calm voice, he spoke again.

"Jody, I'm sorry you never got to know Jimmy. I know it must be confusing for you to learn you had a brother who just died. But Jimmy was my son for eighteen years. I saw him everyday of my life for those eighteen years until last September." He took a deep breath. His voice became shaky. "And I need to go on. Digging this thing up like this might… for you… seem noble and self-fulfilling. But as for me… Jimmy's dead. He fell. It was an accident. This stuff about conspiracy and cover-ups and the sheriff and the John Doe and all that ain't gonna bring my son back. It's only gonna drag out my pain even longer. I honestly don't want to know the truth about his death at this point. I just want it over."

Earl looked at his watch and then, without making eye contact with anyone, he said, "The Yankees 'er on. I'm gonna go inside." He rose and exited the patio, leaving a half-eaten plate of strawberry shortcake at his place.

Elisa said softly, "Jody, Kristel… kids, I'm sorry. Earl just wants it all to end. He thought it was over months ago, and he just wants it to end. We invited you here tonight because he wanted to ask you to put it to rest also."

I was aching to spill the Marilee story upon Elisa, but I held back.

Kristel said, "Mrs. Grandstaff, we want this to be over, too. But we have very good reason to believe that there is something more to Jimmy's death. It's hard to explain right now, and we're waiting for answers ourselves. We just wanted to find out about Sheriff Slater and what you think of him."

"Well, I don't particularly like him, but I don't think he's hiding anything from us."

"But do you think it's possible that Jimmy's death *wasn't* an accident?"

"Yes, I believe it's possible. But just like Earl, I want it to be over." She sighed heavily and batted her wet eyelids.

She rose to clear the table and Kristel joined in helping her again. I stayed put, not wanting to enter the house into which Earl had escaped. Soon enough, the women joined me outside on the patio again.

"I'll tell you kids something," Elisa said. "I don't know if it means much, because it sounds like you have your own suspicions. But that Oliff boy—he's got something to say and he just hasn't said it."

"What do you mean?" Kristel and I asked simultaneously.

"I wanted to say something when Earl brought him up. If there's anybody who might have caused my son to fall from that cliff, that young man would be my first suspect."

"Because Brock and Jimmy didn't get along?" I asked, deeply interested in her opinion.

"Yes. He threatened Jimmy more than once, you know. He never said he'd kill him, just rough talk like boys do who are jealous over a pretty girl." She smiled at Kristel. "But mix drugs and alcohol into a petty little fight, and bad things happen. And when I heard about Brock Oliff attempting suicide and that drugs and alcohol were involved, my heart froze. I think he knows. I think he's got something to say, something heavy on his heart. I saw him in town a couple of weeks ago, and when our eyes met, it seemed like he wanted to tell me something."

"He's in a rehab center now," Kristel said.

"Yes, I know. I'd like to go there and look him straight in the eye and ask him if he pushed my son over that cliff."

"Sheriff Slater already questioned him," I said dejectedly.

"Yes, but now that you mentioned it," Elisa said, "Maybe the sheriff is protecting Brock. Maybe Clive is getting a nice gratuity from Branson Oliff. Lord knows *that* man can afford it."

"That's exactly what we've been thinking."

"But, I'll tell you kids this—for Earl's sake and mine, we want to stay out of this. We don't want any more attention. Our son is gone, and we're starting our lives over. But you kids, don't you give up. Do all you can! And the first place I'd start is going down to that rehab center and having a face-to-face with Brock Oliff. He's got something to say, I just know it."

# CHAPTER 33

## *An Avalanche of Falling Action*

That weekend whizzed by like a blur. Kristel traveled back and forth from the Club to the hospital, and I took it upon myself to be her chauffer. Except for the meal at the Grandstaffs on Saturday, we ate fast food on the way to or from Lake Henry, either after or between my work shifts.

My grandfather still never called back, and Mrs. Schuple, discerning that we were worried about him, reassured us that sudden disappearances and lack of contact were Abbott Marilee's protocol. There was one span a decade ago during which he never made contact with George or Beverly for eight straight months.

With this info, Kristel and I were satisfied to let Abbott be Abbott. Since we had already told everything about him to Roy Anders, and because it didn't seem like Sheriff Slater was pressing the issue about Robert Rothschild anymore, the main reason I wanted to talk to my grandfather was to thank him for the fortune that we had hidden away in the Anders' safe. That could wait as along as necessary.

The tree house visits were now a thing of the past, mainly because Kristel's parents weren't around. Nevertheless, we had plenty of long conversations in my car on the way to and from the hospital. Plus, there was just something discomfiting about going inside the Schuple house while her parents were gone. By this time, I had received two pecks on the cheek from Kristel, a couple of embraces, and enough handholding to wear off its flavor, and the little angel on my right shoulder whispered to me that all this was just fine. Sometimes, admittedly, the little devil on the other shoulder prompted me to make a move, but the only time Kristel and I were actually alone was in my car. So I behaved, and it was clearly the smart decision. Anything else would have been taboo.

Our talks centered mostly on the amazing events of the past month and the people who were part of them: Abbott, Jimmy, Mr. Schuple, the Sheriff,

Roy, and Brock. Ever since my confrontation with the sheriff and our hearing Elisa Grandstaff's suspicions about Brock, Kristel and I were convinced there was something rotten in the town of Abbeyville. If the sheriff and Branson Oliff had conspired to save Brock from a murder trial, it was still all speculation. But mere speculation didn't quench the temptation, during our daily commute, to drive past Lake Henry and continue south six hours south to New Jersey, where Brock was holed up in a rehab center. We believed Mrs. Grandstaff was right: the younger Oliff knew something about Jimmy.

With all this to talk about, the subject of the money from the crate was rarely discussed, other than my saying that I didn't feel I had a right to it, and that was true. The half million in cash didn't feel like mine at all. Because of the sheer size of the fortune, and having known my grandfather for such a short time, I hardly considered it a gift. I settled it in my mind that it was Jimmy's legacy, it was the money was that *he* was supposed to enjoy. If he had never died, it would have been all his anyway.

And that got me thinking: if Jimmy had never died, would I have even been here? Did my mother send me up here to purposely meet my grandfather, thinking that *I* would become the heir to his fortune? It just made me wonder why she had so suddenly presented this summer job opportunity to me, as if she knew all this was going to happen to me. At times, I wanted to pack up that money and drop it back in that vault and forget about everything that had anything to do with it. But Abbott Marilee was *my* grandfather, and Jimmy *was* my brother. Still, the money never seemed like mine, so, for the time being, I let it sit there in Roy's safe.

If life hadn't been crazy enough over the past month, the avalanche of incredible incidences had just begun. To begin with, on Sunday night, six days after the shooting, I was walking Kristel down the dark driveway toward her house when we noticed lights on inside her house. It turned out, innocently enough, to be Darlene, the hostess, doing her laundry, watching TV, and just enjoying some relaxation separate from the other staff for the evening. Kristel had invited her to do that and nearly forgotten it.

With Darlene there, I felt more at ease about entering the house when Kristel invited me in. Darlene had rented a video, some Hugh Grant chick-flick I couldn't care less to see, and she and Kristel sat on the couch in the living room while Darlene folded her laundry. I hung out in the kitchen and read some more *Gatsby*.

I was trying to get back into the novel again. It had been about a week since I had picked it up, and Nick had just helped to reunite old Gatsby and Daisy at his little bungalow. I knew it was supposed to be a significant moment in the story, but it got kind of mushy and boring, especially when they went over to Gatsby's place afterwards. I wondered if I would ever meet Kristel like that again, five years after this summer, and if we would hit it off like time had never passed. Fully distracted, I put the novel down and went into the living room with the girls and tried to get into the Hugh Grant movie.

Kristel had retrieved her photo albums so she could get the picture that Elisa Grandstaff wanted to see. To display a mild expression of my distaste with the movie, I sat next to her on the couch and thumbed through the albums and studied the pictures. Kristel had had so many friends throughout the summers, and although she dated Jimmy for a short time, he did make it into several of the most recent photos from last summer. I then wondered if I'd become part of her photo album. The only thing was, I hadn't noticed Kristel taking any pictures.

"How come you haven't been taking any pictures this summer?" I asked, interrupting what must've been a good part in the movie.

After a moment, Kristel answered without looking at me. "I usually wait until the last few weeks of the summer to take pictures," she said. Then she looked at me. "By then, I have a lot of close friends and I make sure to get pictures of them."

I examined several photos on the last page—pictures of staff members crowding into a group during a beach party and several photos of girls gathered around a dinner table at the dining room. I recognized a few of them who had returned this summer, and then it happened.

One girl in the photographs caught my eye—not her face, but what she was wearing. She sported a Tampa Bay Devil Rays baseball jersey. I had seen this before, and now the girl's face was slowly becoming familiar, too. And there it was!—this was the girl in one of the photographs from the busted camera Slater found at Smooth Rock Falls!

"Kristel!"

"What?"

"Who is this girl? Right here! The one in the jersey—who is this?"

Kristel huffed and glanced down at the album. "That's Kelly Walker. She was a lifeguard last summer."

I tapped my index finger on the photo. "This is the girl who was in one of the pictures that Slater showed me! There was a picture of her in that camera they found at the falls!"

"Are you sure?"

"I think so! When I looked at those pictures in Slater's office, I remember seeing this baseball jersey. This is her! I know it!"

We immediately called Roy Anders for advice. He suggested that Kristel and I go to the station Monday morning to take a look at the Smooth Rock photographs and see if Kristel could identify the girl herself. Maybe this could be a breakthrough. Kristel reluctantly agreed to go, even if it meant having to see Sheriff Slater again.

After my breakfast shift, we arrived at the police station, a full week since I had met with the sheriff there and gave the TV interview in the parking lot. Inside, an overweight woman, not in uniform, sat at the desk where Roy Anders had sat for many weeks when his leg was healing. She was a different lady than the one who was there last week.

"Can I help you?" she said, adjusting the wide-lens glasses on her plump cheeks.

"Yes. I'm Jody Barrett. Is Sheriff Slater in?"

The woman looked down at the phone on her desk. "He's on the line right now. He's been busy. Can I help you with something?"

I answered politely, "We need to look at some photographs that were obtained from a crime scene. We think we can identify somebody in one of the pictures."

"Crime scene? What crime scene?"

"Smooth Rock Falls, where Jimmy Grandstaff died. He was my brother. I'm Jody Barrett, and this is my friend Kristel Schuple."

The woman's eyes darted back and forth between both of us. "Oh my, yes. Just one moment please."

She scampered down the hallway to the sheriff's office. In a minute she returned with Clive Slater shuffling behind her.

The sheriff barked, "Mr. Barrett, what can I do for you today?" He looked intently at me, paying no attention to Kristel, who expected no less.

I answered, "I think we can identify someone in those photographs from the camera you found."

"You don't say!" Slater cajoled, now eyeballing Kristel with curiosity. "Hello, Ms. Schuple, 'm real sorry about your father. We're doing everything we can to find out who fired that gun," he said to her in a sleazily officious tone.

The sheriff gazed at her a moment longer, saying nothing, shifting his eyes down her figure. Then he looked at me and said abruptly, "I don't have the Grandstaff file anymore."

"What do you mean? Where is it?"

"In the system somewhere," he said bluntly, as though he enjoyed being blunt with me.

"What do you mean?" I said again with a crossed look.

"The Grandstaff case is now being handled by investigators in Lake Henry. We don't have a big department here in Abbeyville, as you can see. We normally pass cases like Jimmy's down to Lake Henry, especially when they get all the media attention you attracted to it. Lake Henry's got the time and the manpower there to continue the investigation. Right now, I'm busy with last week's shooting." The Sheriff glanced again at Kristel.

"Why didn't you tell me that when you called me last week?" I asked angrily. "You said you were getting flooded with calls from all sorts of phony John Does."

"We were. So now Lake Henry is handling it. I sent the file to them on Friday."

"So you're not handling the case anymore at all?"

"No. Not directly. Not since you sicked those media bloodhounds on us. An officer in Lake Henry will keep me up to date on anything that comes up."

"And who might that be?"

"I haven't been informed as to whom they've assigned it to yet."

"So they have the photos down there?"

"Uh, yes. They have the whole file."

"How come you didn't tell me this earlier?" I asked again sternly.

He was getting just as annoyed. "It just got transferred on Friday, like I said. Son, it's common procedure. Nothing's changed as far as the investigation goes. I told you I'd keep you informed if anything turns up, and nothing has, okay?"

"Well, something has turned up now. We know someone in those photographs!" I proclaimed.

"Who?" Slater asked, shifting his eyes to Kristel again. "Is it someone you know?"

Kristel nodded.

"How would you know who it is if you haven't seen the pictures?" he asked her sardonically.

"That's why we're here!" I cut in angrily.

"I think you need to calm down young man!" the sheriff growled.

"C'mon, Kristel. Let's go down to Lake Henry." I reached for Kristel's hand and turned towards the doorway.

"Just one minute, Mr. Barrett!"

I stopped and looked back at the Sheriff.

"I would advise you not to go down to Lake Henry and raise a media ruckus like you did here last week. You're only making it more difficult for the investigators. Suppose your brother *was* murdered and the killer sees this case on TV and in the papers. That's gonna keep him on his toes. Now, if I were you, I'd think about where you're standin' before you go shakin' too many trees, if you know what I mean."

I said nothing, but I knew the warning was called for, even from this jerk of a sheriff.

"Now as a matter of fact," Slater continued, "I *do* have copies of those photos here in the office. We've kept them and the camera here just in case the owner comes to claim it."

"Why didn't you tell us that in the first place?" I asked angrily.

He answered nonchalantly, "We sent the file on Friday. I just happened to remember we kept the camera here."

"Can we see them?" Kristel asked sweetly.

Slater looked her over, as if he liked what he saw. "Yes, I'll bring them out in a moment."

He walked back down the hallway toward his office. The fat lady behind the desk shuffled some papers and pretended she hadn't heard any part of the conversation. I stood silently next to Kristel near the door, and in a moment the sheriff returned.

"Show me who you recognize," Slater said, handing a small stack of photographs to Kristel.

Kristel flipped through them quickly as I looked over her shoulder.

"That one!" I said, pointing at one of the photographs. "That's the one!"

"Yep! That's Kelly all right. I don't know who that other girl is, though."

"You sure?" Slater asked, snatching the picture from her hand.

"Yes. The one in the jersey. She was a lifeguard at the Club last summer."

"Do you know if she lost a camera?"

"No, but I can call her."

"Why don't you give the number to my secretary here and we'll give this young woman a call. I doubt if she'll still want the camera because it's badly damaged."

"I'll have to look up the number at home," Kristel said.

"Could you call us with the number? I'd like to speak with her myself and ask her a few questions."

"Okay…"

I interrupted. "But I thought Lake Henry was on the case now. Shouldn't Lake Henry question her?"

"Listen, Jody," Slater said impatiently. "If you want to hear something about the camera a few weeks from now, let Lake Henry handle it. I'm doing you a favor by getting on this as soon as possible. I'll let you know if it turns out to be her camera, okay?" His words sounded as suspicious as they were reasonable. "Son, please believe me. We're doing all we can on this case."

"You mean Lake Henry is," I said curtly before I shoved open the door and walked out. Kristel hurried behind me. I jumped in my car and slammed the door shut. Kristel entered on the other side and stared me in the eye.

"He really got to you, didn't he?" she said.

I frowned ruefully and started the engine.

Kristel exclaimed, "I can't believe you were so sharp with him! It was great!" She laughed, enticing a small smirk on my face. I was still pretty ticked, though.

"You know what?" Kristel said cheerily. "I'm going to call Kelly myself. You could tell right away that Sheriff Slater is hiding something! I know he is, Jody!"

A half-grinning, half-angry grimace consumed my face as I backed out of the parking lot and squealed onto Route 7. "I can't believe it," I muttered. "It's us against the police department!"

Kristel added, "At least Roy Anders is on our side!"

As clear as it was that the sheriff was hiding something, things grew even more interesting when I got off work that night.

Kristel greeted me at the back dock with excitement in her eyes and exclaimed, "Jody, you won't believe what Kelly Walker told me! That camera belongs to Brock Oliff!"

"Are you serious?"

"I talked to Kelly on the phone and told her about the picture. She said Brock Oliff took that picture of her and her friend last August. She remembers it because they ran into Brock in Lake Henry at the end of the summer and he made them pose for that picture! It was Brock's camera!"

"So it *was* Brock!" I exclaimed. "*John Doe was trying to lead the police to Brock!* We've got to call Roy!"

In minutes, we were on the phone, but even before we told him about the camera's owner, Roy Anders was already convinced that Sheriff Slater was indeed involved in a cover up to protect Brock Oliff.

"Jody," he said over the phone. "Slater gave you a bunch of garbage about the case being sent to Lake Henry—it's a lie. The whole file is still in his office!"

"He lied right to our face?! A bold faced lie!" I declared. "I can't believe it! What do we do now?"

"Well, there's more, and I'm glad you called. I got on our computer system to do a search on Robert Rothschild. Our system keeps a log of every file that has been accessed in the last thirty days, and it showed that someone else in the county performed the same search on Robert Rothschild earlier this month."

"Was it Slater?"

"I don't know for sure, but I suspect it is, especially since he asked you about him. The file was accessed from the computer here at the station. Anyway, the search revealed a Robert Rothschild from New York City who died back in July of 1958, the same week as the Marilee tragedy. It looks like your grandfather somehow assumed the dead man's identity. I wouldn't doubt if Slater has learned the same information."

"I wish Abbott would contact us again. We've got to tell him about Slater."

"I know. But listen, I'm going to call a friend of mine down in Albany and let him in on our suspicions about Slater, and about Brock. All this is more than just mere suspicion now, because Slater did lie to you about the file being sent Lake Henry. My friend might be able to help us build a case."

"Are you going to tell him about Rothschild and the money and all that?"

"I don't think I have any other choice."

"Can you trust him?"

"Positive. He and I go way back. He's a good man. Oh, and another thing, I also did a search on anyone with the last name of Emory from this area. There was a family of Emory's who lived near Pokeville, but that was over thirty years ago, and they've all since departed. We need Miss Emory's first name and her year of birth to do a more thorough search. I didn't find any records of a birth to a mother named Emory in 1959 either. If she had her baby, whether it was Zane's or Abbott's, that child wasn't born in any hospital around here."

"Maybe she gave birth at home?"

"Could be. I'll have Walter do a nationwide search from Albany. Our system here only has access to state and county records. Oh, by the way, have Kristel call her friend in Florida again and see if she is willing to submit a sworn statement about Brock taking that picture. That'll stack up pretty seriously against Brock. See if she can fax or mail a written statement with her signature to the Club. Don't have her send it to the station here, because Slater might get it first."

"Gotcha."

"Good. And Jody, tell Kristel we're still praying for her dad. I'll call you if anything new turns up with Slater or Brock."

As it turned out, Roy *would* call again, as things very quickly grew even more interesting.

In the meantime, Kelly Walker was not home for the second call, so Kristel left a message. On Tuesday, Kristel spent most of the day in Lake Henry at the hospital with her mother and father. It had been a full week now since her father was shot, and the doctors were estimating just a couple of more days before he could be released.

That afternoon at about four o'clock, just after I arrived at the kitchen for the dinner shift, I received the phone call in the kitchen office from Officer Anders.

He asked me in a hurried voice, "When do you get off work?"

"About eight o'clock."

"Can you and Kristel come over to my place tonight?"

"Why? Did something happen today?"

"Yes. Lots of things happened. You're not going to believe it!"

"I'll believe anything!"

"I'll see you tonight then."

This had to be something *big*, and as I worked through the dinner shift, dunking basket after basket of breaded butterfly shrimp into hot oil, I imagined what it would be like to see Sheriff Clive Slater get convicted for covering up a murder.

Then I imagined Brock Oliff on the witness stand—would he plead not guilty? Probably. His father could hire the best legal defense team in the nation.

Then I thought about the half a million dollars, and how Jimmy's legacy would live on in the form of an adoption home built at Marilee Manor. I thought about how the rest of my life might play out as the grandson of Abbott Marilee.

What had Roy Anders discovered today? He certainly sounded excited on the phone, and I continually glanced at the clock, anticipating our meeting with him that night.

Expecting breakthrough news, Kristel and I arrived at the Anders home just before dark. Michelle Anders answered the door, holding a little baby in her arms. "C'mon in, kids. Roy is in the living room."

We found her husband sitting on the edge of the couch. The All-Star game was on television, but Roy was paying little attention to it. He was looking over a yellow legal pad on the coffee table. A black pen stuck out from his lips like a long cigarette.

"I'm going to go put the baby down," Michelle said. "I'll be back in a minute."

Roy hardly spoke as he studied his notepad while Kristel and I sat in separate chairs opposite the couch. Our curiosity grew the longer we sat there in silence. Michelle finally returned from upstairs and sat next to her husband. Roy took the pen out from between his lips.

"You won't believe what happened today," he said with a hint of excitement in his voice.

"What?" I asked, ready to hear about the impending downfall of Sheriff Slater.

"Well, for one, Slater fired me!"

# CHAPTER 34

## *Temporary Asylum and Library Research*

Roy made the announcement as if he thought it was funny. His wife even gave an embarrassed smile.

"You got fired?" I exclaimed.

"Yep. Slater up and fired me."

"Why?"

"Probably because he knows his own neck is in a sling."

"Tell us what happened!" insisted Kristel.

"Well, last night I called my friend in Albany and gave him some background to our situation here. I told him about the photographs and how Slater lied to you about the investigation being sent to Lake Henry. He knows Slater; he worked with him for a while down in the city. He told me the best thing to do is to confront Slater directly with the lie, because that's the only way to deal with Slater—boldly and directly. So today, I did."

A grin shot across Roy's face as he added. "And you should have seen him squirm! This morning, I flat out asked him why he lied to you about the file being sent to Lake Henry. He said it was 'none of my business,' so I came right out and asked him, 'what are you hiding from those kids?'

"When I asked him that, his face turned red and he began stammering and pacing around the front office. Then he yelled at me, 'You think I'm covering something up?' and I said, 'You tell me.' Then he swore and pounded the side of the file cabinet with his fist. He started yelling about how a man can't go about an investigation without the town deciding they all want to become a bunch of Matlocks or something. Then he stormed back into his office and came out with a huge file and shoved it into my chest. He said 'There! You take over the case!' Then he cursed some more and stormed back into his office and slammed the door.

"I looked through the file and it was filled mostly with all those 'Ambassador' letters you got from your grandfather. But the pictures from

Brock's camera weren't in there, just the negatives. So I went back into Slater's office and asked where the pictures were. You should have seen his face! He glared at me and picked up the pictures that were sitting right on his desk and he threw them at me. They flew across the room and landed everywhere. I said 'never mind, I've got the negatives here,' and I walked out of the office. The pictures were still all over the floor.

"When I looked over the negatives, I noticed that the one of the two girls at Lake Henry wasn't there among them. So I went back into Slater's office again and asked where that negative was. He said it should be in the file with the rest of them. I said it wasn't, and he said 'You really think I'm hiding something, don't you!'

"I said, 'I know you lied to those kids yesterday, and the negative of that photograph they identified is now missing.'

"Then he yelled, 'Get out of my office!'"

Roy shifted in his chair and continued in an exited tone, "So at that moment, I laid it all out on the line. You won't believe what I said next."

"What!?"

"I said, 'You're being paid off by Branson Oliff, aren't you.' And when I said that, his face froze, and he just looked at me. So I said it again, 'You're helping Branson Oliff protect his son Brock, aren't you.' Slater only looked at me and said nothing. So I said, 'The camera belongs to Brock Oliff. I know it does. You knew that weeks ago, didn't you.'

"Then he yelled at me again: 'Get out of my office!' I thought he was mad enough to hit me, so I left and closed the door.

"A minute later, he comes storming out and yells 'Anders! You're through! Give me you're badge and get outta here!' I said, 'What for?' and he said, 'For making unfounded accusations against your superior!' I said, 'I just wanted some answers" and he said, 'Get out of here. You're done!'

"So I left the office, but I never gave him my badge. I came home and called my buddy in Albany. They're starting a full-fledged investigation on Slater."

"You're kidding!" I exhaled.

"I knew he was involved!" Kristel cried.

Anders nodded his head. "Well, get this. Later this afternoon, Slater calls me here at home to try to apologize. He said he's been under a lot of pressure and he wanted to meet with me tonight to explain things. I told him it was too late for that, because I had already made a report to the department at the state capital. He swore and hung up the phone."

Anders raised his eyebrows and nodded, saying, "This thing is coming down, kids, and coming down fast! Are you ready to be all over the news again, Jody?"

I answered sheepishly, "I guess so. It looks like my grandfather was right—there *was* a police cover-up over Jimmy's death."

"Well, Michelle and I have been talking about that, and here's what we think. Brock is obviously a suspect at this point. And maybe Branson is protecting his son and paying Slater a pretty big sum to help him out. But then we've got to consider Brock's motive for murder. Why would Brock kill for some cash that Jimmy might have received from Rothschild if Brock is already filthy rich?"

"Jealousy over Kristel?" I suggested.

"Maybe. And maybe it was an accident. Maybe they got in a fight on top of that cliff and Jimmy fell accidentally. But think about this," Anders said. "You said that Slater asked you about Rothschild, whether you had ever spoken with him or got a letter from him, right?"

"Yes."

"Then Slater definitely knows something about Rothschild, especially since he's most likely the one who did the computer search on him recently. And if Slater is being paid by Branson Oliff to protect Brock, then it's possible that the Oliff's know something about Rothschild, too. Don't you think Branson Oliff would have an interest in Rothschild's identity, considering he's had an eye on that property for years?"

"Do you think they know he's Abbott Marilee?"

"I don't know, but Slater's after Rothschild for something, and the Oliff's could be connected. Maybe Brock's motive wasn't jealousy. Maybe he knew what Rothschild was going to do for Jimmy. If Jimmy got that land, it would prevent Brock's father from building the hotel for him."

"That could be it," Kristel said. "Brock would kill to get his resort built over there."

"But there's more, Kristel," Anders said gently. "And it has to do with your father."

"My father?"

"I think your father is a victim in all this." Anders tapped his notepad with his pen. "If Jimmy Grandstaff was eliminated to keep the Manor property available for the Oliff's, and if they know who Rothschild really is, then wouldn't you think they would want to eliminate Rothschild also?"

It sounded logical.

"So maybe that bullet was intended for Rothschild and not your father. Maybe they thought Rothschild has been carrying the lantern all this time."

"And they shot Daddy instead!" Kristel cried.

"Who do you think might have shot him?" I asked. "Slater or Branson or Brock?"

"Well, Brock was already in the rehab center in New Jersey. And Branson is too rich to do dirty business like that himself. Maybe Slater pulled the trigger, but it could be someone else. Branson Oliff certainly can afford to hire as many people as he needs."

"A big conspiracy!" I exclaimed. "My grandfather was right!"

Anders added, "No wonder he hasn't contacted anyone since last week. He's probably knows Slater is onto him and he has to lay low."

I said, "But if they already killed Jimmy and now are trying to kill Abbott, who's to say they won't kill anyone else? We all could be in danger."

"That's why we asked you to come over tonight. I think we all have made a few enemies over the past few days."

"Yes," Michelle cut in. "Neither of you should be anywhere alone, not until the department in Albany gets to the bottom of this."

"My wife's right. I saw Slater's face today. He had looks that could kill. And you, Jody, are the cause of much of his frustration."

He was right. Who would be next? First Jimmy was pushed off that cliff, and then Mr. Schuple took a bullet that was intended for my grandfather. I've ticked off the sheriff, and now Roy has been fired. What should we do now? That's exactly what I asked.

Roy's answer proved that this was even more serious than I had presumed. First of all, Roy and his wife were so concerned about our safety that they insisted Kristel and I spend the night with them. Roy accompanied us to the Club to get our things, and by eleven o'clock, we were all back at the Anders household.

Furthermore, Roy and Michelle had already determined that precaution dictated they take their entire family out of Abbeyville, at least until assurance of safety could be confirmed from the department in Albany, and they suggested we come with them, just to be safe. They had already made arrangements at a motel in Lake Henry, and we would all go there tomorrow.

They were drastic measures, none the least, but there was no telling how far this thing could go. So on Wednesday morning, Roy escorted us back to the Club and Kristel and I packed enough clothes for a week.

Chef Al was upset to learn I would be out for a while, but in light of the

Schuple shooting, everyone was forced to be flexible. He said he hoped I would be back sooner than later. Darlene assured Kristel that she could get along just fine for a few days, and not to worry, because Mrs. Schuple phoned at least three time a day to check up on things.

I didn't get a chance to say so long to Boonie, which was probably for the better. He most likely would have teased me about staying in a motel with Kristel, and I didn't feel like giving him an explanation.

The motel in Lake Henry was called the Huron Village Inn, and it was a convenient location for Kristel to be close to her mom and dad. Beverly Schuple was staying in a much nicer hotel on the waterfront, and Becky was still staying with her aunt and uncle.

So in my Mustang on that morning of July 15, Kristel and I followed the Anders family van to the top of the steep driveway of the Huron Village Inn. Together we rented a total of three rooms with double beds. The two oldest Anders boys took one, Roy and I would sleep in the other, and Kristel, Michelle, and the littlest baby in the third. All the rooms were adjoined with connecting doors, and it was like one big family living in a three-room house. The motel had a pool, and a half-hour after we got there, Michelle already had the three kids in bathing suits.

There we were, all of the sudden, gone from Abbeyville and hiding out in Lake Henry. It was obvious to us all that we were not living in absolute seclusion. If someone was after any one of us, they could probably find us if they wanted to. But it was better, for the meantime, to be almost an hour away from Abbeyville, where Branson Oliff, Sheriff Slater, and whoever might be working for him were always lurking nearby. Plus, we were closer to Albany, where Roy's buddy, Sergeant Walter Holliday worked.

In all, each of us felt safer in Lake Henry than we did in Abbeyville, and as a result, The Huron Village Inn would serve as our temporary headquarters, hopefully for only a few days at the most. We figured the critical day was July 27$^{th}$, twelve days from now. That's when the Manor property was to go up for sale, and if Branson Oliff was having people killed to assure his property acquisition on that day, we would make this motel our asylum until then. Hopefully, Roy Anders and Walter Holliday, along with Albany Police Department, could get something done about Slater sooner.

Temporarily out of work, and trapped at the motel, Kristel and I found ourselves with absolutely nothing to do. Roy said it was okay for us to visit the hospital, go shopping, or take in a movie, but we needed to be careful: always be on the lookout for someone following us. So, while Roy and Michelle enjoyed some time in the pool with their kids, Kristel and I decided to visit the Lake Henry Library.

Kristel had visited that library twice last year when she was doing her research paper on the legend of Marilee Manor. Today, we hoped maybe we could dig up something more on the Marilee family, and perhaps something about Miss Emory from the newspaper archives.

The library was an old two-story brick building, with heavy wooden doors and noisy wooden floors. Its books and equipment looked as old as the building itself. Missing were the standard rows of computer stations—only stacks of ancient card-catalogues were extant here. There was only one computer, an old 386 model, sitting in the corner. The next-most modern equipment in the place were those microfilm machines where you could scan images of newspapers and magazines.

The *Lake Henry Gazette* was established in 1921, and the earliest date the Lake Henry Library had of the local newspapers on microfilm was 1949. I flipped through the drawer labeled "Mar.'57- Nov.'58."

Kristel was nearby in a narrow aisle between stacks of books. "There's a book on Adirondack Mountain history here that I used for my research project last year," she said, as I searched through a drawer of microfilm. "It has a chapter just on Lake Marilee. You should see it."

I asked, "You said you found newspaper reports about the explosion in here."

"Yes. Look in July 1958."

Kristel sat at a table and perused a large colorful book about the Adirondack Mountain region. I sat in front of a viewing machine and read through old but fascinating newspaper articles about the tragedy at the Marilee estate. I read reports about the rape accusation against Abbott Marilee, the explosion at the Manor, and the latter discovery of Abbott Marilee's body. The article about the rape did not report the victim's name because she was a minor. Neither did I find anything that mentioned the name Emory in any of the articles, only that the victim was fifteen years old and from the Pokeville area.

What did catch my attention was an article about the missing body of the Marilee infant—my own mother. Investigators presumed the baby's body parts must have been blown into the woods and carried off by animals. There was also an article about the funeral, and I never before realized that there was a small tombstone marking where my mother's drawer full of baby clothes was buried in the Abbeyville cemetery.

All of these newspaper reports sounded like solid fact, and none of them contradicted the true explanation that my grandfather and Kristel's mother told us.

We stayed at the library and read for nearly an hour before Kristel suggested in a yawning voice, "I just wish we could find something about Miss Emory—she's the key in getting your grandfather acquitted."

I was still engrossed in the articles, but finally said over my shoulder, "Roy said he tried to find a hospital birth record for Miss Emory's baby, but he couldn't find anything through their computer system. He's going to have his friend in Albany do a nationwide search. Do you think I should search the newspaper's birth announcement sections?"

Kristel stood up from the table and stretched her arms as she advised, "She could have had the baby at home, or moved out of state, or miscarried, or..." Suddenly, she was re-energized. "Hey—Let's look for Emory's on the Internet."

"Won't the police have a better chance of finding something on their system?"

"Yes, but we could always look. This is kind of fun."

For Kristel, this was like playing detective, trying to unleash the truth about the forty-year old murder of my relatives. Ironically, the very reason we were in Lake Henry was because we had practically uncovered the ten-month old murder of my brother. And if Roy's theory was correct, maybe both cases had something to do with each other.

Kristel and I crowded around the single computer monitor, and she clicked on the Internet icon and waited for the start pages to appear. It was a slow machine—a phone line hookup, and I was convinced that waiting for the police to do their search was a better use of our time.

But Kristel was insistent. She had done this last year: dug up information on the Marilee legend, and searching for Miss Emory was something she hadn't done yet.

The Internet search was slow and netted no results. We hit New York State government agencies, Huron County records departments, and about as many "people finder" dot coms that I could tolerate. We found thousands of Emory's in the USA, with phone numbers listed, but it was useless: we didn't know Miss Emory's first name.

Out of curiosity, Kristel brought up some pages dedicated to the Legend of Marilee Manor, some factual, some as fictional as you can imagine. Kristel was having fun, mesmerized by some sites about the Lights of Marilee she hadn't seen before, now looking at them with the knowledge of her father's involvement. I, on the other hand, was getting hungry. It was lunchtime.

"We should go," I suggested. "I'm hungry, and besides, you told you're mom you'd be at the hospital by one."

"Hang on, Jody," she said, now with a touch of chagrin in her voice. "Look, this site is about my Dad."

It was a site linked to UrbanLegends.com, and it contained a recently posted account detailing the hoax behind the legendary Lights of Marilee. It even showed a photograph of a young-looking George Schuple. A link brought us to a newspaper article written about his shooting.

"Hey, this is the *Gazette* article from last week," Kristel said.

I pointed out, "Look—you're in lakehenrygazette.com. We've been searching through those dumb microfilms all this time when it's right here on the web."

After a few clicks, Kristel added, "No—look. Their archives only go back to 1995."

I left the computer and checked the stack of microfilms; it, indeed, stopped at December 1994. Everything in the last three years was now available online. By the time I returned to the PC, Kristel was enthralled with something she had found.

"I found a Nathaniel Emory!" she said. "Look!"

There was the name Nathaniel T, Emory on the screen. It was in the obituary section of the Lake Henry Gazette published May 23, 1995.

Kristel giggled, "I just typed the name Emory in the archive window, and this came up!"

There was no photo, only lines of text under the bold heading "Nathaniel T. Emory" that read,

*Nathaniel Tate Emory, 67, former resident of Pokeville, went home to be with the Lord on Saturday, May 20, 1995. He is survived by relatives Vernon Emory of Abilene, Texas (brother); Gretta Ardello (Emory) of Bangor, Maine (daughter); and Mary Lee Ardello of Bangor, Maine (granddaughter). A memorial service will be held on Tuesday, May 23, in Roanoke Rapids, North Carolina.*

"Gretta Ardello!" Kristel gasped. "Gretta and Harold Ardello! She's an

Emory?!"

We gazed at the screen in amazement.

I jumped to conclusions: "Miss Emory has been right down the road all along?!"

Kristel cautioned, "She's *an* Emory, at least. Maybe a relative, maybe *the* Miss Emory."

I pointed at the text on the screen. "No, look: the granddaughter's name is *Mary Lee* Ardello. Maybe that's Gretta Ardello's daughter, and maybe she was named after her father—Mari-lee."

In a minute we were speeding in my car back to the hotel. Roy was tickled with the news. If Gretta is indeed the Miss Emory we're looking for, he said, and if she's willing to make a statement, Roy wanted to get it recorded for the Albany department. We dropped Kristel off at the hospital before Roy and I took off for Pokeville.

# CHAPTER 35

## *An Ancient and Essential Testimony*

Pokeville was about a forty-minute ride from Lake Henry, but at the speed I was driving, we might have made it in thirty.

Old Harold and Gretta. Was she tacky enough to name her daughter Mary Lee after the Marilee family? Was she brave enough to drive away in the pontoon boat the night of the killings? Was she bold enough to come up with the rape story to get Zane's thirty grand? Had she become honest enough to confess the truth to Abbott and his parents?

I thought back to that day I first met her at the gas pump, and how she thought I was Jimmy's brother. Later she told Harold it was all just a "ca'incidence." There were those nights down at the Club beach, Gretta and Harold gazing across at the Manor with their binoculars. Did she think it was Abbott himself? His ghost? Is she the Miss Emory we're looking for? Is she even a relative? "It's all jus' a ca'incidence" she had cackled at Harold. Boy, was she wrong. I *was* Jimmy's brother! What a coincidence it would be if Miss Emory was living right there in Pokeville! My grandfather might be found innocent!

"Slow down there Jody, or I'll have to give you a ticket," Anders warned.

"Huh uh. You're not a cop; you were fired, remember," I said with a smile.

"I've still got my badge, and right now I'm on undercover duty!"

I eventually slowed down for the Pokeville exit, and after creeping through that depressing town, my Mustang finally crumbled onto the gravel lot in front of Harold and Gretta's gas station and post office. Gray dust wafted through the air as the vehicle skidded to a halt. We were already out of the car before the flabby old Gretta Ardello (Emory) poked her head out the screen door.

A yellow, toothy grin crossed her face when she recognized me. "Why, I sah yah on TV 'while go, young man! Tahns out yah related to al' Jimmy after all!" She cackled in delight. "An' wasn't that you we sah take aff fram th' beach the night a' the shootens?"

"That's right," I said. I looked at Roy who earlier told me that he would do most of the talking.

"Mrs. Ardello, do you have a moment?" he asked in an official voice.

The woman glanced across the dusty, empty lot, where my car sat alone. "Dahn luhk too busy naah, does et?" Gretta retorted, stepping completely outside the door onto the top step.

"No ma'am." To show his badge, Anders stepped forward and slid out his wallet from his back pocket. "I'm Officer Roy Anders. I just need to ask you a few questions," he said, holding his wallet open.

Gretta's forehead rippled into wrinkles. "Is they'ah trouble?" she asked.

"No ma'am ...."

"Dahs this hav'ta do with Jimmy?" she said glancing at me.

"Yes ma'am," Anders said. "Well, indirectly it does. This actually has more to do with a case that took place forty years ago."

Gretta stared blankly at Anders.

"We are looking for a woman who, back in 1958, pressed charges against Abbott Marilee, for, uh, sexual assault, or, for rape."

Gretta's eyes narrowed as she stared into the air at no one. Her lips moved, but no words emitted from them.

Anders waited before saying, "Her last name was Emory. Do you know of anyone in your family who might have made those charges?'

Gretta shifted her eyes above our heads, beyond us, beneath us, and then they finally connected with mine. Then she turned towards the door, opened it part way and leaned her head inside. She hollered, "Harold, I'm gahin' down to the house to talk w'these fahlks."

Harold's voice could be heard from inside. "They'ah a prahblem?"

"Nah. No prahblem." Gretta turned back towards us at the base of the steps. "C'mon back to the house and we can talk," she said in a low voice.

My hopes swelled and something tickled inside my stomach.

The old woman was wearing oversized leather sandals that slapped against her bare heels as she walked off the small porch and across the gravel. We followed behind her as she slapped around the side of the building where an oily, gravel driveway sneaked into the woods behind the store. Roy was carrying his camera bag by the shoulder strap, and I hoped we would be putting the video camera to use here.

A pile of a dozen or so old tires, an old rusted pick-up truck without wheels, and a scrap pile full of wood planks and aluminum roofing bordered the stony pathway. Just into the woods, we came to a mobile home with a nice, silver, four-door sedan parked in front. The mobile home was not much bigger than the general store, but it certainly looked newer.

"Harold and I moved he'yah 'bout three ye'ahs ago when my father died. He had this plat of land in his name for ye'ahs, so we pahked our own home right he'yah." Gretta pointed beyond the house deeper into the woods. "They'ah's a little lake back they'ah where Harold likes to fesh. Hardly no one knows 'bout et."

The woman invited us inside the trailer where we were surprised to feel the coolness of air-conditioning and the plush surroundings of a new, comfortable living room. A small kitchen was off to the left of the door. "C'mon in and sit dahn. Can I get ya sam'n' to drenk?"

"No ma'am," Anders and I said together.

I sat in a fluffy cushioned love seat under a window. Roy sat on the edge of a leather Lazy Boy, and Gretta pulled over a wooden chair from the small dinette set. "Well na'ah," she said bluntly. "You were asking 'baht a rape case?"

"Yes ma'am," Anders said. "Do you know who made those charges against Abbott Marilee?"

"That's saht've sens'tive infahmation, isn'tit offissah?"

"You're right. You only have to tell us what you want to. This isn't an official investigation."

Gretta glanced at me and then back at Officer Anders. "How much y'all know?"

"About what?" Anders said, prompting Gretta to do the talking.

"Abaht this whole thing. The rape. The Marilees."

"We know some. We're hoping you will tell us more."

"Do ya' know the legend, the Marilee legend?"

"Yes. We've both heard various versions of it."

"Ya' think al' Abbott's ghost still rahms them grahnds over they'ah?"

"I don't believe in ghosts ma'am. The shooting last week proved it all to be a hoax."

"Ya thenk ol' Abbott's stell alive? Maybe stell aht they'ah somwhe'ya?"

Anders eyeballed me, then answered, "I know there's a grave and a tombstone with Abbott Marilee's name on it. What can you tell me about that?"

Gretta's lips puckered and she stared at the carpet for a moment. Then she finally said, "I know he's naht dead. Ehr at least he wasn't dead durin' his fun'rahl when they thot they buried him."

I felt my heart thump against my chest. This *is* Miss Emory!

Roy stated, "Miss Em… er, uh, Mrs. Ardello, we have very good reason to believe that Abbott Marilee is still alive. Were you an eyewitness to the tragic explosion that destroyed the Marilee mansion in July of 1958?"

A quiet moment followed as the old woman began fighting back her emotions. Her chin shook as her flabby eyelids formed a dam against a flood of tears. She sniffled, wiped her eyes, and said in a shaky voice. "Haw did ya fahnd out?"

"We have spoken with Abbott Marilee himself, or at least Jody has," Anders said, gesturing to me.

Gretta looked at me wide-eyed. "Ya spahk ta Abbott? He's stell alive?"

"Yes ma'am," I said softly. "And he wants to come out of hiding."

"Praise Jesus!" Gretta cried, clapping her hands. She looked at Anders. "Abbott is as ennacent as an angel. He ain't no mahduh'ah!"

"Is he a rapist?" Anders asked.

"Gahdness no," Gretta said, wiping her eyes and smiling, all her yellow teeth showing. "Whay'ah is Abbott? Is he he'yah?"

"No ma'am. He's gone back into hiding."

"Well I dahn blame hem, weth everyone thenk'n he's a mahduh'ah an' a rapest."

"Most people think he's dead," Anders said bluntly.

Gretta chuckled. "That's right… heh, that's right. Well, al' Abbott's ennacent. It's his brothah' that's gelty, and he's buh'nen in Hell far it thes very men'et."

"What can you tell us?"

"I can tell ya evra'theng ya need ta know ef et well keep Abbott frahm gahn to preson. I sah the whole theng that night at the Marilee prap'ty. I nah' the hul' truth!"

Anders opened his black camera bag containing the family video camera. "Would you mind if you tell your story on video tape? It could help lead to the acquittal of Abbott Marilee."

"Shu'ah, but well I get ta see Abbott?"

"He's in hiding right now, but we hope to see him soon. Go ahead, tell us everything you want to tell us." Anders said, resting the camera on the arm of the chair and looking down into the viewfinder.

Gretta smiled and sniffled, saying, "Wehl, et was an ahf'l lahn time ago, and I haven't evah told thes story to nah'n—nah'n! Naht even ta any of my husb'ns!"

Anders said, "We know that Abbott Marilee is alive, and there may be some greedy people out there trying to prevent the truth of this story from being known. If you tell us now, he could come clean with his identity. Your story can help clear his name from the crimes that his brother committed."

"Wehl, I'll tahk as lahng as yah cam'ra keeps runnen, offissah!"

"Go right ahead!" Anders said with a grin. A red light on the camera flashed on.

Gretta sat back in her chair and began her story.

"Wehl, et was 1958, in the summahtime. I nevah had any contact weth any Marilees 'fah then. They wah all wealthy an r'ligiss and I was po'ah and bein' raised in a bar b'my fathah. But one night Zane Marilee, the youngah brothah comes into the bar. I had nevah seen him b'fah. He came up ta me an' I was only 'bout 15 ye'ahs old. He said he had jus' graduated from Yale or Hahvahd or some fancy, shmancy school like that. He told me he was a Marilee and he'd soon be runnen' the bank up in Abbeyvelle. Wehl, one theng led to anothah, and you know, et happened en the back seat of hes cah."

"Zane raped you?" Anders asked.

"Nah. Et was cahnsent'l, I hate to a'met et. I said et was rape so my fathah wouldn't kell me."

"But you told the authorities it was Abbott who raped you."

"Yes. When I fahnd aht that I was pregna't, Zane gave me a wahd of cash to put the blame on hes brothah. I hadn't evah seen so much money en all my life. Thety grand et was. I took et without thenken, an' so I passed the blame onto Abbott and publicky accused hem. I dedn't even know who Abbott was. I dedn't know he was married and had kids 'till I read about'm in the papah.

"I felt so gelty abaht et! But then like an angel ahta heaven, Abbott finds me, an' I was glad to tell hem the truth 'bout me being pregna't with his brothah's child. An' then we all went right back to hes home at the Manah an' I told hes pah'ents the truth. They wah so ovahjoyed, an' Zane—that lettle devil—he ran right out the back do'ah when he saw the blame bein' penned on hem.

"Ol' Mr. Marilee, he was a proud man, but he let me stay weth hes fam'ly at the house, an' I was ganna go with the family to tha pahlice and tell the truth. I was glad t'be at the Marilees 'cause I didn't want to face my fathah aftah lyin' about who I slept weth. When the explos'n happened that night, nahbody baht me and the Marilees knew the real truth 'bout my pregna'cy."

"And you were there that night." Anders interjected. "What happened?"

"Whal, I woke up and saw Zane out the window doin' sahm'then' around the yahd. Fahnd out latah, too late, of coss, that he was planten the dynamite. But when I sah hem, I ran and got Abbott who went out to tahk to 'm. Then Zane wanted to tahk to me and try to make me marry hem. We gaht ento an ahgament, and then I was holden Abbott's lettle baby gahl in my ahms, while Zane and Abbott stahted ahguin. We wah standen dahn by the dock wey'ah no one else could hear us. Then Zane pulls out a detinatah box, an' I realized that he had been settin' dynamite 'round the house. I got sca'yahd and ran dahn the dock with the baby towahd the boat. Then the house blew up in flames. I gaht away in the boat with the Abbott's lil' baby gahl.

"Did you see Abbott shoot Zane?"

"Nah, but I hahd the gun fi'yah. I dedn't know who was dead 'tel the next day."

"Where did you go?"

"I stayed with a gahlfriend a' mine up at Wheelahtown. I tald 'er the baby was my cahsin's little gahl who I was watchen. The baby was only about six ah eight weeks ald at the time. I was feelin so galty ovah what I had cahs'd, so I went to chuch to settle my mind. My pray'ahs stell dedn't get me cle'ah of my gelt. All those ennacent people had died, Abbott's sweet waf and son, his parents, and even that devil brothah of hes—all 'cahs of my lies. So one night I left the baby weth my friend and veseted the graves of the family. I evn' considahd writen a cahnfesh'n note an killen myself raht they'ah en the cemet'ray.

"But then en the meddle of the night, right they'ah at the cemet'ray, out of nowhey'ah cahms Abbott an' some othah man. I knew the pahlice wah aftah hem, an' I thought he was long gone. I cahdn' believe he had cahm ta the cemet'ray right they'ah en Abbeyvelle! I hed bahind a tombstone an' watched hem and the othah man. They stahted deggen up Albeht's grave! Et took 'em sehv'ral a'ahs. I saw 'em pull the body out of the casket and re-bary the caffin and replace the dahrt. They feneshed just as the sun was risehn'.

"Then I fahllad 'em as they dragged Zanes's body dahn thrah the woods towahd' the lake. When I saw 'em change the clothes on the body, I knew just what they was dah'en.' I saw Abbott pahl the triggah of the gun and blow Zane's face right aff. Pahts of the face splattahd against the trees. Nobody found that except the 'coons, I suspect.

"The two of 'em left in a hurray—ahmast too fast fah me to keep fahllowen.

But I fahllowed 'em all the way back to a house jus' outside of Abbeyvelle whey'ah they both went inside. I fig'yahd Abbott was hiden' out they'ah weth that man. A few days latah the news comes up that Abbott's body's been fahnd, and I knew Abbott had successfahlly faked hes own death. I was so glad for hem!

"'Ventually, I knew I had to get hes lettle baby back to hem, so I braht hah to that house whey'ah he was hiden and set her on the pahch. I left the lettle dahl right they'ah at the door and watched Abbott come out ahly en the mahnen and fahnd hah. Et looked like he was on hes way somewhey'ah 'cause he had a bag packed full'v staff. I knew Abbott and hes lettle gahl would be alright. He had all the money he needed an' the smahts to get by. That was the last I saw of hem—they'ah at the doorway of that house cradling hes lettle baby en hes ahms."

Gretta stopped speaking and Anders clicked the camera off. He looked at me and said, "Abbott Marilee *did* tell you the truth. Gretta's version matches up perfectly, except that he left out his coroner friend who helped him dig up the grave, probably to protect him."

"We've got to find him and tell him that we've found Miss Emory!" I exclaimed.

"Oh, do! Please find hem!" Gretta cried.

I told her, "It's unbelievable you've been here, ma'am, for the past three years, just miles down the road."

"What dah ya mean?"

I explained, "Abbott has been a guest at the Brown Swan Club for years under the disguise of a rich old man named Robert Rothschild."

"Ya dahn say!"

"Yes, and now that I think about it, he might have been at your little post office. Did you ever see a rich man that kind of looks like Santa Clause come in to deliver mail? He sent me a letter postmarked from Pokeville everyday for a couple of weeks."

Gretta thought for a moment. "Nah, I'd certainly recall that. They'ah was a skenny ol' man who came by 'bout nine 'clahk en the mahnen to delivah a lettah. "He ded that 'bout evreh day fer 'bout two weeks."

Anders and I glanced at each other. "Maybe Rothschild had someone deliver it for him," he suggested.

Gretta added, "Ay'eh, that ol man wahked weth a lemp and he had a terr'bly harse voice. Like he had lahr'ngitis or somt'n."

Now I knew. Whisper!

The woman's words forced the logical explanation to fall perfectly into place in my head: Whisper wasn't just working for Rothschild; Whisper is Rothschild! Whisper is Abbott Marilee, my grandfather! Whisper, the one who told me to look for the truth, the one who himself said the ghost of Marilee was a hoax. He knew it because he *is* Abbott Marilee. He watched from the beach as his old buddy George Schuple played his ghost. He called the emergency crews when he heard the gunshots—shots he probably knew were for him.

I stood to my feet. "I know where Abbott is," I said.

Gretta and Roy looked strangely at my sudden outburst.

"There's a night watchman at the Club who walks with a limp and speaks with a hoarse voice. They call him Whisper, and if you put a beard and a mustache on him and dress him in a fat suit, he would look just like Robert Rothschild."

"Was he still around after Rothschild took off?" Anders asked.

"Yes. He was watching from the beach when Mr. Schuple got shot. He called the police… and now that I think about it, that's the last time I saw him."

"Let's go find him!" Anders insisted. "He's an innocent man, and he's the owner of the Marilee property!"

# CHAPTER 36

## *Puzzle Pieces Falling in Place*

"Beverly Schuple said that Abbott is a master of disguises," I recalled, as we sped north on Route 7 along Lake Marilee. "She was right!"

"That guy's got a lot of guts," Anders added.

It was all coming together so fast: Slater self-destructing, Miss Emory testifying, and now Abbot Marilee can take his story public and terminate his false identities as Robert Rothschild, Whisper, and any others he has invented.

We squealed up the Brown Swan Club driveway and zoomed over the hill, straight to the cabin grove. "There's his golf cart," I said as we pulled to a stop in front of Hawkeye.

The loosely hanging cabin door was unlocked as we quietly stepped inside. The place still looked untouched since my first visit: the tools all remained in their same spots on the tool bench; the utensils were still spread about the kitchenette; and the big half-carved swan on the floor didn't look any more like a swan. Anders noticed the briefcase on the top bunk. He opened it—empty, just like it was when I did the same thing almost two weeks ago. He found the old rusty lantern and lifted it up for me to see. I acted as if I had never seen it before, although I had stolen it when I suspected Whisper to be the ghost. In some ways, my stupid suspicion about Whisper was actually right on the nose.

Anders poked through a few boxes but found nothing significant. "Do you know where Robert Rothschild's room was?" he asked.

In minutes, after Roy showed his badge at the front desk to get a key to Robert Rothschild's summer residence, we unlocked the door to the chalet appropriately entitled, "Tycoon's Roost." The inside was immaculate—not a sign of a man who spent every summer in the place.

"Housekeeping must have been here," I said. "Or he never actually stayed *here*."

Roy and I searched each of the rooms, rummaged through closets, cabinets, and drawers. Nothing. No clue that might lead us to Abbott Marilee.

"I wonder if the front desk has a record of any outbound calls he might have made," Roy pondered, as he rifled through drawers of a small desk. "We've got to find him as soon as possible—before Slater gets to him."

He opened a sliding glass door and stepped out onto a small cedar deck that overlooked the valley. Roy looked down to his feet, stopped, and then crouched, peering through the cracks of the deck boards. At once he scampered down the steps and crawled underneath. Out he came with a few curly particles of wood in the palm of his hand.

"Wood shavings," he said. "You're right. Whisper and Rothschild could be the same guy."

I shook my head in awe. My grandfather was amazing.

Just then, Roy's cell phone chirped and he immediately answered it.

"Kristel, hi, what's going on?"

A long, long pause as Anders listened.

"You're sure you're okay? Where are you?... Okay, we'll be there in about an hour."

Anders looked at me with a worried expression, "Kristel was chased by a strange man at the hospital."

"Is she all right?"

"Yes. She's back at the motel. Let's go."

We zoomed back down to Lake Henry faster than we did up to Pokeville. Kristel was safe with Michelle and the kids at the motel, still a little shaken, but typically Kristel—in amazingly high spirits.

"So what happened?" Roy and I asked simultaneously as we got to the room.

Kristel's story went like this:

"After you dropped me off at the hospital, and when I got to Daddy's room, I heard my mom talking to someone. It was someone I didn't know, so I didn't go in. I just stood by the door. Mom was answering questions about the shooting, and I thought he was an investigator. He said he was working for Sheriff Slater, and he also asked her if he knew where he could find Jody Barrett.

"I didn't know what to do—I figured if he was working for Slater, he couldn't be trusted. I peeked in to see what he looked like, and I didn't recognize him at all, but he saw me. I started walking away from the door really fast, and he followed me out of the room and he shouted, 'Hey, wait!" Then I started running, and so did he. I ran into an elevator just in time, but it was the bottom floor, and I could only go up. So I went up to the fifth floor and came back down a set of stairs in a different wing. When I came out of the stairwell, I saw him standing in the lobby. He saw me just as I was going out the door. I ran as fast as I could across the parking lot to the street. I looked back and I couldn't see him following me, so I kept running as fast as I could, and then I went into a Denny's restaurant. I didn't see him after that."

"Would you recognize him again if you saw him?" Anders asked.

"Yes, I think so. He was kind of tall, had dark hair and a goatee. He was probably in his late thirties or early forties."

Anders asked, "Did you hear if your mom told him where we're staying? —where he could find Jody?"

"No. I don't think so, because he had asked her if she knew where he was, and that's when I looked in and he saw me. He might have gone back to the room and got that information from her. I only heard a little part of the conversation, but he was obviously trying to find Jody."

"Have you contacted your mom at the hospital since then?"

"No. I thought he might have gone back there. I was just paranoid. I waited at the restaurant for a while, then I walked back here to the motel."

Roy thought for a moment. "He could be a legitimate investigator, looking into your father's shooting. But he said he was working for Slater?"

"Yes, but he wasn't asking questions about the shooting, at least when I got there. He was trying to find Jody. Do you think I should have talked to him to find out who he was?"

"No. It's okay, Kristel, you did fine. Slater just better keep whoever he's got working with him away from my family and both of you." Roy sounded quite peeved when he mentioned the name Slater.

This stranger with the goatee could be friend or foe. Maybe he was a reporter; maybe a legitimate investigator; maybe an accomplice within the Slater-Oliff conspiracy.

We considered our safety at the Huron Village Inn. Michelle had been at the pool all day, and there had been no sign of Slater or a strange man with a goatee. The Anders' kids still thought this was their vacation. We decided it was safe to spend the night.

We ordered pizza to be delivered to the rooms. Meanwhile, Kristel was finally able to reach her mother by phone at her hotel. When she told her mother what happened, Mrs. Schuple said the man with the goatee never came back to the room after he suddenly bolted out the door. He had said his name was Michael somebody—she couldn't remember exactly—and he was there on behalf of the Abbeyville police department to get some information for Sheriff Slater. He was only there for a few minutes, and Mrs. Schuple was surprised to learn from Kristel that it was her whom he had chased out into the hallway. It took Kristel over thirty minutes to explain the scenario to her mother, and Kristel managed to assure her that she was safe with the Anders family. She advised her mom to reach her only by Roy's cell phone

Surprisingly, Mrs. Schuple was okay with Kristel staying with the Anders, and she didn't even seem to care that she was sleeping in a motel room next door to mine. It's a shame it took a bullet through her husband's gut to make her stop hating me so much.

The pepperoni pizza arrived, and after we dug in, Roy spent the next hour on the phone with his friend Walter Holliday from the Albany Police Department. Roy brought him up to speed on the day's events, including Kristel's adventure at the hospital and the discovery and taped testimony of Miss Emory.

It was all enticing information for Walter Holliday, but he had as much news for us about the case as we had for him.

The big news Holliday delivered was that Sheriff Clive Slater had skipped town. Slater hadn't reported to work in Abbeyville that day, and nobody at the station or his home knew of his whereabouts. Coincidentally, Branson Oliff was also not able to be contacted. According to his secretary, Branson would be out of town until July 27$^{th}$, the day the Marilee property goes up for auction.

In addition to all this, Holliday informed Roy that Brock Oliff had gone AWOL from the rehabilitation center in New Jersey. He had disappeared late last night, leaving a note to his counselor that he was leaving the country.

All this was absolutely unbelievable news. The cover-up was unraveling for Slater and the Oliffs, while an acquittal was coming together for my grandfather.

"So what's going to happen now?" was the general question that Michelle, Kristel, and I had for Roy after he gave us the low down on the new information.

Roy smiled and said, "The Albany department has already issued a warrant to arrest Brock Oliff for the murder of Jimmy Grandstaff. It's all tied to the camera—that piece of evidence was the precise item of proof John Doe wanted the police to find."

I asked, "What about Slater? Will they arrest him, too?"

"Right now, there's no warrant on him, because we don't have conclusive evidence against him yet. His involvement is still based on speculation—valid as it may seem—but it's still speculation. All we've got is the fact that Slater lied to you, which is not a severe enough offense."

"But he hasn't reported to work and nobody can find him."

"True. But that doesn't warrant an arrest—not yet, anyway. It'll come. Just give Walter another day or two."

"What about Branson Oliff?" Kristel asked.

"There's not enough on him yet either. He may or may not be involved. Brock and Slater could have conspired by themselves—I'm sure Brock is capable of coming up with some cash for a payout—but only time will tell who is all a part of this."

"Branson's *got* to be involved," Kristel averred. "I think it's all tied to the Marilee Manor property, not protecting his son."

Anders agreed. "I'm with you Kristel. Brock may have pushed Jimmy over that cliff, but it wasn't because he and Jimmy were enemies. I think he and his father knew that Jimmy was going to inherit that land. Somehow, I believe, the Oliff's learned about Robert Rothschild's true identity, and when it came time to eliminate Rothschild, they got the wrong man—your father."

I asked, "But how could the Oliff's have figured out who Rothschild really is?"

"Well, Oliff and Rothschild are both very rich men. I know that Oliff has his fingers into just about everyone's business, whether they know it or not. He must have found out somehow. But this, of course, is all still speculation. We've got the camera evidence on Brock, some on Slater, but nothing solid on Branson… not yet, anyhow. So right now, all we can do is chase down Brock and hope that Slater makes another stupid move."

"Do you think Brock could be with his dad?"

"Well, Brock's definitely on the run, and I bet it was Slater who told him he better get on the move after I confronted him yesterday. He may be tough to track down, especially if he did leave the country. His father has enough money to send him anywhere in the world, where he can hide as long as he wants. We might not see Brock for a long time, and I wouldn't be surprised if Slater is planning to leave the country, too. But Branson Oliff sounds like he will stick around. He's gonna do everything to come out of this without a smudge on his reputation."

"So Brock's on the run!" I exclaimed, with a hint of joy in my voice.

Roy concurred, "Is that a sure sign of guilt, or what? You did it, Jody. You unburied this thing. You've practically solved your brother's murder!"

"I hardly did a thing. It all unfolded in my lap—thanks to Abbott Marilee."

"But it was you who got the ball rolling. You went public, like your grandfather wanted."

"No—it was actually John Doe who started the whole thing, whoever he is."

"That's true, but you carried it out. You put your face in the paper and on TV."

"Only because Abbott paid me five hundred thousand dollars to do it."

"You didn't know there was money in that crate until afterwards. You should be proud of yourself."

"I'm kind of stunned right now."

Kristel handed me a styrofoam plate full of pizza and proclaimed it a celebration dinner. Afterwards, the seven of us went for a swim in the pool under the moonlight.

The Anders were a pretty cool family. Roy and Michelle loved their kids, and each other, but what I remember most about them, especially that first night at the motel, is how they treated me like a member of the family. We stayed up late that night, after the kids were in bed, playing a game of Scrabble, and then we just talked, talked, and talked some more. For Kristel and me, it was like one of those tree house nights, this time with adults present.

We yakked about all that had happened with Slater, Brock, and some of the other characters that had advanced upon our lives in unexpected ways.

Then we got on the topic of funny family stories. Roy told a hysterical story about his sister who, years ago, accidentally walked into the wrong hotel room during her honeymoon and almost jumped in the shower with a complete stranger. "Tee, hee, hee!" Roy squealed, holding his gut and nearly falling off the chair. Michelle followed that up with a story about Roy, on a trip to Atlanta, locking himself out of a motel room and getting arrested for trying to break in through the patio door. "If he only hadn't been too proud to go to the front desk," she laughed, "he wouldn't have had to call me from the Fulton County jail!"

Kristel recited a plethora of tales that her father had told to her, most of them about guest mishaps at the Club. A story involving her mother evoked the loudest round of laughter, as Kristel described how a drunken man had somehow passed out in the front yard of the Schuple house. Mrs. Schuple, when she arrived home after dark, thought it was her husband who had had a heart attack. After calling 911, she was discovered by paramedics trying to perform mouth-to-mouth resuscitation on him, in the dark, in the middle of her yard. After they boarded the ambulance and departed for the hospital, she asked the paramedic why her dying husband smelled like alcohol, and it was only then that she learned that it wasn't her husband she had tried to resuscitate. At this revelation, Mrs. Schuple proceeded to vomit in the back of the ambulance. Then she demanded that it stop and let her out in the middle of town, and as she was walking back to the Club in absolute embarrassment, her husband, who had been out on an errand, and who had seen his wife exit the ambulance, pulled up alongside her. Mr. Schuple said it took him twenty minutes to convince her to get into the car, and another twenty minutes to convince her to get out of the car once they got back to the Club, where a crowd had gathered at the house to hold a prayer vigil for the dying George Schuple.

Roy followed those hysterics with a collection of the strangest and most hilarious police stories you could imagine. The night was just like that: knee-slapping, bellyaching laughter. We even got around to finishing off the cold leftover pizza, scrounging for quarters to get some cans of soda from the machine in the hallway.

It was after midnight by the time the two adults yawned enough to convince Kristel and me to call it a night, so finally Kristel and Michelle departed for the "girls" bedroom, while Roy and I got ready for bed in ours.

After the lights went off, I tucked my hands behind my head and considered the impressions that several adults had recently made on my life: Roy and Michelle—two fantastic parents that I would trust with my own life; my grandfather and Mr. Schuple—two men who had fooled the world, whom I would also trust with my life nonetheless; my mother and father—two adults I wouldn't trust for the world; and then there was Mr. Gray, my history teacher. He was right, in a way, about people. Some you could trust, and some you couldn't. But he was wrong about what he said we *could* trust in with absolute certainty. It wasn't myself: I had definitely proven that. I was too young, stupid, and selfish to trust myself. I had learned I could trust people like Kristel and the Anders before I would trust myself.

There was another thing Mr. Gray was wrong about—the existence of truth. What Kristel had told me weeks ago was absolutely correct—the truth is there, no matter how many people believe in it or not, and no matter how strongly you feel one way or the other. Just look: the world had been misled about the truth of Abbott's guilt, and he had misled the world about the truth of his death. And the whole time, the world was wrong. Truth existed, and now Roy, Kristel, and I knew for sure what it was.

Then there was the truth about Jimmy. For weeks the Ambassador, my grandfather, had prompted me to do something about that truth, and I had ignored the calling. It took his dragging me to the vault and paying me off with a fortune to do something about the truth of my own brother's death. And even when I did act, it was just to see what might be in that crate. It wasn't because I cared about the truth or about Jimmy. But now, here it was, all coming to the surface, and it *mattered* now, my brother's death. Just think what I would have missed if I had stuck to my own selfish motives when I didn't want Jimmy or an Ambassador in my life. But I finally, just a little bit, let them in, and now look: I'm the heir to the Marilee fortune, and we're about to uncover a police conspiracy. It was an unbelievable feeling as I lay there on that starchy, cool, motel pillow.

What's more unbelievable was the fact that there was additional truth about to come out beyond what we had already discovered. Slater, Brock and Branson, and whomever else they had working for them, were still on the move, and the truth about their involvement in this case would come tumbling down upon us over the next forty-eight hours like a tidal wave.

# CHAPTER 37

## *Knowledge, Faith, and Action*

Walter Holliday showed up early Thursday morning at the Huron Village Inn to pick up Roy. They had plans to search Sheriff Slater's office up in Abbeyville and would probably be gone most of the day. That left Kristel and me with Michelle and the kids, and everyone thought it best to stay at the motel for the time being. With Slater missing, and Brock missing, and this new guy with the goatee looking for me and chasing Kristel through the hospital, we were happy to remain in seclusion. Besides, it was a dank, rainy day, and we could all use some down time.

With Slater and Brock now on the run, it was indefinite how long we would have to remain in this modest hideout in Lake Henry. I wanted to get back to the Club, not necessarily to work, but so that my grandfather could find us—or we could find him. Somehow we had to let him know that we found Miss Emory, and July 27th was only eleven days away. I wondered where he had gone, when he would come back, and sometimes I thought that I might not ever see him again.

Kristel kindly gave Michelle a chance to take a morning nap by entertaining the kids, and while I tried to get back into *Gatsby*, I listened to her read a story to them about Daniel from the Bible.

"Shadrach, Meshack, and Abendego!" she had the boys repeating. It was a story about a fiery furnace, and I didn't quite follow the plot, hearing about Daniel in the furnace while reading in my book about a near fight between Gatsby and Tom Buchanan on a sweltering afternoon at the Plaza Hotel.

Around eleven, Michelle was awake and she slipped out by herself to pick up some lunch. She returned in twenty minutes with three Happy Meals, and three grilled chicken combos. I hadn't had McDonald's since Ohio, and I even got to finish the youngest boys' McNuggets he couldn't eat.

As we were eating lunch, out of nowhere Michelle asked me a question that Kristel had asked me four weeks ago. "So Jody," she said, with a curious tone, "are you a Christian?"

I knew that she and Kristel went to the same church, and I wondered if their evangelism committee had trained them each how to proselytize out of a how-to book. It was the same question from the tree house, verbatim, and equally inopportune. My mouth was full of McNugget and sweet & sour sauce, and before I could answer, Kristel answered for me.

"He's an agnostic," she said, winking at me, I guess to make me feel better.

Michelle exclaimed, "An agnostic! Jody, here?"

I swallowed and piped up, "I'm a Christian! I'm just a cautious one."

That left both women speechless, so I had to append, "I mean—nobody knows for sure, and if there is a God, then I believe in him. I'm not like an atheist or a Satanist or anything."

Michelle offered a gentle, mocking laugh. "Jody, can you know *anything* for sure?"

"I know for sure that I exist."

"And what *caused* your existence?" Michelle came back confidently.

I knew where this was headed, so I changed directions. "Listen," I said, "Kristel and I have talked about this before." I glanced at Kristel, and she was smiling, kind of egging me on. I then posed the question, "What I'd like to know from you two, since you both seem to believe the same things, is how you know *for sure* that you're right."

"Right about what?" they both said simultaneously.

"Right about Christianity. There are a thousand and one religions out there, so how do you know *yours* is right?"

"It's what the Bible says," Michelle averred.

"Yes, but that's the Bible. What about the Koran or other writings? What would be wrong with being a Buddhist or a Muslim or something? Don't they all worship the same God? Why do you only ask if I'm a *Christian*?"

"Jody," Michelle said calmly. "Do you know what will happen to you when you die?"

"Not for certain. Nobody does until they die."

"Yes, but don't different religions have different beliefs about death?"

"Most of them believe in some kind of heaven."

"Some do, that's right. But think about all the different beliefs about the afterlife. Some people believe there is no afterlife—you just die, and that's it. Some believe you die and go to heaven; some believe you go to a purgatory first." Michelle was creating a list with her hand gestures. "Some people believe you either go to heaven or hell; some believe in reincarnation—that you come back as something else. Some religions teach that when you die you become one with the universe; some say you become the god of your own universe. And some people believe when they die they will meet Elvis up in a spaceship in the sky."

Kristel giggled, and I smiled.

Michelle continued, "It's like you said, there's a thousand and one beliefs out there about what happens when people die, and we all are going to die, aren't we?"

I answered the rhetorical question, "Yes."

"So is what happens when you die, is that based on the religion you follow? Or is there one truth about death that applies to all of us?"

I saw where she was headed, and I let her continue.

Michelle proposed, "Will the Catholics go to purgatory because they're Catholics? Will the Hindus be reincarnated because of their religion? Will the atheists simply cease to exist? Will the Elvis lovers meet the King in the sky?"

"No."

"And what if you, during your life, convert into a different religion?" Michelle continued. "Will what was supposed to happen to you when you die suddenly change into something else when you convert? How hard do you have to believe in it for that to happen to you, and for how long do you have to believe it? And who or what is in charge of it?" She eyeballed me smartly and asked, "Is the truth of what happens after death associated at all with a person's religion?"

"No."

Michelle smiled. "That's right. There's only one truth, and we don't determine it, no matter how *many* people believe or don't believe, and no matter how *hard* we believe or don't believe. There's only one truth about what happens after death, and I have absolute faith I have found that truth. I know that when I die, my sins have been forgiven and Jesus will invite me home to heaven."

She sounded so confident, but I couldn't give up the argument that easy. I questioned her, "But how do you know *for sure* that it isn't one of those other things you listed? Maybe you will be reincarnated or something."

Kristel jumped in. "I can argue this one, Michelle." She looked at me with that familiar, confident, expression. "Jody, all religions except one fall apart when faced with this one issue."

"With death?" I asked.

"No. With the issue of the person of Jesus Christ. That's why we call ourselves Christians, because of Christ."

"Other religions believe in Jesus," I claimed, stepping into unfamiliar territory.

"I know, but only one claims him as the only way to eternal life. Only one religion claims that Jesus is the one true God, and that's Christianity."

I argued, "But you don't have to believe in Jesus to believe in God. I mean, many other religions believe that Jesus was a great prophet or a great teacher, and they also believe in God."

Kristel tilted her head and asked, "Would a great prophet or great teacher lie?"

"What do you mean?"

"I mean, how can these other religions call Jesus a great teacher or a great prophet, if he was a liar?"

She had me confused now, and all I could do was repeat, "What do you mean?"

"Jody, imagine if I were to tell you right now that I am God, and only by accepting me as your Savior will you get into heaven."

"I'd say your crazy."

"That's right. If someone makes that claim, he's either crazy, he's lying, or …" she paused and looked me dead in the eye, "Or he's telling the truth." She paused again to let it sink in. "Jesus claimed to be God's son; he claimed that he was the way, the truth, and the life; he said that he was the only way to eternal life. When he made that claim, that made him either a lunatic, a liar, or the Lord of Lords. C.S. Lewis said to call Jesus a great prophet or a great teacher is just a bunch of patronizing nonsense. Jesus either was God, or he was lying, or he was just plain crazy."

That was a neat argument, but I could cast a big shadow of doubt on it. I said boldly, "Maybe he didn't actually claim to be God,"

Kristel was ready for that. "If he didn't claim to be God, then why did they crucify him?" she asked rhetorically. "It was very clear to the people what he claimed, because they killed him for it."

Michelle added, "And three days later he rose from the grave to prove that he is the Savior of the world!"

"That's right, Jody," Kristel continued. "You have to make a decision about Jesus. He was either a crazy lunatic, a liar looking for attention, or he is the Lord of the universe."

I thought I was pretty clever when I said, "Well, then that leaves only three possible religions: Christianity, the Jewish religion, or agnosticism. And I take agnosticism—because I'm not sure yet, and I can go either way when I figure it out."

"Okay," Kristel conceded. "That's reasonable. At least you're not a religious relativist. But what *will* it take for you to believe that Jesus is the Son of God?"

"I guess he'd have to prove it to me."

"By doing what?"

"Show up here. Maybe perform a miracle."

"He did that already."

"Yeah, but I wasn't there."

The conversation came to a sudden but merciful end when the phone rang. It was Roy, and he wanted to talk to me.

"We're still here at the Abbeyville station going through Slater's stuff," he said to me from his cell phone. "I wanted to get you up to speed."

"What'd you find?" I asked. Michelle tended to the kids while Kristel sat near me and listened to the phone conversation.

Roy spoke, "We've found quite a bit, actually. Quite a bit. The first thing we found were some extra negatives."

"From Brock's camera?"

"We think so. From what we can tell by holding them up to the light is that they look like pictures taken right there at Smooth Rock Falls."

"Are you serious?"

"It looks like it might be Smooth Rock. We'll know for sure shortly. Walter ran them down to the drug store in town to get them developed. But I'm positive they're from Smooth Rock. You could see cliffs and trees and waterfalls. Regardless, Slater was obviously hiding those negatives. I don't know why he just didn't destroy them."

"I can't wait to see the pictures! Does this build a case to arrest Slater?"

"It could help. We'll know for sure in a little while. But listen—we've got several cases going on here all at once, and they all have something in common. First, there's Jimmy's death that seems to involve Slater covering for Brock and maybe his father—and now we've got Slater and Brock on the run. Then there's the forty year-old Marilee murder case, and we've got Gretta Ardello's video-taped testimony to bring that all out in the open. Then there's the George Schuple shootings, and Slater had been handling that up until yesterday. Plus, you've got $500,000 thousand dollars sitting in my safe in my house. I just checked on it; it's all safe and sound."

"So what are you saying?"

"All of these things are tied together, and your grandfather is the common thread. We've got to find him. The Brown Swan Club has no phone records from Rothschild's room. You're sure Mr. or Mrs. Schuple doesn't have any idea where he disappeared to?"

"I wish they did. He's got to be back before the 27th, though."

"I wouldn't be so sure of that. We're fairly certain that the bullet George Schuple took was meant for Abbott Marilee. There might be more people involved in this than Slater and the Oliff family, and Abbott is keeping a safe distance."

"He might be around here in disguise."

"That's true. But we really need him now. No telling what could happen between now and the 27th, especially if someone like Branson Oliff is funding the whole conspiracy. There's that guy with the goatee who chased Kristel to think about, too. He was looking for *you*."

"I know. Do you think we're safe here?" I asked.

"Walt and I have been talking about that a lot. They've already killed Jimmy. They tried to kill Marilee, and if the land acquisition *is* the motive, then the logical assumption would be that you or your mother is next. But, Brock is on the run. Slater has gone berserk, not to mention he's missing, and Branson is nowhere to be found either. Perhaps they're backing off, now that they know we and the Albany department are onto something. But that guy with the goatee has Walter worried. So when I get back down there later this afternoon, we should pack up and head down to Albany. Walter says he has plenty of room for all of us."

I asked, "If Abbott knew *he* was in danger, why would he have asked me to go public if it would make me a target?"

"I doubt he thought *you* would be a target. Maybe he figured that the killers were too smart to kill you just after you began a search for you brother's murderer. That would cause quite a stir. It wouldn't look like an accident or a mere coincidence that two brothers died. It would cause too much suspicion.

"But here's the thing, Jody, and this is why I called, and this is why I think we should get down to Albany tonight. You've already gone public about being Jimmy's brother, and Walter and I think you ought to go public about being Abbot Marilee's grandson."

The implications of that were unnerving. "What? Now? Shouldn't I check with Abbott first before..."

"Maybe this will help bring him out of hiding. We've got eleven days before that land is passed onto the state. Jody, you can't inherit the land after that date because it would belong to the state, or whoever buys it first. We need your grandfather."

"But I can't inherit it before then unless I can prove that I'm Abbott Marilee's grandson. What do we have to prove that?"

"Well, there are lots of things. First, we might be able to delay the July 27th date if you step forward and make this claim. Even though your mother wants nothing to do with her true heritage, she might be willing to come forward if it means your inheriting the estate. And two, you've got your own testimony about what Abbott Marilee, under the alias of Robert Rothschild, revealed to you. You can disclose the passageway to the vaults, and you've got all that cash for proof. And three, we've got Gretta's testimony to support your claim. And four, hopefully Abbott will come out of hiding soon and clear everything up for all of us. Not to mention, he might have some more insight into your brother's death. I'm sure there's a connection with Jimmy and that land."

"So you're saying I should go public now as Abbott Marilee's grandson?" I asked, just to be sure.

"I suppose we ought to call the commissioner of real estate who will be conducting the auction for Marilee Manor on the 27th. It's possible they'll delay the sale of the property once all this comes out."

"Wouldn't this reveal the connection between me, Jimmy, and the Marilee estate? I mean, won't the public start to see what we see now—a link to Branson Oliff and Jimmy's murder, and George Schuple's shooting?"

"That's very true. But that's fine with me if the public starts to make that connection. *We've* already made it, and I bet Branson Oliff knows by now that this is all coming unraveled, because with the way Slater was shaking in his boots when I confronted him, and now his disappearance, I'm sure he and Branson have talked already. I'm sure they've come up with a plan on what to do now. In fact, I'm sure Slater *knows* we've linked him to Branson Oliff. And I wouldn't be surprised to see Oliff back out of the purchase between now and the 27th, just to show he isn't all that interested in the property. He'd be a fool to bid for it now, if he knows we suspect him of foul play."

"Do you think he'll get away with this?"

"Who, Branson? It depends on how clever he is. And again, Jody, maybe we're wrong about Branson's involvement. It might just be his son Brock.

The key to linking Branson Oliff to this whole thing—anybody to this whole thing, for that matter—all comes down to John Doe. John Doe got this case rolling in the first place. John Doe might have information on the larger conspiracy, including Branson Oliff's involvement. Unfortunately, what John Doe didn't know, obviously, was Slater's involvement in the cover-up, which actually may not have occurred until Slater found the camera. John Doe started all this, but we haven't heard from him since early June. He or she is still a complete mystery, and perhaps without his testimony, Branson Oliff may indeed get out of this clean as a whistle."

"Aren't there any grounds to at least *investigate* Branson Oliff's activities?"

"Yes, but when we do that, we'll be pointing fingers at a very prominent—and powerful—local businessman. If John Doe is aware of Branson's involvement, I can see why he wants to remain anonymous. But right now, we need to focus on you coming forward, not only as Jimmy Grandstaff's brother, but also as Abbott Marilee's grandson. How do you think your parents will feel about that, Jody?"

I answered, "My mom still thinks her father is a rapist and a murderer. Maybe once she hears Gretta's testimony, she'll changer her mind."

"Alright, Jody. That sounds good. I'll see you later this afternoon. We'll have the pictures back by then."

"Okay, g'bye."

After I hung up with Roy, I thought more about my mother's reaction to all this. I would be going public as the grandson of Abbott Marilee. In a matter of days, I could be a millionaire! The more I thought about it, the more it began to creep into my head that my coming here this summer was no coincidence. I started to suspect that my mother actually wanted me to meet my grandfather. Maybe she knew her father was going to pass the land onto Jimmy. And maybe when she learned of Jimmy's death, she arranged for me to come up and take his place as the heir to the Marilee estate.

Kristel, Michelle and I never resumed the Jesus conversation. Instead, as the rain outside pattered into the pool, I took a long afternoon nap, dozing off after heavy consideration of what it would be like to claim my place in the Marilee family. It was like being adopted by a king, inheriting riches beyond my wildest imaginations.

Abbott Marilee wasn't a liar, and he wasn't insane. He was the wealthiest and smartest man in the state of New York. He was my grandfather, and soon I would let the world know.

# CHAPTER 38

## *Pictures, Pizza, and a Vanishing*

Roy finally showed up at the motel around six o'clock holding a large, brown envelope. "You guys all packed?" he asked. "We're leaving for Walter's as soon as you're ready. But first, look at these."

He sat at the little dinette table as Kristel and I gathered around. Michelle stayed in the next room to pack up their suitcases. "These are copies of the photographs we got from the negatives in Slater's office. They came straight from that camera John Doe wanted us to find. They're rather incriminating, to say the least."

He spread an array of eight-by-ten photographs on the table.

"These were taken from the east side of the falls, opposite the road," Roy explained. "See… that's the cliff Jimmy fell from. Somebody must've climbed up the other side of the gorge to take these pictures."

"Brock took these photos?" Kristel asked.

"No, I don't think it was Brock. I think it could have been John Doe who took them with the camera, maybe a friend of Brock's. Look closer—they tell the whole story. See… there's two people standing back there in the woods away from the edge of the cliff."

I looked closely at the photographs. "It looks like two men. Do you think one of them is Brock?"

"Maybe, but look at this one," Roy said, moving a second photograph in front of us. This picture displayed the exact same view of the cliff. The only difference was that one of the figures was standing in full view near the cliff. He was a tall, lanky man in a white dress shirt and tie.

"That's Branson Oliff!" Kristel shrieked. "It's him!"

"I know," Roy said. "This is bad news for Mr. Oliff, for sure. But I wonder who the other person is. Look at this one." He centered a third photo, this one showing another male figure near the edge of the cliff with his head turned to the side. "It's hard to tell who this person is, but he's too skinny to be Slater."

"It's probably Brock," I said.

"I don't know," Roy replied. "Look at his hair—it's too dark. It's hard to tell for sure. Walter's got the negatives and he's going to get them blown up and digitally enhanced at the lab in Albany."

Kristel interrupted, "He's right. This guy's hair does look darker than Brock's. Do you think it could be that man with the goatee who chased me at the hospital?"

"That's another possibility," Roy answered. "Hopefully, we'll be able to tell for sure whether it's Brock or not when the photos are magnified."

I interjected, "So it could be that Brock didn't kill Jimmy. It might be this other goatee guy who could have been hired by Branson?"

"Possibly."

"I wonder when John Doe took these pictures and how he got a hold of Brock's camera," I questioned.

"Well," Roy said, "Walter and I don't think these pictures were taken the morning of the accident. We think they were taken the night *before* the accident. Look at the long shadows the trees are making over the cliff. That puts the sun setting behind them. If it was morning, the sun would cast shadows the other way. These pictures were taken sometime in the evening as the sun was going down. And as for Jimmy being pushed—we don't think that's what happened either. Look… do you see something in that guy's hand?"

Kristel and I peered closely at the small, unidentifiable figure. He was holding what looked like a large metal ring in his hand, about a foot in diameter.

"What is it?" Kristel asked.

"We think it's a coil of wire," Roy said. "Look at this last picture."

He flipped a fourth picture onto the table. It was the same view, now displaying Branson Oliff crouching down at the top of the cliff with his left hand holding onto a tree trunk. The dark-haired figure had disappeared from the cliff.

Roy said, "Look—the guy with the wire—he's down here now." He pointed to a white waterfall in the lower left corner of the photo, about thirty yards to the left of the cliff and about ten yards below it, roughly halfway down the gorge. "You can see him behind the waterfall there. See his arm?"

"Yes," Kristel said, pointing at the waterfall. "There's a small cave behind that waterfall. You can crawl back there without getting wet and hide behind a wall of rushing water."

Roy asked Kristel, "If you're standing in there looking out from behind the water, can you see the top of the cliff?"

"I'm not sure. I'd have to go there and see."

"Well, look at Branson," Roy continued. "He's looking right down at that waterfall where the other guy is. So here's what Walter and I think. We think they fastened that wire to that tree there next to Branson and stretched it across the cliff, over top and around those rocks and into the waterfall. We think this guy is holding the other end of the wire behind the waterfall."

"They set up a trip wire?" I asked incredulously.

"That's what we're supposing," Roy said. "Maybe somebody—probably Brock, because he was at the scene first—hid behind the falls and watched Jimmy at the top of the cliff. The wire was there, hidden under dirt or pine needles, and at just the right moment, he yanked it so it stretched tight above the ground about a foot or so."

Kristel said gravely, "That's why Jimmy came over the edge head first. He tripped on the wire."

"He never saw it," Roy said. "And Jimmy never saw his killer."

Kristel added, "That means they all knew that Jimmy and I were going to be at the falls that morning."

"Was it possible any of them knew you were going there that day, far enough in advance for them to have time to set up this trip wire?" Roy asked.

She thought for a second. "I guess so. Brock could have known about our plans easy enough. I told some of my girlfriends that Jimmy and I were planning to go there on his day off. Who knows who Jimmy might have told."

"Then, like Jody said, the question is who took these pictures and how did he or she take them with Brock's camera?"

We were all silent for a moment.

"Wait a minute," I said. "Didn't Kelly Walker say that there was another guy with Brock when he took that picture of them at Lake Henry?"

"Yes," Kristel said. "But she is sure it was Brock's own camera because he had it around his neck. She was sure it was his camera."

I theorized, "But what if that other guy who was with him knew about the plans to kill Jimmy. Maybe he found out about it, and maybe he felt guilty for letting it happen. So he steals Brock's camera and takes these photos of them setting up the trip wire. Maybe one of Brock's friends is John Doe."

"That's a possible scenario," Roy said. "But that also means John Doe knew about the trip wire and allowed the death to happen. I would hope he'd have enough sense to try to warn Jimmy instead of taking these photos the day before and leaving the camera for us to find nine months later."

Kristel said, "I'll call Kelly again and see if she can describe the guy who was with Brock that day. Maybe it was one of the other band members or something."

"Well, whoever took these pictures," Roy said, "and whoever John Doe is, these pictures will nail Slater against the wall for hiding them from us."

"And both the Oliff's too?" I asked.

"Well, Branson is in these photos. It's still speculation as to what he's doing on the cliff. But with enough pressure on Slater, he might break down and implicate both of the Oliff's."

I questioned, "I wonder if this is the murder theory that Abbott thought of."

"Abbott would have had to have known something that we didn't," Roy commented. "Without Slater losing his cool over all this, I never would have built up the guts to confront him in his office, and we'd still be clueless. These pictures tell the whole story, and they're what John Doe wanted us to find. If Abbott *does* know more—I wish he'd come right out and tell us."

"Maybe they already got to him," I said glumly.

"I hope that's not true. Branson could have hired the Mafia if he wanted. But from what we've learned about Abbott, he's probably a step ahead of them. I'm sure he's going to show up any day, especially if he sees you on TV soon, claiming to be his grandson."

At that moment, an unexpected knock at the door stopped everything. Roy looked through the peephole and then turned and asked us if we ordered pizza.

"No," Kristel and I answered.

"That's strange. It's the same delivery kid who was here last night." Roy stepped into the adjoining room. His wife had fallen asleep on the bed with the infant. The kids were watching a video. "Maybe Michelle ordered it," he said.

The delivery boy knocked again before Roy returned to the door and opened it.

"Anders? One small pepperoni?" the freckly face boy asked kindly.

"Uh, I guess my wife ordered it," Roy said, reaching for his wallet. "How much?"

"Paid for already," the delivery boy chirped. "With a credit card. Tip not included."

Roy handed him a dollar and took the pizza.

"Did Michelle say anything about dinner?" Roy asked us. "One small pizza obviously isn't enough."

Kristel and I were both confused. Michelle had mentioned earlier that we should stop at a drive-thru on our way to Albany when Roy got back.

Things quickly grew more mystifying when Roy opened the pizza box and found a grease-stained white envelope stuck to the cheese. He immediately rushed to the door, but the delivery boy was down the hallway and out of sight. Without saying a word, he returned to the table and opened the envelope. His jaw dropped open as he read its contents. Then, without hesitation, he winked at us and suggested, "This isn't enough pizza; let's eat out tonight."

Not more than two minutes passed before Roy awakened his wife and had all three kids and the rest of us, suitcases and all, out the door and into the van. We didn't even leave our keys at the front desk. After letting Michelle read the grease-stained note, he handed it to Kristel and me in the back seat of the van.

It read,

*Your room and phone are bugged. Retrieve an envelope from the men's room at the McDonalds on Highway 7. Follow the instructions.*

John Doe.

In a stern voice, Roy ordered, "Jody, you and Kristel take your car. Let's each drive around a little bit, separately, to see if anyone is following us. Then let's meet at the parking lot at McDonalds in about fifteen minutes and get the next envelope. Then we'll head to Albany."

John Doe. Bugged phones. Secret notes. It was uncanny.

Kristel and I obeyed Roy. We turned north out of the Huron Village Inn and Roy and his family turned south. The McDonalds was not far—just a mile further in our direction, but I took the first right and drove up and down several side streets.

"Do you see anyone following us?" I asked.

"No." Kristel said nervously.

We drove around several more blocks before heading towards the McDonalds on Highway 7.

The parking lot was crowded, but no sign of the Anders' van yet. We looped around the lot three or four times before parking in a vacant spot to wait.

We waited and waited. Nearly thirty minutes passed since we had left the motel.

"Maybe they were followed," Kristel said.

"Maybe."

We waited ten more minutes.

Kristel spoke the obvious, "Something happened. They'd be here by now."

"I know. Roy's careful. He'll know what to do."

"I just wish whoever it is would leave his family out of this. Enough people have gotten hurt already. How long do you think we should wait here?"

"Where are we supposed to go? To Albany without them?"

"Let's get the letter from the bathroom and then drive around the area some more. Maybe we'll see them."

We walked into the restaurant hand-in-hand, and Kristel insisted on coming into the men's bathroom with me. She didn't want to be left alone.

So in we both walked. One man was at a urinal, another in the stall. Kristel received an expected quizzical stare from the man standing up.

"Where is it?" she whispered, clutching my hand.

We scanned the restroom ceiling to floor. I was wondering if it might be in the occupied stall until Kristel stooped down below the sink and found a white envelope taped underneath. She grabbed it and we hastily departed the restroom.

We opened the envelope at my car. A letter in the same handwriting as the first one in the pizza box read,

*Saranac.*

John Doe.

"This is too weird," Kristel moaned. "We're supposed to go all the way to your cabin now?"

"What if it's not John Doe," I cautioned. "What if it's one of them—one of Branson's guys?"

"Let's try to find Roy and Michelle first."

I agreed. If it was John Doe, he could wait. He's used to waiting.

We went back into the McDonalds and used the pay phone to call Roy on his cell phone. There was no answer.

"Are you sure he had it with him?" Kristel asked.

"I'm sure. He had it on the dashboard of his van."

We drove around Lake Henry for the next hour. No sign of the Anders' van. We saw a similar model in the same color—but a different family inside. Four times we drove along the main strip in Lake Henry—a main street lined with shops, arcades, restaurants, miniature golf courses, a water park, dinner theaters, and a wax museum. We passed by the McDonalds repeatedly, and we even looped back around to the Huron Village Inn. We tried his cell phone number a dozen more times. No answer. The Anders were nowhere to be found.

It was almost eight o'clock, the daylong rain had ended, and the streets were getting busier with the evening tourists. Kristel and I realized we had two choices: try to locate Walter Holliday's house down in Albany, or drive up to Abbeyville where there may be another note waiting for us at my cabin.

"Where could they be?" Kristel asked a millionth time.

"Something's definitely wrong," I said. "Roy would have gotten back to the McDonalds somehow. He wouldn't strand us. And he always answers his cell phone."

We called the Albany police department and left a message for Walter Holliday. They refused to give us his home number or address. The person in charge there didn't seem to know anything about Roy Anders or the case in Abbeyville.

Abandoned in Lake Henry, we thought the Club might be the safest place yet. We left the McDonalds and passed by the Huron Village Inn without stopping, and fifty minutes later we were driving up the steep entranceway of the Club. We decided to park in the guest lot so that my car might not be as easily noticeable.

Boonie was sitting on the steps of Saranac when we arrived in the cabin grove after darkness had fallen upon the woods.

"Long time, no see, my friends!" Boonie said. "Are you ever coming back to work, Jody?"

I wanted to tell him everything, but couldn't. I simply answered, "Family emergency."

"Well, I better warn you," Boonie said. "Brock's looking for you. I told him you up and left two days ago and I haven't seen you since."

Kristel and I glanced at each other.

"Brock was here?!"

"Yup. I was surprised to see him myself. He said he just got out of the rehab center yesterday. You should've seen him. He wasn't his usual self. I don't know what they did to him there, but Brock hardly looked rehabilitated.

He looked like he had been to Hell and back. Acted like it, too."

"Did he say anything? Was anyone with him?"

"No. He was alone. His eyes were all bloodshot and it looked like he had slept in the woods all night. He was sittin' right here on the steps when I got back from dinner; said he was looking for you."

"Did he say anything else?"

"He asked if I had seen you or that police officer you've been working with—Officer Anders. He was acting kind of nervous, not cocky like he usually is. He was like really desperate to find you. When I told him you hadn't slept here the past two nights, he just kind of hung around for a while—real nervous like—pacing back and forth across the grove. Then he just took off back through the woods towards town. He was running, in fact."

"Did he say if he'd come back?"

"I don't know. He just bolted into the woods about an hour or so ago,"

"Has anyone else been here?"

"Like who?"

"Like Brock's father, or the Sheriff?"

"No."

"Well, if you see him again, call the police department in Albany."

"Why?"

"He wasn't released from the rehab. He went AWOL—because he's about to get arrested for murder."

"Yer pullin' my leg. He *did* kill Jimmy?"

"He was part of it." I wondered if I should be telling Boonie any of this. "Don't tell anyone else, though, because we don't know for sure. But Brock did run away from the rehab center. They didn't release him. And there is a warrant out for his arrest."

Boonie advised, "He was really desperate to find you."

"That's weird. It doesn't make sense."

"When are you coming back to work?"

"I don't know." I glanced over at Hawkeye cabin. "Have you seen ol' Whisper around, by any chance?"

"No."

"How about Robert Rothschild?"

"The Santa Claus guy? Yep—he showed up at dinner tonight. I guess he had been gone for a while because the waitresses were glad to see him back."

Kristel and I again exchanged glances.

"See ya, Boonie. Thanks!" We immediately turned and walked briskly out of the grove in the direction of Tycoon's Roost.

# CHAPTER 39

## *A Family Reunion, a Framed Comrade, and a Fiend in Bed*

Robert Rothschild, minus the beard, the round tummy, and the three-piece suit, greeted us at the door of his chalet, and for some pathetic reason, I started crying. Never in my life had I cried happy tears, and as sappy and sloppy as it was, it was a moment I'll never forget. He bear-hugged me and patted my back; I buried my face into his shoulder. Kristel started crying, too, and the whole slobbery scene lasted about a minute.

Twelve days had passed since I last saw him, when he boarded the airport van after returning with us from the vault. He was still an uncertain figure to me that night, too ambiguous, too incredible to be believed. On that night I wondered: Was he a fraud? A liar? My benefactor? I not only doubted him, but after talking with my mother, I rejected his story entirely. And after the George Schuple's shooting, I was convinced my mother was right.

But he had promised me a fortune, and so I acted—I gave two interviews to the media, and my generous grandfather rewarded me ten times as much as he had promised.

By now, in the grand scheme of things, the reward was almost forgotten. The man had finally returned, not as Rothschild or as Whisper, but as my grandfather, Abbott Marilee. And now, I believed in him, not because I wanted to believe, but because I would have been wrong not to. His claims were true. Misunderstood by the world, he was true. Rejected by his own daughter, he was true. I accepted this truth, and I believed it beyond a shadow of a doubt. Tonight, he looked at me and embraced me and adopted me as the newest member of the Marilee family. It was like I had a new life, like I was a new creature. That's why I cried, if you can swallow the lame excuse.

He welcomed us into Tycoon's Roost, and the homecoming continued. He filled us in on where he had been for nearly two weeks, admitting that he had actually stayed at the Club dressed as Whisper for the first two days after his supposed departure. He said he left town immediately after the George

Schuple shooting, knowing without a doubt that he himself was the intended target. Since then, he had stayed in New York City, laying low, and when he had tried in vain to contact both me and Kristel by phone two days ago, he knew he had to get back here.

We briefly discussed his identity as Whisper, one he had been using for the past seven years in addition to his long-time Rothschild identity. This summer, he used it as another way to get to know me during all those nights confronting me on my way back from the tree house. It was revealed, too, that Brock wasn't guilty of slashing my tires that night at the roadside. He did it himself, to prevent me from leaving. No wonder he was so eager to help me with the car!

After that, Kristel and I told him all that had happened since he left. He laughed out loud when we told him all about Kristel's mother's confession, and he nodded his head and snickered about how George Schuple loved to prowl those grounds as the ghost of Marilee. He admitted that he avoided telling us that information because he wanted to protect the Schuples. He was pleased that Mrs. Schuple had been honest with us, especially in light of her husband's condition.

When we told him about Slater and Brock and Branson Oliff, he was somewhat surprised. It wasn't a shock that Slater was involved, because Abbott had been suspecting a police cover-up ever since the John Doe story. But he never suspected the Oliffs. He thought someone else was involved, someone he knew, and he didn't discount his original theory right away.

Perhaps, he suggested, the conspiracy goes beyond the Oliffs. Perhaps the Oliffs are just a part of it. The stranger in the camera, and the man with the goatee, and tonight's inexplicable disappearance of the Anders family helped advance this theory. In all, he was unconvinced that Brock and Branson were the brains behind everything. He thought it was someone else, and we would soon find out that he was right.

Kristel and I saved the best piece of information for last. For my grandfather, it would be the news of his lifetime, and when we finally told him that we had found Miss Emory and that she had confessed everything on videotape, my grandfather went speechless. He covered his mouth with a shaking hand, his eyes welled up with tears, and he stood and shuffled slowly across the carpet. He stopped at the sliding glass door and stared out into the darkness for several minutes.

For Abbott Marilee, Miss Emory was the only connection to his past. Yes, he had his daughter, but she had rejected him entirely. Miss Emory knew, and Miss Emory testified, and at that moment the old man was set free for the first time in forty years.

At the news that she had been living in Pokeville for the last three years, my grandfather ended his brief trance and laughed softly. He looked heavenward. "Praise God," he said. "This is His work! This isn't a coincidence, Jody. Miss Emory, Jimmy, and you, all coming together here at Lake Marilee."

I offered the gentle suggestion, "Maybe my mother sent me here because she wanted me to meet you."

He smiled and answered, "If that is true, then her heart isn't so hard after all." He chuckled again and added, "I told you, Jody. God has a plan in all this. He's working through your mother, He's working through old Gretta Ardello, and he's going to use Jimmy's death to bring glory to his kingdom."

I told him right there that I would do anything to make sure that adoption home was built at Marilee Manor.

He smiled again and added, "First things first, Jody. We've got to find the Anders family, and we've got to find out who this John Doe is that showed up in that pizza box."

"I think it's one of Slater's guys," Kristel avowed.

"It could be," Abbott assented. "But there is a real John Doe out there who led the police to the pictures in that camera. He's Jimmy's advocate, and he is the spark that ignited this fire. Maybe he *is* the one who sent the pizza. Maybe he isn't. Still, we've got a missing family."

I asked, "Who else is it that you think is involved in this? You said it was someone you know."

Abbott rubbed his chin. "Mmm. Well, my original theory is that the person behind all this is an acquaintance of mine who has shown deep interest in the Marilee estate. And he could be that fellow you said was in those pictures on the cliff. He could be the same man who chased Kristel. I'm just not certain." Abbott shook his head and said, "But John Doe knows who it is for sure."

"Do you think Slater and the Oliffs know of your true identity?" Kristel asked.

"Yes, they are on to me. And that's why I suspect this other person, because I believe he knows who I am, too. But that's another matter, and Miss Emory's testimony will help clear me of that.

"What I am concerned about is how these conspirators have done such a fine job in making Jimmy's death look like an accident. Look at the effort they put into it. What worries me most is that not everyone is going to take the fall for this when it all comes out. If murder is proven, then someone's going to be in hot water, and that's what the brains behind this outfit is planning. If murder is proven, they'll either pin the whole thing on Brock, Slater, Branson, or all three. Then again, now we know that Branson could be the brains working here. So we've got to find John Doe. John Doe knows. I just hope he gets back in touch with us somehow."

Kristel despondently asserted, "I'm positive that letter tonight was a trap. I'm worried about Roy and Michelle and the kids."

Abbott nodded and said, "The criminals behind this are most likely gathered together right now, just like we are, discussing how to disprove everything we've uncovered. And if they did bug your motel room, then they're probably way ahead of us. Remember, they've got Slater working for them, and who knows who else in the police department."

Kristel said, "But where could the Anders be? It's like they just disappeared. What would they have done with them?"

Abbott looked at Kristel straight in the eye. "Could Roy be part of it?"

She and I glanced at each other. That had never crossed our minds.

"If he is," she said, "he's the best actor in the world. I would bet my life that he's on our side!"

"Me too," I confirmed.

"I'd like to meet Officer Anders," Abbott said. "Do you think he might have returned to the motel?"

I answered, "I doubt it, but they could have. We never actually checked out of our rooms. We just left in a big hurry after that pizza came. Maybe they did go back there."

Abbott retrieved a phone book from a desk drawer and I called the number of the Huron Village Inn and got transferred to room 116. The phone rang eight times. I hung up after no answer. Then I called the motel lobby again and asked if any message had been left for us.

Good news! If only we had done that earlier! There was a message from Walter Holliday for us to call him at a phone number in the Albany area.

Moments later, I was speaking to Walter Holliday at his home.

"Jody, It's good to hear from you. Are you and Kristel all right?" Walter asked. It was the first time I had actually spoken with him.

"We're fine. Have you heard from Roy?"

"Yes. He and his family are here at my house. They're safe."

I expelled a sigh of relief, and gestured the news to Kristel and Abbott.

Walter Holliday went on, "They had a bit of a run in with Clive Slater.

That John Doe note in the pizza box was all a set-up. But they're all right now. Where are you?"

"We're at the Club in Abbeyville. We've got Abbott Marilee with us."

"That's fantastic! That's wonderful news! Here, I'll put Roy on the line. He wants to talk to you."

Seconds later, I heard Roy's jubilant voice: "Jody, you've got Abbott with you?"

"Yes! What happened to you?"

"It's a long story. We were followed right out of the parking lot. Some guy in a Honda, and we couldn't shake him. He must have had a radio or cell phone, because after a few minutes, Slater comes up and pulls us over—in his squad car and all! Then the Honda disappeared."

"You're kidding!"

"Slater was in uniform—flashed his badge and said I was under arrest. I asked what for, and he said for breaking and entering into his office, for conspiracy to cover up the murder of James Grandstaff, and for the attempted murder of George Schuple. Jody, they're trying to pin this thing on me! They had me set up!"

Unreal! Abbott was right. They had devised a counter-attack for everything we had discovered.

Anders continued his story. "I figured it was only me against Slater, so I resisted his arrest, and hit the gas pedal. He followed us in his squad car for about a half-mile. Then it was like the entire Lake Henry police department was waiting for us at a roadblock. Slater had set it all up! He had the Lake Henry police waiting for me, accusing me for covering up Jimmy's murder! There was nothing I could do; there were four cops at their cars with guns pointed. I was arrested right there and taken in, and they took my family to the station, too. Walter here had to bail me out. One hundred grand bail! I tell ya, Jody. I might be able to laugh at this a month from now, but right now Slater and his gang have me framed. I don't know who they're going after next, but you're probably high on their list."

"I can't believe this!"

"Neither can I, but we've got to act fast. Slater's back in control in Abbeyville, and he's got a bunch of people in the Lake Henry department on his side, too. And the way things stand now—we don't have any hard evidence against him. It's only our word against his. What we learned about the camera, the file, everything—he's using it all against me. Who knows what's next? They're probably ready to frame you for something too, or worse."

"But what about Branson Oliff in those photos? Doesn't that incriminate him?"

"Well, Slater searched my van and found the photos and took them. It was like he knew we had them. Luckily, Walter still has the ones he's getting enhanced at his station. But right now, it's just circumstantial evidence, and that doesn't help my situation. More important than those photos is that you've found Abbott, and we have Gretta's testimony on videotape—but stupid me left the camera at the motel!"

"You're kidding!"

"Do you think you can stop by there and get it? We need that camera!"

"I can get it. We'll stop there on our way to Walter's."

"Good. I can't wait to meet Abbott. Just be careful, though. No telling if that room is really bugged or not. The tape in that camera is like gold to us right now, and we need to build this case against Branson Oliff and Clive Slater as quickly as possible. I hope the camera's still in the room. I left it sitting on the table between the beds."

Roy gave me directions to Walter Holliday's home in Albany—about an hour south of Lake Henry on the interstate. "Make sure no one follows you, especially from the motel," were Roy's final words.

Get into the motel room, get the camera, and get out, was all I was thinking during the fifty-minute drive with Kristel and Abbott back to Lake Henry.

Midnight was approaching, and the streets of Lake Henry still hosted its late night tourists who were patronizing its nightclubs, miniature golf courses, and arcades. The quaint Huron Village Inn was calm and quiet. We parked near the lobby entrance, and for safety, the three of us entered.

We cautiously and softly treaded down the motel hallway to the first door of our three connecting rooms. Praying the camera would be an easy find, we were paralyzed by the first thing we saw inside.

Reclining on Roy's bed, with his head propped up on the pillow, and his beady eyes focused on us, was none other than Brock Oliff.

# CHAPTER 40

## *An Astonishing Ally*

He was alone, just lying on the bed, and he calmly sat up when we walked in. He made no sudden move—he just sat there, knuckly old Brock, in a white T-shirt and baggy blue jeans. I figured that with me, old Abbott, and good ol' Kristel here, we could put up a fight if need be. But that was an unnecessary precaution. Brock just sat on the bed, cool and motionless, while we stared at him speechlessly.

His hair was cut short, buzzed close to his head like a Marine. He looked even skinnier than before, if that's possible. The most distinguishing difference in his appearance was the softness of his eyes. Their devilish squint and fiendish leer had dissolved. When the light hit them just right, they seemed to glisten.

I was about to say something when Brock raised two bony fingers to his lips and blew a soft "sshhh." Furthering this form of communication, he effectively lipped the word "bugs" and shifted his eyes around the room. He quietly stood from the bed and walked to the doorway of the connecting room. He turned and motioned for us to follow. Cautiously, quietly, and curiously, the three of us obeyed.

In the next room we saw how he got in—through the shattered sliding glass door from the pool patio. We watched him tiptoe carefully through it, and now outside, he walked calmly across the dark pavement and stopped at the gate of the black iron fence that enclosed the pool. We stood at the broken door, and eventually Brock turned back to us and motioned for us to follow. Again, the three of us obeyed. The potential danger of the situation was negated by our overwhelming curiosity.

After we stepped outside, I remembered the video camera for which we were there in the first place. I whispered, "hang on a sec," ducked inside, snatched the camera, and returned to Kristel and Abbott at the doorway. Brock was still waiting at the black iron fence on the other side of the pool.

Assured that we were indeed following him, he proceeded through the gate and across the side yard of the motel.

We followed him through the wet grass and climbed over a guardrail. Soon, we were weaving between cars in the parking lot of a crowded bowling alley. Brock stepped between two parked SUV's and motioned for us to come closer. We did, but stopped warily behind a beige Buick.

Finally, Brock was ready to speak out loud. He swallowed hard, cocked his hands at his hips, looked directly at us and proclaimed, "I'm John Doe."

A volley of glances, teeming with utter surprise and doubt, kept Kristel, Abbott, and me breathless. Brock stood between the vehicles and crossed his arms in front of him.

"Hello, Jody," he said meekly, looking at me straight in the eyes with a softness that defied his character. He then said hello to Kristel, followed by a nod to Abbott. He must have not recognized him as Whisper or Robert Rothschild.

We each responded with a soft hello. That is all we said, all we could muster at that moment.

Brock scraped a sneaker on the pavement and shoved his bony hands into the pockets of his blue jeans. He turned and glanced around the parking lot, up towards the night sky, and then he turned his head sideways. It was obvious he was trying not to cry. His lips tightened and scrunched close to his nose as he stared at the pavement. We all stood there silently for what felt like about five minutes. Nobody said a word.

Brock shuffled his feet a dozen times and lightly kicked the tire of a Ford Bronco with his sneaker. Then he took one hand from his pocket and wiped his eyes. Finally, he spoke in a broken voice.

"I'm your John Doe… I sent that letter to the police," he confessed softly, his voice cracking. "I sent that letter… to turn in my father… 'cause he helped kill Jimmy."

The son of Branson Oliff pressed his lips shut and lifted his eyes skyward. Then his eyeballs shifted sideways, down to the ground, before going up again. He couldn't look straight at us when he talked, obviously due to shame, not dishonesty.

"My father helped kill Jimmy," he repeated. "And they're gonna get you if you don't get outta here." Finally, his eyes focused straight on mine.

I asked a stupid question, "Did you pull the trip wire?"

"No, I didn't pull it!" he answered firmly, in a voice that sounded more like the Brock we knew. "I don't know who pulled it, but I didn't pull it!"

"Then who did?" I asked.

"I said I don't know, but I know my father helped set it up!"

The lanky figure took a step toward us and the tears were now running freely down his face. He pointed his bony finger at himself and jabbed his ribs as he cried, "I took those pictures! It was my camera and I took those pictures! Only I didn't know until later that Slater was in on it, too!"

This was the truth with a capital T. No doubt.

Kristel cried softly, raising her hands to her mouth, "Oh my heavens! You *are* John Doe!"

"Yer darn right I am," Brock asserted, shoving his hands back into his pockets after wiping his face dry.

He paused again to regain his composure.

"They're after you, Jody," he said brazenly, returning to his typical haughty demeanor. "And they're after Abbott Marilee. They're already after me 'cause they found out I'm John Doe. I came back here to tell you to get outta town before they kill you. I've been trying to get you outta town all summer!"

"Who's they?" Abbott asked.

"My father, Slater, and a couple of other scumbags—they're all after Abbott Marilee's money. You know he's your grandfather, don't you, Jody?"

"I do now," I said before adding, "We've got cops on our side."

"Not anymore. Anders is dead meat. My father and Slater are gonna eat him alive. That's why you've got to leave. There's no way to prove they did it now."

"Not if you tell the truth!" I said.

"No. They've got it all worked out. My father knows now that I'm John Doe—the one who tried to turn him in. He's got a story all worked out that everyone will believe. I'm just a crazy old druggie, remember? He's got the blame shifted on you, me, Kristel, and Anders already. There's no proof against his story!"

"But we've got the photos! The Albany police have copies!"

"They already know you've got them! They've had Anders' house bugged ever since you went public. They bugged your motel room the day you got here. And they know you have the photos and the testimony from old Gretta, and they're already coming up with an explanation for them. Gretta's going to be dead by tomorrow. That's the latest thing I found out. They know you've got her story on video. You're lucky Anders didn't have it on him when they arrested him. They think you have it."

I clutched the newly procured camera bag at my side. "Is the tape still in here?" I asked, lifting it up.

"Yes. I didn't touch it. All I know is they were hoping to get it off Anders. But he didn't have it. They don't care about the photos. They've got a story worked out for that. They say there's no proof in those photos that will hold up in court against my father's lawyers anyway."

"Then why did you want the police to find the photos when you wrote the John Doe letter?"

"I didn't know Slater was part of it! I thought I could trust the police! And now they're going to frame a different policeman—Officer Anders! There's five hundred grand in his safe that'll further prove his guilt!"

Kristel cut in. "Why did you wait so long after Jimmy died to write the John Doe letter?"

Brock calmed down to answer. "It took a long time, but I finally did it, didn't I?"

Abbott asked, "Who is the other person up on the cliff with your father?"

"I don't know who that guy is. Some partner of my father."

Kristel asked, "So you took those pictures because you knew your father was setting a trap to have Jimmy killed?"

"I didn't know it was going to be Jimmy. All I knew was that my father was up to something because I overheard his conversations. All I knew was that they were going to eliminate someone who was supposed to inherit the Marilee property that my father wanted instead. So I took those photos of him and his partner setting up the trip wire, and it wasn't until it was too late that I found out it was gonna be Jimmy. If I had known earlier, I would have warned him. Honestly, I would have! I got to the falls in the morning and I was gonna wait all day if I had to so I could warn the victim. But you guys were there early in the morning and the killers somehow knew you'd be there early. By the time I got there, Jimmy had already fallen. I hoped the police would figure out what happened, but they didn't, and now we all know why. I knew I had evidence inside my camera, but I just couldn't get up the nerve to turn in my father. I knew he could've had me killed, too. But what I finally did was, I threw the camera down to the bottom of the falls and then I wrote the John Doe letter. I figured the police would see my father in those pictures and put the whole thing together. But Slater…."

I cut him off. "But the Albany police have the pictures, and we've got Gretta on video. And with your testimony we can…."

"I ain't testifying to nothing. My father's got it all worked out to turn this whole thing on me and you and Anders and even Kristel. They've got this story that I had the motive to kill Jimmy because we were arguing over Kristel, and… well, I just came here to tell you to get the heck out of town—out of state if you can. I stole a load of money from my father last night and I'm gettin' on a plane as soon as I can. I've spent the last day and a half spying on my father and Slater, and I know what they've got planned. Slater's gonna to take you into custody as soon as he finds you. Who knows what will happen to you then? They'll probably have you killed. They're also after Abbott Marilee, and they shot Kristel's dad because they thought he was Abbott. And I know there's going to be more. I've been listening in on them all night. They're turning this whole thing around."

He sounded credible—unfortunately.

Abbott asked, "You mentioned that Gretta is going to be dead by tomorrow. How do you know?"

"I heard them talking about it. She may already be dead. I'm sure they made it look like an accident."

Miss Gretta Emory Ardello—alive and well yesterday, scheduled to be the next to die. I seriously feared for my own life now. I feared for Kristel, Roy, and Abbott. Who would be next?

"We've got to warn Gretta right away," Abbott said.

Brock cut in. "You think you can beat them, don't you."

Abbott responded, "I think your testimony alone can get a conviction on everyone who is involved in this. Forget the pictures. Forget the video. You know the whole truth."

"They'll kill me first."

"Then let's get your testimony on tape here and then you can get on your jet plane. We can *all* run for cover."

Brock shook his head. "No. You don't know the power they have. I'm getting' outta here as soon as I can!"

"Listen," I cut in. "We're going to make a case against Slater and your father whether you help us or not. But if you leave and don't help us, their argument that *you* killed Jimmy is only going to be stronger."

"We will all be dead before you can make any case against them," Brock insisted.

"Then let's do this now! Let's get your confession on video and get it to the Albany police, and then we'll all get on a plane for somewhere. Officer Anders already has his friends in Albany working on it. They're on our side."

Brock cocked his hands on his hips and began shaking his head and swearing, "God, they're gonna kill me, I know it!"

Kristel stepped forward and rested her hand on his shoulder. "Brock, just get your story on tape. Then come with us. If you don't tell the truth to the police—the good guys—then it only hurts us."

Suddenly, a plump figure darted out from behind a car and barked, "Everyone put your hands in the air! You're all under arrest! Turn around and put your hands in the air!"

Three of us twirled and raised our arms to see Clive Slater in full uniform pointing a pistol in our direction.

His gun fired.

# CHAPTER 41

## *The Escape*

The report cracked an echo against the concrete walls of the bowling alley after the bullet shattered the windshield of the Bronco next to us. Brock bolted away and the sheriff took off in pursuit. Kristel, Abbott, and I watched from behind the vehicle. Slater's head wobbled above a row of cars as he ran, and we heard his gun fire a second time.

The out-of-shape cop didn't keep up the chase very long. He gave up with a curse, turned, and started jogging back in our direction. I remembered that I was holding the camera bag with the golden evidence inside.

"Let's get out of here," I whispered loudly.

Now *we* were fleeing arrest.

Kristel, Abbott and I weaved through a maze of vehicles with our heads ducked down low. I heard Slater swear again when he saw us escaping. Unfortunately, my grandfather could not keep up. When I looked backwards, he was gone, and I was sure he would be an easy catch for the sheriff. As Kristel and I darted across the parking lot, I listened for another gunshot, but thankfully it didn't come. Perhaps Abbott got away; or perhaps Slater nabbed him and needed to keep him alive for a while.

Kristel and I cut around to the back of the bowling alley and didn't stop running until we were completely out of breath. It must have been more than a mile before we slowed down. We managed to run through two soggy irrigation ditches, a K-Mart parking lot, across several back yards in a residential neighborhood, and then onto the fairway of a golf course. We slid to a stop on the steep embankment of a putting green, confident that Slater was long behind us. Several minutes on the wet grass slipped by as we caught our breath and watched pockets of fog swirl over the rain-soaked fairways. I clutched the camera bag to my gut.

"Abbott couldn't keep up," Kristel said between pants.

"Maybe he got away," I said optimistically. "Maybe Slater chased us far enough to allow him to get away."

"I hope so. I hope they don't hurt him!"

We lay on our backs on the cool, wet grass and stared up at the black, starless sky. The crickets, chirping incessantly into the misty night air, were oblivious to our plight.

"Slater must have gone to the motel to get the camera, saw the broken door, and tracked us out there," I said.

"He scared me to death!" Kristel gasped. "I thought we were dead!"

"Me too!"

Instantaneously, a body from nowhere slid down the grassy bank next to us. Kristel yelped and then covered her mouth with her hand. It was Brock.

After catching his breath, he explained how he was hiding in a backyard when he saw us sprinting across the fairway. "Did Slater get the old man?" he huffed.

"We don't know. Probably," I said. "He's my grandfather, you know. Abbott Marilee."

"I thought so. They're gonna kill'm if Slater caught'm."

Kristel groaned, "These people are evil!"

"Listen," Brock said, pointing to the camera bag. "What are you gonna do with that video of old Gretta?"

"We were going down to Albany to a cop's house who's working on the case. Officer Anders is there already."

"Is the cop's name Walter Holliday?"

"Yes."

"They're already onto him. It won't be safe there. Why don't you guys come with me?"

"Where?"

"I dunno… London, Paris, somewhere far away from here." It was a portentous proposition.

Kristel asked, "Brock, how do you know what they're doing?"

"I've been hiding out at home the past two days. My father didn't know I was there. Slater and him have been on the phone constantly, and I can listen to everything through my computer."

"How?" I asked incredulously.

"I have a telephone hookup through my computer in my room. When my father's on the phone, I just click a button and the whole conversation comes through the headphones. I tried recording it as a sound file, but it was too big and I ran out of hard-drive space."

"And you know for sure they killed Jimmy?" I asked.

"Dude, I took the pictures! I'm John Doe!"

"But why did you wait so long?"

Off in the distance, we heard squealing tires and an accelerating engine. The screeching treads sounded like they could have been peeling out of the bowling ally several blocks to our left.

"Must be Slater on the move," Brock whispered.

I waited for him to answer my previous question. He finally did, albeit reluctantly.

"Dude, it's like this. After Jimmy was killed, I coulda turned in my father for murder. I had that camera with those pictures, and well, I was gonna do it, but I was drunk one night and my father and I got in an argument, and it all came out that I knew what he'd done. Well, then he starts makin' up excuses, and lies, and crap like that. And then he made me an offer: he was askin' me to be in on the whole scam."

"What scam?" Kristel asked softly.

"The scam to get Abbott Marilee's property. My father had somehow figured out that Abbott Marilee was Robert Rothschild, and he found out that Jimmy was gonna inherit Marilee Manor. Apparently, there's still a fortune of gold buried over there, and that's what my father is after. When he found out that I knew he had Jimmy killed, he tried to bargain with me. He was gonna build me my own resort over there."

"So you took him up on it?" I asked.

"No, not right away. See—I hated his guts… and I still do, even more now… and… well… it's a long story." Brock was becoming more hesitant the more he spoke.

"Why didn't you turn in those pictures earlier?"

"Well… I… I didn't know what to do. See, I was doin' crack and stuff, and I wasn't thinkin' straight, especially after Jimmy died. An' my father made me that offer… an' it beat goin' off to college… an' so I just went along with it. It was too tempting, an' I just went along with it at first. I figured that's the way things are—that's the way you get to the top. So I hid the camera in my closet and started makin' plans for my big resort."

"You never told me about your resort," Kristel interjected.

"I know, Kristel. See, it was like I was livin' two lives. One around you, when I made good decisions, and one around home where I was the devil's child." Brock stared up into the foggy darkness and explained, "See, I've been two different people this past year. When I was at home and doin' drugs and listenin' to my father, there was somethin' in me tellin' me that I was doin' the wrong thing. So I'd go an' be with you, Kristel, an' think good things, but then I'd get home and get high or drunk or somethin'. But it's been two straight weeks now, not a hit or a drink, although I've been tempted. I'm gonna be a new man. I'm changin' for good."

Kristel asked, "What finally made you write that John Doe letter?"

"I just did it one day. I was sick'a my father, and I was sick'a my own life. I didn't care what would happen to either of us. I could'a committed suicide right there, but instead I sent that letter in to the police. That's when I found out my father had Sheriff Slater coverin' for him."

Brock looked at me as he said, "And then, when I saw you, Jody, for the first time—the same day the news broke about my letter—I about freaked out. I knew you had to be Jimmy's brother or somethin'. At first I thought you might be part of the plan—that you might be working with my father and Slater—you know, eliminate your brother so you can get the fortune. Anyway, that's why I hated your guts so much, because I thought you were a part of it. That's why I beat the crap out of you at your car that night. And that's why I tried to set you up with Mandi, just to get you out of here. If you hung around, I would know for sure you were in on it with my dad.

"But I was still havin' my own problems, too, and I was glad to go to the rehab center. It was like escaping hell itself by goin' there. I was finally at peace. I would have stayed there longer if I could. I met God there, man—I mean I really met him. There's nothing like it now, being on God's side. Dude, it's like I have a whole new life."

Brock spent the next ten minutes explaining how it felt to be a completely new person, saved by Jesus Christ. It was like hearing a preacher talk, but his words were so real and sincere, and I felt I could trust him as much as I did Roy and Abbott and Kristel. Imagine that—trusting Brock Oliff!

Eventually, Brock got back to his explanation, describing the events of the most recent days. "Well, anyway, it was late on Monday night this week, and this guy showed up in my room at the rehab center and said he knew who I was—that I was the John Doe who ratted on my father. He threatened to kill me if I did anything else as stupid as that. He said my only way out of this alive was to go along with their plan."

I asked, "What did that guy look like?"

"He was prob'ly in his early forties, had dark hair and a goatee. I thought I recognized him from somewhere. He said he works for my father, and I'm pretty sure it was the same guy who was on the cliff with my father when I took those pictures, only he had grown the goatee. He told me I could choose to go along with their plan to frame Anders and you, or else I'd die. So I stayed up the rest of the night fixin' to run away from the rehab center. I came back home here and actually hid out in my own room most of Tuesday. I got the keys to my car, stole enough money from my father, and was about to get out of here and move a long way away. Then I realized how easy it was to spy on my father. He didn't even know I was there in the house. I've been listening in on them for two days and I found how many more people they're gonna hurt. That's why I chased you down."

So, it *was* John Doe who had put the note in the pizza box and the McDonald's bathroom. Brock explained how he knew through his father that our rooms were bugged, so he paid for a pizza to be delivered to contact us. He was waiting for us at my cabin, but because Kristel and I had spent so much time looking for Roy and his family, Brock gave up and came back down to the Huron Village Inn to hopefully catch us there. When he saw the camera in the room, he hoped that we would be the first one's to try to retrieve it. Thankfully, we barely beat Slater to it.

"So it wasn't a trap after all," I said. "The guy in that Honda and Slater were planning to trap Roy anyway. They had it all planned out to arrest him."

"You see," Brock said. "That's all part of their plan—to frame you guys, especially Anders, for Jimmy's death."

This was a bigger and more sophisticated conspiracy than Abbott, Roy, or anybody had imagined.

"Brock," Kristel pleaded sweetly. "You need to say everything you've said to us tonight into this camera before you leave."

Brock shook his head. "You guys should come with me! You don't know what they're gonna do next. Just come with me and I'll say whatever you want me to say on tape. You have to believe me—we don't have much time here. They're gonna track us down eventually."

"Are you serious about leaving the country?" I asked.

"Yes. I'll pay for your flights. I've got plenty of cash. We should head up to Montreal and fly out there. They probably have Albany airport staked out already."

The thought of leaving the country was both daunting and marvelous. I could tell that Kristel was seriously contemplating its necessity like I was.

I looked at my watch. It was after midnight.

"We can get to Montreal in three hours from here," Brock said. "We'll be on a plane before the sun's up. Then we can shoot the video, make copies of the tape, and send them wherever we want. At least we'll still be alive."

I thought about my grandfather. What had happened to him?

Kristel looked me in the eye and gave me an approving nod. A second later, we were off to Montreal; from there we'd escape to heaven-knows-where.

The three of us scurried surreptitiously from the golf course to the parking lot of the Huron Village Inn. There, we discovered that Sheriff Slater had secured a boot on the rear tire of my car, effectively disabling the vehicle. Brock, however, was a step ahead of us, having parked his car several blocks away from the motel.

When we arrived at Brock's Porsche, Kristel mentioned, "We should could call Roy and Walter. They're expecting us."

Brock warned, "Walter Holliday's phones are probably bugged, too. I heard them mention his name a lot."

We got in the car, and I wondered how long it would be before we would talk to either Roy or Walter again. Then I said a prayer for my grandfather. I hoped somebody heard it.

As we sped northward in the early morning hours of Friday, July 17th, the tourist town of Lake Henry had fallen asleep under a blanket of wispy mist. It's citizens, like the golf course crickets, were oblivious to the crimes committed in their midst. Last month, I was like one of them—completely ignorant, and I tried the best I could to keep it that way. I was blind then, but the darkness was changed by a light, ignited by my grandfather, the Ambassador for the Dead. He too, had been blind, and his sight was illuminated by Brock Oliff, the John Doe, who, with a small step for righteousness' sake, had brought us all to this very moment of truth.

I wondered what the reaction of the people of Lake Henry, Abbeyville, and all of the Adirondacks would be like when they wake up one imminent sunny morning and read the truth about the legend of Lake Marilee and the murder of Jimmy Grandstaff. I hoped I would be back in the country by then to see it.

I was up front with Brock, who was driving; Kristel had taken the back seat. A green highway sign indicated we were 195 miles from Montreal. From there, off to London, Paris, Rome? Where would we be when the sun comes up again? I glanced backward at Kristel. She had her eyes closed. She wasn't sleeping; she was praying. I heard the name of Jesus amidst her whispered supplications.

Shortly after one a.m., we passed the green highway sign indicating that

Pokeville was the next exit. "Let's check on Gretta," I said. "We've got to warn her." Brock and Kristel assented.

A mile later, we were driving slowly through the empty town of Pokeville, past the old church, down the dilapidated main street. As we rolled through the intersection at Dreary Creek Drive, the town seemed as ghostly and eerie as ever, especially as the thin, misty rain merged into droplets on the windshield.

Just beyond town, past the stony brook and the graveyard, a posse of flashing lights had assembled along Route 7. At least a dozen cars were parked at old Harold and Gretta's gas station. Teams of officials and local citizens were standing in groups outside their vehicles.

"Oh, no," Kristel gasped. "Something's happened!"

Brock slowed his Porsche to a stop. Beyond the post office building and into the woods where Gretta's home was located, we could see the blue and white lights of several emergency vehicles.

"God, they already did it!" Brock moaned.

We jumped out of the car and dashed down the dirt driveway, past the piles of tires and rubbish and into the well lit woods. Two fire trucks, one ambulance, and two police cars blocked the dirt driveway. Thankfully, no Slater.

The scene in the woods was a tragedy. The only remains of Gretta's home were the black-charred shell of a mobile home and a torched Cadillac resting next to it.

We stuck around long enough to learn from some townspeople that the husband and wife were found dead at the mobile home, just before midnight, their charred bodies clutching each other on their bed. No information yet as to what caused the fire.

Kristel cried, "Who's going to die next?"

We didn't dare stick around to talk to any police. Who knows whom Slater had ordered to arrest us? We were determined to continue our flight.

The videocassette in Roy's camera was now more valuable than ever, and I gripped the camera bag as Brock started the engine.

He was about to turn south and head through Pokeville to pick up the interstate from there. Kristel urged him to drive north to Abbeyville so we could stop at the Club. "We shouldn't, Kristel," Brock insisted. "Don't you see what just happened? They could be waiting for us at the Club."

"Can't we stop just for a minute so I can get some things?" Kristel argued. "Besides, I need to get my passport if we're leaving the country."

That made me say, "*I* don't have a passport."

"Got a birth certificate?" Brock asked.

"Not here."

"Then we'll have to stay in the country if we stick together. Maybe Seattle or somewhere out west."

Kristel was still insisting on stopping at the Club. "Please! The Club's probably the last place they think we'll go."

Brock acquiesced. In fifteen minutes, we parked the car on a neighborhood side street in Abbeyville, scampered through town, and climbed the back way through the woods and into the cabin grove. All was quiet as we skulked past the softball field, up the hill beyond the pool and down Kristel's driveway. That's where we saw an unfamiliar car parked at the locked gate.

We froze in our steps, crouched down low, and for the first time ever, I heard Kristel utter a swear word.

"That's a Honda Accord," Brock whispered. Whether it was the same one that followed Roy's van out of the motel parking lot about seven hours ago was undeterminable. And where its driver was presently located, we had no idea. Slowly, we turned around and crept back down the gloomy driveway. At the pool, which was surrounded with illuminated globe lamps, we crouched low into the shadows of the poolside café building. The Coke machine in front of us hummed softly, and, inexplicably, the crickets in the woods behind us were silent.

Then we heard a vehicle crumbling over gravel. It wasn't the Honda coming down Kristel's driveway; it was another car rolling slowly down from the Club building. As it entered into the brightness of the pool deck, our blood turned cold as we saw the unmistakable bracket of lights mounted to its roof. It was a police cruiser.

"Is that Slater?" I whispered.

"Can't tell," Brock answered.

The police car rolled slowly down the hill toward the cabin grove beyond our view.

"They're looking for us," Brock said. "I bet they saw us drive into town."

We both looked at Kristel, who eyeballed us an apology for insisting we stop here.

"With that cop down there," Brock whispered, "we can't get back to my car the back way. And we definitely can't walk to town the front way."

In other words, as long as that police car was in the cabin grove, we were trapped. And even if the cop would leave, cutting through the woods and into town to get to Brock's car was still risky. They may have even found Brock's car and disabled it like they did mine.

"Now what?" Brock asked Kristel, clearly annoyed.

At this moment, Kristel audaciously stood and tiptoed to the gate of the pool deck and opened it. Brock and I watched her prance up to a solid steel door next to the Coke machine. The door was unlocked, and she stepped partially inside and motioned for us to follow.

Soon, all three of us were in a windowless room stacked full of white bath towels on three sides, and a shelf stocked with pool chemicals on the fourth wall. A single light bulb thoroughly illuminated the small linen room, and we stuffed a towel at the bottom of the door to keep the light in.

"Now what?" Brock asked Kristel a second time.

She sternly ordered him, "You're going to shoot this video now, while we have the chance. You're going to say everything into that camera that you told us tonight. If they find us, whoever can run the fastest will take the video."

Her assertive tone allowed no time to argue over who was the fastest runner. So, there, in front of Roy's video camera, into the wee hours of the morning, surrounded by piles of pool towels, we added to the late Gretta Emory-Ardello's testimony our own.

For the next three hours, the three of us described every detail of everything we knew. Brock went first, beginning with what he learned about his father's scheme last September. Kristel added a description of Jimmy's death. I gave background details of my family and linked it to the Marilee family history.

Then we all pitched in descriptions of what had happened in the last few days: the chases; the spying; and tonight's horrifying death of Miss Emory and her husband.

About an hour of blank tape remained on the cassette, and with an electrical outlet in the room we were able to keep the batteries charged. Kristel had more plans for the camera. She wanted us to explain how the trip wire was set up, and she wanted to film it on location—at Smooth Rock Falls.

Brock and I saw value in that and agreed to go there if we could. Besides, it would be a quick stop on the way to Montreal, that is, if we were able to even get out of town.

It was almost six a.m. when we finished our videotaped testimonies; the sun was beginning to paint its colors across the eastern sky. We hadn't slept a wink since our only night at the Huron Village Inn, but none of us yawned even once.

Like fugitives from prison, we peeked outside before creeping through the gate of the pool deck. Still under the cover of darkness, we stealthily and swiftly glided toward the cabin grove.

No police car was in sight in the grove, and we wondered how long ago it had left. We also wondered if the Honda remained by the gate of the Schuple driveway.

Then…

The caw of a crow.

The rattle of a doorknob.

Three heart attacks nearly happened when the door of Saranac suddenly opened.

# CHAPTER 42

## *The Capture*

It was Boonie. Our stomachs untwisted, and the flow of blood through our fluttering hearts resumed. My cabin mate was on his way to work, and, predictably, he was thoroughly puzzled when he saw Kristel and me together with Brock. I gave him the briefest of explanations.

"Boonie, you might not see us for a while. You might hear a lot of things about me, Kristel, Brock, Officer Anders and others. But let me tell you one thing. For your own safety—you know nothing. You don't know anything about Jimmy's death. Okay?"

"Sure, man," Boonie said. "Are you guys in trouble?"

"We're in danger. First it was Jimmy. Then Schuple got shot. Anders got arrested. And now old Gretta and Harold are dead."

Boonie only stared at the three of us with a stunned expression.

"See ya, friend," I said, slapping him on the shoulder before we snuck down the path the back way toward town.

"Good luck," I heard him call from behind.

Brock's Porsche was still on the side street, untouched. As the eastern sky was turning orange, and as Abbeyville slept, Brock, Kristel, and I said very little as we sped out of town and past the northern shore of Lake Marilee.

Brock barely slowed down for the curves, hitting some of them at sixty miles per hour, causing the wheels to squeal and a pair of sunglasses on the dashboard to slide violently from side to side. The road became more tortuous as we entered the valley under Mount Hector, and soon we were alongside Stony River that would eventually lead us to Smooth Rock Falls. A few more miles of hills, dips, and sharp bends were conquered with barely a tap on the brake pedal. Finally, twenty minutes later, after the sun had risen in the east, we were there—at the sight of my brother's murder.

"Let's get this done and get up to Montreal," Brock said eagerly. "I hope they don't have a road block at the Canadian boarder."

We jetted through the woods to the cliff's edge and prepared the camera. The air was cool under the shade of the pines, but the rocky ledge of the precipice was much warmer under the rising morning sun. The sun's rays had not yet reached the deep bottom of the gorge, making the white, rushing water far below us look gray and icy cold.

"We'll get a shot from all angles," I said, speaking loudly above the din of the crashing water. "We'll do a shot from up here, one from those falls down there where they pulled the wire, and one from the very bottom where you were when Jimmy fell, Kristel. Then we'll go across the gorge to where Brock took the pictures. We'll have Brock explain how they set the trap. That should go along well with those pictures that Walter has."

Brock urged, "And then we'll get in the car and get the heck outta here." He and Kristel agreed with the filming plans.

The first thing we did on film was provide an explanation of where we were. Kristel held the camera and I stood at the cliff's edge, much like a reporter, announcing into the camera, "We're now here at Smooth Rock Falls. It's Friday morning, July 17$^{th}$. We're going to show you exactly how Jimmy Grandstaff was murdered."

I pointed across the gorge and reported, "Brock sat right over there on the other side of the gorge the evening before the murder, and he took the pictures that Sheriff Slater didn't want you to see."

Kristel panned the opposite cliff and then did a close up on me.

"He took those pictures because he knew his father, Branson Oliff, along with several conspirators, were arranging for someone to die. And this is how they did it."

Brock then stood before the camera and explained the trip wire. He showed the tree where the wire was tied at the top of the cliff, explained how the wire could have been barely visible across the cliff, and demonstrated how it was stretched across and around the big boulders and down to the middle-level waterfall below. Kristel performed marvelously as a camerawoman.

"I'll take the camera down there to that waterfall," she said, "to show how the person who pulled the wire can see you at the top of the cliff. You stay up here and back up like Jimmy did for a running start."

"Okay," I said. "Then we'll go down to the bottom of the gorge to show how you couldn't have seen anything from where you were."

Kristel took the camera down the path towards the road where she could fairly easily climb down the rocks from the top level of the falls.

I stepped to the edge and watched Kristel descend to the base of the mid-level falls where the actual murderer must have positioned himself to pull the wire. It took several minutes for her to climb down, as Brock, meanwhile, paced nervously in the dirt. Finally, she was there, perched atop a huge, smooth boulder several feet away from white crashing water. The red light on the camera was on, much brighter now in the gray shade of the gorge.

She had to yell so I could hear: "Okay, back away from the cliff so we can show how far back you can go until I don't see you."

I could hardly hear her, but I knew what she said. I slowly stepped away from the cliff's edge to where Jimmy probably stood before he took the last three steps of his life.

Brock stopped me and moaned, "Oh God, they're here!"

Through the trees toward the road, we could see a police car parked behind the Porsche. Behind the police car, another car was pulling up. It was a shiny, silver town car driven by Branson Oliff.

Kristel shouted something about a camera angle from below, so I ran to the edge to signal for her to keep quiet. I pressed my finger to my lips and pointed in the direction of the cars. She knew exactly what I meant. I watched her slip the camera under her shirt and duck for cover in the dry cave behind the waterfall.

Brock was now crouched low behind a tree and I joined him there. Through the foliage we watched Sheriff Clive Slater and Branson Oliff get out of their cars and say something to each other. Then they walked to the railing at the edge of the upper falls.

I looked around and realized there were few escape options should the enemy come this way. To our left was the cliff; behind us was the thick brush that descended rapidly down the gorge towards the river. It would be impossible to cut through it without being noticed. To our right was a steep, muddy embankment that led up to the highway. We could climb that and risk exposing ourselves on the open road. From there we would be chased into unfamiliar terrain.

The fourth option, and the one we chose, was to stay put for the meantime and see what Slater and Oliff would do. Kristel was safely hidden behind the falls, as long as neither Slater nor Branson climbed down there and looked. At first, I hoped they would give a cursory search of the area and leave, but then I remembered they had parked behind Brock's Porsche. They knew we were here.

When Slater climbed over the railing and stepped out onto a large stone in the river at the top of the falls, it was obvious that they would search this area well. Slater leapt from stone to stone to get a look at every angle of the gorge below him. Seeing nothing, he jumped back to the shore, climbed over the railing and joined Branson again. Then they both started walking towards us.

Brock and I crouched lower behind two pine trees as they approached.

"Now!" Brock whispered, "Let's run!"

We bolted to our right toward the steep embankment below the highway. Doing so, we revealed our whereabouts to the enemy, and they started weaving through the trees in our direction.

The embankment was steep and slick from the morning mist. Both Brock and I slipped on our first steps, falling flat on our chests, covering our fronts with mud and pine needles. I looked back at our pursuers and knew it was going to be close. Brock moved to his right and got a foothold on a tree root, hoisting himself to the top.

I lunged for the ledge. The mud on the incline was treacherous, but the foothold of the tree root helped immensely. My head reached road level, and I saw Brock leap the guardrail, landing on the pavement of the highway. He bolted across the road as I stretched out with one hand for the guardrail and pulled my body up. Then I felt the painful grasp of a claw around my left ankle.

I heard Slater growl, "Yer not goin' anywhere!"

The fingers on my right hand caught the lower lip of the guardrail, and I held on for dear life. Slater was pulling me violently from behind; I kicked with both legs. Another firm grasp on my other leg caused me to lose hold of the guardrail and down I went, sliding on my stomach down the embankment.

"Yer not goin' anywhere," Slater growled again as I rolled over to my back. He towered above me and pressed his boot into my ribs.

Branson Oliff jogged up behind him, wearing his typical suit jacket and tie. "Where's the other one?" Branson asked in short breath, referring to his own son.

"This is the only one we need," Slater muttered, yanking me up by my mud-covered shirt. He looked at Branson and urged, "Your boy can't do any more harm."

I glared at the two men—the two men who arranged for the murder of my brother, the two men who had Harold and Gretta killed, the two men who probably shot George Schuple. I wondered what they would do to eliminate me, to keep me quiet, to keep me from making a "big fuss over this thing" like Slater said about my actions a week ago. I thought of Kristel down under the falls. I knew she had the camera; I knew she'd get away. And if I could stay alive long enough for her and Roy and Walter to rescue me, I'd watch these two men be arrested and taken to prison. Then I'd be there for their trials.

Stay positive; stay positive, I kept thinking to myself. It was all I could do not to get sick looking at these two men. Murderers.

"You killed my brother," I hissed at both of them, showing little fear, although I was scared to death.

Slater snickered and shook his head. "I knew you'd say that, Jody. That's why I tried to hide these pictures from you." He took from his pocket a pile of crumpled photographs, probably the ones he had taken off Anders. "I knew if you ever saw these pictures, you'd use that wild imagination of yours to think that I covered up your brother's death." Slater glanced back at Branson who stood quietly, wearing a stern expression. "But I have to hand it to you Jody, you did solve the murder!"

I spoke boldly. "I did. And it was you, both of you. You killed Jimmy to keep the inheritance away from him. You did it for the land, and for the gold you think is still over there."

Branson looked down at the ground.

Slater smiled and snickered again. "No, Jody, you discovered the murderer. It was Brock. His own father here will tell you the same thing."

Branson raised his eyes and looked at me. "Yes, son," he said in a startling, deep voice. "My son Brock killed your brother. I'm very sorry, and very ashamed." He looked back to the ground again.

"You see, Jody!" Slater said with a sinister smile. "Brock did it; he even confessed it in rehab. We were about to have him arrested while he was in rehab in New Jersey, but he ran away before we could get to him. But he'll get caught, and we'll bring this whole thing to an end. You're the hero, Jody! You didn't give up. I have to hand it to you. You solved the murder!"

"I know all about Brock's confession," I said. "He confessed to me that his father arranged for Jimmy to be killed. He confessed to me that he took those photographs of his father setting up the trip wire. And his confession is going to get both of you arrested for murder."

"No, Jody," Slater argued. "Brock set up the wire. He pulled it. These are pictures that someone took during the investigation after the murder. Mr. Oliff came to me after the murder and said that he suspected his son was involved. We've been investigating Brock ever since. We even questioned him directly, and he, of course, denied it all these months. He finally fell apart and he tried to kill himself."

"No, you're wrong, Mr. Sheriff," I retorted. "Brock didn't fall apart. He finally got up the nerve to turn in his father, so he wrote the John Doe letter to the police so they'd find the camera. He's the real John Doe. You know that. Only he didn't know that the Sheriff of Huron County was working for his father. You're both murderers!"

"Son, that's exactly what Brock wants you to believe. Yes, he wrote that letter—because he wants his father to be blamed for the murder. Brock has had a vengeance for his father for many years. Branson here will admit that."

Branson eyeballed me for a split second and then returned to his staring at the ground.

Slater continued, "Branson here is feeling the guilt of his son's crime, and he wants to make it up to you, and to the Grandstaffs, for all the pain you've suffered."

I said nothing. Brock was absolutely right. They had concocted a plan to cover what we had uncovered. The photos were now useless. Our only evidence now was the videotape in Kristel's hands. Even with that, if we pushed this thing to a court trial, it would still come down to a battle of lies between Brock and his father—each implicating the other.

As I stood there and looked at Branson and Slater acting so innocently, I began to realize that Jimmy's death might indeed be ruled a homicide, but the punishment would be inflicted on the wrong person—Brock Oliff—the real hero.

It was at this moment that Brock reappeared at the top of the embankment.

"You worthless snake!!" he screamed, glaring at his father.

Branson looked up at him, emotionless.

"You snake!" Brock screamed again. "I'm not runnin' anywhere! I'm stayin' right here and to watch you go to prison—where you belong."

"Who's gonna arrest him, son?" Slater called, looking up at Brock. "Huh? Me? Why don't you step down here and we'll get this over with. Don't make this harder on yourself."

"I did not murder Jimmy!" Brock growled.

Slater pulled his gun from his holster and pointed it at Brock. "Son, I'm ordering you to step down here right now."

I figured Brock would either bolt away again or be shot, and I'd be left there with Slater who was now waving a gun around again. But Brock didn't run. He slowly stepped over the guardrail and slid down the embankment on his backside. He stood next to me; the anger in his eyes was like an inferno.

"You're going to Hell, Slater!" Brock seethed.

Slater continued to point the gun at his face. "Son, turn around. You're under arrest for the murder of Jimmy Grandstaff."

I couldn't understand why Brock was suddenly giving up. He willingly turned and held his hands behind his back. Slater slid the gun into his holster and clutched Brock's skinny wrists with one hand while he probed around his belt with the other.

"Where's my handcuffs?" Slater barked. He cussed twice.

Branson spoke in a low voice and glanced in the direction of the cars. "They're on Abb, er, uh, Whisper."

Slater peered through the woods toward the vehicles parked along the road. I realized that Abbott must be in Slater's squad car with handcuffs on. Slater must have caught him in the parking lot of the bowling alley in Lake Henry.

"Here," Slater said to Branson, handing him the gun. "Watch these two. I'll be back."

Branson refused the gun. "I've got my own," he said. "He reached into the vest pocket of his jacket and pulled out a small, silver pistol. He cocked it, and with a straight arm pointed the barrel at the back of his son's head.

Slater scampered through the woods to the car, leaving the three of us near the cliff. Branson held the gun firmly, and Brock didn't move, standing with his back to his father, looking at the muddy embankment.

My shuffling feet caused Branson to point the gun at me, but he immediately returned it to his son. He said nothing, sternly and stoically aiming at his own flesh and blood.

Slater returned with his prisoner, poking my handcuffed grandfather along in front of him, with his fat, sausage-pack hands. "I've only got one pair of cuffs," he mumbled. "We'll have to cuff Brock and this one together."

Abbott, alive, but haggard looking, glanced at me, and—in a most peculiar way—he grinned.

Slater began wrestling with the cuffs on Abbott's wrists.

The smile widened on Abbott's face as he looked at Brock. "What are you going to do, Clive—handcuff us together and throw us both over the edge?" he teased.

"Shut up, Whisper. Brock's going to prison for murder, and you and Roy Anders are under arrest for breaking into my office."

"I didn't break into your office!" Abbott said with a smirk.

"Shut up, Whisper. Both you and Anders broke into my office yesterday.

You're in on this with Anders, so I'm arresting you for conspiracy to cover up a murder."

"Then why don't you arrest the kid, too?' Abbott said, nodding toward me.

"Because he's being pardoned for solving the murder. He's a hero—but you and Anders are going to jail."

Slater jerked Abbott's arm toward Brock and he cuffed them both together.

Abbott turned his head to his new companion and patted him on the shoulder with his free hand. Then my grandfather looked at Branson, who had now lowered his pistol, and said to him, "Branson, I've seen family members turn on each other, but never a father passing the blame for his own devilish crime onto his only son!"

"Shut up, Whisper!" Branson snarled.

Abbott only smiled. "Ah, come now, Branson. *You* know my real name. Just say it. Tell everyone here what my real name is. You've known for a while now."

Branson said nothing. His nostrils flared.

Slater clutched the chain on the cuffs between Abbott and Brock. "C'mon Whisper, Brock. Let's go. Jody, you can ride with Mr. Oliff."

Abbott resisted and said, "Wait a minute, Clive. *You* know my real name, too. Why don't you say it?" He looked Slater in the eye. Branson was staring down at the ground as usual.

"C'mon, Clive. Say my name," Abbott again prodded the Sheriff.

Slater's upper lip twitched. He glanced at Branson.

Suddenly, a strangely familiar voice was heard from above. A deep, resounding male voice, one that was incredibly familiar to me, I couldn't place it at first.

"His name is Abbott. Abbott Marilee," the voice declared in a shout.

I turned and looked up the embankment toward the road. There was a man straddling the guardrail—my stepfather, Wesley Barrett.

He looked different since I last saw him a few weeks ago. He had grown a goatee.

# CHAPTER 43

## *The Man Behind the Plan*

My stepfather climbed over the guardrail and slid clumsily down the embankment, muddying one thigh and both hands in the process.

"It's nice to finally see you again, Abbott," Wesley said smartly, as he approached the circle, slapping the mud from his fingers.

Brock raised his free hand and pointed at Wesley. "It's him!" he cried, glancing at me with both a look of joy and horror. "It's him! Jody, he's the one who was with my father here the night before the murder! He's the one who pulled the wire! Jody, this is the one who talked to me at the rehab center!"

My heart stopped. My brain churned like a hurricane.

"I think you're mistaken, son," Wesley said calmly to Brock.

"No I'm not! It was you!"

I asked, "Wesley, what's going on?"

I wasn't sure if I really wanted to know. Things were becoming clearer, and as the truth came into focus, my past looked even darker now.

Wesley answered me with only a pitiful facial expression. Then he glanced around at Brock, Abbott, Slater, and Branson.

Slater and Branson both looked dumbfounded, as though my stepfather's appearance here was, to them also, a surprise.

"What's going on?" I demanded again.

Abbott answered, "This affirms my hypothesis, Jody. Your stepfather has been conspiring with Branson, not just to get the land, but my whole estate."

Wesley's facial expression neither confirmed nor denied Abbott's claim, while every facet of the possibility of his involvement crashed through my brain in seconds. My stepfather: partner with Branson Oliff in Jimmy's murder. To get the land—his wife's father's land, and the entire inheritance, too.

"He's the other person in those photographs, Jody," Brock said. "He's the one who pulled the wire."

What Abbott and Brock were saying was unbelievable—but the truth of their words was entirely possible. Wesley had found out about his wife's heritage when Abbott contacted her last year to say he was thinking of coming clean. Wesley wanted the fortune; his wife didn't, so he teamed with Branson to have Jimmy killed. It was all very, very possible, and by the look on Abbott's face, I knew it was most probable.

"You did it," Abbott said to my stepfather. "Didn't you Wesley. You killed your wife's son to get my money, didn't you."

Slater suddenly blurted, "Shut up, Whisper! Just shut your mouth!" He looked at Wesley and said, "And sir, just who are you?"

Wesley turned and faced Slater who was standing alongside Branson. "It's all right, Clive. We don't have to play this game anymore. They have discovered everything."

Slater glanced at me and then at Branson, before looking at Wesley again.

My stepfather looked back at Brock, Abbott, and me. He repeated sternly, "They've discovered everything."

I asked him, "*You're* the one who killed Jimmy?!"

Wesley shook his head. "No, son. Brock killed Jimmy."

"You're a liar!" Brock screamed. "You were here on this cliff! It was you I took pictures of settin' up that wire! You and my father and this crooked sheriff killed Jimmy!"

Slater shouted, "Now that'll be enough, Brock! You two come with me." He again grabbed the chain between the cuffs on Abbott and Brock, but they both resisted, pulling back.

"Not yet, Clive," Abbott said calmly. "First, I want you to tell everyone here what my real name is."

Slater backed off and looked around. He glanced first at Wesley, who seemed to have blown part of the cover-up. He then looked at Branson, who remained sternly emotionless. Then he looked at me standing next to Brock and Abbott. He looked at Wesley again.

As the sheriff stood dumbfounded between my father and Branson, I glanced beyond them through the trees and noticed Kristel climbing up from the lower ledge, with the camera strapped around her neck. She ducked behind a thicket and held the camera to her eye. The red light went on. She was being very brave, and very risky—perhaps stupid—and I prayed to God she wouldn't get caught.

Then Wesley said to Slater, "Go on, and say it, Clive. It's all right. Say his real name. It doesn't matter now. The truth's out, and, in fact, it's better this way."

Slater looked at Wesley in the eye and said nothing. He seemed as if he wasn't sure what he should do. It was as if Wesley had arrived on the scene and fouled up the story that Branson and he had concocted.

"His name is Abbott Marilee," Wesley proclaimed to the rest of us when Slater refused to speak. "Forty years ago he raped a fifteen year old girl, and then he murdered his mother, father, brother, wife, and son. Only his daughter survived—my wife Madeline, who has hated this man ever since she learned of his heinous crimes."

For the first time this morning, Abbott wore an expression other than one of haughty pride. He now looked angry. His jaw clenched shut and his eyes narrowed in fury as he listened to Wesley speak.

"And this murderer," Wesley continued, pointing at Abbott, "with the aid of an innocent and unknowing George Schuple, has lived in hiding ever since. And I'm glad that he now has the courage to reveal his true identity, so that his surviving family can share in the fortune that is due them."

"You won't get a dime," Abbott said grimly.

"I will after you die," Wesley responded with an evil smirk. He reached to his belt behind his back and pulled out a handgun.

My face flushed in horror.

Slater shouted, "All right, Wesley! This has gone too far! I don't want any part of this."

Wesley glared at him and growled, "This was your deal, Slater. You and Oliff! You both wanted the land, and I got it for you! You won't have to pay a penny for it, cause I'm giving it to you!" He looked back at Abbott. "Ol' Abbott's done us a favor by coming out of hiding. Now we won't have to buy the land from the state, we'll inherit it, including the fortune that goes with it!"

"That's not part of the deal, Wesley," Slater said. "One person lost his life, and that was supposed to be it. You killed two more last night. What are you going to do? Kill three more here on the cliff?"

"Only one more will be necessary," Wesley said. "Brock's going to prison for killing the first kid." He looked at me. "And the second kid is coming with me."

And it was now that I fully understood. My stepfather had wanted to get his hands on the Marilee inheritance ever since he found out about it, but Madeline had refused to accept it. So Wesley partnered with Branson Oliff and Clive Slater to obtain the Marilee Manor property and the entire Marilee fortune. Because Wesley knew of Abbott's plans to come out of hiding and grant everything to Jimmy, he killed Jimmy before it could happen. But since we had uncovered everything, he was going to let the world learn of Abbott's identity, and, I fear, lay claim to his share of the inheritance as the husband of Madeline Marilee.

"You're not getting a dime of that money," Abbott insisted again. "I've already changed the will. It's all going to Jody."

Wesley smiled and looked at Abbott. "Jody's not old enough yet, and because his mother still hates you, just yesterday she signed a statement that grants me power of attorney over the fortune until Jody comes of age." He looked at me. "So Jody, if you want to see any of that fortune which your mother has so stubbornly refused, you're going to have to be nice to me. I can do with it as I please until you're eighteen."

"Why don't you kill me like you did Jimmy?" I said rashly.

"That thought did cross my mind, son, but I thought I'd give you a chance to cooperate with me."

"Don't call me son!" I shouted. "I'm not your son! And when mom learns that her father is really an innocent man, she'll accept the fortune and embrace her true family heritage! You won't have any right to it!"

Wesley shook his head and snickered. "She's never going to believe that he's innocent. No one ever will. There's no proof."

I thought again of Gretta's testimony on the videotape and I eyeballed Kristel who was still behind the thicket with the camera running. I prayed again she wouldn't get caught. She could be our last hope.

"There's plenty of proof," I said to Wesley. Then I stupidly added, "You'll have to kill us all before you get away with this."

"If that's the way you want it, you can die with your grandfather," Abbott said, waving his handgun in front of him like a toy.

Slater shouted again, "Wesley, that's enough! Let the old man live, and let the kid go! There's nothing they can do! They can't prove anything! It's all covered. We're clean! All we're up against is an old man and a bunch of kids and that cockamamie cop of mine comin' up with an outrageous conspiracy story with no proof to back it up."

Wesley spun and faced Slater. "You're an idiot, Slater! I know all that! God, do you think I'm as stupid as you are?" He crammed the gun in his belt behind his back. "Nobody else has to die! Did you think I'd go and knock off the cop and the entire Schuple family too?"

Suddenly, Wesley stopped his diatribe and bolted from the circle to the woods in Kristel's direction.

"Where in the heck are you going?" Slater shouted.

He soon knew the answer. In a split second, Wesley seized Kristel from behind the tree and yanked the camera from her hands. The red light was still on. He locked Kristel's neck in a half-nelson, pulled out his pistol, pressed it to her temple, and dragged her to the clearing near the cliff where the rest of us were watching in astonishment.

Wesley tossed the camera to Slater and then transferred his gun to his free hand. Kristel let her body go limp as Wesley struggled to hold her up straight. "Stand up, you little spy!" he said, pulling her up with his forearm under her neck. "Branson, give me a hand."

Branson Oliff cautiously approached Kristel and clutched his forearm around her neck from behind as Wesley released and stepped away. Branson steadily held his silver pistol to Kristel's temple while Wesley began waving his own gun at us.

"She's no threat either," Wesley huffed at Slater, heavy in breath.

At that moment, Brock bolted forward towards his father, dragging Abbott with him by the arm.

Branson let go of Kristel and fell flat to his back as his son tackled him like a linebacker. Abbott fell to his side, wreathing in pain as his cuffed arm bent backward behind him. Kristel dashed to my side as Brock started throwing punches with his free arm into his father's face. "You're a murderer! A cold-blooded murderer!" the younger Oliff screamed as he bombarded his father with blows.

Branson, a man of fuller stature than his son, slower to react but obviously much stronger, managed to lock Brock's head under his elbow, thus limiting Brock's ability to use his free arm as a weapon. Abbott screamed in pain as his handcuffed arm got contorted around backwards. The two Oliffs rolled over twice, wrestling like two dogs, and Abbott flopped over top of them to keep his arm from being ripped from its socket. The rest of us stood by and watched with dumbfounded expressions.

During the struggle, the shiny pistol remained in the clutches of Branson's hand. He tried pointing it at his son, but Brock snatched his wrist and pinned it to the ground.

Slater reacted by pointing his own gun at the chaotic mass of limbs squirming on the dirt. We all ducked as Branson's pistol was pointed in every direction during the struggle. Poor Abbott appeared to be unaware of the gun. His eyes were clenched shut in pain as he tried to maneuver his arm in the midst of the struggle. Brock was using his chained arm to hold Branson's right arm down while his free hand struggled to keep the gun out of range.

Bodies flopped over and over again, and it was hard to tell who had the advantage. Abbott ended up sprawled on top of both of them at one point. It looked like his arm was bent completely backwards, obviously broken.

And then it happened. A shot rang out and echoed across the gorge. The struggle went still. Kristel covered her face.

I watched the three bodies lying in a pile near the muddy embankment, neither of them moving. I looked at Kristel standing next to me with her face covered. Her eyes peeked out between her fingers. I looked at Wesley who stared at the bodies with a smirk. Slater stood above Abbott with an idiotic expression, his gun pointed loosely at the bodies. The camera was still in his other hand, the red light still on, the lens pointing backwards over the falls. I looked at the Oliffs and at Abbott lying on top of them, his chained broken arm buried under someone's torso.

Then the bodies moved slightly. Wesley and Slater stepped closer.

Abbott rolled to his back, his arm still chained to Brock's. Blood oozed from his wrist, pinched in the steel cuffs. Branson rolled off his son and flopped on his back. He was still holding the gun, but not clutching it tightly. The gun was pointed limply at his chest where a large mass of blood had stained his white shirt.

Brock sat up and looked at his father. "Oh God," he cried, seeing the wound in his father's chest. Branson laid still, his eyes staring straight upward in utter horror. "Oh God," Brock wailed again.

Wesley stepped closer to the pile. Slater stood next to him, still pointing the gun with one hand, still holding the running camera with the other, and looking stupid. I stepped between Kristel and Slater. We huddled around Brock and his father as we watched Branson Oliff breathe his last breath.

"Oh God," Brock cried once more.

Abbott sat up and observed the results of the struggle. Then he checked his maimed wrist and arm, wincing with pain.

"Well, this is perfect!" Wesley proudly announced, as if people dying in front of him was a common occurrence. "Brock Oliff kills his own father just before his father is about to turn him in for murder. Perfect. This is perfect!" He wasn't being sarcastic. He truly liked what had just happened.

I couldn't believe how brazen he was. How many other people had he watched die in his lifetime? How many other people had he killed?

My hurting grandfather looked at me and then at the camera in Slater's hand. His eyes returned to mine and then quickly to the camera again, and quickly back to mine. I knew his eyes were telling me, "Grab that camera and run!"

I hardly thought about his command before I acted. I lunged forward and snatched the camera from Slater's fat hand. Before I could leap away, Wesley lunged forward and grabbed me around the legs. I tossed the camera toward Kristel, but it hit the ground, causing several pieces to snap off. Kristel picked it up as both Slater and my stepfather hurled toward her. She faced them, looking at me ten yards behind them, and like a quarterback, she tossed the camera through the air over their outstretched hands.

Her pass was too strong. The camera sailed completely over me, smashing onto the rocky ground near the edge of the cliff, sending more pieces shattering. The bulk of the camera in which the tape was encased bounded towards the rocky ledge of the cliff and wobbled to a stop. I rushed to pick it up and found myself at the very edge. I spun to face the two enemies who had now turned away from Kristel to focus on me. Kristel was still standing behind them and Brock and Abbott were further behind her, near the muddy embankment, still cuffed together, kneeling around Branson Oliff's body.

"Alright, Jody," my stepfather said calmly. "Just give me that camera."

He pointed his gun at me, and Slater copied him. I now had two loaded barrels locked on me no less than ten yards away. The edge of the cliff was less than a yard behind me.

I examined the broken camera and managed to pull out the videocassette from its innards. Then I tossed the remains of the camera at my stepfather. He dodged it with a sneer. Slater watched it bounce against a tree behind them near where Kristel was standing.

"Now give me the tape!" Wesley demanded, still pointing his gun at me.

I looked backwards over the edge of the cliff. The thought crossed my mind.

"Step away from the cliff and give me the tape!" Wesley yelled.

I looked at Brock and Abbott who were gazing at me while they kneeled over Branson's body.

Then I looked at Kristel who seemed to be gazing beyond me over the cliff.

"Step away from the cliff and give me that tape!" Wesley yelled again, still pointing the gun. I gave no attention to Slater, who stood there like Wesley's oafish shadow.

I again noted Kristel behind Wesley and Slater. Her eyes told me to do it.

I glanced backwards over the cliff again and down at the shady gorge below where white water bubbled under the crashing cataracts.

Then I heard a shot ring through the air and echo across the gorge. Kristel screamed. I spun around and checked my body to see where the bullet went in. I didn't feel a sting or see a hole. I looked up and saw Wesley, Slater, and Kristel staring in the direction of the three men near the muddy embankment.

My grandfather was now slumped over on top of Branson's body. Wesley had shot him.

"Oh God, you fool!!" Brock shrieked, bending over to check the old man who was still attached to him by handcuffs. My grandfather was motionless.

I heard Kristel whimper softly, covering her mouth.

Slater shouted a sentence full of swear words and cursed at my stepfather. "Wesley! You stupid idiot! Not here! You didn't have to kill him here!"

"It's all right, Clive," Wesley said calmly, pointing the gun towards me again. "We can blame this one on Brock also."

I glanced again at my wounded grandfather. He was now moving; his free arm was clutching his stomach. Brock was sitting helplessly alongside him, their arms still attached. Slater rushed to them and tended to Abbott's wound.

I looked again at my stepfather standing ten yards away with his gun pointed at me. There was now no doubt now that he had the mind to shoot me, too.

"I'll shoot *you* if you don't step forward and give me the tape!" Wesley confirmed.

"No you won't!" Slater shouted. "Not here, Wesley! Don't shoot anyone else!"

"Shut up, Clive, and let me handle this!" Wesley snarled, still pointing the gun at me.

I looked beyond Wesley at Kristel and feared for her life, too.

"Okay," I said. "I'll give you the tape. Just don't shoot anyone else."

I started walking forward towards my stepfather. My plan was to walk up to him, and, just before handing him the tape, spin around and throw it far over the edge. I hoped it would divert the gun-holder's attention long enough for Kristel and me to run for our lives.

I stepped slowly towards Wesley with the videotape held out in front of me. I was now five yards away from him.

Kristel inexplicably ran towards me. She passed by Wesley, not looking at me, but at the cliff.

Following her lead, I faced the gorge and stepped towards the edge. I heard Wesley yell something as I turned away from him. I reached for Kristel with my right hand and held the videocassette in my left. Two more strides and we were both holding hands in mid air.

# CHAPTER 44

## *The Shot*

The rocks at the bottom swooped into view behind my heels. The deep crystal pool was in reach, sixty feet below. We soared outward and then began an arch downward, falling toward the water, holding hands as the air rushed past our ears like a storm wind.

As the gust intensified, I heard a shot ring out overhead.

I never let go of Kristel's hand, even when we hit the water. That was a mistake, as the action caused our arms to smack hard and jerk brutally upward when we went under.

We shot deep into the icy pool like torpedoes, plunging twenty feet down. Millions of bubbles swirled in our wake as I searched for the shining surface. With the videocassette grasped firmly by my left hand, my right finally let go of Kristel's so we could swim.

We both reached the surface at the same time and paddled toward the waterfall at our right—the nearest area of cover. I glanced up at the cliff and saw Slater up there with his gun pointed at us. Wesley had disappeared, scampering away towards the cars and the pedestrian railing where he could more easily climb down the falls towards us.

We found temporary asylum from Slater behind a planet-like rock near the crashing lower cascade.

"Are you all right?" I asked Kristel as we treaded water behind the rock.

"Yes! We made it!" she panted, grabbing onto the large boulder. "What now?"

"I think my stepfather is coming down from the top of the falls." I peered around the boulder and looked up at Slater who was still pointing his gun in our direction. I paddled back to Kristel and held up the videotape.

"This is all they want," I said. "Wesley knows this has Gretta's testimony on it. He's gonna kill for it."

I looked across the open pool and down the stony river beyond. "If we can get to the far side of the pool, we can run down the river's edge and up the other side of the gorge down there. I think we can out run them from there."

"We better go now!" Kristel said, looking across the pool in the direction we would go.

"I know. But Slater's up on the cliff."

"He's not going to shoot us," Kristel assured. "But your stepfather will. C'mon lets go!"

She pushed off from the boulder out into the open pool. I followed, glancing up at Slater on the cliff. He kept his gun pointed at us, but he didn't fire.

When we were halfway across the pool, I turned backward towards the falls and saw Wesley climbing down from the top level. He was crawling gingerly down the steep rocks, looking over his shoulder at us, far at the bottom. When he saw us swimming toward the stony river, I heard him yell to his accomplice on the cliff, "Don't let'm go, Slater! Don't let'm go!"

We reached the edge of the lower pool on the opposite side of the falls and climbed up into the knee-high water, which from here flowed calmly across the bottom of the gorge. Wesley shouted at Slater again, "Don't let'm go!"

We heard a shot fired from above and a bullet ricocheted off a rock near my leg. Slater had fired his gun.

He fired another shot and it again ricocheted off a nearby rock. He wasn't shooting to kill, only to keep us from going any farther. We stood straight up and watched him, ignoring the power of his weapon. I looked across the pool and saw Wesley continuing his careful descent down the rocks.

We started down the river again; another bullet was fired. Kristel fell to her knees in the water, and I saw a faint swirl of blood cloud around her.

"My leg," she cried, wincing as she sat down in the one-foot deep river. "I think he shot my leg!"

As the current swished the cloud of blood away from her thigh, I could see through the clear water a clean hole the size of a pinky in the side of her calf. I glared up at Slater on the cliff. He wasn't looking at us, and his gun was lowered. He was looking back up the gorge at Wesley. Slater yelled at him, "Barrett! You hit her! You hit her, you fool!" What do you think you're doing!?"

Wesley was now standing upright on a lower ledge about twelve feet above the lower pool where Kristel and I had landed. He was at least fifty yards away and he had his gun pointed firmly at us with both arms. It was his bullet that pierced Kristel's leg.

"Wesley, you fool!" Slater kept shouting.

I kneeled in the water and put my arm around Kristel as she gripped her wounded calf. This was the moment of decision: give up now, or risking getting shot at again.

Wesley yelled, "Jody, give me that video tape!" His gun was pointed firmly at us. "Or I'll fire again!"

I considered what would happen next if I didn't obey. He *would* fire another shot. He would actually kill one of us or both of us. He was an avid hunter, and he had the marksmanship skills to do so.

Then I considered what would happen if I gave up and handed the tape over. He'd destroy it, thus eliminating the critical testimonies it contained; thereafter, he would have all the bases covered. He had a scapegoat in Brock and the popular opinion of the people of the Adirondack region that Abbott Marilee was a cold-blooded rapist and murderer. How could the stories of a couple of teenage detectives and one disgruntled police officer fare against a forty-year legend and a sophisticated conspiracy?

The truth resided in the video, particularly in the late Gretta's testimony. If I handed over the tape, I'd be putting the truth in the hands of its destroyer.

"Jody, give me that video tape," Wesley demanded again. His gun was still pointed at Kristel and me.

I don't know how long we stood facing each other across the pool. The waterfalls pounded behind Wesley, and I began feeling the aching chill as water swarmed past us.

I looked at Kristel, who, incredibly, wasn't crying. She was holding her wounded leg tightly with her hands under the chilling water while looking at me with pleading eyes. Does she want me to hand over the tape? Just one word from her and I will.

"I will not hesitate to fire this gun again, Jody," Wesley shouted. "And your stubbornness might force me to, so just give me the tape and nobody is going to get hurt anymore."

I held the cassette behind me, sandwiched between my back and Kristel's. I moved in front of her to shield her from his aim. Her body shivered, both from fear and from the chilling water.

Then she spoke the bravest words I've ever heard someone speak. "Don't give it to him, Jody! Get out of the river and run through the woods! Drop the tape near the bank where he can't see it. One of us will get away and come back to get it."

I glanced up at Slater standing high above on the cliff. His hands were cocked at his hips as he ruefully watched the scenario below.

"Give me the tape, Jody!" Wesley shouted again.

I didn't move, considering Kristel's plan and all its implications: leaving her wounded in the river, hiding the tape, and more gunshots from Wesley if I fled.

After too much time passed, Wesley kneeled down and started climbing down from the mid-level pool, careful to keep the gun pointed in our direction the best that he could. This climb was easier than the one from the upper falls. He could do it mostly by scooting down on his rear end, but it took time. If I was going to run—this was the most opportune moment.

Before I made the critical decision, another figure appeared at the very top of the falls. I didn't know if I should praise God or fear the worst when I saw none other than Boonie start climbing down the gorge high above and far behind Wesley. He reached the ledge around the upper pool at the same time that my stepfather reached the edge of the bottom pool.

Wesley stood up straight on the edge of a dry boulder and raised his gun again. Now he was twenty yards closer, and the best moment of flight had now passed. I had been distracted by Boonie's appearance, and now everything was up to my old cabin mate.

Boonie stood two levels above Wesley, about forty feet up. He could see from his high perch my stepfather pointing the gun in our direction. Then he turned and quietly scampered back up to the upper river nearest the road. I feared Wesley might spin around and shoot him before he could get away and go for help.

Then it was clear that Boonie was not planning to run for help. Wesley was yelling something at us, but I was hardly listening, trying to watch what Boonie was doing without giving him away with my eyeballs.

Boonie picked up a stone from the upper river near the railing. The stone was about the size of a cantaloupe, and he held it at his belly with both hands and stepped to the ledge where the first waterfall cascaded next to him. Then he jumped feet first into the waterfall and landed without a splash in the foaming bubbles of the upper pool.

Wesley still had the gun pointed at us, advising me I could set the tape down on the rock and walk away without getting hurt. He kept repeating, "I'll fire again, Jody, if you don't give me the tape."

I saw Boonie reappear soaking wet at the front ledge of the upper pool, now about thirty feet above where my father stood. The cantaloupe-sized stone was still cradled at his belly as he hoisted himself onto the rocky ledge.

"Just give me the tape," Wesley repeated again.

I did nothing, waiting for Boonie.

"Just give me the tape," he said again in a deeper voice. Then he stiffened his arm and fired a bullet that grazed my wet shorts. It stung like a burn, and I examined the clean hole in the cuff of my shorts. The skin underneath was not broken, only red and stinging.

Kristel yelped when the gun fired. She wasn't facing my stepfather, sitting low in the water behind me. The bullet probably just missed her.

I felt her head turn as she buried her face into my back. "Just run," she said in a steady voice. I was sure she couldn't see Boonie's movements.

After I examined the bullet's path through my shorts, I saw that Boonie was about to take the one and only shot he had.

He climbed gingerly down to the mid-level pool with the rock buried in his skinny chest. He stood to his feet at the edge of that pool, fifteen feet above and about twelve feet behind my stepfather. Wesley was obviously not aware of his presence. Above, Slater had inexplicably disappeared from the edge of the cliff.

Boonie hoisted the stone to his chest like a basketball player ready to take a foul shot. If he missed, I assumed Boonie would dive back into the pool behind him and somehow try to escape.

Boonie leveled the rock in his palm, bent both knees slightly, and launched his shot. The stone sailed through the sky like a cannonball and Wesley was oblivious to its presence above him. The stone reached its apex, sailed downward, and landed perfectly on top of the devil's head with the full brunt of its force. It didn't bounce at all. Wesley's skull absorbed every pound of the shock.

He never knew what hit him. His arms went limp, his jaw dropped open, and his body tipped off the ledge like a platform diver who had suddenly fainted, dropping his gun and splashing along with it in the water of the lower pool.

I waited for the blood from his cracked skull to cross the basin and wash past Kristel and me, but it never came. The body sank, having to be retrieved by a rescue diver one hour later.

# CHAPTER 45

## *The Conclusion*

On TV, in the newspapers, and mostly to the waitresses in the kitchen, Boonie bragged for the rest of the summer about the foul shot he took with the cantaloupe-sized stone that killed my stepfather. Actually, it wasn't the stone that killed him. It only knocked him unconscious. Wesley Barrett died by drowning, because neither Kristel, Boonie, nor myself had the urge swim after the man who had sunk to the deepest abyss of Smooth Rock Falls.

Because Wesley Barrett was dead, and because Branson Oliff was dead, the only guilty party remaining alive was Sheriff Clive Slater. As it turned out, he wasn't a part of the murder conspiracy from the very beginning. In fact, he wasn't a member until Wesley and Branson paid him off to keep quiet about the photographs in the camera he discovered at the falls in early June. In exchange for his cooperation, they had promised him a sum of one million dollars when the land purchase was finalized. So good old Clive never knew anything about Jimmy Grandstaff or Robert Rothschild, not until he joined ranks with Wesley and Branson after Brock wrote the John Doe letter.

Regardless of his late entry into the scheme, Slater was charged with conspiracy to cover-up the crime of murder. Needless to say, he lost his job and was sentenced to forty-five years in prison, minimum thirty. Roy Anders, who testified against him in court, is the new Sheriff of Huron County.

My grandfather, thankfully, survived the gunshot wound he suffered at the hands of my stepfather at the top of the falls. The bullet punctured his palm, which he had raised in a desperate form of defense, and lodged into his stomach. It was a less severe stomach wound than the one suffered by George Schuple, but Abbott lost full motion of his right hand.

According to Clive Slater's testimony, the two men who suffered wounds in their guts did so at the hands of the same shooter, my stepfather. The bullet Schuple took was, indeed, meant for Abbott Marilee. Both Schuple and Abbott were released from Lake Henry General on the same day, Abbott having spent two days there, and Schuple nearly two weeks. They were both bombarded outside the hospital by an army of reporters, and the media onslaught on Lake Marilee continued throughout the summer.

There was no formal trial for Abbott Marilee on forty-year old rape and murder charges. The judge in Huron County was satisfied with the results of the internment of both Abbott and Zane Marilee's coffins. Zane's was, of course, empty, while his own body was found in the casket under Abbott's tombstone. That, combined with the videotaped testimony from Gretta, a.k.a. Miss Emory, was enough evidence at the pre-trial hearing for the judge to declare Abbott Marilee a free and innocent man.

Within three weeks, my grandfather appeared on a plethora of television programs, including *Prime Time Live, Geraldo, Dateline, and Good Morning America,* just to name a few. Kristel, Brock, Roy, and I also made appearances, and Boonie managed to get his smile into some of them, too

Currently, two big-time movie studios in Hollywood are bidding for the movie rights. Abbott hopes they get Sean Connery to play his role. I hope they find some up-and-coming heartthrob to play me. As for Kristel, she should play herself. I'm sure she could do it, because there's no beauty queen in Hollywood with enough spunk to fill her shoes. She was back on her feet the same day the doctors removed the bullet from her calf. That's Kristel for you.

Meanwhile, it's taken some time for my mother to adjust to the truth of her heritage. Wesley is dead, and it was her family fortune that lead to his downfall. She did make things right with my grandfather, as hard as it was for both of them, although they still feel like strangers to each other. Hopefully, time will apply its salve to their wounded relationship.

The most unexpected ending to this whole story was the fate of Brock Oliff. He will work at a brand new facility on the Manor property after all. It's going to be called the Marilee House and Academy, an orphanage and boarding school for children at risk. Abbott promised him a position there, as soon as he graduates from college in four years. Brock was perfectly willing to accept the deal, and two weeks ago he left the New Jersey rehab center and enrolled at a Christian college out in southern California.

The town of Abbeyville now boasts of its own *living* legend in the person of Abbott Marilee. The mayor gave him the key to the village during a highly publicized Labor Day celebration. Since then, Abbott has purchased a lakefront home near the Manor where he can oversee the construction of the new Marilee House.

He insisted that I keep every dime of the half-million he gave me, but I managed, at the least, to donate a chunk of it for an indoor swimming facility at the Marilee House, dedicated to the honor of Jimmy Grandstaff. Abbott was pleased to spare no expense on the rest of the building project, including an elaborate playground dedicated to his deceased son and a beautiful greenhouse and atrium named in the honor of his wife. The whole facility is going to be a fantastic place, and Abbott's buddy George Schuple is as excited as ever about its development. He guarantees summer employment to young residents of the Marilee House and Academy if they want it.

As for me, I'm sixteen going on twenty, and I've got a fortune put away in the bank. But this summer was more than about getting rich: I gained a lifetime of knowledge about my family and myself. Most of all, I learned that trusting only in me is pretty stupid at times. I can see only so far, know only so much, and understand so very little about the bigger picture. There is truth beyond what my own limited faculties experience, truth that matters and plays upon me. I can't manipulate it. It's out there, and I only need to understand and know it.

Much to Kristel's chagrin, I haven't come to terms with God yet, at least not to the extent that would satisfy the Brown Swan Queen. She says I need to accept Jesus as my savior, but I prefer to be a skeptic for now. I'm not quite ready for that Jesus freak stuff yet. I need more proof—more hands on knowledge, a more direct, validating message from God than I've seen so far.

It's kind of like the Bible is a collection of Ambassador letters, and I want God to drive me to the Manor and take me down into a vault and tell me the whole truth face-to-face. I'm pretty sure the proof about Jesus and the Bible is out there somewhere; I just haven't found it yet. This summer I learned it's waiting to be discovered, but only for those who care enough beyond the boundaries of their ego to search for it. Kristel taught me that, and so did George Schuple, and an old man named Whisper. They taught me more in two months than I ever learned in two years of Mr. Gray's honors History. And that's saying a lot. So for now, I'm what Kristel calls a soft agnostic, and I'll stick with that until a new revelation comes along, no matter how guilty she makes me feel.

I finally finished *Gatsby*, but I never got around to *Mohicans*. It didn't matter; our American Lit teacher left for Texas, and our new one couldn't care less about her predecessor's summer assignment. I'm glad I finished

*Gatsby* though. It's kind of funny—old Nick Carraway returned to the Midwest at the end of his summer in New York, and so did I.

Nick said his was a story of East and West. Mine, I suppose, is a story of black and white, which is the way some important things in life really are, more than I knew before this summer, anyhow. Black and white; right or wrong; guilty or innocent—when it comes to absolute truth, it's an either-or situation.

Kristel told me that Jesus is either a liar, a madman, or the Lord our God. I finally came around to trust in a man named Marilee, and that took a load of prodding. What will it take for me to trust in a man from Nazareth? That's a good question.

It's September 1998: Sosa and McGwire are turning the baseball world upside-down; the President is casting doubt on the meaning of the word *is*, and the world of technology is in a frenzy about the coming Y2K. But in my life, shades of gray are thinning, darkness is fading, and truth is rising from the oblivion of relativism.

The clarity is rather liberating, if you ask me.

CPSIA information can be obtained at www.ICGtesting.com
Printed in the USA
LVOW091026280312

275092LV00002B/5/P